Simon Miller has a PhD from Durham and has taught history at universities in the UK and USA (Manchester, Essex, Cambridge, Belfast and UC Davis). He has published work on the Mexican Revolution and the English culture of land and landscape, but was always drawn to a more flexible genre of writing about the past. His first attempt, *The Wrong Domino*, was shortlisted for the Crime Writers' Association Debut Dagger award.

Praise for Ebolowa

Thank goodness, a historical political thriller that delivers! Simon Miller's novel puts us vividly there and then, amid people who are acted on by History while having agency, and it is page turning to the point I had to make an effort to slow down. It offers individuals and places and times I feel fuller for having encountered. EBOLOWA is what readers hope for – at once an education and an entertainment.

Andrew Greig

EBOLOWA

EBOLOWA

SIMON MILLER

This edition first published in 2017

Unbound

6th Floor Mutual House, 70 Conduit Street, London W1S 2GF

www.unbound.com

ISBN (eBook): 978-1911586432
ISBN (Paperback): 978-1911586425

Design and illustration by Mark Ecob based on images from:
©Shutterstock.com

For Su, with love: and thanks for the title and the rest.

Dear Reader,

The book you are holding came about in a rather different way to most others. It was funded directly by readers through a new website: Unbound.

Unbound is the creation of three writers. We started the company because we believed there had to be a better deal for both writers and readers. On the Unbound website, authors share the ideas for the books they want to write directly with readers. If enough of you support the book by pledging for it in advance, we produce a beautifully bound special subscribers' edition and distribute a regular edition and e-book wherever books are sold, in shops and online.

This new way of publishing is actually a very old idea (Samuel Johnson funded his dictionary this way). We're just using the internet to build each writer a network of patrons. Here, at the back of this book, you'll find the names of all the people who made it happen.

Publishing in this way means readers are no longer just passive consumers of the books they buy, and authors are free to write the books they really want. They get a much fairer return too – half the profits their books generate, rather than a tiny percentage of the cover price.

If you're not yet a subscriber, we hope that you'll want to join our publishing revolution and have your name listed in one of our books in the future. To get you started, here is a £5 discount on your first pledge. Just visit unbound.com, make your pledge and type KAPLAN17 in the promo code box when you check out.

Thank you for your support,

Dan, Justin and John
Founders, Unbound

Super Patrons

Pablo Casares Arrangoiz
Anna Baddeley
George Baddeley
Graham Frost & Miranda Baddeley
Wendy Balloteaud
Anna Bannister
Trisha & John Bannister
Huw Beynon
Caroline Bond
Valerie Bradley
Francis Byng
Marion Cadman
Ramsay Cameron
Orla Carley
Mercedes Charles
Eva Chen
Derek Clarke
Pat Cochrane
Tony Cook
Bob Cowen
Nick Davidson
Max Farrar
Adam Forman
Eddie Frost
Rick Gaehl
Amy Gordon
Susannah Hall
Hal Hampson
Lydia Hampson
Lalage Hampson
Hannah Hassan

Emma Hawtin
Kit Hawtin
Janey Hawtin
Jeffrey Henderson
Sandy Hogarth
Bronwen Holden
David Hughes
Dave James
Judy Gordon Jones
Jenny Keating
Paul Kelemen
Caro Kennewell
Dan Kieran
Alex Latsis
Marina Lewycka
Stephen Little
Karin Maddock
John Maddock
Jean Maddock
Joe Maddock
Kate Maddock
Su Maddock
Sally McGill
Sam Miller
Katherine Miller
John Mitchinson
Stephanie Munro
Hugh Nankivell
Julia Neal
Pat O'Donnell
Martin Orbach
Michael Page
Inga Page
Richard Parker
Steve Pearce

Justin Pollard
Helle Porsdam
Stephen Quilley
Jane Roberts
Julie Schaper
Karen Stafford
Mark Steedman
Marilyn Taylor
Cathy Terrill
Kiran Vithaldas
Hilary Wainwright
Perry Walker
Mark Whitaker
Wilbur
Martin Yarnit

'By power I mean official, political power – what we know in Latin as *imperium* – the power of life and death as vested by the state in an individual.'

—Robert Harris, Cicero trilogy: *Imperium*

'Reality is always more complex than invention: less kempt, cruder, less rounded out. It rarely lies on one level.'

—Primo Levi, *The Periodic Table*

'En France on n'a pas de pétrole, mais on a des idées.' ('In France we don't have oil but we have ideas' – the buzz phrase commonly heard in France amidst the 1973-74 oil crisis.)

North and West Africa

Author's Note

It is in the nature of all human communities to memorise and construct the past. We do so as families, tribes and nations, twisting threads of myth and memory together with the facts of verified history. The question of who we are becomes ever more insistent as the world shrinks.

Emmanuel Macron, the new president of France, received a sharp reminder of this when he sought to update the national story of Empire as 'truly barbarous'. He was immediately caught in the flack of convention and had to backtrack. It turned out that, as William Faulkner said of his own contested history of the American South, 'the past is never dead. It's not even past.'

Ebolowa ventures into this terrain. Based on a true story of courage, complicity and murder, it blends facts with fiction in a version of the past that answers the question of not just *what* happened but *why*.

1

Chicago

He wasn't expecting a woman. Sal had just buzzed the intercom and said, 'New client, Harry; a Dr Fayol...' and here she was, a 30-something medic rattling on about how her sister Annie had drowned in a riptide off the coast of Cameroon way back in '56. Private eyes are like priests, inviting confidence and promising redemption, and Harry was used to clients arriving strung out. Sometimes all they needed was to talk, but this one looked like the real thing.

'It was here,' she said, unfolding an old map of French Equatorial Africa on his desk. 'A beach in the middle of nowhere called Mile 12.'

Her hands were slender and her nails neat but unpainted and she wasn't wearing a ring. She had blue eyes and her dark hair was tied back in a ponytail as if she'd been in a hurry or unsure about coming. With flat heels and minimum make-up, she looked the part of a hard-working medic but Harry had been in the business long enough to mistrust first impressions, especially when the woman in question was wearing an expensive watch.

He wiped off the seat of his spare chair and drew it across to the desk. His cheap metal desk felt pleasantly cool in the clammy months of the Chicago summer, but it was barely spring and the top felt chilly to the touch. A fly was fizzing angrily behind the venetian blinds, probably stirred out by the thin spring sunshine, and he cast it an irritated look.

'Please sit down, Dr Fayol,' he said with an apologetic gesture, as if he knew the place was shabby. He didn't get that many clients from her side of the city.

'Thank you,' she said and sat down, still clearly agitated. 'He must've been with her.'

'Who must've been, where?'

'This guy.' She passed him a faded postcard of a crater taken from the air: 'Mount Cameroon and at twelve thousand feet the second highest peak in Africa.' There was no address or stamp on the card and the message was short. He read it.

Hi Candy, you're not going to believe this but I've met SOMEONE. Really – at the top of this mountain! I'm sky high, but our secret OK, because it's complicated. Annie X

PS I'm onto a big story too.

The forceful handwriting jumped off the card as if the dead woman's excitement was still alive.

'Huh,' he said, watching the sister carefully. 'Trouble is, "complicated" usually means somebody else's husband.'

'I know that,' she said. 'But he didn't even make contact after she died.'

'That's too bad, Dr Fayol, but guys who cheat on their wives don't tend to do the right thing.'

'I know that too.' Now she was angry, her fists clenched. 'But Annie didn't have butterflies for brains and she didn't fall for guys; they fell for her. She was dedicated to her career and didn't let romance distract her. She just used her looks to get her way.'

'What way was that?'

'Getting stories. She was a photojournalist working for *Life* magazine on an African story and she told me Cameroon was perfect because it'd had the dubious benefit of the impact of all three big imperial powers: Germany, Britain and France.'

'There's no stamp or address on the card,' he said, looking up.

'She didn't want anyone else to read it. She sent it in a sealed envelope addressed to me in a package of undeveloped film.'

Harry nodded. 'You think this guy had something to do with her big story?'

'That's what I want you to find out.' She spread the map again and pointed at a blue line circling a town called Ebolowa. 'Could've had something to do with this place.'

He looked at the map. Ebolowa was the largest town in the coastal belt in the southern part of Cameroon. 'That's not much to go on for a case as cold as this,' he said. 'She must've kept a log.'

'Of course she did, but the gendarmes said it must've been stolen along with her cameras and the wheels off her car.'

'OK,' he said, frowning, and tilted back in his chair. 'So we've got a two-timing husband, a lethal riptide, a missing log and a place called Ebolowa. What happened to the film?'

'We got it developed. I've got some of the photographs here,' she said, emptying a thick manila envelope onto the desk. They were granular black-and-white shots like from some French art movie, mostly men of different ages and demeanours.

'Well,' he said after a minute's admiration, 'they're very good. Quite a range of guys too. Any of them strike you as her type?'

'She didn't have a type.'

'In my experience everyone does. What about the men she brought home?'

'She didn't bring any. I already told you she was in love with her career, and home wasn't the kind of place you brought a date.'

'Why not?'

She waved his question away. 'It just wasn't.'

'You must have some idea of the kind of guy she went for.'

'Well, she certainly wouldn't have fallen for a guy who let her drown and then scuttled back to his wife.'

'That's a pretty serious accusation.'

'Not really.' She gestured at the map. 'According to the gendarmes she went to the beach on her own, but that was before we knew about this guy. You don't need to be Sherlock Holmes to figure out they'd arranged to meet there.'

'Maybe so but you haven't got any evidence he was there or watched her drown.'

'But that's why he didn't come forward after she died!' Her eyes flashed. 'He just kept his head down.'

'That's possible, but the rest of it doesn't add up.' He ran his finger along the track leading to the beach. 'This is a dirt road and the gendarmes would've found two sets of tracks if they'd met there.'

'They must've gone together,' she said hotly.

'So how did he get back to his wife if her car was found at the beach?'

Her mouth clamped into a thin line and she coloured slightly. He folded his arms and waited.

'Alright,' she said, 'I haven't got any evidence of him being there, but something's not right – I can feel it in my bones. I just can't believe she would've fallen for a jerk like that.'

Harry nodded. He took his clients' hunches seriously, even when they were as out of date as this one. 'How come it's taken you this long to ask the question?'

'I've only just found the card.' She stopped abruptly. 'It's a long story.'

'I've got time – and I need to know, if I'm going to take the case.'

'I'm not sure it's relevant.' She looked away and when she turned back her eyes had hardened. 'OK, well, the fact of the matter is that my father had taken off with another woman and my mother was getting through a bottle of bourbon a day. Alcoholics can't face the world, Mr Kaplan. They can hardly get the garbage out on the right day and they dump the mail without opening it, especially personal stuff. In my mother's case it was stockpiled in the bottom drawer of a big oak chest. She died last year and it's taken me a while to clear the house.' She shrugged. 'It's sold now and I guess that's partly why I'm here.'

'You never checked your sister's effects before?' he said, deliberately incredulous.

She looked at him with narrowed eyes. 'You ever spent time with an alcoholic, Mr Kaplan?'

He shook his head.

'Well, you spend what time you have checking for bottles.'

'Sure. It must be tough—'

'It was,' she said. 'And anyhow I was in my freshman year at the time and no better than my mother at facing the world.' Her mouth was a thin tight line. 'I am now.'

Harry took stock: it looked as if his new client knew what she was getting into. The past was a dangerous country and finding the guy wasn't going to bring her sister back, but she was still going to have a shot at making sense of it.

He liked that; and anyhow 1956 had been a turning point for him as well. They'd leaked Khrushchev's secret speech condemning Stalin and people across Eastern Europe had risen up against Soviet oppression. He'd had the choice of joining the Hungarian Revolution or escaping to the West and it turned out that he hadn't been any better at facing reality than Dr Fayol. Maybe they had something important in common.

'You sure you're ready now?' he asked.

'Yes. Now that I've got a target. I just want you to help me find out what really happened.' She tilted one shoulder in half a shrug. 'I'm a medic, Mr Kaplan; I don't believe in astrology or the afterlife, but there's something about chance and fate that I can't resist and finding Annie's card after so long felt like a sign. Or at least a spur to action.'

'I know what you mean,' he said and grimaced. 'But it's too bad we don't have his name.' He scanned the faces and figures in front of him. 'None of them look as if they were taken on the mountain. Is this all you've got?'

'The Shultz gallery is printing the rest – they're putting on a retrospective of Annie's work and want a story to hang it on, with names for the people and places.' She paused. 'That's the other reason for hiring you; the easy bit – if you're interested?'

For a second she looked him in the eye and he nodded as if to say that sometimes the loose ends in life couldn't be left any longer.

'OK, Dr Fayol,' he said. 'Yeah, I'm interested alright. I'll take the case but I'm sorry to say it's going to cost you. This oil crisis has pushed air fares through the roof, so I'll need at least eight hundred and fifty up front.'

'That's OK. I know this inflation is crazy but storm clouds can have silver linings—' She looked at him and smiled for the first time.

'Real estate has been going up too, so I've had a lucky windfall. When can you start?'

He had nothing pressing and could see that she was in a hurry. She'd arrived in two minds but was now bursting to get on with it. He understood how she felt: he wanted to get going on a new case and anyhow fancied a stint in the African sun. Plus, he thought with a wry grin, it would give him a break from waiting in line for gas with guys bitching about how OPEC and the 'Ayrabs' were ruining the American way of life. His fellow citizens were suffering severe short-ages for a change and they didn't like it. The American Dream was fading and people were looking for scapegoats.

'I can start right away,' he said, putting his hand out. He could already feel that sun on his back.

'Excellent,' she said, shaking his hand with a firm confident grip. 'I'll have the gallery send the rest of the photos over this afternoon.'

'OK. Meantime I just need your signature.' He took a contract out of his desk and she glanced quickly through it before signing.

'You came highly recommended, by the way,' she said, passing the contract back. 'Denise Ferris—'

'Oh right, yes,' he said. 'I remember.' Mrs Ferris's son Jake had dodged the draft and disappeared in a cloud of drugs and Harry had tracked him down to a shack on an Indian reservation north of Van-couver. Mrs Ferris was just happy to know he was still alive.

All of Harry's early business had come from people like Mrs Fer-ris – anxious parents or siblings who'd lost contact with loved ones over the Vietnam War, either as draft dodgers or GIs who'd had a belly full and gone AWOL. It'd all started when Harry had volun-teered at a day centre for vets and fell into helping find people who'd gone missing.

A few early successes gave him the credibility and confidence of a pro and people started to hire him. He had what it took: he knew the country, spoke French and understood them whether they were draft-dodger or deserter. They said he had a nose for it and it helped him come to terms with what he'd been through.

'I'm glad to say that Jake is doing OK,' Dr Fayol said. 'He keeps in touch with his mother – discreetly – and now that the whole disastrous mess is over maybe there'll be an amnesty.'

Harry closed his eyes and pressed hard on his temples. 'Mess' didn't come anywhere close but there weren't the words to cover it. He'd looked.

'Yeah,' he said, shaking his head. 'I sure hope so.' How many lives had been devastated by such pointless destruction? One day there would be a memorial, a place to visit the dead.

'You were there, weren't you?' she asked, her voice hushed. Photojournalism, TV and magazines, the last days of *Life*, had all brought the war right into everyone's homes, a relentless catalogue of detail and death that no one could hide from.

'Yes,' he said. 'I was.'

They fell silent for a second, each lost in their own thoughts.

'One more photo,' she said, catching his eye and taking a studio portrait out of her bag. 'This is what my sister looked like.'

Harry took it. Annie Fayol had been a striking young woman with thick black hair and blue eyes full of youthful ambition. With her full mouth and confident tilt to the jaw she looked like a younger version of the woman across the desk, but the face opposite was thinner and more angled; the blue eyes were deeper-set and clouded.

'She was real nice-looking,' he said.

'So everybody used to say.'

'And she was going to make the big time?'

'She thought so and so did I. So did *Life*. She was going to tell the story of awakening Africa—' Her voice got husky. 'But instead she wound up under a bridge here.' She smoothed out the map and pointed to a port called Douala.

'I thought you said it was in the middle of nowhere,' he said.

'It was. She drowned in the riptide here' – she followed the coastline with her finger – 'and was washed in on the tide. Douala is as humid as hell so people used to go down to Mile 12 to cool off. They told Dad that skinny-dipping under the stars was a craze. All the kids were doing it.'

He gave her a sharp look. 'You didn't say anything about skinny-dipping.'

'Yeah, well…' She looked away in obvious discomfort. 'That's the way she was when they found her, and that's another reason why I think he was there. OK she was reckless right enough, but only to get a good story. I just know she wouldn't have gone skinny-dipping on her own. I said so at the time but nobody listened. Dad just went on about the riptide; absurd stuff like there should've been danger signs up – in Africa, for God's sake! The gendarmes told him it wasn't their business because the beach was in the British Cameroons.'

Harry nodded and made a mental note: Annie Fayol had drowned in one police jurisdiction and been washed up in another. Straddling jurisdictions was always complicated. He looked up. 'Did your father identify the body?'

'No. They'd already buried her by the time he got there.'

'Really—?'

'The journey from the States took three days and they said the morgue was out of action. Apparently, the body was in bad shape.'

'I bet it was.' Harry knew what the tropics did to the dead from Vietnam. 'So who did identify her?'

'The US *chargée*.'

'I'll need to talk to him—'

'Her – but I don't know her name either. She was one of those Wellesley College types and Dad just called her the Ice Maiden.'

'Meaning?'

'Chilly.' She shrugged. 'You know, East Coast; a bit stuffy.'

'A lot of women in the Foreign Service are like that.'

'Sure they are, but I imagine you can get her name from the State Department now you know the post and when she was there.'

And with that, Harry's new client got up with her shoulders back and head held high. He'd seen it before, the surge of hope that came with the promise of action, but all too often it ended in heartache and disappointment.

She smiled and shook his hand. 'It's not quite the right expression, but I'm looking forward to working with you. It's been a long time.'

Sal was at the window watching Dr Fayol turn up her collar and get into a battered two-tone Ford estate. A police car hurtled past, blue lights blazing, swiftly followed by a fire truck.

'Nice legs and fancy Gucci bag,' she said, 'but she needs a tip on where to get her hair done. Strikes me Dr Fayol is a pretty woman who doesn't know it. She's still in her sister's shadow.'

Harry had noticed. He'd also sensed her state of mind.

'She's at a crossroads,' he said. 'In shock. Her mother's died, her routine has gone to hell and then she finds out her career-driven sister was in love with a guy who dropped out of sight. Plus she's suddenly got some money to play with; options, decisions—'

'Lucky her.' Sal prodded a finger at him. 'I told you, Harry, Gucci bags are not for the downtrodden. Mind you, she could do with a better car.'

'True.' Harry watched the midday traffic on Blue Island Avenue and it occurred to him that she hadn't shown any reluctance to cross town to see him. Not everybody took to his neck of the woods, least of all women on their own. Maybe Dr Fayol was more like her sister than she thought. 'She's split down the middle,' he said. 'Caught between blaming the boyfriend and hoping he'll turn out OK.'

'You don't even know his name.'

'But he might be one of these,' he said, spreading Annie Fayol's photographs across Sal's desk. 'What d'you make of them? Any heartbreakers?'

She bent over them one by one, nodding occasionally. 'Mmmm, I wouldn't trust this guy in a matinee concert hall, let alone at the beach after dark.'

It was the guy on the riverbank in cut-offs and a sleeveless singlet with biceps like Charles Atlas.

'Maybe not,' he said, 'but remember Annie Fayol was head-over-heels.'

'Meaning she was a sucker?'

'No, meaning love is blind – especially if it's Cupid's first hit.'

'Forget about arrows, Harry,' Sal said, gathering up the photos with a grim look, 'what you've got here is a needle in a haystack. Where are you going to start?'

'The *chargée*,' he said, 'and the gendarmes, and whoever stole Annie's cameras. Maybe they saw something. And whoever she took photos of. But the *chargée* first, so I need to talk to Brad. Can you get him on the phone?'

'Sure.'

Sal sat down and flipped through her card index. Bradley Hastings had been in the Embassy in Saigon and Harry had dragged him out of a bar seconds before a bomb tore it to shreds. Ever since, Brad had dined out on how Harry's sixth sense had saved his life, even though he'd told Brad he was just hungover and needed some fresh air.

'Brad, it's Harry Kaplan—'

'Harry, always a pleasure,' said Brad. 'What can I do for you?'

Harry gave him a quick summary of the case and why he needed to find the US *chargée*.

'No problem, Harry,' Brad boomed down the phone, 'we've processed the data on 1950s personnel already. Ike probably knows the colour of her underwear.'

Ike was Brad's pet name for the Foreign Service's computer. After Saigon he had taken a desk job in DC in what he called IBM's brave new world of machine intelligence and now he couldn't talk about anything else.

'Just her name and telephone will do,' said Harry.

'At your command, Jefe. Give me an hour.'

Harry winced: Brad was one of those Americans without an ear for languages. He got up and reached for the C volume of the *Encyclopaedia Britannica*. Some poor idiot before him had swallowed the salesman's patter and not met the payments. The guy hadn't paid the rent either and Sal was forever complaining about bills and circulars cluttering up their mailbox.

Harry blew the dust off the volume and flipped through to

Cameroon, a German colony, Kamerun, until the First World War. In 1918 it was divided between France and Britain into League of Nations mandates. Its range of flora and fauna earned it the title 'Africa in miniature' and it was also known as 'de Gaulle's gift to Churchill' on account of the titanium mines in the French mandate, crucial for the manufacture of fighter planes like Spitfires and Messerschmitts.

An insurrection in Douala in 1940 against Vichy gave the Free French control of the titanium and de Gaulle flew out to feature in a propaganda newsreel on how his gift to Churchill would turn the tide of the war in Europe. In the 1950s a movement for independence got under way and France, already smarting from colonial struggles in Indo-China and Algeria, came down on it with a mailed fist. Thousands of Cameroonians lost their lives.

Harry cut the pages out of the encyclopaedia with a Stanley knife and sat back. No wonder Annie Fayol had said Cameroon was perfect: it had gone through imperial rule of almost every variety, it possessed a mineral resource crucial to the outcome of World War Two, and at the time of her visit it was beset by a brewing guerrilla war for independence.

Harry was putting the encyclopaedia back when he got the word from Sal that Brad was on the phone and sounding very pleased with himself.

'You got a pad and pencil, Harry?' Brad asked.

'Sure.' Harry pulled a legal notepad across the desk.

'Ike's got quite a story for you,' said Brad. 'Even better than the colour of her underwear.'

'Shoot.'

'First thing, her name is Eileen O'Connell; a high-flying French major from Wellesley College. Went straight into the Service and was political attaché in Paris when the Nazis rolled in. Relocated to Vichy and was then seconded to FDR's team liaising with the French Resistance. By '45 she was a very well-regarded specialist, a rare breed back then.' Brad laughed loudly, a braying sound that Harry always thought of as a guffaw. 'What did I say about you needing that pencil and paper?'

Harry grunted. 'What else you got?' he asked.

Brad could barely contain himself. 'I told you Ike would deliver—'

'Yeah, you did.'

'Well, get this, Harry. After the war your dashing diplomat took on some kind of roaming responsibility for French West Africa. There were very few qualified people available and the CIA was just starting up—'

Harry interrupted: 'Hold it, Brad, are you saying she was CIA?'

'As good as. Ike doesn't fill every gap, but it looks as if she fed Langley information but wasn't, as far as I can see, involved in any covert action. Pretty good eh?'

'Yeah, for a machine.'

'Right, Harry, but here's the cream! One of her briefs refers to the rape and murder of an American woman in guess where?'

'Cameroon.'

'Exactly and the timing is right as well.'

'No kidding.' He sat forward. 'Who was it?'

'Sorry but it's classified.'

'That's too bad.'

'Maybe, but the timing is right and all you have to do is ask O'Connell.'

'Where's she posted now?' he asked.

'She's not, and that's another interesting thing about her. She was thrown out of the Service for associating with NORAID.' Brad paused for dramatic effect. 'You know who they are, don't you, Harry?'

'Sure I do,' Harry said. It was a funding front suspected of supplying the IRA with money for arms and explosives. Only the other day a coach carrying soldiers and their families had been blown up on a British freeway. He exhaled: the world was a mess. 'You saying Eileen O'Connell was sacked for aiding and abetting terrorism?'

'Not quite but it's what the Service calls "inappropriate association". She denied any wrongdoing of course and got any mention of dishonourable discharge erased from her record.'

'D'you where she is now?' Harry asked.

'Ike does know,' Brad said proudly. 'Place called Port Jefferson on Long Island. Number 1 Beach Street.'

Harry used the pad and pencil for the first time. 'Thanks.'

'All down to Ike, my friend. Aren't computers amazing!'

'Yeah. Truly amazing.'

But he hadn't sounded enough of a convert and next thing he knew Brad was halfway down the phone on behalf of IBM. 'I'm telling you, Harry,' Brad was saying, 'computers are the future! Paper is on the way out! Imagine a world without filing cabinets or you'll be joining the dinosaurs.'

'OK, Brad. I'll watch out,' he said and rang off.

He wasn't too sure what the future held and he liked the past on paper and he liked handwriting – people revealed themselves in it. He tapped his front teeth with a fingernail and gathered his thoughts. Talk about an ice maiden: a high-flying French expert with White House connections and party to a possible CIA cover-up before being dumped for associating with terrorists. He tilted back in his chair and his inner sceptic wondered if a woman with a CV that good could really have fallen from grace.

He went through and gave Sal the gist of Brad's information and she recoiled in horror.

'Oh my God, that's terrible,' she said, wide-eyed. 'Horrific.'

She wasn't normally thrown by his cases, but he'd never had a homicide before, let alone what might turn out to be a CIA cover-up. She shook her head in shocked disbelief.

'Jesus, Harry, that's just awful and somehow it's worse knowing about it while Dr Fayol is in blissful ignorance – well, not blissful exactly but you know what I mean.' She reached for the phone. 'You going to tell her?'

'No, not yet. Not until we're one hundred per cent sure it was her sister.'

'Oh come on, Harry!' Sal gesticulated in exasperation. 'Remember what you always say about coincidences.'

He grinned. 'I don't believe in them.'

'Exactly. How many other American women were out there back then? It's got to be her.'

'That's what Brad said.'

'OK, so we're all agreed; what now?'

'Get me a meeting with Eileen O'Connell ASAP,' he said, passing her the phone number. 'Make out I'm from the Shultz Gallery and say we're putting on an exhibit of Annie Fayol's long-lost photographs. Tell her the log book was lost and we'd appreciate some help identifying people and places.'

'OK, chief. Good as done.'

'And while I'm away see if the people at *Life* know what big story Annie was working on when she drowned.'

'I thought it had closed down.'

'It has but there'll still be people around who knew her,' he said. 'We can exchange notes when I get back.'

'Assuming Eileen O'Connell agrees to see you.'

'Bet you five bucks she jumps at the chance,' he said, putting his hand out dead certain he'd win. 'She'll want to make sure that Annie's photos don't shed any light on a murder that's been buried for close on 20 years.'

2

Long Island, New York State

Harry ransacked his wardrobe before leaving for the kind of gear somebody working in a gallery might wear. Sal had reckoned they all wore bowties but he figured that was a caricature and settled instead on an old kipper tie of his father's and a Harris-tweed suit he'd bought for a bar mitzvah a few years before.

He'd put on a little weight since Vietnam, back to 80 kilos, and the waistband was slightly tight; but he liked what he saw in the mirror, even though there were a few more grey hairs on view. It crossed his mind to get a crew-cut again: he'd need to keep cool in Cameroon. There was a jaunty spring in his step and a twinkle in his eye: it was a relief to be working again and the case looked interesting. Something different to get stuck into.

He caught an early flight to New York and took the Long Island train from Penn Station. He wanted to see the setting for *The Great Gatsby*. They'd read some wooden analysis of the book at school that had pitched it as a satire on the decadence of American capitalism in its death throes. Of course it hadn't worked out like that – there had been no revolution and millions were still on the breadline. Meantime NASA had put a man on the moon, which supported his brother László's view that capitalism could only harness technology to the beast of profit rather than the good of humanity.

At Port Jefferson dirty snow covered the sidewalks and a chilly wind whipped the Sound into white crests. He strolled down to the ocean and stared out towards Africa as if he could conjure up the whole troubled tangle of the Annie Fayol case. He wondered how much deception had gone into the making of Eileen O'Connell and how many other fathers had trekked halfway around the world to be told a pack of lies. It irked him: people deserved better.

He turned around and took a shortcut across the supermarket parking lot. Neon lights were flashing out messages about miraculous cut-price deals to beat the recession. He stood back and surveyed the scene: it was materialism gone mad and it made him wonder why he'd abandoned the so-called socialist utopia in Hungary for the US in the first place.

Eileen O'Connell lived in a big Victorian clapboard with a porch, a wide bay and gabled windows in the roof. Out front there was a birdhouse with a half coconut hanging from it. He knocked on the porch door and after a moment she appeared at the inner door and smiled. He watched her move nimbly down the steps in stilettos: an attractive woman wearing a perfectly pressed apron over a cream silk blouse and a light-grey pencil skirt. She had a shock of artfully streaked black hair and was wearing make-up that belied her age and for no good reason the phrase 'dressed to kill' popped into his mind.

'Mr Kaplan, welcome aboard,' she said, shaking his hand. 'I like your tie. Very Chicago. Could've been worn by Al Capone.'

'Thank you,' he said. 'We really appreciate your seeing me at such short notice.'

She waved airily. 'No problem, I assure you. I know what tight schedules are like. Tyrants!'

She took his coat and led the way through to the main room. The house was warm, the air thick with the scent of baking and wood smoke. The walls were a mustard yellow that gave the room a comforting glow and in the corner there was a cast-iron stove with flames flickering through the glass door. A neat stack of logs suggested hired help and a signed photograph of Franklin Roosevelt with his trademark bowtie was hanging on the wall next to an alcove full of books.

Strewn across a big oak table were newspapers with headlines in English and French on the Arab oil embargo and Watergate. The *Wall Street Journal* had 'Nigerian crude at an all-time high' and on the front page of the *Enquirer* was a blurred photo of Patty Hearst wielding a gun under the caption 'BRAINWASHED'.

Eileen O'Connell gestured at it with a snort. 'Old man Hearst must be spinning in his grave.'

Harry nodded: one of America's great capitalist barons had been humbled by conspirators on the lunatic Left and he wondered if it was a harbinger of the times or just a girl waylaid by fate in the kind of case that might turn up at his door. He took another look round: it reminded him of his grandfather's apartment before it was sacked. 'Nice room,' he said. 'I like the colour.'

'Thank you. So do I.'

'I heard you were a French specialist,' he said, picking up a special issue of the *Express* on the prime minister's plan for nuclear power. 'What d'you make of this? It's very sudden.'

'Hobson's choice,' she said with a Gallic shrug. 'They've got no oil or coal, but some uranium in Niger. Messmer is risking a back-lash by going for it without a peep of public debate. He's planning on eighty plants in ten years!'

'That's what I mean about sudden.'

She nodded. 'Right, but it isn't sudden for him. He and the nuclear project go way back. He was at the Test that went wrong.'

An alarm clock suddenly went off and she gestured at the settee. 'Sorry, Mr Kaplan, but the kitchen calls. Make yourself comfortable. I won't be long.'

'No problem.'

It was just the chance Harry needed. He moved quickly over to the roll-top desk, passing two framed photographs – one of the *Lusitania* steaming out of Liverpool and the other a familiar shot of a gaunt woman surrounded by children and staring out of a roughly erected tent. It was signed. The books in the alcove were in alphabet-ical order, a good number of them French paperbacks.

Busy noises were coming from the kitchen and with one eye on the door he half-opened the roll-top desk. Next to an old portable typewriter was a torn package covered with colourful stamps, one of which he recognised as Mount Cameroon and dated 1 December 1973. Underneath was a book by Thyraud de Vosjoli called *Lamia*, a bestselling exposé of the KGB's penetration of the French secret ser-vice with dozens of double agents. A photocopy of two pages from a spiral notepad fell out of the back of the book covered with Arabic script and the letters 'BP' written in the margin.

Harry's antennae quivered: spooks and oil were a toxic combination at the best of times and these were very far from the best of times. The world was reeling from the first-ever energy shock and oil prices had increased fourfold in just two years. The West was devastated, mired in the worst recession since 1929 and paralysed by Watergate, Pompidou's illness and Britain's bankruptcy. It felt as if the world was teetering on the edge and one nudge was all it needed.

Harry put the photocopy back and pulled open the central drawer. Inside were neat stacks of household bills and a standard CIA-issue Beretta and an opened box of shells. He just had time to shut the desk and pretend to be looking over his hostess's library before she swept out of the kitchen with a tray of coffee and croissants. She set it down briskly and the cups rattled.

'Black or white, Mr Kaplan? Or perhaps nowadays I should say with or without milk?'

'Black, please,' he said, still weighing up what he'd found. The gun and the book fitted her profile except for the Arabic and BP connection.

'Croissant?' the woman in question asked. 'Freshly baked. A habit I picked up in occupied Paris. The Nazis monopolised the supply.'

Harry took one. 'Must've been tough.'

She closed her eyes for a second and then looked at him in silence, her hands clasped tight. 'Tough?' The word hung between them. 'Seeing fascism at work, a daily routine—' She broke off, suddenly looking her age. 'Humanity at its worst, but I have happy memories too and I have Aznavour.' The stereo was playing the French crooner. 'What do you listen to, Mr Kaplan?'

'Jazz,' he said. 'Monk, Charlie Parker – Miles Davis.'

'Very modern.'

'No words,' he said, bending the truth to fit his gallery persona. 'I like that. Every time a new story.' He actually listened to Bob Dylan and Janice Joplin too, not to mention Motown.

'Stories seem to loom large in your life,' she said.

'Don't they in everybody's?'

'True.' She brushed flakes of croissant onto her plate and then looked up. 'You actually hear a lot of them in the Foreign Service. People are travelling through and don't expect to see you again. It goes to their heads, they get giddy and carefree, keen to cut loose and confide. My god – if only I'd written them down.'

'Maybe you should've been a writer.' He was pretty sure she had written them down. The best were probably classified.

'I might still.' She seemed on the verge of saying she was still young enough. 'Although fiction is all my contract allows.'

'All those memories going to waste,' he said. 'Shame.'

'You're right, Mr Kaplan, and exotic places.'

'Any favourites?'

'Dakar was very lively, Timbuktu was as romantic as the name and, well, Casablanca, obviously,' she said with a sly smile.

'With or without Bogart?'

'Need you ask?' she laughed.

'No, I've never met a woman who didn't like him.' He chewed a mouthful of croissant. 'Delicious. You could be a pastry chef as well.'

'Ha! Thanks but no thanks.'

'So it's the novel then. Anyhow, was Annie Fayol one those giddy travellers?'

'No, she wasn't the least bit giddy.'

'What was she like? I think Dr Fayol has her on a pedestal.'

'I didn't know her that well.'

'Well enough to identify her body,' he said.

'Only in an official capacity.'

'Exactly, she wasn't just travelling through. Two career women in a man's world, fellow Americans on the frontier: you must've have had a lot in common.'

'We didn't,' she said crisply. 'She wouldn't have trusted me with the time of day. I was part of the wicked establishment, as bad as the French.' She pointed to an oil painting of makeshift barricades and classical columns wreathed in gun smoke. The only bright colour came from a fluttering green, orange and white flag. 'That's Dublin

1916, the Easter Rising, painted by my cousin. Anti-colonialism runs in my veins, Mr Kaplan – Irish and American – but Annie Fayol wouldn't have it. I told her I worked with FDR on the Atlantic Charter, but she still thought she was the first white woman to stand up for Africa.'

'What Charter?' he asked.

'FDR's principles for a democratic post-war world, including the rights of colonised people to self-determination, co-signed by Churchill.'

'Really—?' From where Harry came from Churchill was the arch imperialist. 'You couldn't have been too happy dealing with an old enemy like him.'

'It was actually kind of fun.' She shrugged an elegant shoulder. 'We had the old rogue over a barrel – or, even better, looking down one. Of course he reneged after FDR died, as they all did.' She took a packet of Gauloises and a Zippo lighter out of the drawer. 'Another habit I picked up in Paris. Care to join me?'

'Sure.'

He was trying to quit but still getting through half a pack a day.

'You still seem pretty attached to France,' he said.

'I'm half-European. From day one I was straddling the Atlantic, born midway across on the *Lusitania*.'

'I saw the photo.'

'I still have my Irish passport.' She slipped into a beige camelhair coat with big lapels. 'I do my smoking in the porch. Do you want your coat?'

'I'm OK,' he said. 'I grew up with the cold.'

'On the Prussian plains? You sound like Kissinger.'

He shrugged; everybody said so. 'I'm actually from Budapest but we spoke German at home.'

'So you're Hungarian.'

'Like you're Irish.'

She looked at him quizzically and tied her belt. 'Well, I am Irish. We always leave the back door open.'

'Yeah, well, I've never gone searching for a homeland.'

'Out of sight, out of mind?'

'Something like that.'

She led the way into the porch and opened the front door. Cold air blew in off the water and in the distance he could see the chimneys of a power station trailing grey smoke into the blue sky. Down below, the ferry was approaching the quay with a few cars lined up to go aboard. Two more were in position for the drive-thru bank and a hobo was rooting through the garbage bin. All the pieces were in place for an average day in Main Street America.

'How d'you like banking with a robot?' he asked.

'I don't. It's mechanisation gone mad.'

'Right.' It was another of László's man-on-the-moon moments of technology and social need being out of synch. He lit her cigarette with a newfangled gas lighter.

'Thanks.' She drew on it hard and the end burned bright. 'I don't even have a colour TV and I don't like shopping malls. I'm a city girl like Jane Jacobs; streets and markets.'

'Me too,' he said, although he didn't know who Jane Jacobs was. 'So how come you ended up out here?'

'I haven't ended up anywhere, thank you very much, young man.' She blew smoke into the air. 'My father couldn't afford Manhattan. This was his house.'

'Well, at least he left you a great view.'

'Didn't he just? I can keep an eye on what's going on. I watched you arrive and was struck by the way you moved.'

'Really—'

'Yes, the way you ambled. Not at all like someone from a gallery. And then you remarked on the *Lusitania* rather than Dorothea Lange's *Migrant Mother*. Somebody from a gallery would've been all over it. So my deduction, Mr Kaplan, is that you're here on false pretences.'

She was enjoying herself, a big smile on her face.

'Looks like you've got too much time on your hands,' he said smiling back, 'but nice work, it's a fair cop.'

He showed her his PI licence and she clapped her hands and gave a hoot of pleasure. 'Perfect, a private detective! I should've guessed.'

'Yeah well, I am working for the Shultz Gallery as well. Like Sal told you, they want a story to hang the exhibit on.'

'Why didn't you come clean?' She leaned back and laughed, a deep throaty gurgle, before fixing him with a challenging look. 'Worried I wouldn't have a private detective in the house?'

'We don't enjoy the best of reputations.'

'I've dealt with worse, Mr Kaplan, a whole lot worse.' She examined her nails as if they'd scraped the bottom of the barrel. 'The Foreign Service isn't all black-tie receptions and cocktail parties you know.'

'I bet it isn't.'

She drew on her cigarette and blew a smoke ring into the air.

'Very clever,' he said, smiling.

'You were clever finding me,' she said, turning it back on him. 'I'm supposed to be ex-directory.'

'Well, you know how it is—' He tapped the side of his nose as if private investigators had their methods.

She leaned towards him, a glint in her eye. 'No, I don't know. That information is supposed to be confidential. Where did you get it?'

It was clear she wasn't going to let him off the hook so he conceded. 'Contact in the Foreign Service,' he said.

'Ah,' she said, leaning back, 'of course, the Foreign Service, good old purveyors of the Truth. And no doubt they told you the truth about why I ended up out here? Was that their expression? I bet they told you about NORAID as well.'

She'd wrong-footed him. 'Yeah,' he said. 'Yeah they did. The Irish connection—'

She cut in: 'My cousin, Connor.'

'They didn't tell me his name.'

She stubbed out her cigarette. 'Well, now you know – and just to put the record straight it was only a pretext. NORAID is totally legit but Nixon's crowd never misses a chance to get rid of bleeding-heart liberals like me. Too preppy East Coast.'

'OK,' he said. 'Factions in Washington – they're a mystery to me.' He drew hard on his cigarette and looked out towards the power station.

'It's closing down,' she said, following his gaze. 'We're taking a tip from the French and building a nuclear plant instead. By the way, you were probably up too early to hear that President Pompidou died last night.'

'Really?' he said, taken aback. 'How?'

'Cancer. Another president who's been living on borrowed time just when we need leadership.'

'First I've heard of it.'

'I'm not surprised,' she said. 'The French are very good at muzzling the media.'

Harry didn't really need to be told: second stage of his journey out of Hungary had been France during the Algerian War, and he remembered the bodies in the Seine after the Long Night in '61 just before he left for the USA. The press had barely reported it.

'Did they do the same in Cameroon?' he asked.

'And more. They didn't even have to tread carefully out there.' She raised her eyebrows. 'What did you have in mind?'

'Well, Annie Fayol was onto a big story when she died,' he said, 'and I was wondering if anyone tried muzzling her.'

'I don't know.' She stubbed out her cigarette. 'She was always treading on people's toes.'

'Anybody's in particular?'

'I already told you she didn't share anything with me.'

'Like the name of the guy she fell for?'

She snorted. 'Not a chance – although I heard it was the guys who fell for her, with a little come-on flirting on her part of course.'

'She really got under your skin, didn't she?'

'Not half as badly as the French memsahibs. They threw a champagne party the day she was buried.'

'Maybe she'd been seeing one of their husbands?'

'I don't know anything about that.'

'Come on,' he said, 'you must've heard rumours.'

She looked at him, staring him out. 'There are always rumours about women like her in a place like Douala.' She paused as if she was picking her words carefully. 'Young, attractive, unmarried – back then we'd have called her fast, so of course there were rumours, which is not to say they were true or that gossip is the same as intelligence.'

'Sure it's not,' he said, 'but it's not far off with know-how like yours, or mine come to that. I'm not saying we're in the same game but we both trawl in dirty water and have to figure what to throw back.'

'OK, Mr Kaplan,' she said, conceding the point, 'you're right. My work did involve trawling in dirty water, which is why I used to frequent some pretty rough bars.'

'On your own?'

'I know how to look after myself.'

'Sure you do, but what about Annie? Wasn't she taking a risk using herself as bait?'

'Your words not mine.'

'Maybe so, but she was naked when you identified her wasn't she?'

O'Connell's flighty demeanour dissolved and she was suddenly gathered, almost prim. 'Yes, that's right, she was,' she said, 'but it wasn't the way it looked. Skinny-dipping under the stars was a craze and the new bridge over the Wouri put Mile 12 within easy reach of the city so all the young folk were doing it.'

'Not on their own.'

'Maybe not, but Annie wasn't that young and anyhow figured she could look after herself.'

'Maybe she miscalculated,' he said. 'Maybe somebody was with her that night and things got out of hand.'

'Nonsense.' The ex-diplomat folded her arms and drew herself up haughtily. Her tone changed. 'Absolute nonsense. There was no sign of anybody else or of things getting out of hand, whatever that means.'

'It means foul play.'

She looked shocked and paused a second. 'That's an absurd suggestion, Mr Kaplan,' she said. 'Annie Fayol drowned in the riptide

at Mile 12 and there was never the slightest sign of anything untoward—'

'Untoward!' He raised his voice. 'Oh come on, Miss O'Connell,
don't tell me a smart operator like you didn't think about it. An attractive young American woman is found floating naked in the river –
the same woman who's been playing fast and loose with every man in
town – homicide has got to cross your mind.'

'Alright Mr Kaplan, yes.' She glared at him. 'It did cross my mind
but the pathologist found no evidence of violence.'

'I heard the body was in bad shape.'

'It was, but only from being in the water with barracuda and the
coroner returned a verdict of misadventure.'

'OK, I believe you,' he said, unconvinced but beating a tactical
retreat. 'But you can see where I'm coming from, a cynical PI with a
lot of bad experience of human behaviour.'

'The path of the diplomat is strewn with the same sorry stuff.' She
shivered and made for the door. 'I'm getting cold and it's time we did
what you came for.'

He followed, realising he'd been manoeuvred away from the
question of Annie Fayol's death. Once back in the warm he took the
photographs from his bag and his wily hostess eyed them with undis-
guised interest.

'I always wondered where they'd got to,' she said.

'They've been lying at the bottom of a big wooden chest in
Chicago.'

She cleared the newspapers away while he spread the photos out.

'OK,' she said, picking up a set of a gauche young man looning
around on a quay under a net of bananas on a winch, 'this is an Englishman called Ronald Uttley. He was one of Annie Fayol's many disappointed suitors. He'd be a good source for you.'

'D'you know where he is now?'

She nodded. 'Back home in Manchester, England. I can give you
his address. I'm sure he'd appreciate a visit.' She picked up a photo of
the Charles Atlas type. 'He got his fingers burned by going into business with this guy, Victor Castile. Illegal business, smuggling cloth

into French Cameroon. Ronald had the cloth and Castile had the boat – and a criminal record.'

'What for?'

She shrugged dismissively. 'Some drunken squabble. But it was always going to end in tears. They were totally different types.' She smiled sadly. 'And apparently Annie preferred Castile.' She spun two photos across the desk with a weary sigh. 'You can see why.'

She left him comparing the two men and crossed the room to take a thick leather-bound file from a side drawer in the desk. 'The miraculous Time Manager,' she said, turning back with a theatrical gesture. 'Something the Modern Woman cannot afford to be without!'

He laughed, watching her undo the strap and flip through the pages. After a while she stopped to make a note on a blank index card.

'Uttley's details in Manchester,' she said, finishing off with a flourish. 'He'll know where everybody is.' She flipped through the file again and made another note. 'And this is somebody you'll find useful: a journalist called Jules Raymond, the best on the coast.' She picked out a photo from the desk and gave it to Harry. 'Currently convalescing after a coronary and supposed to be finishing his magnum opus on the French in West Africa.'

Jules Raymond was a tall, spindly middle-aged man in a Panama hat with a posture that reminded Harry of an upright wading bird.

'Please give them both my regards,' O'Connell said.

'Of course.' Harry nodded. 'What about these guys?' The photos had been shot in a dim-lit bar with a bunch of white guys dancing close with beautiful African women.

'That's La Frégate,' O'Connell said after a close look. 'They're all Scots working for an oil-prospecting company called SSI. They made the big strike for Shell in '55 over the border in Nigeria.' She sat back with a dreamy look in her eye. 'They'd be out in the mangrove swamps for weeks at a time and then hit town like a bunch of gold miners from the Old West. A barrel of fun, you might say.'

'It looks like it.' The women were very beautiful and very young. 'So Shell was big out there then?'

'Still is – West Africa is the leading alternative to the Middle East.'

'Yeah, I saw the headlines.' He tilted his head in the direction of her newspapers. It crossed his mind to push her directly on BP but decided not to risk anything so explicit. 'Doesn't Shell have any competitors out there?' he asked instead.

'Yes, Total do a lot of prospecting but Shell was in very early and played a canny game during the Biafran War. They've pretty well got the region stitched up.'

Harry studied the atmospheric scenes of the steamy dive. 'Was this one of your rough bars?' he asked.

'It was actually a cut above the rest, owned by a couple of Frenchmen and run by a mesmerising madame called Violetta.' She stopped abruptly and picked up one of the photographs featuring an artistic array of empty bottles. She narrowed her eyes and nodded. 'Yeah, that's her there.'

Harry looked: an indistinct detail at the edge of the shot. 'Hard to tell,' he said.

'You couldn't miss it in the flesh,' she said and pointed to the woman's companion. 'And that's Marc Benet, one of the owners, a legend in his own time, an ex-Legionnaire and the wounded hero of Douala's insurrection against Vichy in 1940. De Gaulle flew over specially to shake his hand under the flag and dubbed his shattered hip as "the most celebrated limp in France". She tossed the photo onto the desk and wrinkled her nose. 'Everybody was incredibly impressed – except Marc, who couldn't have cared less.'

'Why not?'

'He didn't count himself as French. His father was a Romany and had been hounded out of the country before he was born. That's why they called him Gitan.'

Gypsy: Harry nodded – the guy was hard to make out but he sort of looked the part of a Barbary pirate.

'Poor guy had more than his share of bad luck,' she said. 'His wife died in childbirth a few years later, beautiful woman called Monique, and he sold up and left for Niger. He said he belonged in the desert but it was really that he couldn't bear the associations – or the possibility of running into the doctor who fouled up the operation. He was drunk.'

She broke off and picked up a couple of shots of a kid at the top of a very high palm tree tied to the trunk by a belt.

'He brought up Monique's kid as well,' she said. 'They called him the Monkey – climbed trees like one.' She put the photos down with a shake of her head. 'Real withdrawn and sad, poor kid, even before. It always felt as if his antics were some kind of death wish.'

'Jesus.' Harry said studying the photo. 'That must be about fifty feet high—'

'Yes, fifty, sixty feet,' she said. 'It's how they harvest the oil. Anyhow, it's a real sad story.'

Harry looked at the bar scenes again. 'Worth a trip then?' he asked. 'To La Frégate, I mean.'

'Yeah, definitely. They used to do great live music, best on the coast,' she said, brightening up, 'and good food as well as a floorshow. And the girls were very discreet thanks to Violetta. Nothing tacky or sordid. Ronald Uttley was a regular, soothing his sorrows, poor fool, or bitching about his ex-business partner.'

'Did Castile go there as well?'

She frowned and shook her head slowly. 'I don't remember seeing him there much. He was a colon from up country. A different crowd.'

'What's a colon?' Harry asked.

'A settler. Born and bred out there and hanging on to what they've got. White supremacists. Like the Klan.'

Harry put the index card in his pocket while O'Connell gathered up a series of shots of guerrilla fighters sitting round the remains of a campfire.

'Here's what scared them,' she said passing Harry the photos. The young men had taken their boots off as if they were uncomfortable and their camouflaged fatigues looked a size too big. Some were smoking; one was cleaning a machete and another was stripped to the waist washing a gash in his side with a ragged cloth. In the close-ups they looked young and inexperienced.

'These guys are freedom fighters in the early days of the UPC's armed struggle,' she said with a rueful shake of the head. 'Up against the government as well as the colons. Probably training. Could be Vietnam, which only goes to show how little we learn from the past.'

'I'll second that – but no American woman ever got that close to the Vietcong, except maybe Jane Fonda. You've got to be impressed.'

'I already told you Annie knew how to get a story.'

She picked up a photo of a handsome black man with a pencil moustache reading a newspaper and smoking a cigarette at a café. With the bentwood chairs and striped awning he might have been on the Left Bank.

'Annie got that close to the frontline,' she said holding her finger and thumb a fraction apart, 'thanks to this man, her good friend Dr Félix Moumié, deputy leader of the UPC, the party fighting for independence.'

'An intimate friend?'

'If you believe the gossip.' She paused. 'And it's '56, so this was taken in Bamenda.'

She broke off and picked out the shots of two other black men. One was much the same age and leaning happily against a tree, while the other, an older man in his forties, was sitting soberly behind a typewriter. Harry took the pages from the *Encyclopaedia Britannica* out of his pocket and looked at the map.

'Bamenda was in the British Cameroons,' he said.

'Exactly.' She had a triumphant gleam in her eye. 'You said the gallery needed a story.'

'That's what I'm being paid to get.'

'Well, here it is, readymade. Once upon a time there were three young men, idealists, dreamers—' She broke off and shook her head. 'There's no way I can make light of it. The facts of the matter are that Annie Fayol met them in British Cameroon because the French had just outlawed the UPC. The idea was to throttle it at birth, but they simply set up on the other side of the border.'

'The British let them?'

She shrugged. 'The French and British have a lot of bad history.

They might've ganged up against a juvenile imperialist like Germany in Europe, but in West Africa they were always furious rivals. They also had very different imperial styles: the British only cared about trade whereas the French were on a civilising crusade.' She held out the photo of the most boyish of the trio. 'This is Ernest Ouandié, executed for treason only a couple of years ago. He'd been on the run for years.'

Harry took the photo: the young man was beaming into the camera. He looked happy, brimming with energy.

'Too bad.'

'Too damned right,' she said with a flash of anger. 'They thought they had everything to live for. They'd read the Atlantic Charter and put their faith in it and when it wasn't honoured they turned to the Soviets. We let them down, which was the one thing Annie was right about.'

'What happened to the other two?'

'French got them. Nyobé was "killed in action".' She rolled her eyes. 'And Félix Moumié was poisoned by an agent in Geneva posing as a sympathetic journalist. Very nasty – thallium.'

'What's that?'

'Radioactive material. Absolutely lethal.'

'That's a dirty trick.'

'Yeah well, you can't teach the French secret service much about dirty tricks, except in Moumié's case they screwed up. It was supposed to take a bit of time and look like natural causes, but they overdosed him and he died a few days later accusing La Main Rouge – if you remember them?'

'Sure do,' Harry nodded: a terrorist organisation fighting to keeping Algeria French and specialising in booby-trap car bombs.

She spun the photo of Moumié round and watched it come to rest. 'You might recall that some people suspected they were supplied and protected by the French secret service.'

'Were you one of them?'

'Yeah.' She shrugged. 'It was very possible. Every intelligence service has a few bad apples, someone exceeding a brief.'

'That's putting it mildly,' he said, arranging the three freedom fighters in a line. 'The UPC could've been Annie's big story, but she already had these shots in the can, so why was she driving through a war zone to go skinny-dipping under the stars? This border must've been as busy as Checkpoint Charlie.'

'Come, come, Mr Kaplan,' she said leaning back and smiling. 'Romance doesn't only happen in Hollywood you know. It's obvious she'd fallen for someone and couldn't wait to see him again. And it wasn't quite a war zone when she was there.'

'So you agree he was at the beach with her?'

Her smile faded. 'I didn't say that, but it's possible they had a rendezvous and he didn't show up. If I were you I'd want to know why not.'

3

Chicago

Before she left, Candace had a couple of stiff drinks to calm her nerves. Everything was moving so fast and she couldn't tell if she was in control or just hanging on. She'd sold the house, which was a big step, but there were still loose ends to attend to and then Bill had called; passing through, he said, and wanting to meet.

She knew only too well what guys like him had in mind when they said they needed to talk, especially when the talking was scheduled for the Departures lounge at O'Hare with a bottle of cheap Italian fizz for company. It was typical Bill: just like the motel rooms he'd been booking – shabby, out-of-town places with nylon sheets on the bed and reeking of cheap deodorant.

Anyhow, all she cared about was getting in first. She found the bar, picked him out and had crossed the room before he spotted her. She stopped him getting up with a hand raised like a traffic cop, no physical contact thank you. She could see he was all set to break it to her gently, his hand poised and his eyes all dewy as if the situation was hard for him too. Laughable.

'It's perfectly alright Bill,' she said in the tone reserved for malingerers at the clinic where she worked. 'I want out of this mess much more than you do.'

At first she'd thought of staying home and standing him up, but after a couple of drinks felt good enough to dress up and remind him what he was missing. The jarring contrast between her appearance and her attitude took the wind out of his sails and he gaped, his plan in ruins.

'Really—'

'Yes, really,' she said swiftly, 'so no rationalisations thank you very much. I've got too many of my own.'

She couldn't even summon up the cliché about it being fun while it lasted because it hadn't been, but most of all she dreaded him saying it'd been complicated. It wasn't, it was dead simple, and the word had taken on a whole new charge since she'd found Annie's card. Complicated meant somebody else's husband – infidelity, lies, and betrayal. She couldn't imagine Annie being any more comfortable playing the other woman than she'd been, although neither of them was immune to the frisson of forbidden fruit. Nobody was, unless they'd been locked away in a convent. She'd even succumbed with the sorry instance of masculinity across the table, although it was easy enough imagining him scuttling home to his wife.

'Well, Candy—' he said, fiddling with his glass.

'Don't call me that,' she hissed, stifling an urge to send it flying. 'I told you before.'

'Sure, sure, sorry—'

'Just don't do it.' Her tone was curt and icy.

'I won't.'

He wasn't going to get another chance.

She studied him anew, taking in the middle-aged spread she'd once seen as robust and the come-hither macho look that was no better than a barroom leer, and marvelled at her poor judgement. It had all been so damned corny, meeting in a bar and already the worse for wear. Mom had died a few weeks before and she'd been suffering grief and guilt. She'd had to deal with Dad and Marie Claire too – whoever said funerals rounded things off? And that particular night she'd postponed sorting out the house. The attic and Annie's trunk had been preying on her mind and one drink seemed harmless enough. She'd told herself she was entitled to a break but no way had she planned on ending up in bed with a stranger. She couldn't even remember what it was like and the rest had followed like a bad script. It didn't deserve to be called an affair.

My God. Enough already.

'Right, I'm out of here.' She pushed her glass across the table, slopping the wine. 'Celebrate on your own.'

He struggled to his feet and she eyed his waistline with distaste.

'And by the way, Bill, a word of medical advice: get your wife to put you on a diet or she's going to lose you.'

He gaped some more and she pointedly put a hand on her chest and said, 'And I'm not talking about another woman.' With that she turned on her heel and headed for the El, the rapid-transit system that served Chicago. Swarms of people were going the same way and it felt as if she was floating on a tide of humanity – and in the same direction for a change. She was lightheaded, relieved, liberated, but also pricked by a bad conscience: he'd been such easy meat but she'd enjoyed watching him squirm. Had he deserved it? Definitely, but it still felt a tad gratuitous.

The more she thought about it the more she figured Annie would've trashed him and not given it a second thought. She had been the ruthless one, Mom had always said so – which was the other reason Candace was feeling better than she had for years: she'd finally made up her mind to confront the past. She'd talked to her cousin Hélène long distance and they'd decided she should hire a private detective. Now they knew there'd been 'SOMEONE' in Annie's life when she died and they had to find out who.

It was amazing what a difference a decision could make to your morale and weird how coincidences happened. Normally on a Tuesday evening she'd be nowhere near O'Hare, but here she was because Bill had called out of the blue – and right there, standing on the platform ahead of her, was none other than that same private detective, Harry Kaplan, wearing a very handsome flying jacket. She nearly called out his name in surprise.

'Dr Fayol,' he said, clearly taken aback. 'What are you doing here?'

Her mind went blank. 'Seeing off my cousin,' she said. 'She lives in Montreal.' Idiot: the man was a private detective and used to seeing through lies. 'Second cousin technically; she shuttles between Montreal and Paris.' She babbled on: 'Rags to riches, literally, in the lingerie business. Anyhow please call me Candace. Dr Fayol sounds like you're my patient when actually it's sort of the other way round. That's a great jacket by the way.'

Harry smiled, showing his dimples. 'Memento from Long Island.'

'Sal told me you'd been to see the Ice Maiden. I called the office this morning.'

'Anything she couldn't handle?'

'No. I was just touching base.'

'She's booked me on a flight tomorrow via Manchester. I'm going to pick up the tickets now.' He glanced at his watch.

'You don't hang about.'

'It's your money—' he said.

'You don't have to rush for that.'

'I'm not. It's just the way the case is going.'

Why did she feel let down? She'd only just hired him and somehow she'd imagined them covering the ground together. She still had some of Annie's stuff to go through. 'Who's in Manchester?' she asked.

'He's called Ronald Uttley. The guy fooling around under the bananas.'

'I remember him,' she said. 'So the Ice Maiden was useful?'

'Yeah. She gave me a couple of contacts: Uttley and a journalist called Jules Raymond who's still out there, plus a couple of candidates for your sister's boyfriend.'

She recoiled from the word and shot him look of distaste.

'OK,' he said, 'whatever you want to call him. Mr X?'

She nodded: it was better but not by much.

'These are the guys she was—' He paused and then said, 'who she was associated with, Dr Félix Moumié and Victor Castile.'

She studied the photographs with an unsettling flutter of nerves. Dr Moumié was the suave black guy at the café, and Castile the thick-set man on the riverbank. She went from one to the other and back again, her mind invaded by questions. She looked at Harry. His dark eyes seemed softened.

She nodded, 'I remember them. Actually I probably would've picked them out.' She smiled. 'They're Annie's types. You were right about that. People do have them.' An unwelcome picture of Bill came into her mind: corporate lawyer, tight-fisted, Republican, and a chauvinist pig: no way was he her type. She went back to the photos.

'They're very different,' she said, catching his eye, 'and I don't mean just because this guy is black. You can see. He's – well, urbane—'

She looked at the photograph and the more she looked the more he looked like Annie's type: handsome, confident, stylish, and a bit of an egghead – a Left Bank intellectual. Her type as well.

'He was a medic like you,' Harry started but broke off as if he was in two minds about something.

'What?'

'Well,' he said carefully, 'unfortunately he's not going to be able to help us. He's in the cemetery in Geneva.'

She looked up from the photo. 'What was he doing there?' she asked sharply.

'Avoiding the French, I think.' Harry shrugged. 'He was high up in the struggle for independence.'

'I remember those young freedom fighters,' she said, as Annie's pictures of the young guerrillas in the jungle came back to her and in a flash she knew what'd happened. 'They killed him, didn't they?' she said.

Harry nodded.

'I guessed as much.'

It made sense: Annie had gone out there to tell the story of Africa rising up against their colonial masters. It was bound to be a story of national liberation and bloodshed. She looked again at Félix Moumié: the man was dead – the thought sank in – the guy Annie had fallen for had been assassinated.

'How?' she demanded. 'How did they do it?'

'Poisoned him,' he said, his voice quiet, 'with thallium.'

She recoiled. Jesus. She threw her head back. My God. She knew what thallium could do. For a moment the word escaped her and then burst out. 'That's totally barbaric,' she cried clenching her fists tight. Thallium. It had to be against the Geneva Convention, for God's sake.

Outrage surged through her. 'Jesus, Harry, you can't get that stuff across the counter!'

'Yeah I know.' His expression was sombre and he was nodding. 'It was the French secret service.'

'It's monstrous,' she said. 'How come I never read about it?'

'I hadn't either.'

'My God.' She was all shaken up inside. The good feeling of a fresh start had gone. Suddenly she knew who Annie's guy was and she could guess why it'd been complicated. She looked at the photo of Castile. She didn't like his muscles or pose and shook her head. 'It wasn't this guy,' she said, 'he's too crass – too macho.'

'Macho's the word,' Harry said and took the photos from her. 'Sal – my assistant – said she wouldn't trust him in a matinee concert hall let alone a beach after dark.'

'Nor would I.'

He hesitated and then said, 'But it looks like Annie did.'

She shook her head. She was certain. 'Not him,' she said. 'Dr Moumié was definitely more her type.'

'Maybe,' he said, 'but you said Annie used her looks and was used to operating in a man's world—'

'Yeah, that's right—'

'Eileen O'Connell's word for it was "reckless".'

'Really.' Her coldest tone. She didn't care what the Ice Maiden thought, but Harry had got something out of her. 'So what's she like then?' she asked as if she had no choice.

'Smart, very sure of herself, no ice on show, charm itself.'

'No ice?' She frowned. 'I'm surprised. My father normally gets on with women like that.'

'She's a woman of many parts.'

'A fake you mean?'

A train was coming up the track and he took her by the elbow. 'There's a bar down here,' he said. 'I'd rather not talk on the El.'

His grip was firm but gentle and she didn't want to shake him off.

'Is something wrong?' she asked, glancing sideways at him. He had a strong profile and a few grey hairs at his temple.

'I don't know yet,' he said and eased her through the crowd into a bar, an ersatz Western saloon with double doors, polished wood, stuffed bison heads and wagon wheels. The girls behind the bar were wearing suede-leather skirts and vests with fringes. It sounded like Patsy Kline on the jukebox, all broken hearts and deserted women, the sort of place she'd normally avoid like the plague.

'Sorry to drag you in here,' he said as if he'd picked up her vibe, 'but we need to talk.'

'Fine.' An unfortunate phrase, but how was he to know? She headed for an empty booth and smoothed her skirt before sitting down.

'Drink?' He still seemed on edge.

'I get the feeling it's time for something strong.' She smiled. He was a very welcome change from Bill Holden, she realised. 'On expenses of course. Bourbon, on the rocks.'

He nodded and she watched him cross the room. Damn: bourbon, the family poison – what was she thinking? She stole a quick look in her make-up mirror and then focused on the Frederic Remington print pasted onto the booth wall. The 5th Cavalry was arriving in the nick of time to save a plucky family of homesteaders from a circling pack of heathen Sioux and she half expected there to be some blonde damsel tied to a stake.

It was exasperating: what chance had the future got when the past was doled out like this? Men like Remington, along with Hollywood and TV, were all wielding the power of image to the wrong effect, no better than propaganda. She knew that line about art and propaganda, but there had to be a difference.

She looked up as Harry came back from the bar.

'Here we go,' he said, putting down a tray with two glasses and a bowl of peanuts.

'Thanks.' A double: the glass was cold and heavy, the bourbon matching the colour of the pine table.

'Good luck,' he said and clinked her glass.

'Well?'

'I'm sorry, but I didn't expect to run into you like this.'

'Nor did I.'

'Maybe it's all for the good. I was going to call but it's better to talk face to face.'

'What is it?' She tried to quell the flutter in her stomach and watched him gather his thoughts in what Mom used to call a pregnant pause. She knew it wasn't fair but it always sounded like a jibe about her not having any grandchildren.

'Well for a start,' he was saying, 'like I said, there's more to Eileen O'Connell than meets the eye.' He swilled his drink round. 'She didn't hide the fact that she and your sister didn't hit it off.'

'Annie didn't hit it off with a lot of women. She was too busy making it in a man's world.'

'That's the impression I got. Somewhere else they might've got on but Douala wasn't big enough for both of them.'

'Annie didn't give way to anybody.'

'Right, but you said she used her looks to get stories and she was with the guy the night she died—'

'I said she wouldn't have gone skinny-dipping on her own.'

'That's my point. Skinny-dipping with a guy you'd only just met is reckless, whoever it was.'

She felt suddenly cornered and the flutter got close to panic. 'What are you saying?'

'Nothing yet.' He drained his glass. 'It's normal in a new case. The assumptions get thrown in the air.'

'What assumptions?'

He shrugged. 'Who was there and what happened. Eileen O'Connell reckoned Annie had a rendezvous but the guy never showed.'

'Well, I don't think she's right about that. I think he did.'

'That's why I'm keeping an open mind.' He sipped his drink and rubbed his forehead before carrying on. 'Look, Dr Fayol—'

'Candace, please.'

'OK, Candace, I don't want to spook you here – it's early days, but there are things that worry me; not just the rendezvous at the beach and the guy disappearing. Basically, it turns out that Annie was getting in the face of the French authorities out there, and it's quite likely that skinny-dipping under the stars wasn't the only risk she was taking.'

Now panic gripped her. 'You mean it wasn't an accident. Are you trying to say that she was murdered?'

A dam burst and the words leaped out at her as if they'd been waiting for the chance. Somebody killed her. She'd always suspected something but had only managed to utter the words out loud over her mother's open coffin in the chapel of rest, muted like the whisper of dry leaves, but now they were as deafening as if she was trapped in a bell tower.

'I've got to consider it,' he said.

She took another swig and the bourbon hit her stomach and radiated in every direction. It didn't take much for alcohol to cloud her perspective on an empty stomach. A new thought raced through her mind: she'd been waiting for this revelation for years without having the slightest idea how it would be triggered. Now she knew.

'How?' she asked.

He didn't have to say anything. The slightest movement of his head was enough to fill her mind with a kaleidoscope of horror.

'I'm sorry,' he said, 'but I have to check out all the possibilities.' He was trying to pacify her. 'It's not your fault—'

Fault: the word caught in her throat. It was somebody's fault, for God's sake – blood pounded in her ears, waves were crashing on a shore and somebody was tearing at a skirt – a scream ripped through the night. Annie: a hand reached up before disappearing below the surface of the water.

Suddenly she was trembling uncontrollably. She threw off the rest of her drink and tried to focus.

'It's only one scenario,' Harry was saying, getting up, 'I just need to get out there and ask a few questions. I'll keep in touch via Sal. She'll call you if I find anything.'

'It's better knowing,' she said, her head swimming. 'A whole lot better.'

But she didn't know what she was saying: it wasn't a whole lot better. Horrific images of Annie at the beach crowded into her mind and wouldn't let her alone. She looked up: he was shaking her hand and saying something more about keeping in touch.

'You've got to find him, whoever he is,' she said, grabbing at his arm. 'It's the only way.'

Harry was late, but so was Sal. He could see her hurrying along under an umbrella. He'd called her from the airport in New York to give her the run-down on Eileen O'Connell and the two prime suspects. They'd arranged to meet at 9.30, but that was before he'd run into Candace. He called out and jogged across the street.

The Bull was one of those basement dives on the South Side designed to make would-be bohemians feel safe as well as chic, but Sal liked it because there was an old pinball machine with Snow White and a jukebox that played her kind of music. She could also do a bit of celebrity-spotting and had once seen the guy with the bushy beard from *The Chicago 8*.

'Oh wow, Harry, neat jacket!' she said, shaking off her umbrella and pulling him into the light. 'That's genuine USAF. Kent used to have one.'

'That's what they said in the store. Beaver collar and a single piece of horsehide.' He opened it up. 'Wool lining too. Apparently it got real cold up there.'

'Talk to Kent about it,' she said, rolling her eyes. 'How much they charge you?'

'Twenty-five bucks.'

'That's a steal. It really suits you.'

'Thanks.'

They went through to an empty booth in the back room and she put a red folder on the table.

'What kept you?' he asked.

'Getting your trip to the sun fixed up,' she said, pointing her chin at the red folder. 'Your tickets – and I talked to Ronald Uttley. He carried on like it was a local call, but you know I can't resist those British accents.'

'I sure do.' It was an American weakness he couldn't relate to; all he ever got was grief for sounding like Kissinger.

'Anyhow,' she said and blew her cheeks out, 'it sounds as if they're in even worse trouble than us. He said the government was on the rocks and someone had burned the lifeboats.'

Harry grunted. 'I know. I caught up with the world on the flight.' He put his copy of the *New York Times* on the table.

'Anyhow I got you a date with Mr Uttley on Thursday night and he knows where you can find Castile. He's still out there.'

'Nice work,' he said. 'That's a great start.'

'I'm not so sure, Harry,' she said, looking gloomy. 'You're putting a lot of trust in O'Connell's word.'

'I don't trust her.'

He'd thought a lot about the ex-diplomat since leaving Long Island but wasn't any the wiser. He *didn't* trust her. Obviously not: she was a spook. But it wasn't that simple – something else was going on.

'Why didn't you confront her then?' Sal asked, bringing him back with a bump. 'Annie's killer is still out there free as a bird!'

'We can't be sure it was her,' he said, 'not yet anyway.'

'Oh come on, Harry,' Sal cried, 'you can't be serious. It must be her. Brad thinks so too.'

So did he. O'Connell had more or less admitted it with all those dark hints about the French being good at muzzling the media.

'I know, Sal, and that's how I feel too,' he said, gripping his jaw in frustration. 'I ran into Dr Fayol at O'Hare and had to tell her something. That's why I was late.'

'Jesus – what did she say?'

'She already had her suspicions, but didn't want to admit to them.'

Sal looked stricken, a hand on her forehead, 'Oh my God, Harry, you don't think it was the boyfriend?'

'It wouldn't be the first time, would it?'

'No. Oh God. All the more reason to confront O'Connell: she must know who did it.'

He shook his head. 'She's too smart. Nothing has ever come out.'

'Yeah, up to now.' She leaned across the table. 'But we can blow it open. It's a scandal, for God's sake! Annie was raped and murdered—'

'Probably.'

'OK, probably.' She shook her head angrily. 'But her and Castile don't make sense.'

'Dr Fayol doesn't think so either,' he said. 'She thinks Moumié is much more likely, but I can't see him halfway up a mountain. He's not the type.'

'No.' Sal studied the photo and shook her head. 'No he's not, but how could she fall for a jerk like Castile?'

'His rugged good looks?'

'Yuck.' Sal wrinkled her nose.

'Some women like that kind of thing,' he said. 'Really. You don't need me to tell you. They lap it up.' He kept the next thought to himself: that some people were addicted to danger and that maybe Annie couldn't help herself.

But Sal was shaking her head. 'No, no, no – I don't buy it. It doesn't ring true to what she wrote on the card. She was smitten for sure, but not with a guy like that. Up the mountain or at the beach I wouldn't want him near me.' She passed him the file. 'Anyhow, here are your tickets and itinerary: British Airways via London and Lagos, where you can get a visa under the counter. Plus a non-smoker on the train to Manchester and a room in the Midland Hotel.'

'Thanks Sal.'

'My pleasure, but what about taking in Aberdeen while you're over there?'

Harry had thought about that on the flight back as well. The theme of spooks and oil kept popping up, but he wanted to tackle Castile first.

'It's not worth a detour,' he said, 'they don't feature in the gossip.'

'Not in O'Connell's gossip you mean!' Sal looked exasperated.

'Come on, Harry, you just said she's up to no good but now you're taking her word for it. She's probably trying to throw you off the scent.'

'Maybe,' he said, 'but I can always take in Scotland on the way back.'

'You should,' she said. 'Big oil companies like Shell didn't get rich by playing to the rules. They could bury something if they had to.'

'True,' he said. So could BP. 'And while we're on the topic of conspiracies, could you get me a copy of that bestseller *Lamia*?'

The waiter appeared and Harry ordered a bottle of a tried and tested Italian wine and, after a quizzical glance at Sal, a side order of fries.

She sighed. 'I got to watch my waistline.'

'You're looking fine,' he said, but knew what she meant. They'd spent too much of the winter cooped up in the office.

'By the way,' she asked, 'did you tell Dr Fayol about Eileen O'Connell being in the CIA?'

He shook his head. 'She's got enough on her plate.'

'Come on, Harry, you mean you didn't want her bawling O'Connell out.'

'Yeah OK, that too, but I need a bit of space to work out what O'Connell's up to.'

'How about obstruction of justice, for a start?'

'I told you, she's too smart. We've got nothing on her. I'm waiting for her next move.'

'While she warns whoever did it and they go to ground.'

'I know how you feel, Sal, it's frustrating, but we can't rush it. I think we're up against some big players.'

'That's exactly what Annie told the guy from *Life* magazine. I told you on the phone.'

'Yeah but you didn't say who.'

'I was saving it up.' She was smiling again. 'A Puerto Rican called Manuel who used to print Annie's photos. Apparently she called him to say she was using the British mail because she didn't trust the French and that she was up against some big players.'

'No kidding.'

'You don't have to sound so surprised. Anyone would think I sit around all day painting my nails.'

'I don't,' he said, 'really; it's just that it's beginning to fit together.'

He sat back and rubbed his forehead. It'd been a long day but it was beginning to look as if Annie had stumbled onto the big stage. The waiter interrupted his thoughts and he watched him uncork the bottle and pour it without inviting him to taste it. It was that kind of place and anyhow Sal was not a big wine drinker.

She took a sip. 'Mmmm, nice.'

'Did the guy from *Life* say anything else?' he asked.

'No, but he did wonder where the last batch of her photos had got to. He's wild keen to see them.'

Harry nodded: a lot of people were going to be wild keen to see them and maybe Sal was right – maybe they should rip the whole thing open in time for the exhibition. That would make some story for the gallery to hang it on.

4

Chicago

Candace had retched twice jogging on the shore and looked round to make sure no one had seen her, but at least she was beginning to feel better. Her eyes were sore, her head still throbbed and her mouth tasted like mildewed oats. She hadn't been able to face breakfast. The thought of eggs had been enough to make her stomach heave so she'd just nibbled on dry toast and wrapped her hands round a mug of hot black coffee.

She dialled the number on autopilot and waited. Thankfully, Dana picked up. She didn't think she could cope with one of the others: they'd just be too intense when all she wanted was a familiar voice and no interrogation. She didn't want to tell them about Annie. Not yet.

'Candace – you alright?'

Dana's drawl was sharpened with anxiety and Candace remembered leaving a message on the answerphone at a bad time. She took in a deep breath and tried to smile.

'Yeah, yeah, really,' she said, 'thanks. You know, one of those super-bad nights when all your demons turn up—'

'I know those, you poor kid.'

Dana was the founding member of the clinic's team and nearly 60: old enough to be maternal as well as a matriarch.

'Yeah. The worst. Horrific.'

'You sounded in bad shape.'

'I was. Can you erase it for me?'

'I already did.'

The soft smile in Dana's voice was enough to make Candace's eyes prick and suddenly she was pitching in with the whole story, the words tumbling out about what'd happened to Annie and how she needed that leave she'd never taken when her mother died even though everyone told her she should—

'What a nightmare,' said Dana. 'You poor thing, no wonder you're all in. You've got no choice, honey; you're taking the time off.'

Candace blew her nose as if she had a cold. 'Thanks, Dana. I know it's my stupid fault. I just thought it would be best to work through it, but this was the last straw—'

'You need a total break, somewhere in the sun. As much time as you like.'

'Thanks. Really. I feel bad leaving you in the lurch.'

'You're not and anyhow you always pull your weight. I wish everyone did. The only condition is you send us a picture postcard.'

The word 'postcard' brought on a wave of associations, a delayed reaction as well as the king-size hangover. She marvelled at how her mother had put herself through it, day-in day-out, and swore she'd never go near another bourbon for as long as she lived. She showered and put on loose drawstring pants and an aubergine-coloured sweat-shirt softened by years of wear and washing. It was her secret Linus blanket. She made another pot of coffee and looked out at the dark clouds gathering over the lake. Spring was slow in coming.

She tore open the Shultz envelope and shook the last set of photos onto the table. The editor, a young blonde woman called Sophie, had bunched them together with rubber bands into five stories with num-bered yellow stickers and a separate sheet with notes on what she guessed was going on. Candace spread the first one out, a collection of a good-looking man, with a beard and thick dark hair, handling a variety of wild animals from snakes to small monkeys. The notes said: 'Gerald Durrell, brother of Lawrence, out there collecting animals for private zoo, wrote a book about it, *My Family & Other Animals*. Good intro to the British Cameroons.'

She'd never heard of it but somebody had given her one of Lawrence Durrell's Alexandria Quartet, which she hadn't been able to get through. She glanced through the photos and hovered over a close-up of a snake before concluding that there was something to be said for a cold climate or living in a big city.

The second stack was a rag-bag of subjects titled 'Village Life': girls with braided hair looking into the camera with huge eyes; a voodoo man brandishing a chicken and a knife; a drummer with action so fast his hands were just a blur; a colossal man in traditional indigo robes measuring out a glass of palm wine from a gourd as if it was a vintage Margaux; a collection of wooden masks; and finally a kneeling woman blowing on the coals of a small cooking brazier. The notes just said 'unknown locations'.

The next, 'Marches & Vigilantes', showed a political demonstration of Cameroonians carrying UPC placards under attack from white men with clubs and baseball bats. It looked as bad as the American South and some of the whites had been caught on camera beating up guys pinned to the ground. One man in a bloodstained shirt was receiving first aid and one youngster pulled his sweatshirt up to show the flesh torn by a dog. There were shots of gendarmes, black and white, standing by and doing nothing, and a further sequence of a terrace café crammed with jeering whites throwing bottles at cowering marchers. The white guys could've been in the Klan but the notes just said that Annie had been shooting with a zoom.

Candace sighed and sipped her coffee. She knew what Annie had in mind for the project and remembered her saying that Cameroon had been perfect. Memories invaded Candace's mind, a jumble of random fragments of a childhood with a big sister before the images dissolved into one long memory of them looking through a back number of *Life*'s coverage of the D-Day landings. The sea was thick with drowning men, floating bodies and the debris of war and she remembered Annie saying how hundreds had drowned weighed down by their gear. Candace had wondered aloud how photographers could just take photos and not help – and now Annie's response came back to her, still hurtful after all those years: 'Because their job is to record events, not rescue people.' That night Candace wrote in her diary: 'BIG row with A. Have decided to be a nurse when I grow up.'

The next collection was of a rusting old cargo ship in the docks. She got out the other photos and checked: it was the same one they'd been loading bananas into with the young guy, Uttley, joking around on the quayside making an ass of himself. There wasn't anything special about it: she guessed it was seaworthy even though it looked wasted. The paint was peeling and the name was barely legible. A very faded GDANSK was written across the stern and a ragged flag was flying. The notes said it was a flag of convenience. Panamanian.

The last set startled her. She noticed the title, 'Mile 12 Beach', and her hands trembled slightly as she pulled the photos free. She spread them out: huge gnarled trees, hard hot sun you could almost feel, and lots of white families sitting under parasols with coolers and bottles of wine and women in bikinis getting a tan. There were hardly any black figures: a nanny rocking a baby in the shade of the jungle, a young kid in shorts twice his size trailing round the parasols with a bucket of soft drinks, and a couple of older guys in pressed khaki uniforms serving food as if they were in the Ritz. Kids were splashing at the water's edge and a couple of adult heads bobbed further out where the profile of an island cut the horizon. The notes said it was 'Fernando Pó, a Portuguese possession'. There was no mention of the riptide.

Candace leaned back and took a deep breath, waiting for a reaction. This was where Annie had drowned – or was murdered and thrown into the ocean like a bag of garbage. But by whom? She put the photos together to get a sense of the panorama, tracking the people from the bobbing heads to the playing kids and indolent families and their cars all parked up by the dirt road. Two sets of tracks, Harry had said; there would've been two.

She'd been too much in shock to think straight, and the bourbon hadn't helped. She got up quickly and then cursed out loud: he'd gone already, probably halfway across the Atlantic and they hadn't even made a firm arrangement to keep in touch. Idiot. She looked at her watch and dialled the office but Sal wasn't there and she got their answering service instead, a nice friendly woman she could hardly bawl out so she just left the message for Sal to get back to her right away.

The hair of the dog: that's what Mom called it and Candace knew she was giving in but surely a glass of wine with her food didn't amount to a total failure. She pulled the cork on a Californian red and took some blue cheese, crackers and gherkins out of the fridge. She loaded a tray and went through to the spare room, where the removal company had stacked the boxes. She took a record at random and put it on, a Sinatra collection it turned out, and left the door open so she could hear it.

Empty moments like these were lonely, times when she missed the phone ringing even though she knew it would only be Mom, and for sure, these were the times when she lapsed into feeling sorry for herself. She called Karen, wondering how she was dealing with her newfound freedom from ex-boyfriend Drew, but there was no answer and she put the phone down before she got the answering service. She took a bite of the cracker and savoured the salty cheese and crisp gherkin and scanned the boxes for one marked 'AF', the stuff they'd packed up in Douala and put on some tub of a cargo ship for the US. By the time it reached Chicago her world had changed beyond all recognition.

Damn. The box was heavy, and tipped off the top nearly falling on her, but she managed to half hold it up before it slid down sideways. She put down her cracker and opened the Stanley knife to cut through the packaging. Her heart was thumping inside her ribcage. She put a hand under her breast: Jesus, what was her blood pressure? The last time she checked it was way up. She started counting to 10 very slowly and breathing from the bottom of her diaphragm. Get a grip, for God's sake – there was totally nothing to get freaked out about; just a box of old clothes and a few fragments from way back.

She bit into another cracker and almost choked with fright as the phone started to ring – jangled – and she nearly knocked over the bottle of wine getting to it.

'Candace.'

'My God, Karen, you scared the life out of me!' She realised she was trembling.

'I bumped into Dana at the supermarket. She told me.'

'Oh—'

'I'm coming round.'

'Great. I could do with your company.' Her heart crabbed and she couldn't keep the croak out of her voice. 'Really. I was just about to go through Annie's things.'

'You what—?' Karen's normally calm delivery exploded into a squawk. 'Just you wait right there, girl. Watch TV or something. Anything – I'm on my way.'

Candace was left holding the phone and smiling with relief. She went into the bathroom and washed her face and gave herself a lift with some bright-red lipstick. By the time she'd finished and fluffed up her hair the bell was ringing.

'Now then.' Karen looked her up and down. 'You look tired, girl—'

'Don't say that.'

Karen hugged her. 'But gorgeous as ever. Troubled and interesting – how about that?'

Candace smiled: Karen thought of herself as wild and inscrutable, which tended to mean she stuck out her bottom lip and let her Afro go crazy.

'Thanks. You want a glass of wine and some blue cheese and dills?'

'Just eaten,' she said, shaking her head. 'But yes to a glass of wine and this shit needs to go right now.' She stopped Sinatra in mid-croon and ran her finger through Candace's chaotic record collection. 'Muddy Waters, that's more like it! What we need is a hoochie-coochie man.'

It sounded right. They raised their glasses and drank.

'Thanks K – I really didn't want to do this on my own. Not now—'

'Now that this private dick has told you it wasn't an accident?'

She nodded. 'He says it's something we have to consider.'

'Well, sure—' Karen rolled her eyes. 'How much is the dude charging you, for God's sake? I always thought the whole gig was suspicious, the first time you told me.'

'Did you?'

'Of course. First thing that came to mind, but maybe I've got a morbid imagination. You never said much about her.'

It sounded like a reproach and Candace sighed. 'I'm sorry, K, but I've only just put it all together for myself.'

Karen had been running the office for 10 years and really held the whole thing together. Nothing got her down for long.

'And you had your Mom too,' she said. 'A crock of shit to deal with.'

'Right.' She and her mother never said a word about her sister and every year the anniversaries would loom up and pass in silence – Annie's birthday, the day she died, the day she left, the day Dad left, Dad's birthday… There was always something to remind them of their losses but never a word, just one endless treadmill of denial.

Karen jumped to her feet. 'OK, girl, let's do it.'

Candace followed, crunching the last cracker. It dawned on her she hadn't eaten anything else all day.

'I'm going to call up for a pizza,' she said, pausing by the phone.

'If it's deep pan with olives and anchovies I'll steal a slice.'

'You're on.' Candace ordered two. She never liked to eat alone but it happened all the time and was one of the reasons for Bill Holden.

'Mother—' Karen was rooting through the box. 'Nobody been near this stuff since we coloured people got the vote.' She shook out a bin bag of T-shirts and underwear, fishing through it with a pointed foot. 'What goddamned size was she anyhow?'

'Skinny.'

'I guess she never had to diet.'

Karen ripped open another box. 'Books—' She recoiled from the dust with a lot of drama. 'And bugs – weevils – we need the people from Pest Control.' She turned round and did a kind of curtsy. 'I'm real sorry, ma'am, but you happen to have rubber gloves? I mean, I'm not accustomed to cleaning without them.'

Candace drew herself up, the very picture of high and haughty. 'Well, I do recall precisely requesting your people to send you all over here fully equipped—'

Karen hooted. 'C, your Scarlett O'Hara act isn't worth a crooked dime. Just get me some gloves or at least a cloth.'

'I got gloves. What d'you take me for?' She came back from the kitchen smiling and laughing. 'I did better: two pairs and a bug spray. Says it kills all kinds of vermin.'

'Foreign vermin like Drew?'

'No mention of him.' She studied the can. 'But termites, cockroaches, scorpions—'

'Give me that.' Karen blasted the box and an acrid vapour filled the air. 'You got masks?'

Candace laughed and opened a window. 'Just fresh air.'

'It's not that bad.' Karen was famously part of the no-jogging set. She stood back from the box as if something might crawl out of it. 'Jeez, I hate bugs.'

'How d'you feel about snakes?'

'Worse.'

'This guy likes them.' Candace took the photo of Gerald Durrell with a snake wrapped round him out of the file.

'Strange guy.' Karen opened her eyes goggle-wide. 'Wait – this isn't him, is it?'

'I don't think so. Apparently these two are the frontrunners.' She gave Karen the photos of Moumié and Castile.

'They're more like it.' Karen looked closer at Castile and wrinkled her nose. 'But the white guy looks like a redneck. Mean son of a bitch—'

'That's what I thought,' Candace said, 'but the trouble is the black guy is dead.'

The bell went again just as she was going to tell Karen how Moumié had died.

'Pizzas already,' she said, putting her glass down. 'They're only just down the block.' She left Karen with the boxes and went to answer the door.

She paid the kid with a tip big enough to send him off with a smile as wide as a pizza slice. She had one as wide as well – she loved being with Karen and was lucky having a boss like Dana. She was feeling high: she'd dumped Bill Holden and was clearing the decks. It was a fresh start. She was as thrilled as she used to be with a new notebook at school. She undid the pizza boxes and was just thinking about making a salad when a shout came from the spare room.

'Candace, come here, for God's sake—'

She dumped the pizzas and ran up the corridor. Books and crumpled clothes were lying on the floor and Karen was standing amid them in bright-yellow gloves. 'It wasn't those other guys at all,' she said holding out a studio portrait. 'It was this brother here. Look.'

It was an old-fashioned setting from the fifties. Candace's heart thumped hard in her chest: a handsome young man looked back at her with shining eyes and a nappy hair style, a big smile and a zoot suit with a thin bootlace tie. He was standing in a studio with a corny down-home frame and a scroll in one hand – graduation. The studio had cleverly typed his name, D. Nkumbé, into the scroll.

'Look on the back,' said Karen, her voice quiet.

Candace turned it over. The top edge had been eaten away and a dark stain had seeped across the card. All but the last two lines of the dedication had gone but it was just possible to decipher it: 'I adore you, dream of you, and can't wait to be with you at the beach as well as on the mountain. I long for you and will wait forever, Didier.' Her heart raced and she turned the photo over and gazed into his eyes, willing him to speak. Thoughts and words hurtled through her mind too fast to catch. This was the man Annie had fallen for.

'This guy,' she said, a dry whisper. She was fighting with her feelings. 'He looks so young—'

'Annie was too.'

'True, but it never felt like it. She was always my big sister.'

'But she never got to be as old as you are.'

'Yeah, right.' Candace drooped: never a day passed without expecting her big sister to walk through the door.

'Anyhow,' said Karen, 'he looks old enough to me.'

'I can see that,' Candace said, still trying to get her head together, 'but he's not wearing a ring.'

'So what?'

'He was married. Annie said it was complicated.'

'Sure it was,' Karen gripped her arm, 'the guy was black, for God's sake. Race was complicated, Candace – it still is!'

Candace recoiled in shock as Karen's words took their toll one by one. Suddenly it was obvious. Of course.

'You're right,' she said, finally finding her voice. 'We've had the wrong idea from the very start.'

'Happens to the best of us,' said Karen, squeezing her arm.

'I guess so.'

Candace was speechless.

She stared at the photo. Things were tumbling into place and her heart leaped – he looked like the kind of guy Annie would've fallen for: handsome, stylish and over the moon about her. He wasn't married at all – that wasn't the issue; *he* was. It was incredible, he'd been nameless and out of sight for nearly 20 years, but now he'd come back to life, he was black and where he came from was stamped on the back of his photo. Ebolowa.

No wonder Annie had circled it.

'Jesus,' she said, looking up at her friend. Her head was crammed full of questions but she fended them off. It was enough to know who he was – Didier Nkumbé – and where he was from, but she could tell Karen wasn't thinking the same way and before she could stop her she'd put into words the turmoil that was erupting in the pit of her stomach.

'So this was the dude at the beach with Annie,' Karen said, reading the dedication again. 'He says so here.'

5

A thousand miles to the east, Eileen O'Connell was smoking another cigarette. The wind had dropped and the sky was clear. Across the water the power station was ablaze with security floodlights and down below the ferry had closed for the night. She was still mulling over yesterday's visit from Chicago.

Harry Kaplan was an attractive man and a smart operator. Growing up under Stalinism had given him a nose for politics and an instinctive mistrust of the state machine, whether it was Stalinist Hungary, Nixon's Watergate or the French hanging on in West Africa. He had a perceptive eye for Annie Fayol's photography and a good grip on her character.

Ever since Paris Eileen had learned to be watchful; and it hadn't taken much wit to check his fake gallery credentials or to catch him out with her 'little woman in the kitchen' act. Just as she'd planned, he'd gone through her desk. He knew about her all right, and not just where she lived, but she didn't know how much more he knew. At the moment she was one step ahead, but staying there would be difficult once he started picking up the threads from Uttley and Castile.

She stubbed out her cigarette and went back to the dinner table and her half-finished bowl of pasta. She pushed it aside and sipped the wine. She missed the buzz of work and for a fleeting moment had considered inviting him to stay for dinner. She'd enjoyed flirting with him and the cut and thrust, that unstated recognition of something else going on, but it hadn't all gone to plan.

She'd thought she was ready for the photos but their emotional impact caught her off guard. It turned out that Annie Fayol, for all her arrogance, knew how to capture a moment and they'd all come flooding back: the mountain, Mile 12, the African market, the oil rig,

Bamenda, but most of all, Aberdeen Alistair and late nights in La Frégate.

She wondered how he was managing family life with his in-laws round the corner in Fife and about as enlightened as John Knox – and about as much fun. Maybe Britain's economy would be salvaged by the good fortune of North Sea oil but the good times with Ali had been collateral damage after they'd called him home. Violetta had told them the best things in life had to end and hosted a special farewell party somewhere between a wedding and a wake. It'd struck a chord with quite a crowd and most of them were still there at dawn.

She held her glass up and watched the candle flame flicker through the light brick-red colour of the Californian Pinot. Piaf was playing on the hi-fi and her heart sank. She wasn't ready to retire and had been poorly treated, which, as her lawyer said, was scant reward for everything she'd done for the government over the years.

She got up and crossed the room to her desk, her gaze coming to rest on the Cameroonian stamps and the book Jules had sent. Her fancy high school had taught classics and she remembered Lamia being some crazed Greek goddess who'd devoured her own children. The image seemed over the top for ordinary French mortals accused of spying for Russia, but who was she to say? Revenge and resentment knew no bounds.

She took out her gun and tested the mechanism. It needed oiling but it was a while since she'd carried it and times had changed. Thanks to the sudden increase in the incidence of hijacking, airport security was much tighter and of course she'd lost her diplomatic status. With a slight shake of the head she put the gun back and locked the drawer. She hesitated a second over the phone, wondering if Langley had put a tap on it, but then picked up and dialled the number for Western Union.

She had already composed the telegram: 'Harry Kaplan hooked and on his way. Thinks you're a good contact. I'm coming Tuesday. Regards EO'C.'

She dictated it and repeated the Douala address to make sure they got it right. The operator read it back to her.

'Correct,' she said, 'thank you.'

'Pleasure, ma'am. Western Union aims to please.'

She glanced at the clock. It would arrive in time for Jules' breakfast. She thought back over everything and grimaced: getting a hood like Victor Castile involved would've been a bad mistake at the best of times, but given Jules' health it was lunacy. What the hell had he been thinking?

Of course Jules hadn't been thinking at all because he'd been scared out of his wits by his cousin. He always had been: she had a clear memory of him telling her how Victor was 'as bad as a rattlesnake'.

His exact words came back to her. 'The noise they make,' he'd said, 'your blood runs cold. I always dreaded them coming into the city.'

It'd sounded as if he meant rattlesnakes but he'd actually been talking about Castile's family, who lived upcountry and seldom made the trip to Douala. She remembered that she'd seen him in La Frégate, which was unusual for him – she could picture the occasion exactly but couldn't remember when. The date didn't come back immediately. She wouldn't see 60 again and some of her faculties, once the sensation of Wellesley, were not what they used to be.

She remembered that Alistair had been out of town on the rig and she'd invited Jules to join her. She snapped her fingers in triumph: of course, he'd been on his own and looking a mess – drinking too much and not that long after his young wife's spectacular suicide. It must've been '62 – September or maybe October. Yes, that was it, just before the Cuban crisis.

She poured herself another glass of wine and put another log on the fire before sitting down on the window seat. She gazed out across the water to the power station. A trio of massive trucks, reduced to the size of toys by the distance, were unloading coal and it crossed her mind that the move to nuclear would cost a lot of drivers their jobs.

The local campaign to keep the old plant open had pointed to issues of employment as well as safety and she'd taken a passing interest and even made a donation. She wasn't a diehard opponent of nuclear power but was vaguely sentimental about the view of industrial vitality across the water. It seemed a shame to lose it.

Chicago

Candace hadn't wanted Karen to leave. She looked around at the mess and grimaced. Neither of the pizzas had been finished but there was an empty bottle of wine on one of the boxes. Candace sat down and put her head in her hands. She'd tried calling Hélène but she was out. Tonight of all nights!

She needed company. That's how she'd made the disastrous mistake with Bill. It was weird: all those years since Annie had disappeared from her life and yet she'd never got used to solitude. It wasn't as if Mom had been company – and now that she thought about it, maybe Dana had been right about getting a dog. She put the TV on and was flipping through the channels when the phone rang.

It was Hélène.

'Thank God,' Candace said. 'I had to talk to you.'

'I got your message. Deirdre just said call.'

'I don't know where to start.'

'Calm down.'

Hélène's voice was reassuring. Ten years older and a woman who always seemed to be in control. It was late but Montreal was an hour behind and Hélène didn't go to bed early as a rule. She lived an enviably social life whether she was in Paris or over this side. It came with being the glamorous and unattached head of an upmarket lingerie manufacturer. She was also the only other person Candace trusted with her secrets, although she'd almost drawn the line over the Bill Holden fiasco. She was ashamed to admit she'd made such a dumb decision.

'What's happened?'

Candace told her, one thing jumbled after the other.

'My God,' Hélène said. 'I always had my doubts about the

skinny-dipping thing. Annie was never going to do something like that on her own.'

'Exactly.'

'So you think she went with this guy Didier Nkumbé?'

Candace was totally torn. 'I don't know,' she said. 'He's Annie's 'someone' on the mountain and he comes from Ebolowa, but—'

She broke off and gazed at the 1950s studio portrait propped up on the bedside table and Didier Nkumbé smiled back at her, oblivious of the doubts and suspicions that Karen had sown in her mind. Now the question wouldn't let her alone: had he been at the beach with Annie and scuttled home after watching her drown – or done something worse?

'I don't know, Hélène,' she said, gripping her head furiously. 'I just don't know what to think. He looks like butter wouldn't melt—'

'You can't tell – not from a photograph.'

'Course not,' she said. 'I know that, for God's sake.' How many times had Annie told her?

'Well, at least you know who he was.'

Candace studied the face for the 100th time. 'Yeah.' It was amazing, nearly 20 years had passed not knowing and suddenly it was a fact she was already used to. What he looked like, his name – Didier Nkumbé – his style, his words and where he lived, Ebolowa. 'Yeah, after all this time. It's incredible.'

'Yeah, and somehow it makes sense him being black,' Hélène said.

'How d'you mean?'

'Well, you know what Annie was like. She'd go in real deep wherever she was, whatever she was doing.' Hélène paused and Candace could almost see her picking her words and shrugging in that cute French way. 'I just mean she wouldn't have gone all the way to Africa to fall for a white guy. Or at least it seems real unlikely. She was too full of adventure.'

'I see what you mean,' she said. 'She *was* like that. Always buzzing with ideas. She'd get talking about what she was going to do and I'd be goggle-eyed listening. I was just her kid sister but somehow she didn't make me feel it.' Tears filled her eyes and she wiped them away with the back of her hand.

'You know, Hélène, it took me ages to admit that she wasn't coming back. I'd sit on my bed and watch the door, waiting for her to come racing up the stairs and onto the bed beside me. "Guess what, Candy," she'd say – and she'd hit me with another new plan or story; and that's how I knew she was going to be a great photojournalist. You could literally see her stories and she'd always be making a frame with her fingers and thumbs the way film directors do – framing the shot, even if it was just the Kellogg's packet on the breakfast table or the guy next door shovelling snow off his path.'

Candace got up and tried to make one of Annie's frames out of the scene through the window and nearly dropped the phone.

'She wanted it all,' said Hélène, her voice suddenly sounding a long way off.

'Like you?'

'More than me. Nothing scared her.'

'Or you?'

Hélène laughed. 'Plenty scared me, including not having my own money and being stuck with Hugo. Anyway, what's this private eye like? Where'd you find him? You know I could've got you a good French speaker.'

Candace smiled. Sometimes Hélène's help turned into a hand on the tiller.

'I know,' she said, 'you told me, but actually Harry has French too. A woman friend whose son disappeared after getting his draft papers recommended him. He's got a rep for working with casualties from the war.'

'He must be super busy then.'

'I'm not so sure. Nobody's got any spare money at the moment.'

'Anyway I'm intrigued,' said Hélène. 'It was my idea in the first place, remember.'

'I remember.' They'd had a laugh about which fictional version of a PI he'd resemble.

'How old is he?'

Candace had tried to work that out and guessed he was younger than he looked. 'Mid- to late thirties.'

There was a crackle on the line and Candace missed something. 'What did you say?' she asked. 'I missed that bit.'

Hélène came back loud and clear, saying that Candace had saved Harry a lot of legwork by finding out about Didier Nkumbé.

'You can just send him the photo,' she said. 'Piece of cake.'

'Yeah.' She hadn't thought that far ahead.

'Though he might be pissed with you too,' she said. 'You've kind of stolen his thunder. Private eyes like to have a little job satisfaction too, you know.'

There was a pause on the line as if Hélène was thinking. 'Still,' she said, sort of blurting it out, 'a black guy – maybe that's why she never said anything. Your mom wouldn't have been wild about it. Didn't she ever suspect?'

'Who knows? She just drank all the more.' Candace tucked her legs under her and hugged a cushion with her free arm. 'I told them Annie wouldn't have gone skinny-dipping on her own but nobody paid any attention. I was just a teen; what would I know? Dad never said anything either. It didn't occur to him to question the official line.'

'That's weirder, given your dad's politics.'

'Yeah.' The more Candace thought about it, the more she realised that Dad had been out of it too. Not as much as Mom, of course, but still out of it. 'Marie Claire was eight months pregnant with Sophie.'

'Tell me about it. Your dad was on everyone's shit list,' said Hélène.

'Yeah.'

Candace didn't want to remember, but her father had actually dithered about going at all. 'What if it's early' – his words came back to her, followed by the sound of her mother's glass crashing against the kitchen wall. She remembered running upstairs and smoking one of her secret supply of cigarettes. Jesus – it was no wonder nobody had asked the right questions.

'We were all so screwed up,' she said.

'No more than the rest of us.'

Candace laughed. 'Come on, Hélène, you're a jet-setting top designer. You'll probably make the cover of *Time* magazine.'

'Don't you dare, Candace!'

'Well, I've always been impressed by the way you do things—'

'Ha! And what about Yves?'

Yves was Hélène's errant son, about seven years Candace's junior. He had no career to speak of. 'How is he?' asked Candace.

'The bills get bigger with every new fad. This time it's a blues band.' She snorted. 'He thinks he'll get to lay a lot of groupies.'

'He's handsome enough.' Candace caught sight of herself in the mirror across the room, suddenly an observer on her own life. She stared and straightened up with her shoulders back.

'Skin deep, like his father,' Hélène was saying about her son.

She'd been an adventurer in Paris after the war and fallen for an older man with a chateau and aristocratic ancestors. They'd ended up on opposite ends of the political spectrum and gone their own ways. Hélène had made a point of never taking a franc from him and now she could buy him several times over.

Candace squeezed the cushion tighter and arched her back. She wanted a cigarette badly. She had tried to quit the day after her mother's funeral. She'd wanted to mark the occasion with something that demanded strength and fortitude, a fresh start, but it'd been brought to nought by a moment's stupidity in some bar.

'You still smoking, Hélène?' she asked.

'The occasional Sobranie—'

Candace laughed. 'You're such a style freak. I can see you with one of those holders and long gloves like Leslie Caron.'

'I make my own style thank you, Candace.'

'Sorry, I'm a bit drunk.' She looked around for the bottle. 'It's been a bit hectic. I dumped that jerk Bill Holden. Got in before he did.' It seemed ages ago but she was still jubilant. 'You should've seen his face!'

'You never introduced us—'

'And you know why. Talk about a passing phase – and talking of passing, what a shock about Pompidou.'

'Yeah,' said Hélène. 'I should've guessed because he was hardly around but they kept it hushed up.'

'Another mess,' Candace said: everywhere was afflicted by scandal, bankruptcy, or terrorism and to her the world had never seemed so unstable. 'Will it affect your business?'

'Depends who wins the presidential election.' Hélène paused, thinking about it. 'I'll get a better idea tomorrow when I get back. I'd better go and pack. Why don't you join me? You've got the time off and need a break and I'd love to have you.'

Candace sat up with a start. She looked at the studio portrait and seized it. An idea exploded in her mind. She'd been marking time for years and there'd always been a sound reason. Mostly Mom, but not any longer. Now she had the perfect opportunity to wrap things up and start afresh. Find Didier Nkumbé and discover once and for all what happened to Annie that night at Mile 12.

'I'd love to,' she said, startled and ebullient. 'I'll get a ticket to Cameroon and come through Paris.'

'Attagirl!' said Hélène. 'Call me with the flight details.'

'I will,' Candace said and put the phone down. Memories of her mother and Annie came flooding back. The past was over. It had to be, and yet it was still in front of her.

6

Manchester, England

The Midland Hotel reminded Harry of Gresham's in Budapest, the same seedy grandeur redolent of times past, except it fronted onto a boarded-up railway terminal instead of the Chain Bridge and majestic Danube. The Midland's reception hall was dim and desolate but there was a middle-aged woman behind the desk clearly determined to add a glimmer of colour with a high-collared red dress and lipstick to match. Harry had barely had a chance to put his valise down before she welcomed him with a smile.

'Mr Kaplan?'

'Yes.'

'I thought so,' she said with brimming satisfaction. 'I've just spoken to Mr Uttley. There's a problem at the mill and he asked if you could reschedule—' She gave the word an American drawl and smiled by way of an 'old country' plea for indulgence. 'He promises to meet you in the bar at six-thirty sharp.'

Harry smiled back. 'No problem.'

She pressed a bell on the counter. 'I'll have your luggage taken up to your room.'

'Thank you, but I can manage fine.'

She smiled again with a nervous flutter of her hands and Harry wondered when they'd last had a foreigner visit.

'It's just that Mr Uttley thought you might like to acquaint yourself with some of our local landmarks. He reckons the past is more entertaining than the present.' She put a sheet of paper on the counter between them. 'He suggested I show you on a map.'

'Fine,' he said, without much confidence.

Another smile and another flutter and she spun a sheet of paper around for him to get a good look at her hand-drawn map. Her nails were painted the same colour as her dress.

'We're here,' she said pointing, 'and this is our main shopping street, Deansgate, with Kendals, Manchester's Harrods, at the far end, although I'm sorry to say it's closed on Wednesdays and Thursdays.' She shrugged mournfully. 'I expect you know about our three-day week?'

Harry nodded. The derelict state of the British economy had been clear from the moment he'd touched down at Heathrow with government and unions locked in mortal combat. No one was certain what was left to fight over and some of the most alarmist commentators were saying the future of Britain would be decided on the streets.

'Beyond is the cathedral and Boddingtons brewery, which Mr Uttley swears by, and Strangeways, the prison. It's high security; even you won't want to go that far.'

'Even me?'

She coloured under her thick make-up and was momentarily lost for words. She shook her head and said, 'It's just that – well, Chicago is the world's capital of crime isn't it?'

'It was in Al Capone's day,' he said. 'But I think New York claims the title nowadays.'

'Of course, silly me,' she said, taking refuge in the map. 'Anyhow, this is Albert Square and the Town Hall and just here in Lincoln Square there's a statue of your President Lincoln. Mr Uttley was sure you'd want to take a look at that.'

'Really.'

Her composure largely restored, she smiled and said, 'Yes. The thing is, Mr Kaplan, Mr Uttley's family has been in the cotton trade for generations and he says it's one of the things that made Britain Great. Cotton, coal and cargo – that's what he always says – the Three Cs; and he should know. Such a charming man, quite the gentleman. His aunt is Alison Uttley, the famous children's author. I gather she has quite a following in America.'

'I don't read too many children's books,' Harry said.

'Princess Anne has the whole set.'

'No kidding.' People's obsession with monarchy baffled him.

She leaned forward, her voice lowered as if she didn't want to be overheard: 'They say she's a very difficult woman.'

'Princess Anne?'

'No, no, Mr Uttley's aunt. Very difficult indeed: her husband drowned himself in the Mersey.'

'Did she push him?'

'Gracious me, no.' She recoiled, looking startled. 'Whatever do you mean?'

He shrugged. 'You made it sound like she was responsible.'

She coloured a little. 'That's what people say—'

'Yeah, well, people say a lot of things.' Like his grandfather had fallen down the stairs, stairs he'd used a million times, and that Annie Fayol had been asking for it.

The woman now turned crimson but a balding man in a worn uniform came through the revolving doors and rescued her.

'Ah, here's Aubrey. He'll look after your luggage, Mr Kaplan.' She handed him a key. 'Room 134 Aubrey. Mr Kaplan is from Chicago.'

Aubrey gave Harry a stony look as if Chicago, whatever its reputation, was not going to impress him, and picked up the valise without a word and Harry let him.

'The other thing Mr Uttley suggested,' the woman said, pointing again at the map again, 'is the Free Trade Hall. It's not great architecture but Mr Uttley regards it as a famous monument because free trade was Britain's great gift to the world. He said you'd know all that from your Boston Tea Party, but it's all a bit over my head.' She giggled. 'I've never really understood what he means by "cargo".'

Harry took the map. 'I'll ask him,' he said and with a quick wave spun through the doors into an evening of thin drizzle and underpowered streetlights.

'You'll need an umbrella!'

He turned back to see the receptionist brandishing a sturdy black umbrella with a hooked wooden handle.

'April can be wet,' she said with another smile.

He was glad of it because the drizzle got heavier and beat a steady rhythm on the umbrella as he walked alongside a brick viaduct down to the main drag. At the junction he passed a pub called the Briton's Protection with stained glass windows like a church and a dim light within. A man in the porch was regaling a woman about the state of the country and 'the bloody miners'. The area had the feel of the previous century with massive iron pillars and rusting girders plastered with peeling posters of a yellow flower saying 'no thanks' to nuclear power and others asking the question, 'Who Governs Britain?'

Harry had shared a compartment on the train with a young man keen to acquaint him with the details of the British economic crisis and the imminent collapse of capitalism. He'd unloaded a lecture onto Harry about how the dictatorship of the proletariat would bring justice to the masses and Harry had cut it short by buying one of the man's newspapers. Harry knew only too well that there was nothing to be gained by pointing out that it hadn't worked out like that in Hungary. He'd had the same argument with László often enough and it always came back to a question of a faith he didn't believe in.

A flow of people under umbrellas climbed the red brick stairs to Deansgate Station, sober and stoic – seemingly accustomed to making do rather than raising the Red Flag. Was that the famous Dunkirk spirit? By the time he got to the darkened department store it was raining hard. The 1930s façade reminded him of pictures of stores that László had brought back from Moscow but on a more modest scale. In the brighter lights on Deansgate he could make out the shop-window mannequins and three-piece suites, but walking away towards Lincoln Square the street lamps weakened and the statue loomed above him like a rocky outcrop.

He peered at the plinth but it was impossible to read the inscription. Suddenly the beam of a flashlight behind him lit up the familiar bearded image of Lincoln and a rasping voice came out of the darkness.

'There's more to Manchester than cotton and Bobby Charlton you know.'

Harry turned round: the man was just about visible but the peak of a cloth cap cast a shadow across his face. 'Down there in the university,' he said, raising his voice as if Harry might disagree, 'they split the atom! Ernest Rutherford. Now there's somebody to commemorate. The father of nuclear power.'

Harry gestured towards the walls of peeling posters. 'Not much commemoration going on round here.'

'That's what I mean. It's ironic but we've been skewered by the Empire and cheap oil. Look where it's got us.' The voice fell away and the flashlight went out. 'We should've followed Rutherford and made our own energy. Good night to you, sir.'

'Good night,' Harry said as the retreating figure disappeared. Harry was a soccer fan – everybody in Hungary was – and Bobby Charlton was a household name, but Ernest Rutherford meant nothing to him. He shook his head, a bizarre moment, and turned back to the hotel. He'd done enough sightseeing.

'Mr Uttley is in the bar,' the red dress told him as he returned the umbrella. 'His usual table.'

The bar was cavernous and at the far end a man was stirring the fire with a poker to such poor effect that it occurred to Harry that there could be smoke without fire.

'Mr Uttley,' Harry said and the man straightened up and turned towards him.

Annie Fayol's callow youth from Cameroon with the unkempt hair and gangling limbs was recognisable, but he had filled out below the neck and thinned out above it. He was wearing a tweed jacket with leather patches and a green necktie and on his upper lip there was a passable version of a toothbrush moustache. A half-full glass of beer sat on the table with a newspaper and pipe.

'Damned coal,' he said, casting the poker aside, 'it's full of slack. Welcome to Manchester, Mr Kaplan. I'm sorry we're not on better form.' He shrugged. 'But what can we do, caught between OPEC and the National Union of Mineworkers?'

Harry took his outstretched hand. 'Good to meet you. Eileen O'Connell sends her regards.'

'Ah, yes, thank you. Your charming secretary told me she suggested you got in touch.' He turned to the bar. 'A pint of Boddy's for our American guest please, Fred.'

'Coming up, Mr Uttley.'

Harry could just make out the figure of a man behind the bar.

'They don't light the candles until seven o'clock,' said Uttley with a hollow laugh. 'As I said you catch us on an off day. Three-day week.'

'Off year more like,' said the barman pulling at the pump.

'How did you like Meg's little tour?' Uttley asked.

'She said it was yours.'

'She's modest.'

'She gets the point of cotton and coal,' Harry said, 'but doesn't understand cargo.'

'Ah, she told you—' The Englishman filled his pipe from a soft leather pouch and tamped down the tobacco. 'It's shorthand for the fact that the British merchant fleet dominated world trade – or, in other words, cargo. Cloth woven here in Manchester was transported to every corner of the globe!'

'Right,' Harry said, 'I see.' Lenin and László had called it imperialism, the last stage of capitalism before being brought down by its internal contradictions, an image which always put him in mind of Samson tearing down the temple.

The barman passed him the glass of beer, a golden yellow colour with a head of thick cream.

'Cheers,' said Uttley, raising his glass. 'Welcome to the home of free trade and the three-day week.'

'To free trade then,' said Harry, raising his glass and taking a swig. 'That's pretty good.'

'Isn't it? Brewed for the Empire, IPA, or Indian Pale Ale. Out on the North-West Frontier in Afghanistan a fellow needed a quenching drink, not the heavy stuff they drank at home.'

'How about in Cameroon?'

Uttley nodded sagely as his mind travelled back. 'The French brought in Trente-Trois, which was a bit thin but still hit the spot.'

'I think it features in a couple of Annie Fayol's scenes at La Frégate.'

'Ah, La Frégate! What a place!'

Uttley emptied his glass with a flourish and waved at the barman for a refill. He lit his pipe with a spluttering match and said, 'You know, Mr Kaplan, I've been waiting to see those photographs for years.' He drew on the pipe and leaned back. 'A reminder of the good old days is just what we need. How are you managing across the pond?'

'Badly. Gas-guzzlers are a part of the American Dream but they're running out of oil and blaming the Arabs for wrecking the fantasy.'

Uttley swigged at his fresh pint and wiped the cream off his moustache. 'They should've seen it coming. At least the penny dropped at Shell.'

'How d'you mean?'

'Well, they anticipated trouble and started drilling in places like the Niger Delta.'

'That was one of Annie Fayol's stories,' said Harry, starting to get the file out of his bag. 'Young Scots on a rig in the jungle.'

Uttley stopped him. 'Let's wait for the lights to come on,' he said, puffing on his pipe. The embers glowed in the semi-dark. 'But you're right. SSI, they were called, still are actually, and making money hand over fist working like blacks – oops, pardon my French – on the North Sea, including my friend Ian McIntyre. He wanted to meet you but they're on emergency shifts to get the field into production. Talk about desperate times needing desperate measures – Aberdeen is overrun with Texans and property is going through the roof. Reminds me of what my parents used to say about the Yanks in the war – overpaid, oversexed and over here!'

Harry raised a half laugh. 'I was thinking of going up there on the way back.'

'Good idea. Ian had a soft spot for Annie.'

'Didn't everyone?'

Ronald Uttley snorted. 'You're talking about me, Mr Kaplan,

aren't you?' He took another long drink. 'I was a fool. I should've stuck with the girls at La Frégate.'

'According to Eileen O'Connell,' he said, 'Annie Fayol was a flirt and used her looks to get the best stories.'

Uttley studied his drink, rolling what was left in his glass from side to side, and didn't comment.

'Like the one about free trade,' Harry continued, 'and smuggling Manchester cloth into French Cameroon.'

Uttley laughed nervously. 'You heard about that?'

Harry nodded. 'Only the bare bones. It'd be good to have the full story from one of the smugglers.'

'Actually it was fair enough,' he said defensively. 'I do believe in free trade.'

'Even if it means breaking the law?'

'Yes, unless the trade is trespassing on a higher level of liberty. The American Civil War is a case in point. Did you read Lincoln's inscription on his statue?'

'It was too dark,' Harry said.

'Well,' said Uttley, draining his glass. 'Basically it's a tribute to the mill workers of Manchester for refusing to work with cotton from the slave plantations in the American South. They brought production to a halt but my great uncle put free trade above liberty and tried to break the blockade. Split the family business down the middle and the brothers never spoke again.'

Harry nodded. He knew about family splits. His brother rose through the ranks of the party to become a member of the Central Committee just as Harry was mixing with a bunch of young tearaways suckered by the myths of Levi jeans, Coca-Cola and the American way.

'So,' he said as if it was faintly amusing, 'it was family tradition and high principles that drove you to break the law and smuggle Uttley calico across the border?'

'French law,' Uttley snapped, 'which contravened their vaunted principle of liberty.'

'You didn't get on with them very well then; no Entente Cordiale?'

'Absolutely not!' Uttley shook his head. 'It's amazing,' he said, 'we're separated by just 22 miles of water but are worlds apart on everything important—'

'Like free trade?'

'Exactly,' he said and stabbed the air with his pipe. 'Look at our attitudes to empire. They see it as some sacred mission to make everyone French – exporting French food or cuisine I should say, French culture, the French language, French style, the flag, "La Marsellaise"; the whole bloody project – while for us British the priority has been just trade and anything that opens it up, like Pidgin!'

The word exploded in his mouth and he stabbed the air again. 'Can you imagine the French violating their precious language for the sake of what you Yanks call a quick buck? It's quite simply inconceivable.'

'Right.' Harry nodded; the Englishman had a point. He was going to ask him about the English exporting cricket but that was even further from the Fayol case. 'So how it did feel having a French partner like Victor Castile?' he asked instead.

The Englishman bridled at the mention of Castile and glared into his glass. 'Biggest bloody mistake I ever made,' he said, scowling, 'but it wasn't just that Castile was French – he was also totally untrustworthy.'

Harry turned the knife. 'In love or in business?'

The Englishman's mouth pursed as if he was about to spit and he cursed under his breath.

'Both,' he said and put a hand to his forehead. 'This smuggling caper is actually misleading. It was just an episode that suited him, a rung on the ladder to something much bigger. He's a very unpleasant and dangerous man.'

'It was still against the law,' said Harry. 'What would've happened if you'd been caught?'

'I hate to think.' He shook his head. 'Castile bragged about having friends in high places but he was a big mouth, what you Yanks call a mobster. He had a criminal record too. I don't know what for exactly but it wasn't for evading Customs and Excise that's for sure!'

'That side of him didn't seem to bother Annie much.'

'No it didn't.' Uttley stared into his empty glass. 'I could never understand it. Still can't.'

'What did you think when you heard she'd drowned?' Harry asked.

'Crying shame. A tragedy.' He looked at him as if he was stupid. 'Goes without saying.'

'Didn't foul play cross your mind?'

'No,' he said after a slight hesitation. 'The riptide was notorious.'

'Come on, Mr Uttley,' said Harry. 'You knew she was naked when they found her.'

'Of course I did,' he said, 'but skinny-dipping was a craze back then. Everybody was doing it.'

'On their own?'

He wavered. 'I don't know—'

'Exactly,' said Harry, 'You don't go skinny-dipping on your own; and now we've got new evidence that she met someone there.' He let the revelation hang between them. 'Someone like Dr Félix Moumié or Victor Castile or somebody else – any ideas who?'

'I haven't got a clue.' The barman passed him a fresh pint and he drank deeply from it. 'I didn't even know what fucking Félix Moumié looked like.'

'But you were crazy about Annie—'

He went bright red. 'I told you I was too young to know any better.'

'Come on,' Harry said, 'you weren't born yesterday. If you're crazy about someone, you know who else is. It's the competitive instinct.'

'Not to me it isn't.' Uttley looked away.

'The photos might help,' Harry said, getting them out.

The Englishman sighed with exasperation. 'OK, Mr Kaplan, I give in. You're right, I did wonder about foul play, everyone did; and I did wonder about Castile, but I just couldn't bear to think about it.'

'You suspected him?'

'I could imagine the bastard doing it.' He looked crestfallen. 'When she was shooting the smuggling story – well, it was disgusting, she was like a bitch on heat. I couldn't stand being around the pair of them and went back to Lagos. A few weeks later she was dead.'

'Didn't you discuss your suspicions with anyone, like the British consul or the US *chargée*?'

He shook his head. The zip had gone out of him, like a deflated beach ball. 'I didn't know Miss O'Connell that well, and I steered well clear of Douala.'

'Did you see Castile again?'

'No, I made bloody sure I didn't.'

'Didn't you go to Annie's memorial service?'

'No. I went home.' He stared morosely into the smoking fire. 'Seems like another life somehow, another person.'

The hotel room was chilly and the bed linen almost damp with the cold. Harry sat at the shabby desk and mulled over his meeting. As the night had worn on, the Englishman had slipped further into a fog of bitter resentment and incoherent nostalgia. The wound Annie had inflicted was still raw and his language got increasingly blue. At one point he even called her a cunt but the worst of his venom was reserved for Victor Castile.

He had no idea where the fucking bastard was and he didn't give a shit, but in the end he'd given Harry the name of someone who would: 'an utter turd who still drinks with him', he'd said. 'Frank Stokes. Pathetic washed-up relic of Empire, a total drunk. Would never have survived anywhere else. Brain's addled. Fucking pickled. Don't believe anything he says about me and Annie either – but he'll know where Castile is, even if he says he doesn't.'

He had given Harry the names of a couple of places to check out for Stokes. 'The Country Club at Tiko,' he'd said, 'and the Mountain Hotel in Buea. Just go into the bar and ask around for Frank Stokes ex-PWA – that's Public Works Administration. He used to run the vehicle depot in Victoria, although the cunt couldn't tell a Ford from a fucking Ferrari. He won't be too difficult to find. Just put the word out that you'll buy him a beer and he'll come running.'

Ronald Uttley had gone quiet at this point and looked at Harry mournfully as if he should understand. 'It's a small place, Mr Kaplan. You know what it's like: people talk. Nothing better to do.'

Harry had nodded, sure, and asked him if Castile had frequented La Frégate in Douala at all, but the Englishman told him that Castile was banned after a nasty scene over the mistreatment of one of the girls.

'He'd knocked her about,' he said, 'and the madame, Violetta, banned men who mistreated her girls. She and one of the owners, Marc something but everyone called him Gitan – he looked like an Arab, not big but very still, calm; you didn't cross him. Anyway that's how they ran it, but there were plenty of other places where you could get away with murder.'

Harry made a note and put the word 'murder' in inverted commas because Uttley had said he'd meant it only metaphorically. 'Or at least,' he'd said as an afterthought, 'as far as I know, though of course Douala was a port.'

At this point he'd shrugged, as if what he meant was obvious, and when Harry queried it he'd said with weary resignation, 'Oh, you know what I mean, Mr Kaplan. The kind of place where alpha males are passing through after months afloat with no female company. It's a sort of no-man's land, lawless, like the Wild West.'

7

Friday, 5 April 1974

Rhone Valley, France

He could have had the most celebrated limp in France. That's what they used to say in the Piscine, and they probably still did.[1] De Gaulle had seen to that with his newsreel on the Douala insurrection and how his heroics had seized Cameroon's titanium for the Free French. Marc grimaced at his reflection in the mirror, the leathery skin and grizzled hair. They'd called him a fucking gypsy too and that hadn't changed either. He tugged at his tie and cursed them all.

'Papa,' a small voice piped up behind him.

Madeleine.

'Papa, why are you in here again?'

He gathered her up, warm and tousled from sleep. She clung onto him like a primate and he clung back.

'You could've helped me with this,' he whispered, squeezing his tie. She opened her mouth to speak but he shushed her with a finger on her lips. She giggled and they covered their mouths like conspirators. Then he picked up his jacket and carried her downstairs into the kitchen.

'Papa,' she asked climbing onto the bench, 'why were you in the spare room?'

'I didn't want to wake anyone up – especially you, *chérie*. You should still be in bed. Look at you – you're half-asleep.'

He watched her rub her black eyes, as deep and dark as his own, and glared round at his wife's usual debris of cigarette ends and empty bottles. He wiped the table before lifting her onto his lap. She wriggled round and searched his face with an unspoken question they both knew he couldn't answer.

---

1. The HQ of the French secret service, SDECE, was next to a famous swimming pool and became known in the French press as Le Piscine.

'I have to go, *chérie*. Thérèze will be here soon to make you breakfast.'

'I wish you didn't have to, Papa.' Her eyes filled with tears.

'I'll be back soon. Cross my heart.' He grasped her so tight that the letter in his pocket pressed into him. 'Anyway, I've got a surprise for you.'

'Oooooh, Papa,' she shrilled so loudly that he had to shush her again. A sunny smile beamed out at him. 'Beautiful new stamps.'

Mount Cameroon half-hidden in cloud, Bamenda coffee beans spilling out of a basket and the bridge the French had built over the Wouri a few years before he left. They weren't new to him.

'They're from Cameroon, where I got this,' he said, rubbing his hip. The scar tissue was ridged and he could feel the steel splinter under the skin. He remembered the noise as the bullet hit, a whine and thwack, and then the blood, famously shed in the first victory of de Gaulle's battle to save France. 'Lucky it didn't smash the femur,' the surgeon had said, wiping his glasses.

Madeleine wriggled off his lap and he was back in the present.

'I'm going to stick them in now,' she said.

'*Voila*.' He held her tight and kissed the top of her head. 'Be good. I'll send you some more.'

'From Cameroon?' She drew out the last syllable so far that his heart nearly burst.

'No, *chérie*, from Niger. Where our paddleboat is. That's in West Africa too, remember?' He'd called it *Madeleine* in her honour.

She nodded, her dark head bobbing as she slid off the bench. He yearned to take her with him right there and then, consoling himself it wouldn't be long. Everything was ready in Morocco: the house, the nanny, the Montessori school – he had the money; all he needed were the Swiss passports. He grabbed his coat and was opening the door when the phone rang, the so-called safe line Jacques Foccart had insisted on as part of the deal.

'You'll be able to reach me any time of the day or night,' the bastard had promised, but Marc knew better. It meant the line was tapped and the master of information had another chance to play the puppeteer. Dealing with Foccart was like dicing with the devil – you were doomed to lose – but this time fate had dealt Marc a wild card, something that might inflict a mortal blow on his old enemy.

He picked up the phone. '*Oui*.'

'M. Benet?' It was some ENARC minion, the voice vaguely familiar. '*S'il vous plait* – Colonel Foccart would like to speak with you.'

The minion left the line and Marc waited, his grip tight on the phone.

'Gitan—' said Foccart, finally. The nickname went back as far as the limp.

'I thought we'd got rid of you,' Marc said. 'The news was that the interim president had sacked M. Afrique.'

'True, but nothing else has changed,' said Foccart. 'You still answer to me, and we're bringing the date forward to the fourteenth in case the new president tries to block Messmer's nuclear plan.'

Before the election for Pompidou's successor: the bastard thought of everything. 'That's a risk you'll have to take,' Marc said. 'It's too soon; the shipment has only just reached Douala.'

'Don't tell me what risks I have to take.'

'I'm just telling you—'

'And I'm telling you it's going to be the fourteenth,' said Foccart. 'Just remember, Benet, screw this up and your pretty little darling will be staying behind in France. Bye bye, baby.'

'Fuck you, Foccart.' He picked up a paperclip and bent it open.

'I'd be worried if I were you, a little girl all alone in the sticks with no father to protect her – you know what those peasants get up to. You were one yourself.'

'You bastard.'

'Cool down and concentrate on the job in hand. What about Castile? I sent you his details.'

'I got them.'

'And you've dealt with him?'

Marc pushed the paper clip into the soft wood as if it was a knife slicing into the flesh below the fat man's ribs. 'Easier said than done,' he said. 'All you ever do is sit behind a desk.'

'I told you to get it sorted.'

'And I told you that hoods like Victor Castile don't drop out of sight just because Pompidou wanted the Piscine cleaned up.'

'And I told you to deal with whatever and whoever got in the way—'

'I am dealing with it.'

'Good, because I've got problems with the passports. The Swiss are still smarting about Félix Moumié. They know who killed him.'

'Your problem.' Marc pushed the paperclip under his thumbnail until it hurt. 'The deal was two Swiss passports.'

'But as you said, easier said than done. Geneva has applied for extradition.'

'Let them have him then.'

'Out of the question. We take care of our own.'

'That's not what the part-timers think,' said Marc. They both knew that the days of recruiting part-timers from the underworld were over.

'Francois was not a part-timer.'

'That's why they're spitting blood. You ditched them without even saying goodbye.'

'They were on a contract basis. Anyway it's your problem now. Deal with it or there'll be no pink sunsets in Casablanca. Your little darling will be wriggling on a pole in the Rhone.'

'You bastard. I'll—' Marc ground his teeth: how he loathed this man. 'One day—'

'No you won't. Calm down and concentrate on the fourteenth.'

'The dates on the visas will need changing, which means bigger bribes. Five thousand.'

'Five—'

'Yes, five,' said Marc. 'Our lives are on the line and Gaddafi's men are all over the place. They've tapped my phone.'

'I know, and that's the other reason for bringing the date forward. Gaddafi is planning a federal union with Niger and to use Arlit's uranium to make a bomb.'

'Tough shit.' No wonder Foccart was in a flap. 'He's got as good a claim to it as France.'

'You never did have much feeling for your country, did you?'

'It's not my country. You people hounded my father out of it before I was born.'

'So why all the heroics for de Gaulle in 1940?'

'They weren't for him or France,' he said. He knew what Hitler had lined up for his people.

'Just a business transaction—'

'No transaction,' he said. 'I was never one of your part-timers.'

'But now you are, *mon ami*. Your precious integrity sold for the piffling price of a Swiss passport: how cheap can you get?'

Marc closed his eyes and clenched his fist: one day... 'What do you know about integrity?'

'I know about loyalty—'

'To someone dead and buried.'

There was the sound of a sharp intake of breath. 'To a great man who saved France—'

'Fuck France and fuck de Gaulle.'

'Watch your tongue, Benet—'

'You watch your back.'

'No problem.' The bastard chuckled mirthlessly. 'I don't have the worry of my pretty little darling being all alone in the woods to distract me.'

'Just get me the extra money for the visas.'

'I'll send it over with Luc Pleven.'

'I told you I wanted Guy Martin,' Marc said, gripping the phone tight and clenching his teeth in fury. 'He can pass as an American.'

'No chance. He betrayed us in Biafra.'

'He took a different line, that's all.'

'He misappropriated funds.'

Marc grunted: he knew Guy was a lost cause – he'd intercepted blood money intended for Foccart's mercenaries. 'So I have to make do with some fucking greenhorn?'

'Pleven is no greenhorn. He's the best of the new intake and can pass as an American even better than Martin. He went to school there. His father was our man in the Embassy.'

'Oh, that's just fine then.' Typical: a snot-nosed college boy with the right connections. 'I hope he can pick up a gun without filling his pants.'

'He can, never fear.' The bastard was suddenly brimming over. 'Imagine, Gitan, it'll be like old times again! How is the celebrated hip, by the way?'

'Whinging about the fucking French weather,' he said and slammed the phone down.

Outside the cold hit him and he pulled his hat down. He glanced back. There was no sign of Madeleine and the house glowered after him, the windows wall-eyed and morose.

Douala, Cameroon

The flight from Lagos got in early afternoon and Harry had taken a short siesta like every other breathing soul in Douala except the rooster tied up in the yard below. The sound would come back to him as one of his first impressions of Africa, like the smell of the earth steaming after the rain and the bleating goat tethered down the street waiting to have its throat cut.

The countryside seeped into the city on every corner, as Eileen O'Connell had said. She had been right about the descent into Douala too, the mist hanging close to the mountaintop and not a sun-swept beach in sight. Instead, the monotony of the mangroves and the promise of black gold hidden below the surface. No wonder the hotel in Lagos had been bursting with Texans talking up the future. Top price and top quality, they said, and outside the Arab world a bonanza just waiting to happen.

O'Connell had been right about that too; his problem was to

work out when she was lying and when she was deliberately misleading.

He watched a cockroach scuttle across the bare floor and mulled
over the state of the world: back home Sal would be rushing to get in
line early for gas, which was tough on her but then somebody always
made money out of a crisis. It was fair enough the OPEC countries
were finally reaping the rewards – they'd supplied the life-blood for
the West's post-war recovery on the cheap. Now was payback time
and maybe Pierre Messmer and the guy at the Lincoln memorial in
Manchester were right – after 30 years of cheap oil it was time for
nuclear.

It was nearly nine in Chicago; time to call her up. The guy at
reception was wearing a big bowtie and a bigger smile and pointed
him into a booth across the lobby of the hotel. The phone started to
ring before he'd had time to close the door.

'Harry—' Sal's voice echoed down the line.

'Hi Sal. How's life in the windy city?'

'Freezing. It got colder again. I'm blaming you.'

'Not fair—'

'Yeah but I can just see you loafing around in some hammock
and getting a tan.'

'No such luck. It's been cloudy and I haven't set eyes on a hammock; I actually feel a bit queasy – probably something I ate in Lagos.'

'I told you to be careful.'

'Yeah,' he said and massaged his stomach. He'd had a bout of the
runs. Sal was right: he should've been more careful.

'How was Manchester?'

'Dark. Power cuts and jaded glory, Budapest minus the secret
police. Jittery about the possibility of IRA bombs and people taking to
the streets.'

'Sounds worse than here – and Ronald Uttley tried talking me
into a visit!'

'Yeah, well, he's short of company.'

'What's he like?' she asked.

'Bitter but brighter than he looks,' Harry said. 'And he gave me a contact for Castile called Frank Stokes.'

'We already knew that,' said Sal. 'Didn't he give you anything else, like on O'Connell?'

'No, he hardly knew her. He was just an occasional guest on a long official list.'

'What did he say about Castile?'

'Well,' he said, 'he obviously couldn't stand him but it took a bit for him to admit he suspected Castile of foul play, but he wasn't around at the time. He left as soon as Annie dropped him.'

'Nothing new on who it was then?'

Harry shook his head. 'Sadly, no. Nothing solid.'

'What about Jules, the journalist?'

'You can tick him off too,' said Harry with a smile: he could see Sal working through one of her famous lists. 'Just knew him by reputation—'

'What reputation?'

'No, not that sort. He had – still has I guess – a rep as a journalist. O'Connell called him the best on the coast.'

'OK.' Sal sounded disgruntled. 'Was Uttley any help with the photographs?'

'Uh-uh. He drank too much and unravelled. Started calling Annie an unrepeatable name.'

'Oh come on, Harry; it's me you're talking to not Dr Fayol – who by the way should be here any minute. She's got some big news she wants to give you.'

'What about?'

'God knows. She wasn't going to tell the receptionist, for God's sake—'

'Don't upset her, Sal, she's paying the bill.'

'I'm as nice as pie with her, Harry. You know me.'

'That's why I'm mentioning it.'

'OK, Harry I hear what you're saying – anyhow I think she's just arrived.' He heard the phone drop and clatter as it was dragged across the desk.

'Hello—'

'Dr Fayol—'

'Mr Kaplan, Harry, hello—' She sounded breathless. 'Good to hear you got there safely.'

'Yeah, it's all going fine.'

'Was Manchester worth the trip?' she asked.

'Definitely. I'm hot on Castile's trail, so it's not so much of a needle in a haystack—'

'It isn't one at all,' she said, breaking in. 'I know who he is.'

'What?' Harry was stunned. 'Who?'

'The guy Annie fell for. He was a young Cameroonian guy called Didier Nkumbé. Not married, so the complication was race. I found his picture in one of her books. I'm bringing it with me.'

'Doing what?' He couldn't have heard right. 'I'll check him out. Ask Sal to send the photo.'

'I said I'm bringing it with me to Cameroon.'

He had heard right. 'That's crazy,' he said. 'Poste restante works fine.'

'No, no, you don't understand.' Her voice got a little shrill. 'I'm coming out. I should have years ago.'

He understood alright: she'd signed a contract and it was his case. He'd never let a client tag along even if they were loaded and as nice-looking as this one.

'That's your business,' he said, 'but now is totally the wrong time. We have a contract. I'll deal with Nkumbé. Just get Sal to send me the photo.'

'I'm sorry, Mr Kaplan, but I'm leaving today for Paris. I'm not putting it off now I know who he is. I'm going to confront him face to face.'

'You can't know it was him.'

'I can. He wrote her a dedication. It all fits. He comes from Ebolowa, the place Annie circled on the map.'

'You told me you'd checked her stuff.'

'I had,' she said, quieter. 'But I must've been distracted. It's not the same as going through anyone's old stuff.'

'You should've let me do it.'

'There wasn't time. Anyway I should have gone out there years ago,' Candace repeated.

Harry was silent. The line boomed and crackled like an electric storm in tune with his mood.

'Have you seen Jules Raymond yet?' Her words were barely audible.

'I've had my hands full finding Castile.'

'He's not a priority now, although you can still get his story for the gallery. Nothing's changed on that count.'

Bullshit: everything had. He couldn't stop her coming but he wasn't in the habit of accepting the say-so of the client. 'We can talk about the contract, but Castile is still the prime suspect.'

'I don't see how.'

'You haven't talked to Ronald Uttley,' he pointed out.

'Obviously not—'

'And anyhow this isn't how I run a case.'

'You said it wasn't a regular missing person's case.'

He clenched his fist. 'All the more reason. You'd be much better off calling Eileen O'Connell. I don't trust her. Ask her what she knows about this guy Nkumbé. She was a key player, for God's sake—'

Crackling static buried her reply.

'I can't hear you,' he shouted.

'I said I'm coming anyway – I'd appreciate it if you met me—'

The line echoed like somebody pulling on a gigantic piano wire and her voice disappeared. All he could make out was 'Tuesday night, ten o'clock'.

Tuesday: he had just three full days to find out who had killed Annie.

'You'd be far better going to Long Island—' He was shouting but the line was dead. He slammed the phone down and almost tore the flimsy door off its hinges. The guy with the bowtie glanced up. The smile was still there but it was just hovering.

'Everything alright, sir?'

'Fine thanks.'

But it wasn't. He already had a CIA agent meddling in the case – and now the client was coming over. He actually liked her but it wasn't the way he worked. He'd never even had a partner.

Saturday, 6 April 1974

Niamey, Niger

Abandoning Madeleine in France left Marc with a sapping ache he couldn't reach. The pain of the famous bullet and, as a child, the battering he'd taken from his grandfather were nothing to compare. He hadn't cried as a baby, or at least that was how he remembered it, and he'd wished his grandfather dead with every conscious moment, a primal urge that overtook him whenever the old man came at him with those huge red fists. Marc learned to expect nothing else, a dread that hounded his every step from the peasant hovel of his birth to the great green outdoors. His mother dared not show him affection and his solitary refuge was the village blacksmith, who could see he had his father's rare gift with horses.

His father had escaped when his mother started to show under her peasant smock. They would have strung him up and let the crows pick his bones clean, but he'd slipped away in the depth of night – albeit, as Marc chose to believe, torn with anguish for the unborn hostage he left behind. The village said he took after his father, a gypsy bastard with an eagle nose and black eyes, the left clouded with a smear like chalk, and half-sighted, a daily reminder of his grandfather and the foreign land he'd been born into.

'M. Marc.'

He looked up, brought back to the job in hand.

'The minister's assistant is on the phone. He has the visas.'

Marc nodded. 'Tell him I'll pick them up in an hour.'

He took the legal document out of his drawer and crossed the office. It was all part of his plan for Madeleine and he needed to recognise how good Yasmin had been to him over the years. He'd been ready for her sadness but was still touched by the moment. It was another milestone: normally he didn't dwell on death, he'd been too close too many times, but the plan reached into the depths of his being. His time was running out, no question, but maybe he would live to see Madeleine married and raising children in a universe totally different from his own. The idea filled his heart with light and he smiled.

'Yasmin,' he said, flipping through the document to where they would both sign. 'Don't be shocked but I am taking steps to move to Morocco with Madeleine and I want you to take over the business for me. You pretty much run it already.'

Yasmin reeled back, her hands flying across the keys of her typewriter.

'But M. Marc, why?' she said, breathless, not knowing how to respond. 'I don't understand.'

And why should she, Marc thought. He'd said nothing about it, even though she was one of the very few people he could trust. He held out the document like a dead bird. Words on the page were not his milieu.

'It's fairly simple,' he said softly. 'I'm transferring control of the business to you. It's what I want and you deserve it and anyhow it's in the spirit of the times.'

Yasmin gaped, her eyes shining with tears.

'Please make sure it's all in order,' he said and for the first time in 17 years he almost reached out to touch her face. 'The money taken here will be yours and my share will be the thirty per cent paid upfront in France. If you have a bad year the losses will be covered by my share.'

'But M. Marc,' she said again, looking at the document as if it was about to strike her. 'I don't understand.'

'I'm nearly sixty,' he said, smiling at the thought.

'Impossible!'

'But unfortunately true,' he said and put his hand on his hip. 'In France I feel it.'

'Will you go to France?' Her brown eyes widened with disbelief.

'Just to get Madeleine.' He looked at her very steadily. 'You know why.'

She gulped and nodded.

'Nobody else knows.' Their eyes locked and the emotion between them was palpable. 'Our secret until we're safe and sound in Casablanca and then you must come and see us.'

She dabbed on the corner of her eyes with a tissue and gave him a dazzling smile. 'I will pray for you,' she said. She picked up the document. 'I'll put this in the safe. Nobody else will know.'

Marc smiled. 'Read it first and then sign. I'll be back soon.'

Yasmin stood up and bowed. 'Thank you, M. Marc. I don't know how to thank you.'

His smile widened. 'You can thank me by getting a passport and coming to see us,' he said. 'That's all the thanks we want.'

But she hesitated as if there was still something on her mind. 'What is it?' he asked.

'Marcel,' she said. 'What will he do?'

'He's coming with us,' he said reassuringly, 'don't worry.'

He turned and left the office, nerves tightening his chest. He hadn't told her the whole truth: one other person knew his plan, the last person in the world he would've chosen, but the only person with the power to make it happen: Jacques Foccart.

By the time he left his office, the street was a glaring contrast of black and white with long shadows cast by the late-afternoon sun. It was the last month of the dry season and the air was full of dust. Marc took the turning towards the souk and stepped through the arched gateway into the shade. He strolled past the stalls of tradesmen selling traditional gowns and waved a greeting at some he knew. On the next corner an old man was frying doughnuts in a vat of oil, manoeuvring them with a stick as they fizzled and spat then lifting them out as they turned golden and threading them onto long stems of grass.

Marc took a string of four and followed the arcade deep into the heart of the souk and the stalls of jewellers and silversmiths. He paused to admire a necklace of heavy amber beads held in place by ornate silver claws. Long ago he'd bought one just like it for Monique from an itinerant Mauritanian in Douala and for a second he was dragged back in time to the terrible moment when he heard that she and the baby were dead.

'M. Marc—'

A hand was laid on his shoulder and he turned, his mind still caught up in the mists of the past.

'Abdullah,' he said and shook the hand. He held up the string of doughnuts. 'I was just on my way.'

'Come—'

Abdullah steered him into a cool interior with low couches and velvet cushions. Marc removed his shoes and took up a reclining position on one of the couches. On a low circular table there was a pewter teapot and a set of short glasses. Abdullah poured two and the clean scent of mint filled the air.

'How are you, M. Marc?'

Marc rubbed his hip and smiled. Once, long ago, he had told the old trader about the life he had lost and left behind in Cameroon. 'A lot better for seeing you,' he said, 'but I have to change the dates of the next tour.' Abdullah acted as an agent for Marc's business, an intermediary who could bring together events and entertainments.

'No problem,' said Abdullah. 'I even have a new attraction for you – a snake charmer just in from Marrakesh. He's small and child-like and his flute is crystal clear and high-pitched. Very dramatic.'

...

8

'Sir! Just a minute, Mr Kaplan, please—'

Harry turned around. Jean, the receptionist, was coming out of the side office holding an envelope. 'This just came from the US Consulate for you by special delivery.'

'Thanks.'

'And I found you a car, sir.' Jean also had a key in the palm of his hand. 'Nothing special. A green Deux Chevaux, just outside, I'll show you. M. Ricard is going home to France and is happy to sell it cheap for a hundred and fifty dollars. Says test it out and he'll be in the bar later tonight if you want to do business.'

'Thanks,' Harry said, but was distracted by the special delivery. It could only be from Brad. He turned to Jean and said, 'I'll give it a run. How far is Tiko?'

'Half an hour, forty minutes maximum, sir,' Jean said with a worried expression, as if a birthday surprise had turned into a catastrophe. 'Is anything wrong, sir? You want me to show you the way?'

'No, no thanks,' Harry said. 'It's fine.'

He stood in the only shade in the hotel parking lot with the unopened envelope in his hands, wondering why he didn't get it over with. He was normally decisive, even when he sensed bad news. But as soon as he'd torn it open and glimpsed the contents he knew he'd been right. It was from Brad and the news brought the whole house of Fayol cards crashing down.

Dear Harry,

Ike fallible after all. Dead American woman not Anne

93

Fayol after all – – date of homicide Feb '54, long before
her visit to Cameroon.

Human error!

All the best, Brad.

Damn. He read it through a second time and beat his hand on the
hood of the car. Human error all right – they'd all whipped themselves into a certainty that the dead woman was Annie and that Eileen
O'Connell had covered it up. He'd gone along with it because he'd
been too darned keen to put the CIA in the dock. He almost crumpled the telex in his hand – how could've he been so dumb? Like an
idiot he'd been seduced by the idea of playing on the main stage and
it'd just taken them up a blind alley.

Action came to his rescue. There was nothing like it to beat the
blues or shift his mood. The car started on first shot and took off pretty
well. Getting through the city's crazy traffic consumed his concentra-
tion, but as soon as he crossed the river the city faded away and the
road got rougher.

Tiko was the first place on the other side, the old British mandate
of West Cameroon, and he found the Country Club easily enough.
Just as Uttley had told him, it was set back off the road, a long
ramshackle single-storey building with a surrounding wooden porch
made from bamboo and a rusty tin roof of flattened kerosene cans.
The gateposts were absurd, massive concrete posts supporting imperial lions that had seen better days. One had lost its head.

What remained of a Union Jack was flying from a flagpole at
nowhere in particular and at the back there were trees full of chat-
tering birds with long drooping tails. He cut the engine and got out
with an appreciative glance at the car – it didn't have air con, but otherwise it was doing fine. The sun beat down on his back and he pulled
his shirt away from his body. The air clung to his skin like damp cob-
webs.

'Good afternoon, sir,' said a tall African emerging from the shadows on the porch. He wore a spotless long white tunic and a scarlet

wraparound cummerbund that matched the fez on his head. 'Welcome to the Tiko Country Club.'

'Thank you,' Harry said and took the rickety steps two at a time. 'Glad to be here.'

Inside the ceiling was low and a fan rotated slowly. A bar ran from one end of the room to the other and double doors gave onto what looked like a restaurant with a chaise longue backed up against one side. Nobody was about and the man in the fez had moved soundlessly inside and was standing behind the bar.

'We have bottled Trente-Trois, sir, French, and Guinness on tap.'

Harry went for the bottle – the same light lager he'd had the night before in a bar in the docks watching a woman in a diamante G-string wriggle out of a coiled snake. Harry didn't like snakes and he'd seen enough floorshows in Saigon. He sat down under the fan and undid another button on his shirt. His drink was quick in coming and the glass was perfectly chilled in his hand. He took a long swig and wiped his mouth with the paper napkin. The place deserved to be busier.

'You always this quiet?' he asked.

'Gets better later, but business went down after the British left.'

'Yeah, too bloody right it did!' rasped a voice from the restaurant.

Harry looked round. A gaunt head was sticking out from the chaise longue. The eyes were bloodshot and deep in their sockets and the skin was drawn tight across the skull like parchment. His forehead glistened with sweat.

'What's it to you, Yankee?' the skeleton demanded, staggering onto its feet. 'Bastards—'

'You Frank Stokes?' asked Harry.

'Who wants to know?'

The old drunk was holding a handkerchief in one hand and his crotch in the other as if he needed to relieve himself. He wore a stained shirt and long shapeless khaki shorts. His arms and legs were spindle thin and he was white enough to pass as a ghost.

'Harry Kaplan,' Harry said, turning right round. It was as close as he wanted to get. 'Ronald Uttley told me I'd find you here. He sends his best wishes.'

'You know Ronnie?'

'I stopped off to see him on the way over.'

'How is ruddy Ronnie? Still tied to his mother's apron strings?'

'Seems to be.' Harry remembered the Englishman going on about his mother. 'Can't get away like he used to.'

'Yeah well, he never got far enough to wet his willy I can tell you.' Stokes cleared his throat with a nasty rattle. 'Swear to God, Ronnie Uttley will be a virgin to the day they carry him out.'

'That's not the way he talks.'

'Phwaw – you shouldn't take his word for it!'

'He was telling me about an old flame he had out here called Annie Fayol.'

'That Yankee tart! Fanny Fayol more like. Bitch used to drive him up the wall.' The old drunk broke off into a storm of coughing. 'The stupid prat proposed to her on his bloody knees with a bunch of red roses that cost a fortune. I told him she was running around like a bitch on heat with half the Frenchies in Douala but he wouldn't listen.' He snorted and wagged his finger. 'You Yanks have got a name for women like her – "prick teaser" – and that stupid berk Ronnie fell for it.'

Uttley's warning was fresh in Harry's mind: don't believe a word the washed-up bastard tells you, he'd said, especially about me and Annie.

'I heard she got it on with a guy called Nkumbé,' he said, floating it like bait.

Stokes stared at him, his eyes foggy. 'Who?'

'Didier Nkumbé.'

'She got it on alright, but it wasn't with him.' He looked confused, staring into the distance before his expression slowly morphed into a toothless grin. 'You know what they used to say about knickers in the Blitz don't you? One good Yank and they're off.'

His hoot of laughter knocked him off balance and he sat down heavily. His shoulders shook and he spat and then wiped his mouth on the back of his hand. He slumped back panting, sweat glistening on his brow.

'Here, Mr Frank – drink this.' The barman supported him with one hand and held a glass of water in front of him.

'Bollocks, get off—' Stokes knocked it over. 'I haven't lost my marbles yet.'

The barman avoided Harry's eye and went back to the bar. Stokes was leaning forwards again, his body heaving. Something splattered onto the floor. The air reeked of piss and body odour.

Harry recoiled, 'Jesus—'

'Fucking Jesus got nothing to do with it, or any black bastard either. Fanny Fayol liked red meat in her sandwich.'

At this the old drunk broke into such a fit of cawing that Harry was hard pressed not to slap his face.

'What d'you mean?'

'You born yesterday?' Stokes rolled his eyes.

'Who said that about her?'

'Wouldn't you like to know, Yankee?' His eyes sharpened and he made a lewd gesture. 'Want a test drive with her or something? You're a bit late.'

Harry stepped in and grabbed the old man's arm at the elbow and pressed his thumb hard into the bone.

'Get off—'

'Who said it?' he said, close enough to smell Stokes' breath. He squeezed tighter, digging deep into the joint, and the old drunk jerked around like a puppet.

'Pal of mine—' Stokes was gasping with pain. 'Tougher than you.'

'Who?'

Harry could feel the barman standing behind in silent disapproval but he tightened his grip and Stokes kicked out and knocked the bucket over.

'Victor Castile.'

Harry let go and wiped his hand on his pants.

'He's an old man,' the barman said quietly.

'He should have more respect for the dead,' said Harry.

'Ask Vic what she liked if you don't believe me,' screamed Stokes, spittle hanging off his lip. He made the same lewd gesture.

'Where can I find him?'

Stokes managed a last defiant shot: 'It'll cost you.'

Harry gave the barman a bill. 'Keep him topped up.'

Stokes grabbed at the beer when it arrived but Harry got there first. He held the bottle out of the old man's reach.

'You bastard—'

'I asked you where I could find Castile.'

Stokes glowered some more. 'He's got a shack on the old Calabar road, about 20 miles from Kumba. Up a track on the right just after a bridge, but watch out or you'll miss it. If you get to the Hi Life you've gone too far.'

'That's more like it,' said Harry and put the bottle on the table with the air of someone training a dog. 'Easy, wasn't it?'

'You bastard. I'm not telling you any more.'

Harry waved him away, 'No problem.' He wanted to get away.

'You'll see—'

'Yeah?'

'Yeah. Vic will show you.' Stokes suddenly grabbed Harry's arm. His fingers were skin and bone and his grip dug deep like a claw. 'But don't let on it was me that told you. Bastard's got a mean streak. Killed a guy in Douala who got in his way. Beat the life out of him with his bare hands.'

Harry shook him off and stood back. O'Connell had skated over it – some drunken squabble she'd said.

'He used to slap Fanny around too – boasted about it. Said it turned her on.'

Harry left without saying goodbye, but he'd only got as far as the steps when Stokes hollered after him.

'Best time to get him is early morning. He'll be sleeping it off.'

Harry slammed the car door with Stokes' words ringing in his ears. The old drunk had a filthy mind all right but he wasn't smart enough to cook up a story like that, least of all under the painful pressure of a crushed elbow. But as Harry drove off a question kept coming back to him: why hadn't Eileen O'Connell told him the truth about Castile?

She'd bragged about drinking in dives and the Frenchman was a hood, no question about it. Harry wondered again about his gun: he'd thought of bringing it, but Sal had warned him off. Given the spate of airline hijacks, she said that travelling with a gun was just asking for trouble and he'd listened.

Back at the hotel he was steered into the bar by Jean to do the deal with M. Ricard. He paid up in full, no hard bargaining because it was Candace's money and she had enough to fly out on some wild-goose chase; so tough, the woman obviously had money to burn.

'Does the name Didier Nkumbé mean anything to you?' he asked after he'd got himself a cold beer and they'd exchanged a few routine pleasantries typical of men-of-the-world encounters in far-off unlikely places. Ricard had complimented him on his French – 'sounds Swiss' – and Harry had nodded: that was where he'd picked it up.

'Not particularly,' said Ricard, a short wiry man with a pepper-and-salt Van Dyke beard and a cheroot to go with it. 'It's quite a common name.'

'What about Ebolowa?'

'It's down south near the border with Equatorial Guinea and Gabon.'

'Any oil down there?'

It was a shot in the dark and Ricard looked startled. 'No, it's cocoa territory. But now you come to mention it, I think there's a big shot called Nkumbé with Total.'

'Really. Didier Nkumbé?'

Ricard frowned and flicked the ash off his cheroot. He shook his head. 'No – sorry, it's gone, but it's something like that. Could be, or David – damn – my memory's going. Too many years in this sauna!'

'How many is that?'

'Hate to think.' He stubbed out the cheroot and drained his glass. 'Over 20 in one place or another.'

'Ever heard of a guy called Victor Castile? Bit of a crook—'

'Yeah, Castile, mean bastard. Got into a fight with a young hot-head we had working on our project.' He shook his head again. 'One of the reasons I'm glad to be going home, guys like him.'

'Like what?'

'He's a colon, a settler,' he said, getting up to go. 'They give the rest of us white men a bad name.'

9

More than 1,000 miles to the north Marc Benet was on the terrace of the riverside Sahel Hotel watching the sunset, a giant orange sliding into a shimmering surface of red and gold. It was one of the scenes on the postcard 'the Glories of Niger' he had just written to his daughter. He licked a stamp, a new one for her: a silver and beige graphic of the uranium mines at Arlit. He put the card into his bag and in his mind crossed off another day. He glanced at his watch and right on cue the head waiter came through the doors from the main restaurant.

'Phone for you, M. Benet,' he murmured as he reached the table. 'Mlle Yasmin.'

'*Merci*,' Marc said and followed the man back to the booth in the lobby.

'*Bonsoir*, Yasmin.'

'*Bonsoir, monsieur*. Two calls – from Marcel saying he was there and it was hot as ever, and from M. Dayak reporting that the truck is on schedule to cross the border at ten o'clock.'

'Did Dayak say anything else? His exact words?'

'What he said,' she said firmly, 'exactly, was that it was always a pleasure to do business with Destination Sahara.'

'Thank you, Yasmin. And the American?'

'I took M. Blake to the hotel. He loved the air-conditioning!'

'They can't live without it.'

'He speaks some French, but with the funniest accent.'

'It's Cajun – from Louisiana.'

'I know,' she said, sounding slightly put out.

'Of course you do. Well, thank you so much for working today and remember, please take Monday off if it suits you. I'll be leaving tomorrow unless we have trouble at Customs.'

'Last time it took all night.'

'Don't remind me.' It had been the first sign of Gaddafi's meddling. 'Hopefully tonight will be better.'

'God willing.'

'Yes,' he said, 'God willing. Thank you, Yasmin. Good night.'

'*Bon nuit*, M. Marc.'

He put the phone down, ruminating a moment and rubbing the scar on his cheekbone. He mailed the postcard in the lobby and bought a bottle of cheap cognac from the bar. He had just settled the bill when a tall man took him gently by the elbow – Seyni Amadou, the main Citroen dealer in Niamey. They shook hands.

'How is business?' asked Amadou, wrinkling his nose at the brand.

Marc gestured with the bottle and lowered his voice. 'I've got a consignment coming across at Malanville—'

'Ah, I see – and you don't want to be there all night. Naturally.' Amadou nodded and looked around. 'This Libyan business is making life hell.'

'Us too. Bookings from France are down,' said Marc with a grimace. 'Maybe Gaddafi will find somewhere else to meddle.'

'Don't count on it.' Amadou dropped his tone to a whisper. 'I hear he has set his sights on the uranium at Arlit.'

Marc feigned world-weary surprise. 'That's the last thing we need,' he said, 'but don't worry, I'm not counting on anything any longer. Except the sun.'

Amadou nudged him with his elbow. 'A little bird told me you were making plans.'

'I'm always making plans.'

'Huh.' Amadou waved an elegant hand. 'Anyhow, good luck tonight.'

'Thanks.'

Marc had learned never to rely on God or good luck and wasn't about to start now. He went out into the balmy air and followed the river. His paddle steamer was the largest and most ornate vessel moored at the quayside. He paused at the broad stern to look at the repairs before continuing to the gangplank. Halfway across he was caught in the beam of a powerful flashlight.

'*Pardon*, M. Marc,' called a voice as the light was promptly switched off. 'I didn't realise it was you.'

'That's alright, Albert. It's your job. I'm expecting a visitor. An American called Blake. Show him up.'

Marc's office was one of the more spacious cabins on the upper deck. He dumped his bag before crouching down and twirling the combinations on the safe. On the top shelf was a Colt .44 Magnum and a box of shells. He loaded it and put it into the desk drawer before going out to watch a taxi swing off the main road and freewheel down to the quayside. A lithe young man climbed out of the back. He was dressed in a light linen suit with soft loafers and white socks. His blond hair was cropped short like a GI and he carried a smart brief-case.

Marc looked on, sizing the man against his paper profile: Luc Pleven, late twenties, background haut bourgeois, powerful patron, arrogant, glittering CV and a novice, wet behind the ears, a risk. Marc cleared his throat and leaned out of the shadows and into the moonlight. The young man looked up and nodded before crossing the gangplank and taking the stairs two at a time. Marc waited for him at the top.

'Welcome to Niger, M. Pleven,' he said.

It should have been Guy Martin, not this upstart.

Pleven grasped his hand and Marc watched the young French-man savour his moment of triumph: his first mission in the service accomplished and the perfect rendezvous, a paddle steamer on the Niger. It was the ideal script and Marc could see the young man wanting to punch the air.

'It's a beautiful boat, M. Benet,' he said instead with half a bow. 'Everyone talks about it in the Piscine.'

'Really?' Marc turned into the office, a converted cabin with two portholes and a desk and chair. 'Sit down. Can I get you anything? A coffee or a glass of Evian?'

The young Frenchman couldn't suppress a smirk and Marc read his mind: mission accomplished, it said, and he's offering me fucking mineral water. So uncool, what a jerk! That was what they said in the Piscine: the fucking gypsy didn't drink; he'd converted to Islam and he never, ever joined in. No style, no sense of occasion: he just didn't belong.

'I said, coffee or Evian?'

The young man's smirk disappeared. '*Non merci.*'

'Hotel OK?'

'Fine.'

'What about Customs? They've been tightening up.'

'No problem,' Pleven said, putting his US passport down with a snap. 'Piece of cake. This would fool the CIA.'

'And the package from Foccart?' The whole point of the mission.

'In here,' he said, flipping the brass locks on the case. 'It's real genius, straight out of James Bond – look—' He opened the lid and slid his hand under the lower flap to release a false bottom and reveal a stack of pornographic pictures.

Marc looked on. 'What's the point of those?'

Pleven smiled, a hint of condescension. 'In case Customs found the compartment. I was going to say I was smuggling a bit of porn on the side.'

'Not from France.' Marc gave the postcards a dismissive glance. 'They've got Pigalle written all over them. You're supposed to be from New Orleans.'

Pleven coloured. 'But with a ticket via Paris.'

'I know. I planned it.'

'Not this bit with Customs.'

'No. At least your crew-cut and accent seem to work with them.'

Marc had created the cover persona: Collis Blake, a paddle-steamer technician and the only guy who could be trusted to refit the boat. It was just a courier job, nothing glamorous but close enough to the frontline to make it a tough first assignment.

Pleven was fiddling with the lining in his case and triggered a second-level secret chamber. '*Voila*, the package,' he said, 'clever, eh?'

He held Marc's eye, no doubt taking note of the damage. 'Clouded like a smudge of chalk on a blackboard', somebody had said; and, like everything else about de Gaulle's trip in 1940, the impression had lasted. Ever afterwards Marc's reputation preceded him, the famous limp, chalk-smudged stare and not giving a damn.

Pleven emptied the package in front of him: two stacks of banknotes and a bankbook for Credit Suisse.

Benet flipped through it angrily. 'Where are the passports?' he asked.

'They're not ready. Colonel Foccart said you'd understand.'

'I don't.'

Pleven shrugged as if he was just the courier and put a counterfoil on the desk.

'You need to sign this. They've tightened up since your day.'

'I didn't have a day,' Marc said, signing the counterfoil.

'Oh really,' Pleven said, closing the case. 'Well, that's it. My job done.'

Marc stopped him and put the money back inside the case.

'You've just signed for that,' Pleven told him with exaggerated patience. 'You're responsible for it now, not me.'

'What did Foccart tell you?' he asked.

'The global situation obviously,' said Pleven airily.

'Meaning?'

'Well, the problems of the Arab oil embargo and our switch to nuclear power.'

'I meant what did he tell you about the operation here?'

'Well, the arms are coming in from Dahomey and the Commando unit will come over undercover as one of your tours, like a Trojan horse. They're expecting the Paras so the ground attack will catch them off-guard. We'll take control of the presidential palace and the radio and TV station before anybody knows what's going on and Colonel Kountché will do the rest.'

'You're telling me that Foccart briefed a courier with all that?'

Pleven reddened furiously. 'I needed to know—'

'You needed to deliver a package, that's all,' Marc said. 'Anything else puts the operation at risk. Somebody else told you.'

'I was fully briefed by the Piscine—'

'Like hell. Even they aren't that dumb.' The idiot was lying. 'What if Customs had bust open your fancy case?'

Pleven stood up defiantly. 'I've done the service's course on interrogation.'

'Bullshit,' Marc sneered. 'You'd have been babbling before they'd even pulled your pants down.'

Pleven leaped forward. 'How dare you—' but his voice turned into a piercing screech as Marc slammed a hand into his crotch and crushed his testicles.

'Who told you?' He pressed his face tight to Pleven's. 'They're a security risk. Foccart should be informed.'

Pleven was standing on tiptoes to ease the pain. 'Mmm-y father—'

'Your fucking father!' Marc pushed him back into the chair. 'I should've guessed. Did he clear his breach of security with Foccart?'

'He's in the colonel's confidence.'

'Not if I have anything to do with it.'

'They have a long history together in the service of General de Gaulle.'

'Sure they do! You all do, but right here it's my life on the line and my business. I don't give a fuck about your father or de Gaulle. Did your father also tell you I had a different first choice? Guy Martin. A renegade, thrown out of the service in Biafra – I'm sure they told you all about him as well.'

'No – I didn't even know his name.'

'What did they call him then? Casanova?'

'I haven't a clue. I told you I don't know anything about him.' He struggled to his feet and started to take the money out of his case. 'I'm finished here and I might as well warn you now that I intend to file a report for assaulting a fellow officer.'

Marc seized the idiot's wrist. 'Go ahead! Do it in triplicate for all I care, but leave the money where it is.'

Pleven shook him off and glared. 'Why? You requested it.'

'You're not taking the case back yet.'

'Then what the hell is going on?'

Marc ignored the outburst and asked calmly, 'How's your shooting, M. Pleven?'

'I came out joint second.'

'Bravo.' He reached into the desk drawer and came out with the Magnum. 'Here.'

'What?' Pleven gawked at it, his face agog.

'Try it.'

'It's too big – not my style.'

'Get a feel for it, you'll need to.'

Pleven's face paled with panic. 'I was only briefed for a courier job.'

'Come come,' said Marc, turning the knife, 'a young lion like you with such a distinguished father should jump at the chance of a bit of real action.'

'I don't like not being prepared—'

Marc thrust the gun into his hand. 'That's why I'm giving you a little practice.'

'It's not practice I need,' he said, passing it back.

'You sure about that? They can be pretty scary you know.'

'Who? The Libyans?'

'Libyans!' Marc snorted. 'No, not Libyans, but big scaly bastards more than thirteen feet long. You need something like this to stop one. Feel the weight of it.'

'I thought you meant really using it.'

'Really using it? On Gaddafi's men? Is that what they tell you in Foccart's seminars? Heroic deeds on the frontline?'

'Of course not.' Pleven put the gun down, clearly fuming: he looked as if he would've happily shot Marc stone dead. 'What's all this about crocodiles anyway?'

'Just a diversion.' Marc put the gun into the case and shut the lid. 'Gaddafi's guys have made things a lot tougher.'

'But what's it got to do with me?'

'You're coming with me to meet the shipment and it's a good spot to hunt crocs.'

'But I'll stick out like a sore thumb,' Pleven said, his voice rising with panic, 'posing as an American.'

'That's the idea. You're a diversion. *Sécurité* knows all about you already. They've tapped my phone and listened to us talking.'

'But I haven't talked to you on the phone—'

'The real M. Blake has.'

Pleven looked stunned. 'Blake is real?'

'Sure, an old friend from the Legion, a good old boy from the Bayou who likes to hunt alligators and fancies a pop at a croc. You should know your cover story, for God's sake.'

'I should've been briefed. Colonel Foccart said it was just a courier job—'

'You have to think ahead in this game and it's not a good idea to put everybody in the know. People leak, even top brass from the Deuxième.'

'You should've cleared it with Colonel Foccart. He's running the operation.'

'Not out here.'

'But it could go wrong—' the young Frenchman said. 'They might find the guns.'

Put into words, the prospect was clearly appalling, and he looked up into Marc's dark, deep-set eyes with something akin to a plea, but Marc just pushed the case across the desk and picked up his walking stick. The handle was knobbed like the knot of a thorn tree.

'You're on the frontline now,' he said and Pleven flinched. 'Not some pampered office in the Piscine.'

And with that Marc turned away, leaving Pleven to follow. The Magnum banged against the side of the case and for the first time the young recruit wondered if he'd made the right career choice. He felt sick. He was breaking a cardinal service rule by exceeding his brief without authorisation and for a second he panicked and thought of pleading illness – he was going to throw up; the unfamiliar diet; he was sorry – but one glance at the forbidding figure ahead was enough to stifle the thought and he trudged after him across the quay to a battered four-door Toyota Land Cruiser.

'Give me the case,' said Benet, unlocking the tailgate.

Inside there was a concealed space big enough to take the new-fangled attaché case.

'That's not going to fool anyone—'

Benet slammed the door. 'They're interested in what's coming over the border, not what's hidden in here.'

'How can I pose as a crazy crocodile hunter when my gun is buried back here?'

'Just take your cue from me.'

Luc moved away from the Toyota as if he was making a stand. 'I shouldn't have been bounced into this without authorisation.'

'You have mine.'

'Yours—' he sneered before he could stop himself.

'It's all you've got.'

Luc smashed his fist into the seat and turned sideways, his head resting on the window. He pretended to doze all the way and made a show of waking up as they pulled up at the Customs post at Gaya.

'Stretch your legs,' Benet said as he got out. 'You'll need to be alert.'

Luc delayed just to spite the bastard but then got out to smoke a cigarette. He watched the door of the Customs office and kicked at the ground under his feet. The smoke calmed his nerves and he wandered along the rough sidewalk and looked up at the star-studded sky. He'd never seen anything like it, even in the High Atlas or Colorado, and it should've been memorable, something else to brag about, but instead he turned back to the Customs post and wished the job was done.

The door swung open and Benet appeared.

'We won't need the cognac after all,' he said. 'The corporal doesn't drink.'

'But you said—'

'He's a Moslem,' said Benet getting back into the vehicle.

'You said everything was covered—'

'Bad luck. You can't plan for it.'

'Jesus Christ!' Luc exploded. 'We should postpone the shipment.'

'It's coming over tonight.'

Luc's stomach seized up. 'How far away is it?'

'You can see for yourself,' said Benet. 'Just up here.'

At the top of an incline Benet pulled over and cut the engine and took a pair of binoculars out of the glove box. The bank rose sharply from the roadside and a clump of trees cut a dark profile against the starlit sky. They walked to the edge and looked down at the moon-lit river and the bridge was visible as a chain of faint lights linking the shores. On the distant bank of the River Niger were barriers and guard huts and a flickering of miniature figures moving to and fro.

Luc stared down at the scene. The bored sentries, the barbed wire, the barriers and searchlights were straight out of a Cold War spy movie but they were real and he was in the middle of it. Fear closed on his heart. Benet was leaning against a tree trunk with the binoculars. He grunted and passed them over and Luc raised them to his eyes.

'See the truck?' Benet asked.

'Yeah.' A lumbering shadow with dim headlights was approaching the barrier. It ground to a halt and a figure dropped to the ground. 'Your man has just got out.'

'Right on time.'

They returned to the Toyota and Luc watched the toy buildings and miniature figures become lifelike as they came closer.

Within 20 yards of the barrier Benet cut the engine and picked up his stick and the official papers. Luc lit another cigarette and trudged towards the bridge. A sentry came out of the hut but Luc kept going towards the river.

'I'm looking for crocodiles,' he called to the man.

The silver surface of the water stretched away flat and undis-turbed. Soft murmuring croaks floated up and the stiff river grass crunched under his feet. Suddenly, so close that his heart leaped, a long log shape got up and slithered into the water before gliding out of sight. At the same moment the truck's engine coughed into life and the bridge above him began to shake and rumble – Colonel Foccart's consignment of arms was on the move. He watched the metal and canvas monster heave and hiss its way across the bridge and was momentarily mesmerised by the thought that he was witness to history in the making. The truck above him might be no less momentous than the little biplane that had carried General de Gaulle to London in 1940 or the train that had taken Lenin to Finland Station in 1917. He took in a deep breath and squared his shoulders: this was what he'd signed up for; the chance to make history.

He met Benet coming out of the Customs office.

'What about the Moslem?'

Benet shrugged. 'He's in a bad mood.'

'Fucking hell—'

'Keep calm. Play your part, that's all you have to do.'

'That's all—' he hissed but Benet was already on his way to meet the truck. The driver leaned out of the cab and shouted something and a couple of youths emerged from the hut and climbed up inside.

'What's going on now?' Luc asked, catching up. Relief flooded through him. 'You mean we're OK?'

'Yes.'

'Why didn't you tell me?'

'You're here for the crocodiles. Why would you be interested in the consignment?'

'But that's just my cover—'

'So just play it.'

Benet started back towards the Toyota and Luc had to stifle the urge to kick the old bastard's stick from under him. He'd just caught up with him when a siren cut through the night. Over the rise came a fast-moving vehicle with flashing lights, followed by another. Benet thumped his stick into the ground and swore.

'What's going on now?' Luc asked, panic jumping at him again.

'Gaddafi's men.'

10

Niger, Benin border

The youths leaped out of the truck and the Moslem corporal came out of the Customs shed. They all watched the leading car skid to a halt. The doors flew open and officers in laundered uniforms with ribbons and epaulettes spilled out. Luc's heart hammered against his ribs as Benet's official papers were dismissed with a wave of a baton and a swarm of men got into the back and started to unload the crates. Luc was transfixed. A hand gripped his arm from behind.

'You are Collis Blake?' The name rang out like a roll call.

'*Oui, c'est ça* – that's right, that's me.' His stomach turned over. '*Moi* – American – Yankee!' He pointed at himself like an imbecile and took his passport out. The soldier took it and steered him towards the shed. At the door Luc glanced back: the crates were lined up on the ground like a row of coffins with Gaddafi's men attacking them with crowbars and jemmies. As the soldier pushed him inside he heard the first lid cracking open.

Luc answered the man's questions with the sound of splintering wood filling his ears. He pictured guns and ammunition being spilled onto the ground and fear gripped at his stomach. He looked over his shoulder but all he could see were paddles for Benet's steamer strewn across the ground. The scene unfolded in front of him, split wood and mounting tension as each of the opened crates yielded yet more paddles. There were no guns, nor ammunition; nothing.

Relief overtook him as the men reached the last crate and scattered more paddles across the road. Benet was standing with the senior officer clearly expressing confusion as to why his legal consignment had been subjected to such a furious assault. He appeared bemused and wished the senior officer a cordial goodnight. The men kicked their way furiously through the paddles and got back into the truck.

It was only as the convoy disappeared over the horizon that Luc's relief turned into rage. He'd been made a fool of. He stomped down to the ruined crates, which Benet and the guards were packing with paddles.

Benet handed him a hammer. 'Make yourself useful.'

He shook with fury as he hammered the lids in place, pounding away so hard that sweat soaked his shirt and dripped into his eyes. When he'd finished he flung the hammer into the back of the truck and a chorus of laughter broke out behind him.

'They say you work like a crazy man, M. Blake; better than a gang of Hausa.'

Luc rounded on them with clenched fists. The oldest sentry, who Luc realised now was Benet's inside man, offered him the bottle of cheap cognac, half-empty now, and he accepted it with a nod and took a long swig, letting the coarse alcohol burn deep into his throat. The driver got back into the cab and the truck spluttered into life and pulled out of the bay, and the little cluster of guards broke up to let it through. The Customs detail went back to the shed, leaving the two of them finally alone.

'Fuck you, Benet,' Luc exploded and slammed his fist down on the hood of the Toyota. 'Was that your idea of a joke?'

Benet got in without a word and put his stick on the back seat. He started the engine and waited for Luc before driving off. 'It wasn't a joke.'

'What the hell was it then? You had no right—'

'I had every right. In this business, all that matters is the result.'

'Result! A stack of fucking paddles! We were supposed to be meeting a shipment of arms.'

As if in reply, Benet braked and Luc was pitched forwards as the Toyota pulled off the road and bounced down a hidden track. Bushes caught at the wing mirrors and slapped at the windows.

'Where we going now?' he yelled.

But Benet didn't answer. He steadied the Toyota and sped along a sandy piste.

'You should count yourself lucky,' he said at last. 'Everyone has a first time to taste fear and normally the danger is real.'

'You should've told me!'

Benet just drove, leaving him to seethe. The undergrowth was thinning out and in the distance he could see the river glinting in the moonlight.

'You should've told me—' he said again.

'I told you what I needed to. That's how to stay safe on the front-line. They should've taught you that at the Piscine.'

'They taught us about trust and teamwork.'

Benet face took on a long-suffering look. 'You can only earn trust,' he said, 'and it takes time.'

'I bet Guy Martin had time.'

'Yes, as a matter of fact he did. We worked together. I saw him deal with pressure and fear.'

'Well he's not trusted in the Piscine any longer, not after Biafra!'

Benet ignored him and slowed up to bump through a ditch. They were closer to the river.

'What're we doing now, or don't you need to tell me that either?'

'We're going to pick up the guns.'

'What?'

Benet glanced at him. 'They're coming across down here. You're going to help me load up.'

'So I'm just muscle—'

'Nothing wrong with that.'

Benet eased down a steep slope onto a strand of shingle. Down-stream Luc could see the outline of an island. In front of them was a sandbank. Benet drove across it and reversed up to an inlet. He cut the engine and climbed out.

'Somebody's used this before,' muttered Luc, his hand on a moor-ing post. 'How big is the boat?'

'You'll see.'

They crossed the shingle and Benet seemed to need his stick

more. They stood and looked out across the river, a vast uninterrupted shimmer of moonlight. A couple of crocodiles flopped into the water and glided away and a flock of waders fluttered into the air and resettled at a safe distance. Benet raised a hand.

'Listen—' From far out there came the faint throb of a diesel engine. 'That's Dayak.'

'Somebody else you trust?' Luc said and then wished he hadn't.

Benet ignored him and took a hand-held searchlight from the Toyota. Its powerful beam leaped out at the riverbank, picking out the yellow eyes of a crocodile.

'Yes.'

Benet looked at his watch. Thick cloud threw a dark shadow across the water. The thudding tremor of the engine was louder and Luc swallowed. His heart was racing again. A light flicked on and off. In reply Benet switched on the beam – two long flashes and two short, followed by another long. The engine slowed as if it'd been throttled back and a return signal lanced through the night: three short, one long, and one short. Luc strained his eyes. A shadowy shape was just visible and the steady beat of the engine grew clearer; and then suddenly there were two splashes.

The blurred outline sharpened into a boat and Benet guided it into the inlet with his torch. It bobbed and churned up dirty white foam and bumped against the bank. The engine died and a substantial figure appeared and threw a rope ashore. Benet wrapped it around the post. In the murky moonlight Luc could see crates lying in the bottom of the boat, identical to those on the truck. The big man steadied himself and Luc reached out to take his hand but the man barged past, knocking him sideways. He was still staggering when Benet's quiet voice broke the silence.

'Where's Dayak?'

Instead of answering the man took a gun from his belt and pointed it at them.

'Get over there with Grandpa,' he rasped at Luc.

Luc froze: he couldn't see much of the man but the accent was a giveaway – coarse and from Marseilles.

'I said move, asshole – and get your hands up!'

Luc moved alongside Benet with his hands up. He felt the older man wobble while they were being frisked and he cursed him for leaving their only weapon in the back of the Toyota.

'Where's Dayak?' Benet asked again.

Marseilles laughed. 'He got this crazy urge to feed the crocs so I gave him a hand. Weird guy. Was he a friend of yours?'

'He did the job.'

'That's right, he delivered the goods! You're welcome to them. They're weighing me down.' He shoved Luc into the boat with the point of his gun. 'Unload them.'

Luc heaved the first crate onto the edge of the boat. Benet grabbed the rope handle, and pulled it up. Luc was surprised how much of the weight the gypsy took. They shifted them and Luc climbed out, his chest heaving with the effort.

'How did you find out?' Benet asked. 'I thought I'd covered our tracks pretty well.'

Marseilles waved the gun. The moon was bright enough for Luc to make him out – a big-boned guy, muscled and maybe running to fat, dressed in a T-shirt and loose jacket, dark-skinned with black hair and a moustache.

'I got a hot tip of something big coming through Douala.'

Benet rubbed his hip. 'I need to sit down.'

'I heard about you, Gitan. You're famous.'

'That's right,' said Benet, 'famous limp and lip and for being kicked about, a Tuareg they could never trust. I'm not on their side either.'

'I heard you were out for yourself.'

'That's why they never trusted me with the money. Why d'you think they sent this snot-nosed brat over? He's the Piscine's poodle.'

Luc tried to protest but Marseilles smacked his mouth with the gun. Panic throttled him: they were going to do a deal over his dead body. 'I'm just the courier—'

'From his own mouth, poodle, courier, what's the difference? If you want the money, ask him. Leave me out of it.'

Marseilles pushed the barrel of the gun up Luc's nose, lifting him onto his toes. 'Where is it, poodle boy?'

Luc's eyes and nose smarted but his mind was racing ahead. The gun was in the case with the money in the Toyota. He cried out as if he was the office wimp. 'Let me get it, it's in my bag.'

'Where?'

'Under the spare, hidden in the back,' he said, his nose feeling scorched.

'Get it – you too, Gitan.'

They retrieved the attaché case. Marseilles grabbed it and set it down on one of the crates. He swung the gun at them.

'On your knees!'

Luc hesitated, the familiar phrase flashing through his mind – dying on your knees.

'Now!' Marseilles drove the gun into his ribs and twisted it. Benet was leaning sideways on his stick like a fucking supplicant. Marseilles swung the beam into Luc's eyes. 'Open it.'

The brass clasps shone in the flashlight and Luc's fingers trembled as he turned the numbers. His heart was thumping: he was going to die if he didn't get to the Magnum. The pain of the gun was excruciating. He held his breath and slipped the numbers into place and half-opened the lid. The flashlight picked out the money but he'd only tipped the case slightly and the gun was out of sight. He made out the lid was stiff and was just about to reach inside when Benet leaped up with a shout of warning.

'He's got a gun,' Benet screamed and smashed his walking stick on Luc's wrist. Pain shot through his arm and the case fell onto the ground. Marseilles stabbed at him with the gun barrel and his head snapped backwards.

'You stupid fucking hero,' the man snarled. 'You're dead meat.'

Luc's arm was limp, his wrist numb. He was going to die. The words 'on your knees' swarmed over him. He tried to focus. Marseilles cursed and hit him again, this time with the Magnum. He tried to put a hand up but the barrel smacked him in the eye. There was blood in his mouth and his mind was going blank.

The man loomed over him, a huge towering shape, but at the edge of his vision there was a flash of moonlit steel followed by a horrible gurgling sound that filled the night air. Marseilles buckled and juddered forwards like a pole-axed bull. Blood pumped out hot and thick into Luc's face and he flailed furiously with his good arm. Nothing made sense. He thrashed out and his mind cleared as he realised that the weight pinning him down was dead – Marseilles, his throat slashed open from ear to ear gushing blood everywhere while Benet stood casually to one side wiping the blade of a knife and slipping it back into his walking stick.

Luc screamed. 'Get the bastard off me.'

He scrambled out and plunged into the river. He ripped his shirt off and wiped his face and body clean. His wrist was numb and he was trembling from head to toe. His stomach heaved and he retched. Footsteps crunched in the shingle behind him.

'You bastard,' he shouted at Benet. 'What were you playing at?'

'Saving our skin.'

'That's why I was getting the gun!'

Benet waved him away contemptuously. 'You'd have never got near it.'

'Don't tell me you saved my life.' It was too much. 'Where's your fucking walking stick?'

'Over here.' Benet began to walk away.

Luc caught him up. 'You fucking fake. You don't need it at all.'

Benet gave him a pitying look. 'I needed it alright. We both did.'

'You set me up again. You knew what was going to happen.'

'I told you, you have to think ahead.'

'You've used me all along—'

'Don't worry, I'll tell Foccart you didn't let the service down.'

Luc snapped. He swung with his left but Benet ducked and let fly a fierce blow to the body that blew the wind out of him. He buckled and Benet hit him again. With more humiliation than pain he fell to the ground. Benet slapped his face.

'Get up and hold this,' he said giving him the torch. 'I want to find out who this guy is.'

Luc directed the beam at the body while Benet took a bunch of keys, a wallet full of money and a French passport from the dead man's pockets. He checked the passport and emptied the wallet, pausing briefly to look at a couple of cards. One of them had a picture of a naked woman with a snake and a telephone number scrawled on the back.

'Wait,' Luc brought the beam closer, 'that nightclub is in Douala.'

'So?'

'It's your old stamping ground. You knew him—'

'He's called Louis Dupin, a thug from Marseilles.' Benet tossed him the passport. 'I've never set eyes on him but you might have. He's one of Foccart's part-timers.'

'That's absurd.'

'Think about it. For years those guys did the dirty work and suddenly they're out on their ear just because the Piscine needs a squeaky-clean image. Guys like him aren't going to take this shit lying down.'

Luc glared at the body, training the beam on the slashed throat and turned-up eyeballs: Benet had a point. His cohort at the Piscine had been left in no doubt that the new director had drawn a line under the past and there were to be no more Ben Barka-style abductions in broad daylight or elaborate murders of anti-colonialist opposition like Félix Moumié. Nor was there to be any more raising money through drug-trafficking, high-class call girls or counterfeiting money. It was all change: the service was turning over a new leaf.

'Get his feet,' Benet said, lifting the dead man's shoulders.

Luc's arm hurt but Benet was taking most of the strain and they tipped the body over the edge into the boat. Benet stepped nimbly after it.

'Throw me the rope.'

He slung it at Benet and watched him tie the body to the seat. 'What now?'

'He can feed the crocodiles as well. Dayak was a good man.'

'That little detail wasn't in your grand scheme, was it? Didn't go according to plan—' But before he could finish Benet had stepped back onto the land, the dark craggy face close enough for him to feel his breath hot on his cheek.

'Grow up, Pleven. Stop feeling sorry for yourself.'

'You took me for a ride—'

Benet pushed him away and opened the back of the Toyota. He took out a short axe and plastic shoes, the kind Luc had seen in the bazaar, and stripped off to his shorts. His body was lean and muscular and Luc couldn't help staring at the famous hip.

'You knew about this guy, admit it,' he said.

'Dayak warned me about him.' He shoved the searchlight into Luc's hands. 'Listen, I'm going to scuttle the boat and swim back. Chase off any crocodile that get close. They don't like light.'

'So now you trust me—'

But Benet was already climbing into the boat. Luc watched him start the engine and cast off. A cloud shrouded the river in shadow and he had to narrow his eyes to follow the boat as it dipped into the distance. He shone the searchlight up the river and onto the boat just as Benet swung the axe with a shattering crack. Another crack ricocheted across the river, followed by a soft splash and the sound of Benet swimming. Luc kept the beam moving, skimming the surface. The motor thudded gently, taking the body further from the shore, and Luc wondered what he'd do if a crocodile got close to the man who'd made him feel such a fool.

He was still wondering when Benet splashed onto the shingle. Luc picked out the boat with the beam and they both watched as it dropped lower and lower before slipping below the surface altogether.

'Good riddance,' muttered Luc, 'bastard.' It was cold. He dumped his wet shirt and put his jacket on. He got into the Toyota and Benet handed him the attaché case; it was as light as a feather. He shook it: not a sound. He could barely believe it. Outrage overtook him.

'You've stolen the money.'

'It's for Dayak's family. The Piscine only looks after its own.'

Luc was left gaping and Benet pushed past him.

'Come on,' he said, 'we've got to get these guns to Niamey or his death will be for nothing.'

They loaded the crates into the back of the Toyota and onto the roof rack. It hurt Luc's wrist but he felt his spirits lift and his resentment yield.

'How did Dayak tip you off?' he asked.

'He used a prearranged phrase on the phone.'

'You knew something was going to happen—'

'I knew Foccart had left a lot of part-timers with a bitter grievance,' said Benet. 'One of them was bound to turn up one way or another.'

'Maybe more than one—'

Benet looked at him. 'Now you're thinking –'

In spite of himself Luc glowed in the warmth of the man's hard-won praise. Something about him, his ruthless consistency, was winning Luc over. 'I'm sorry,' he said, 'but I'll have to report the loss of the money to Colonel Foccart. I signed for it.'

'Don't worry, I'll tell him myself, and about you too. You did OK.'

'You're seeing him?'

A curt nod. 'More's the pity.'

'He didn't tell me he was coming over.'

'He's not. I'm leaving. My job's done.'

'What about the coup?'

'It's not my business.'

'So you're running?'

'No, I'm leaving.' Benet broke off and held Dupin's gun out, a new Makarov. 'You want a souvenir, something to brag about when you get back to the Piscine?'

Luc took it, the handle fitting neatly into his hand. The cool metal and balance felt good.

'Isn't it against the rules?'

Benet gave him a look of stunned incredulity. 'I don't give a fuck about the rules. I'd have thought you'd picked that up by now; but while we're on the subject, stay away from those young whores in the hotel. They work for Gaddafi.'

Luc nodded and tucked the gun into his belt. All he wanted now was a bed to sleep in and a safe return to Paris.

11

Sunday, 7 April 1974

Road to Calabar, Cameroon

Harry was pissed with himself. Yesterday had been a mess. Frank Stokes had left a very nasty taste – sure, the old lech was a total louse but Harry had bullied him and that wasn't right. The bastard was probably twice his age, for God's sake, and the expression on the barman's face had said it all. He'd wanted to forget the whole thing so he'd gone back to the hotel and sat in the bar drinking the way he used to in Munich after leaving everything in Budapest, and then again in Saigon – that savage self-loathing attempt at amnesia, which really never worked; and like a total idiot he'd tried it all over again.

He knew full well he'd wake up with a hangover, but that was only half the story. The other half, the vicious sting in the tail, had hit him hard at dawn with a wrench at his guts and an explosive visit to the john. He'd been dumb about eating the greens in Lagos; either way he felt a total fool. On two counts he'd made a mess of things and wasted half a day, and now he only had 36 hours before Candace arrived.

And that was the other thing bugging him: her finding Nkumbé's photo. It was puerile but he couldn't help resenting it – cracking a case was the bit that made up for all the rest and her triumphant tone had reminded him of László leaning over his shoulder to make the winning move at chess. Checkmate. Damn! It used to drive him wild, which back then was maybe fair enough but this was later and he should've been able to handle it.

Jean on the desk gave him a couple of aspirin and he drank too much black coffee. By the time he got to Kumba he was thirsty and yearning for a long shower. On the edge of town he stopped at a Total station and watched as a guy in a blue overall laboured over an ancient hand pump. Harry waited for him to wipe off the windscreen with a dirty cloth before walking back to pay. 'Business tight?' he asked.

The guy wrung his hands. 'Very bad. Prices up every day.'

'This your place?'

The guy shook his head. The whites of his eyes were yellow and bloodshot. Sweat stood out on his forehead and he looked all in.

'You don't look too good.'

He let out a deep sigh. 'Bad fever,' he said. 'Very bad.'

'You should be in bed,' Harry said, stating the obvious and feeling ridiculous.

'They would kill me dead.'

'Who's they?'

'My boss. Here he is.' A shining black Merc swept into the forecourt kicking up dust and the sick guy gave Harry a mournful sidelong look. 'New model every year.'

Harry waved and left. A short way down the road he passed a guy selling Coke from a bucket of ice and Harry stopped to buy one. He asked about the Calabar road.

'Not good,' the man said as he flipped open the bottle. 'It's a dirt track.'

'I thought Calabar was a big port.'

'It is, but Biafran War killed the connection. Now it's just the back door for the oil mafia. Don't take it.'

'I've got to,' Harry said. 'It's the only way to the Hi Life bar.'

The man clapped his hands and did a couple of dance steps in the dust, 'I know it! The place used to really jump.' His feet quietened down and the grin faded. 'But it's dead now, that's what I heard. Like the road.' He looked at Harry as if he was making a big mistake. 'Those guys don't like strangers.'

'Thanks for the warning.' He drank the rest of the Coke, bought another and got back into the car. Down the road a way he could see what the guy meant: the further he went the more the jungle was taking it back. Dark clouds were gathering and the air was so tight it felt ready to snap – and then it did with a blinding flash and a clap of thunder that rebounded on the car's thin roof. A splatter of rain hit the windshield followed by a sheet of water like somebody was emptying out a colossal bucket. The wipers couldn't cope and he slowed down and looked for Castile's track, but all he could see was the jungle wall.

The rain got heavier and he'd slowed to a crawl when a white car swept out into the middle of the road. He braked and wrenched at the wheel but the car started to skid. The white car spun round and he took his foot off the brake and swerved into the gap between it and jungle wall. It wasn't wide enough and he braced himself as the high-pitched screech of metal cut through the steady bass of rain drumming on the roof. The wheel twisted in his hands. His wrists and shoulders jarred and the hood bounced up as the car lurched into a tree and died.

His forehead stung and blood was running into his eye. He brushed it away and scrambled out of the passenger's door. Through the curtain of water he caught sight of the white car careering away. He cursed and smacked the wheel: he was miles from anywhere and hadn't seen a soul since Kumba. He tried the engine and it caught on the second shot and sounded OK. He slammed the gearstick into reverse and eased out the clutch. The wheels spun but then gripped and popped and suddenly he was out on the level and looking down a dark track. It had to be Castile's place: an aperture as tight as a tunnel with only a hint of light at the other end.

The rain had stopped and sunlight cut though the foliage, filling the track with steamy mist. He drove carefully forwards until the jungle gave way to a clearing about 100 yards across. The trees had been felled leaving thick stumps with weeds and jungle shrubs taking their place. A troop of monkeys emerged from the rain arguing about something pretty serious. On the far side there was a single-storey shack with a pickup and it took Harry a second to realise that smoke was coming from a half-open shutter and it was getting thicker.

He accelerated across the clearing and pulled up, ducking under the smoke and sprinting over to the door. It gave a bit but then jammed up against something soft and heavy, like a body. No wonder the white car had been going like a bat out of hell. He stepped back and rammed his shoulder into it, forcing it enough for him to squeeze through.

Inside was filled with hot smoke but he could just make out a body lying face down and half-hidden behind the door. Despite the rain, the partition wall quivered with heat. He grabbed the man's jacket and pulled. The fabric oozed between his fingers but he managed to haul the body halfway through the door. Flames crackled through the roof and the stench of scorched flesh filled his nostrils. Blood pounded in his ears as he pulled and wrestled the body all the way out and dragged it clear. He collapsed and gulped at the fresh air while the clouded sky spun crazily above him. He got up just as the shack's roof caved in with a whoosh of scalding air.

He turned the body over. Victor Castile was recognisable as much from his build as from what remained of his face. His jacket was soaked with blood and his right arm had been shattered at the elbow and hung at a crazy angle. His eyes had been savaged and his mouth was wide open in a silent bellow of pain. Below the waist was worse. His cut-offs were a tattered mess of frenzied butchery and someone had wrought a terrible vengeance on his genitals.

Harry looked away and stared across to the track. The clearing was cloaked in an eerie silence: the monkeys had gone quiet and the fire was just a heap of smouldering ashes. He looked up for vultures like in the movies but the sky was empty and the only sound came from an excited buzz of insects. He found a tarpaulin in the pickup and was just about to throw it over the body when he noticed a screwed-up ball of paper caught up in the Frenchman's collar. Flattened out, it turned into a topless blond pointing a handgun at the camera. Another ball from Castile's gaping mouth revealed a woman in boudoir lingerie standing astride a steel pipe.

Harry went through the Frenchman's pockets and found a bunch of keys, a pocketbook and a thick envelope. The wallet was stuffed with cards for nightclubs, including La Frégate, and a touring company in the desert called Destinaciones Sahara. The envelope was full of press cuttings on the OPEC oil crisis and French plans for nuclear power. There were a few photographs of the French prime minister and President Pompidou – and, to Harry's surprise, one of the prime suspects for Annie Fayol's Mr X, Dr Félix Moumié.

Questions crowded his mind before caution kicked in. Castile wasn't his case and he was a long way from home; and anyway it was always a bad idea arriving first on a crime scene, especially a homicide. He threw the tarp over the body and drove back down the track with Stokes' words ringing in his ears: if you get to the Hi Life you've gone too far.

The Hi Life had seen better times. The wooden steps up to the double doors were splintered and a gutter was hanging loose. The bar was empty except for a young guy wiping off the tables.

'I need to call the police,' Harry said. 'Your neighbour is dead.'

The barman froze, his cloth poised above the metal table. 'M. Castile?'

'Yes, murdered. Where's the phone?' The man seemed paralysed. 'It's urgent.'

'I'll get Madame.'

The barman disappeared through a curtain of plastic ribbons next to a poster of a man with a beaming woman leaning against him. She had a baby in her arms and was surrounded by smiling children with the slogan 'Guinness Gives You Strength'. The ribbons swirled again and a woman swept in dressed in a full-length traditional gown in indigo blue, a high turban to match and huge gold hoops. The fierce look in her eye suggested she'd been dragged away on a fool's errand. Harry wiped his hand on his pants.

'I'm Harry Kaplan. I need to call the police – your neighbour's been murdered.'

She declined his hand. 'You sure it's him?'

'Yes. The killer is on the road to Kumba in a white car.'

'He deserves a medal.'

'That's for the court to decide.' He made a move towards the office. 'Please.'

'Wait a minute.' She unlocked the door of a room hardly big enough for the desk and filing cabinet. The phone was an old black model like the one Harry's family had in Budapest. It was padlocked and it took her a long minute to find the right key.

'His body is out there in the sun—'

'It can cook to a crisp for all I care,' she said, pulling the lock free. 'Dial 999, the old British system.'

The phone rang in stretched solemn tones but nobody answered. He glanced at her.

'Let it ring,' she said, sitting down heavily on a small office chair. 'They'll answer.'

They did: a booming voice told him that he was through to the Kumba police station but it sounded more like a club.

'I want to report a homicide—'

'What? I can't hear—'

'Murder,' he shouted. 'A man's been murdered, Victor Castile—'

'Castile?'

'Yes. His killer is getting away.'

The loud music in the background was suddenly muffled as if a hand had been placed over the mouthpiece. Harry could make out a shout for quiet and then the music cut out. The man came back to him.

'You are serious? Victor Castile?'

'Yes. I'm calling from the Hi Life bar.'

'Wait—' The phone clattered down.

'Inspector Takere speaking.' It was a different voice, slightly high-pitched with an accent as crisp as David Niven's. The background quietened to a hush. 'You say Victor Castile is dead?'

'That's right. Out at his place. The killer is driving a white car, heading your way.'

'Are you a friend of his?'

'Never met him in my life. I just pulled him out of the fire. He'd been butchered.'

'Good riddance,' said the woman across the room.

'Did you get the number of the car?'

'No, it was raining too hard.'

'Don't worry. I'll meet you there.'

The line went dead and Harry looked at the woman. 'Sounded like a party, but an Inspector Takere is on his way.'

'His farewell, last day on the force,' she said and laughed, a deep gurgle of pleasure. 'Castile dead! He wouldn't miss it for the world.'

'You didn't like your neighbour much.'

'Nobody did.' She snorted. 'People will be fighting to dance on his grave.'

'What's he done to get so popular?'

She looked at him goggle-eyed. 'Ask the inspector.' She shook her head and rocked from side to side. It sounded as if she was singing. 'We should've killed him years ago.'

'Whoever did made him suffer.'

'Good for them,' she said. 'I saw the car, a brand-new Hertz hire car—'

'We should tell the inspector—'

She snapped the lock back in place. 'You already made your call.'

'If you say so.' He looked at his hands. 'Any chance of getting cleaned up?'

'Not in my bathroom,' she said with a shudder that shook her gold hoops. 'There's a tap outside.'

She waved him down the corridor as if she was sweeping up and he picked his way past crates of Fanta and casks of Guinness. Outside the air was fresh and cool and he took a deep breath and looked around. There was a rough wooden privy at the end of a worn path with a black bird sitting on the roof like a sentry. On his left a faucet was dripping into a heavy porcelain sink stamped with a blue logo of a lion and crown and the words 'Made in Great Britain'. It seemed an apt comment on empire, random but enduring.

He washed his hands and arms and scooped water over his head. It ran through his hair and down his face and stained the sink a muddy red.

12

Close to the Nigerian border, Cameroon

Harry drove back to Castile's place, pulled up in the shade and took the envelope out. The address, a PO Box in Douala, was typed and the stamps had been torn off leaving behind an airmail sticker, the date 15 March and the letters NIG from the Nigerian postmark. He tried to shake the contents out but the blood had dried and the opening was stuck. He prised it open and shook harder and the cuttings suddenly fell into his lap.

This time he caught sight of one in English: bizarrely, a review from the *New York Times* in 1970. He ran his eye down the titles past *Love Story* to one circled in red that swept him back to Eileen O'Connell's house on Long Island: *Lamia*. His pulse quickened as he recalled the blurb, 'a shocking exposé of KGB's moles in the French secret service'. Espionage and realpolitik made sense for a shadowy French specialist in the US Foreign Service, but it wasn't the kind of stuff he expected a crook like Victor Castile to be interested in.

He hadn't got anywhere near figuring it out when the sound of a vehicle coming down the track interrupted him. He pushed the cuttings back into the envelope and waited to play the good citizen. A dark-blue box-shaped police jeep came into view and accelerated across the clearing. It pulled up and a big cop with a shaven head as black as polished ebony got down and fanned his face with a peaked cap. He was wearing a broad grin and neatly pressed khaki shorts that half-covered his knees.

'Inspector Takere of the Kumba Police,' he said with the same clipped vowels from the phone. He put his cap on and stretched out a big hand. Harry took it, a surprisingly soft grip for such a big man.

'Harry Kaplan. Pleased to meet you, inspector.'

'The pleasure is all mine,' the inspector said with a mischievous giggle and looked past him at the lumpy tarpaulin and smoking ruins. 'Hmmm. So they burned the little pig's house down as well.'

'Yeah, I pulled him out.'

'Now that was definitely beyond the call of duty.' The inspector smacked the short baton against his trouser leg and set off across the clearing. Harry followed in his wake and watched as the two young constables, hardly more than boys, pulled the tarpaulin clear. They stood over the body with their eyes wide and jaws dropped like characters out of a pantomime.

'It's Victor alright,' said the inspector with merry satisfaction, 'and it looks as if they got their message across.'

'What message?'

'Keep off our turf. Lagos oil mafia.'

'But he was choked on soft porn,' Harry said, holding out the picture of the busty brunette.

'Guns actually.' The inspector hardly gave the woman a glance. 'That's a bazooka between her legs.'

'Oh right,' said Harry, nodding. 'I thought he was running girls. His wallet is stacked out with cards from dives in the docks.'

'The white slave trade?' The inspector dismissed the idea with a sweep of his baton. 'No, no, that's what he spent his money on. He made it by running arms in the Biafran War.'

'I wondered why he was so popular at the Hi Life.'

The inspector laughed. 'The redoubtable Mrs Bankole?'

'Yes.' Redoubtable she was. 'She saw the killer's car, a white Hertz, but she made it clear she wasn't going to help.'

'There're no flies on that lady, I can tell you, Mr Kaplan; no flies at all.' He pointed at the body with his baton. 'This is the Douala gendarmes' case now and they won't get any help from people round here, or from me. Tomorrow I start as head of security for Shell Nigeria.'

'Really?'

'Yes. So I'll be keeping an eye on the crooks who did this.'

'It looks as if they aren't the only ones with a motive.' Harry nodded at Castile's mutilated genitals. 'Somebody certainly wanted to make a point.'

The inspector shrugged. 'Who knows? Or cares? I don't. All that matters is he's dead. Let his French friends figure out who did it.'

'These might help them,' Harry said, handing him Castile's things.

The inspector put the keys in his pocket but passed the wallet and envelope straight on to one of the young constables before barking out an order in Pidgin. They jumped to and rolled the body into the tarp and threw it unceremoniously into the back of the pickup.

'Revenge is sweet,' said the inspector. 'People round here had good cause long before Biafra.' He took off his cap and fanned his face. Beads of sweat shimmered like tiny pearls on his nose. 'Can you give me a lift back to Kumba?'

'A ride? Sure. I'm spending the night in Buea. I can drop you off on the way.'

'Buea's even better.'

The inspector shouted something more at the young constables, who jumped into the cab and drove off across the clearing.

'Let the famous gendarme sort it out,' he said with caricatured mispronunciation and opened a gap between his finger and thumb. 'I had a file on Castile this thick, but they never let me bring him in. Bastard had friends in high places.'

'Because he was white?'

'French.'

'They seem to have let him down all of a sudden.'

The affable inspector was suddenly seething. 'I knew what he was up to. I even knew where he kept his gun.' He hit the battered Peugeot with his baton and wrenched the door open. The passenger seat was littered with pages of half-naked girls selling military hard-ware and on the floor there were some empty beer bottles and a used rubber. In the glove box was a handgun, which Takere picked up.

'Russian,' said the inspector, tapping the side of his nose, 'spoils of another war.'

But Harry knew better: it was Czech, a CZ52, the same model as the one he'd left behind in Chicago. The one Judit had given him in the cellar in Budapest with the sound of Russian tanks crushing glass on the streets overhead. She'd taken it out of the box and stood on tiptoes to kiss him. 'Now you're really one of us,' she'd said and he remembered the scent of her perfume mingling with the oil from the brand-new pistol.

'Which war was that?' he asked, struggling to banish the memories.

'The guerrilla war against the French,' said the inspector. 'Some of them are still hiding out in the jungle.'

'I heard about it from an Englishman called Uttley. Imported textiles from Manchester.'

'I think I know who you mean. Used to operate out of Lagos.'

'He's retired now.'

'Probably couldn't take the climate,' said the inspector, slapping at an insect. 'Even I can't.'

'More a case of being allergic to Victor Castile I think,' said Harry. 'They smuggled cloth into Douala together.'

'I know.' The inspector nodded so vigorously that his cap slipped. 'Victor's little project. I'll show you how he ended up.'

He strode off across the clearing and Harry followed. All Harry could hear was the damp soil giving way under his feet and the same mournful birdsong. They reached a shed half-hidden in the jungle and the inspector rammed his big shoulder into the big door. The clasp and padlock creaked but held fast. The inspector tried the Frenchman's keys but none fitted and he stood back and pulled the CZ52 from his belt.

'Stand clear,' he shouted and fired three rounds into the rotting timber.

The shots reverberated round the clearing and a cloud of birds burst into the sky. As the echoes faded the monkey clan started up again, screeching and howling as if in protest. Cordite filled the air and Harry's eardrums sang. The inspector blew smoke out of the barrel and pushed the gun back into his belt before leaning in to admire his marksmanship. The timber was shattered and the clasp hung loose from one screw.

The inspector ripped it free and hurled it into the jungle. He hauled at the door and the hinges groaned as the door opened. Inside he spread his arms out wide like a welcoming impresario. It took Harry a second to adjust to the gloom. They were standing in a shed with two medium-sized oil trucks painted in drab brown and olive.

'Spoils from the Biafran War.' The inspector's voice boomed through the half-darkness. 'I knew the bastard was running stolen diesel but I wanted to catch him red-handed. That way his friends in Douala would've had to put him away.' He struck the side of the truck with his baton. 'No matter. He finally picked on somebody his own size.'

On the way to Buea Harry told the inspector he was working for Dr Fayol. 'You've probably heard of her sister.'

'Everyone has.' The inspector replied shifting around. His considerable bulk was crushed into the seat. 'I was in GB at police college at the time and heard about the fuss when I got back.'

'What fuss?'

'Jurisdiction. She drowned over this side but the body was washed up under the bridge in Douala. Always happens. There was another woman ended up there but she was a suicide. Walked straight into the riptide like Lady Godiva.'

Harry didn't know who Lady Godiva was and anyhow needed to slow down to go through a village where swarms of kids streamed out of their houses to wave and shout at the side of the road. The inspector waved back and then harrumphed. 'We wanted the Annie Fayol case but the message from upstairs was loud and clear: hands off, boys; Douala's got it. My pals in Victoria reckoned they didn't ask the right questions.'

'What kind?'

'Oh, like why a woman like her was skinny-dipping on her own and why they couldn't find any of the gear stolen from her car.' He threw his hands up and nearly hit the low ceiling. 'They tried all the usual suspects but it'd disappeared into thin air.'

'Did your pals suspect foul play?'

Takere nodded. 'That's why they wanted the case. They suspected she had company and they'd run for cover. Somebody who shouldn't have been there.'

'Somebody's husband?'

'Exactly.'

'But nobody came up with a name?'

'It was Douala's case.'

'And you think they bungled it.'

'Off the record until tomorrow, yes. But I'm biased.'

They were on the edge of Buea and the Citroen's small engine laboured on the lower reaches of the mountain. The air was cooler and the vegetation along the road less tangled as if the fight for survival wasn't so fierce.

'Does the name Didier Nkumbé mean anything to you?' Harry asked.

'Nkumbé—' The inspector frowned and pursed his lips. 'I think there's some Minister in Yaoundé by that name, but I'm the last person to ask. They're all Frogs to me.'

'What about Eileen O'Connell? She used to be US *chargée* in Douala.'

He wrinkled his nose. 'Not that I remember. To tell the truth, I don't take to Yankees any better than the French. We got the Peace Corps running all over the place telling us what to do.'

The road steepened and Harry shifted down. The buildings looked like government offices with signs in English and French. A signpost off to the left welcomed them to the Buea Mountain Hotel. It was a stern, solid building, vaguely Alpine, in stone that looked like granite with a slate roof.

'The Germans built it,' said the inspector, squeezing his considerable bulk out of the car. 'With a hut near the top, ten bloody thousand feet up – in stone! Can you imagine! Incredible, but you know what they say: where there's a will there's a way. Especially if you've got masses of forced labour.' He gave the mountain a jaunty wave and set off for the entrance. 'Come on, Mr Kaplan, I'll buy you a drink. I've got time.'

The bar was cool and dim and at the far end there was a big chimney breast and a deep open fireplace. The barman poured them two long glasses of Trente-Trois.

'Careful,' said Harry, 'it's French.'

'The exception that proves the rule. Everything else they do is crap.'

'What about wine?'

The inspector made a face. 'Never drink the muck.'

'French food?'

'Frogs legs and snails – yuck.'

'How about French women?'

The inspector grinned. 'I haven't had the chance to test them out, more's the pity.'

'You haven't tested the food or wine either.'

'And I'm not going to.' He laughed. 'Nigeria here I come!'

Harry raised his glass. 'All the best for your new job with Shell. They're Dutch, aren't they?'

'Anglo-Dutch.'

'There was a bunch of them staying at the same hotel as me in Lagos. High on the oil boom.'

'That's why I'm leaving, plus I don't appreciate being spied on in my own station.'

'Who by?'

'Douala. Gendarmes planted one of their poodles to get the dirt on me. I couldn't move without the little shit making a note, but I beat them to the punch! Cheers!' The inspector sunk half his glass and then raised it. 'Here's to you too, for closing the Victor Castile case.'

'Douala isn't going to see it like that.'

'That's why I'm drinking to you.' The inspector beamed. 'They'll be running around like headless chickens and I'll be laughing myself silly on the other side of the border.'

'Hardly thanks to me—'

'Without you I'd never have known, or had the privilege of sending Victor on his way.'

'They'll want to talk to us.'

'Indeed they will, but I'll be out of reach.' The inspector drained his glass with the air of a job well done and ordered another for Harry. 'Sorry, but I've got to make a call: 36-22-36 – and that's not her phone number.' He winked and got up.

Harry got up and shook his hand. 'OK, inspector. Nice meeting you.'

'Ditto, but I'm just plain Mr Gideon Takere now. I'll send my Shell card over. There'll always be a welcome in Port Harcourt for the man who brought in Victor Castile.' He smiled. 'You know, Mr Kaplan, that's got a real ring to it. It could even be a Western with John Wayne. I can see it now. You've made quite a mark already.'

13

The inspector had made his mark too and Harry was left marvelling at how the big man had survived so long. Maverick cops were rare enough and Takere had been looking for trouble. He sipped his beer and glanced through the brochure for the hotel's unique attractions: the delicious prawns (the Portuguese word *camaron* had given the country its name), the mountain (second-highest in Africa and porters available on request) and 'the famous' Mile 12 beach within easy reach. There was no mention of why the beach was famous.

A couple of girls barely out of their teens came into the bar and sat down on the bar stools. They crossed their legs to make sure he noticed how short their skirts were and the barman gave them Cokes that would last until business arrived. He was just about to take his beer into the garden when the double doors burst open and a large man in a short-sleeved shirt strode towards him with an outstretched hand.

'Welcome to the Mountain Hotel, Mr Kaplan,' he said in a deep bass. 'Hans Ouweneel. I manage the place, for my sins.'

'Good to meet you.' He shook the man's hand.

'You've made quite a splash.'

'Really?'

'Well, we don't get that many private eyes from Chicago.'

'News travels pretty fast round here.'

'Jungle drums—' The man laughed, a big sound to go with his size. 'And I happened to see ex-Inspector Takere on the way in.'

'Ah, that explains it.'

'He's over the moon, a guy like you closing the Castile case! He says you couldn't make it up.'

Harry shrugged. 'I just passed on the news.' The case wasn't closed but it wasn't his job to say so.

'Still makes you a hero in Takere's book. He can't wait to see Douala jump.'

'He told me.'

'Let me show you round my estate.'

They walked out onto the lawn and the same mournful whistle that Harry had noticed at Castile's place piped up again.

'What's that bird?' he asked.

'Haven't a clue. I'm only interested if you can eat them.'

They stopped and looked out over the distant ocean. A single church bell was ringing.

'Beautiful,' said Harry.

'It's even better at sunset.' It sounded like a sales pitch. 'Another beer? Takere is picking up the bill. He said he owes you.'

'He doesn't, but thank you.'

Ouweneel gestured towards a parasol of thatched leaves and put his fingers in his mouth to produce an ear-splitting whistle. A man in a white jacket appeared on the terrace. 'Two beers, Paul, from the cold fridge!' said Ouweneel.

They sat down in the deckchairs and Ouweneel shifted around from side to side in his. It wasn't built for his size but he eventually settled and lit a cigarette.

'You've got quite a place here,' said Harry.

'You should've seen it when I arrived. It was supposed to be a temporary break from marital trouble in Rotterdam but turned into much more.' He sighed. 'I really should've moved on by now.'

'Easy to see why not.' Harry nodded at the view but privately he was struck by an image of the big Dutchman as a beached whale.

'No, I should've done something else with my life.'

Harry looked around and said, 'It's pretty impressive. I read your brochure.'

'Arrrgh. It's so out of date! The photographs!'

'Well,' Harry said, smiling, 'I guess they don't quite do Mile 12 justice.'

'That's because you can't fake it!' hooted the Dutchman. 'But it's the only beach near Douala, which is lucky for us. The French go down there to cool off and come up here for Sunday lunch. You should've seen us earlier. Heaving—'

'Even with the riptide?'

He shrugged. 'As I said, it's the only beach around.'

'How bad is the rip?'

'Bad. Very bad. One minute it's like a Dutch canal and the next a raging torrent. Comes out of nowhere, bang!' He snapped his fingers. 'Apparently you have to let it take you and swim back. Trouble is it goes a hell of a long way out.'

'I suppose you know Annie Fayol drowned in it?'

Ouweneel nodded. 'It's morbid but I think it's one of the reasons people go there; and she wasn't the only one either. A French woman killed herself by walking into it exactly five years after Annie Fayol drowned, like an anniversary. Stark naked too as if she was making a point.'

In Harry's experience all suicides made a point, but getting into the mind of the suicide was something else. He was on the point of asking who she was when the barman arrived with the beers on a tray, the chilled green bottles glistening in the sun. He flipped off the tops and poured them out.

'Cheers, as the English say,' said the Dutchman, raising his glass. 'Welcome to West Cameroon.'

Harry raised his glass in reply. 'Did you know Victor Castile?'

'Hardly, but I heard a lot about him. The inspector was one of our regulars.' He rolled his eyes and held his hands out like an angler showing off the size of his catch. 'You can get a reputation round here without going so far as the Lagos oil mafia, but don't believe everything you hear. Otherwise we'd have more affairs than Peyton Place.'

'Like the one between Castile and Annie Fayol?'

He wrinkled his nose. 'That's what I mean about moving on. All we get is gossip, gruel for the undernourished – thin stuff at the best of times but it gets thinner every time it's served. You must get the genuine thing as a private eye, haute cuisine.'

'Only in Hollywood.'

But the Dutchman wasn't listening: everybody thought private eyes were like Philip Marlowe. They'd read the books or seen the movies.

'I wish I had the figure for it,' he said sadly, tapping his waistline with fingers that showed no sign of knuckles. Damp patches were spreading under his armpits.

'Actually it's mostly desk work and chasing leads that go nowhere, like the name Didier Nkumbé. Ring a bell?'

Ouweneel frowned. 'Isn't he a minister or something?'

'Could be.'

'I'll ask my bar manager. He pays much more attention to what happens in the French sector.'

'The French sector?'

'Douala, Yaoundé, the government,' he said. 'I know it's more than ten years since unification but it still feels like two countries.'

Harry nodded. 'What about Eileen O'Connell, the US *chargée*?'

'We hardly overlapped.' He struggled out of the deckchair. 'Look, I've got to get into the kitchen now, but I'd like to share a brandy later. I recommend the francolins by the way. They're like guinea fowl but gamier and we do them with lemon and garlic and a touch of chilli.'

Harry grinned. 'Sounds great.' He downed his beer and got up. 'Could I check your old registers? I want to see if Annie Fayol stayed here.'

'Be my guest.'

They were locked away and covered in dust but the Dutchman loaned Harry a senior member of staff, a grizzled old guy called Noah who'd worked at the hotel all his life. Together they dug out the volume for 1956 and Noah wiped the book clean with a damp cloth. It took only a minute for Harry to find the entry he was looking for: Annie Fayol had stayed for just one night, 15 May, two weeks before she drowned; but there was no entry for any of the prime suspects.

'We used to keep a visitors' book,' Noah said, arriving with another thick volume.

Harry flipped through it, skimming over phrases like 'superlative views' and 'glorious gardens!' until he came across an entry written in the same emphatic hand as the faded postcard: 'A comfortable stay,' it said, 'but the operation of a colour bar is deplorable. Annie Fayol.'

'When did the hotel start accepting black guests?' he asked the old man.

'After Independence, sir. 1960.'

'Huh, it figures,' said Harry, conjuring up the past. It fitted together all right, Annie meeting her man on the mountain and him being barred from even having a drink. Presumably they'd left after she'd made her feelings known. He checked the visitors' book some more before closing it thoughtfully.

Back in the lobby he was lucky enough to get an international line almost immediately and Sal picked up right away.

'Harry—'

'Sorry to bust into your busy week,' he said, 'but it's urgent. Castile is dead—'

'What—'

'Yeah, murdered, so can you stop Dr Fayol getting on that plane? Tell her I've found Nkumbé.'

'Where?'

'In the government.'

'Wow. Like Annie said, big players—'

'Right. Another reason for her not coming.'

'How, for God's sake? She's dead set.'

'Just say I need her to figure out what O'Connell's playing at'

'Oh yeah, like she's going to take it from little old me.'

'Tell her she's pulling the strings.'

'Is she?'

'She's definitely mixed up in it.'

Sal sighed. 'OK, Harry, I'll try.'

'Thanks. I owe you,' he said and rung off.

He found Jules Raymond's number in his book and dialled it. A woman answered and told him in poor French with an excruciating

English accent that M. Raymond was asleep. He was supposed to be convalescing.

'My news will do him the world of good,' Harry said, reverting to English. 'Greetings from an old friend. Tell him when he wakes up that Harry Kaplan came all the way from Chicago to deliver them.'

'Ooh, you're American,' she said, relieved. 'Chicago! What do you do over there, Mr Kaplan?'

'I'm a PI – private investigator.'

'Oh,' she said, impressed.

She had a nasal accent like John Lennon. 'You're from Liverpool,' he said.

'Yes – how did you know?'

'I was there just the other day.' A little white lie. 'Great city, fab music.'

'Really – that's amazing. What a coincidence. I miss home so much.'

'Yep, it's a small world but Liverpool is at the centre of it.' He didn't give her his line on coincidences. 'I promise not to get M Raymond too excited.'

'He's actually a very difficult patient. He doesn't listen and is used to getting his own way.' The nurse was coming to the fore. 'He's still smoking.'

'Jesus,' said Harry, laying it on. 'That must be tough for you, Miss – sorry but I didn't catch your name?'

'Jenny Fitzgerald, but everyone calls me Fitz. My friends anyway.'

'Fitz is great. Call me Harry. Maybe you'd like to show me round on your day off?' he said boldly.

There was a short pause. 'Oooh yes, I'd like that. You can tell me how you liked Liverpool.' She sighed. 'Beatlemania's gone off a bit. Anyway I'm free all day Fridays and some Wednesday nights.'

'Friday should be fine. I'll call you midweek to confirm.'

'Great. But don't call this Wednesday. I'll be out. Girls' night.'

'I'll remember, no mixing with the girls.' He paused. 'I suppose you have to help him out?'

'How d'you mean?'

'Work stuff, you know, little errands.'

'Oh yes, I see,' she said, sounding relieved. 'Yes, I do, he's always asking to run little errands, like the post – or the mail as you'd call it.'

'So, would the name Victor Castile be familiar?'

The line went very quiet after the sound of a sharp intake of air.

'Fitz – you OK?' he asked.

'Yes.' Her voice trembled slightly. 'I'm sorry, but can I leave the subject of Victor Castile until I see you?'

'Sure, no problem. I take it you know him?'

'Unfortunately.' And with that the young Englishwoman said goodbye and rang off.

Harry put the phone down and gathered his thoughts. There were a lot of tangled connections, past and present, and now there was a dead body. He went through to the restaurant and Ouweneel showed him to his table. Most of the others were taken.

'Busy—'

Ouweneel smiled. 'Thanks to our chef's reputation and the joys of Mile 12. I took the liberty of opening you a bottle of Aligoté. On the house.'

'No need—'

Ouweneel waved away his protests and poured him a glass. 'Like I said, Mr Kaplan—'

'Harry, please.'

'I told you, we don't normally get private eyes staying here, least of all witnesses to murder—'

'I wasn't a witness.'

Ouweneel chuckled. 'Poetic licence, my friend, for us undernourished.'

Harry sipped the wine. It was cool and crisp. He started with a chilled melon spiced with cinnamon and ginger before the waiter brought him a plate of tiny deep-fried fish 'caught on the dawn tide in the Wouri' served with fresh garlic mayonnaise. They tasted of the ocean and he'd just scooped up the last when the waiter struck a glass with a knife. Everyone looked up as Hans Ouweneel stepped up on to a small podium with a glass of wine in his hand and a big smile on his face.

'Good evening, ladies and gentlemen,' he said and then repeated himself in French and Dutch and Pidgin. 'I don't want to distract you from what I hope is another wonderful meal from our kitchen—' He broke off and bowed as warm applause swept across the room. 'But tonight is not just any old night, which is why we are treating all our honoured guests to a bottle of Burgundy.'

Harry joined in another round of applause before Ouweneel waved it away and continued. 'I wanted you to join me in a toast to my time at the Mountain Hotel. When I arrived it was mainly a British affair, but now—' He looked around and smiled with pleasure. 'I can proudly lay claim to a truly cosmopolitan dining room with guests from all over the world. Tonight we have people from Paris, Geneva, Amsterdam, Lagos and even Chicago. May I offer you all my congratulations on finding us and wish you *bon appétit* and a speedy return. *Salut.*'

There was another burst of applause as Ouweneel stepped down and made his way across the floor of the restaurant, pausing here and there to accept the praises of his guests and respond to the occasional raised glass. By the time he got to Harry's table his glass was empty.

'A very pretty speech – congratulations.'

Ouweneel grinned. 'More poetic licence. The dates have got a bit blurred and I'm the guest from Amsterdam.'

The waiter arrived with the main course on a tray: half a francolin garnished with fresh parsley and surrounded by glistening shallots, buttered baby carrots, boiled potatoes and a pat of steaming spinach. Harry leaned over the plate and inhaled the rich aroma.

'Smells fantastic,' he said and raised his glass. 'Here's to more of these while I'm here.'

They both drank deeply and Harry popped a shallot in his mouth, sweet and perfectly cooked. He cut into the thigh of the bird and the bone fell away from the body.

'Perfect.'

'This is for later.' The Dutchman passed him a folded newspaper with the headline in view. 'NIGERIAN OIL RACKET: TOTAL BOSS SLAMS OPEC'. 'I was wrong about Nkumbé. He used to be a minister.'

Harry took it and was just about to glance down the column when they were both distracted by a disturbance in the restaurant entrance. The head waiter was in discussion with two very tall gendarmes. It seemed to be getting heated and the head waiter looked across the room at Ouweneel.

'Ahhh,' Ouweneel said. 'Excuse me but I see we have visitors.'

He gestured and set off in their direction but before he'd taken a second step the gendarmes had taken off towards them. Harry watched as they glided with sinuous ease between the crowded tables and the contented murmur of well-fed diners gave way to an expectant hush. Harry put down his knife and fork and braced himself for something bad. Late-night calls from the cops had never been good news in Budapest and Chicago and he couldn't see Cameroon being any different.

14

Buea, West Cameroon

'I'm sorry, Harry, but it's you they've come for,' Ouweneel said, looking pained. 'They want to search your car and room. I can't stop them.'

'No search warrant?' Harry said with heavy sarcasm.

'*Maintenant*,' said the paler-skinned gendarme, stepping forward and gesturing Harry to his feet.

'*Pourquoi?*' Harry asked.

'Routine—'

He grimaced: the same cliché the world over.

'OK,' he said and turned to Ouweneel. 'I won't be long.'

'I'll keep your food hot—'

'Thanks.'

The gendarme led him across the floor and as they passed the hushed tables stirred with whispers. The word 'Chicago' stood out. He shook the gendarme off and marched out into the lobby, taking his keys from his pocket. Two police vehicles had been parked across the forecourt and there were two more gendarmes lurking outside the front door. They fell in behind and together they crossed the parking lot like a posse with the gravel crunching under their boots. A mosquito whined in Harry's ear and a bat flew a jagged course across the dark sky. Somewhere a dog should have been howling at the moon.

'*Votre voiture*, M. Kaplan?' enquired the senior gendarme, still icily polite.

'Obviously,' Harry said, but before he'd had a chance to use the keys, the man had snatched them and he was grabbed from behind. They unlocked the car and flicked on the interior light. The seats were bare but for a bottle of Evian and the map of Cameroon that belonged to Annie Fayol. They opened the trunk and the torchlight picked out the spare wheel and a small backpack from Abercrombie & Fitch.

One of the minions shook out the contents: a Swiss Army knife, an ancient Christmas gift from his father; a Fruit of the Loom T-shirt still in its cellophane wrap; a spare notebook; a soft case of pencils and ballpoints; a small flashlight; the gallery's Canon Pellix and some spare film; and a dogeared copy of Graham Greene's *The Quiet American*. Nothing remotely incriminating.

'OK now?' Harry asked, slamming the trunk. 'Can I go back and finish my dinner?' The senior gendarme looked at him as if he was butchering the French language so he added, 'You really should try the food here. It's as good as anything I've had in Paris.' He made a move towards the hotel.

'Wait,' the man said, and his minions made sure Harry understood by pinning his arms behind his back. The officer leaned into the passenger seat and opened the glove compartment with an exclamation of satisfaction. Harry's heart beat faster. He was pulled backwards and twisted round so he could see the bad news. There had to be bad news, he was expecting it, but he was still taken aback: it was Victor Castile's CZ52.

'Your gun, M. Kaplan,' the officer said and sniffed the barrel. Everything he did was mannered. 'The murder weapon.'

'It's Victor Castile's, not mine,' he said, just as a small figure leaped out of the shadows. A flashbulb popped and he blinked and it popped again.

'You're under arrest for the murder of Victor Castile,' said the senior gendarme. The grip on his arms tightened and he was frog-marched towards the Peugeot. A small motorbike sprang into action and careered down the drive. Harry was going to be front-page news.

Jesus F. Christ. What a damned fool he was.

The two gendarmes tossed him into the back of the Peugeot and slammed the door. He heard the lock click. Between him and the front seats there was a metal grid that reminded him of a dog kennel. Outside the junior gendarmes saluted and the big bruiser got in and the engine jumped into life. He punched the seat hard and cursed: he might've been right about late-night calls from the cops, but he'd dropped his guard and got the genial Inspector Takere totally wrong.

Long Island, New York State

Eileen O'Connell was packed and ready to go and had just zipped her valise when there was a rap at the door. She stopped a second, wary and alert: she was expecting a young Iranian friend but it was a bit early and the knock was too urgent – too masculine.

It was Western Union, a telegram. She took it with a slight tremor and smiled with relief at the message:

> He bought my car. No hitches. He asked about Victor Castile, Nkumbé and Ebolowa. See you in Paris sometime? Ricard.

No hitches: a gleam of satisfaction came to her but she turned it back and locked the telegram away in the desk drawer. There was time aplenty for something to go awry.

She went back upstairs to put on her expertly streaked hairpiece. She tugged gently at a few strands and pencilled in a little eyeliner. Nobody took her for more than 50, even guys like Kaplan who knew how long she'd been with the Service. The funny thing was that in her youth it had worked the other way round and men took her for a woman of experience. Gérard had been amazed when he found out – one spring day when they'd walked across the cemetery Père Lachaise and ended up making love on the floor of his garret apartment.

She shuddered with wistful pleasure at the memory and had to take a deep breath. The Gestapo had taken him away in that autumn. Everything came back to her, the slate-grey sky and the rain-slicked sidewalks, the old butcher closing his peeling shutters and above all the creepy sense of surveillance and sullen despair.

Mona's tentative knock drew Eileen back from the past. Her

young friend had tied her thick black hair under a red woollen scarf and was dressed modestly in a topcoat and trousers. Eileen took her coat and showed her into the front room. Flames were leaping behind the glass door of the wood-burner and the room felt like a warm embrace.

'Sit down,' she said, 'it's cold out there. How are you surviving our Long Island winters?'

Mona smiled. 'It's the wet summers I don't like.'

Eileen smiled back. 'You shouldn't have done your doctorate on the West Coast. It spoiled you.' Mona had done a PhD in Middle Eastern history at Santa Cruz and was now a tenure-track assistant professor at NYU Stony Brook. 'A cup of tea? We've got time.'

'Please.'

She poured black tea into a glass Iranian-style and Mona smiled her appreciation. 'Thank you. Just like home.'

'You must miss your family.'

'I do, of course, but I'm going home for the summer.'

'Your parents must be excited.'

'So am I.' Mona sipped her tea. 'Don't get me wrong, Miss O'Connell, I like it here, the freedom and the scale, people as well as places, but – you know – roots, they go pretty deep.'

'Sure.' Eileen had heard the story often enough to know but for her the drive had been restlessness, the desire to be the stranger. Her roots had tied her down. 'My Irish cousin says you can travel the world but what you're looking for is in your own backyard.'

Cousin Connor was big on his roots even though they were largely invented.

Mona smiled again. She leaned down to take a manila envelope out of her briefcase.

'I'm glad you enjoyed working on it.' Eileen opened the envelope and glanced through the text. There was nothing she wasn't ready for but it was good to have it pinned down in black and white. Jules Raymond had got that much right. 'Thank you. It's perfect.'

'It's dynamite, isn't it?'

'It might be,' she said airily, as if it wasn't too important which way it went.

This part was tricky: she didn't want to give Mona the idea that the material might be top secret and she'd originally passed it off as something from her time in West Africa like someone sticking a final photo in a family album. But the document had piqued Mona's interest – and why the hell wouldn't it, for God's sake? Dynamite didn't get close: it was more like nuclear.

'I mean, this guy,' said Mona leaning forwards, 'he's the same Messmer who's prime minister of France isn't he, the guy who's pushing for nuclear power and messing up Kissinger's plans to oppose OPEC?'

'That's right, typically French to rock the Western boat,' Eileen said with casual indifference. 'Oddly enough I had a bit to do with him in London during the war. He was one of the first to join de Gaulle and sign up for the Free French.'

'Amazing,' Mona said, the historian clearly warming to her theme. 'I've read quite a bit about de Gaulle, but who's this Foccart?'

'He's more of a bit player, in the shadows,' Eileen said vaguely, playing him down, although he'd been one of de Gaulle's key supporters and run covert operations like the abduction of Ben Barka and murder of Dr Félix Moumié.

'He's never had Messmer's profile,' she said, waving a hand, 'although he used to be his minister for Africa and Madagascar.'

She glanced at her watch and tidied the envelope into her bag. It wasn't the right time to dwell on its contents. 'Please excuse me but there are a couple of things I have to get together before the taxi arrives.'

'I don't want to hold you up.'

'You're not.' She gestured at Mona's glass. 'Take your time.'

'You didn't say where you'd decided to go.'

'I've always hankered after Timbuktu,' Eileen said with a careful mix of truth and lies. It was at least in the right corner of the right continent. 'I was mostly posted to steamy places on the coast, so I thought I'd try the desert.'

'You'll love it.'

'I'm sure I will.' She was turning towards the kitchen when the phone started to ring. She checked her stride, stopped by a sense of foreboding. 'I'll take it in the kitchen,' she said and pushed open the door.

The phone was set in the wall next to the fridge with a long spiral extension. As she closed the door behind her and picked it up she recalled what Connor had said about the technological leap in so-called 'listening devices'. She wasn't as conspiratorially minded as him but she'd been halfway convinced and ever since had wondered if they'd bugged her house. It just seemed absurd when there were so many other pressing needs for reliable intelligence.

'Hello,' she said as she picked up the phone, but had to hold the earpiece at a distance. The noise was high-pitched and very loud, a squawk of something between agony and relief and in French.

'Eileen, *chérie, merci beaucoup – mon dieu—*'

It was Jules, clearly in a bad way.

'What's the matter?' she asked, acutely aware that there was no chance of him being discreet.

'They've killed Castile—' Shit. Eileen closed her eyes and breathed out. Jules was babbling on. 'Butchered. Burned his place down—'

'Who, for God's sake? Who has?' She tried to keep her voice down.

'The oil mafia. He was muscling in on their business.'

'He was always a crook. You shouldn't have brought him in—'

'That's why I did,' he screamed. 'He had the contacts.'

'Calm down, for God's sake,' she said in a loud whisper. 'You'll kill yourself. Where's that damned nurse?'

'Asleep—'

'Wake her up then! She should be looking after you.'

'No, no, I have to tell you, they've arrested Kaplan.'

'What?'

'The private eye you sent over. He's working for Lagos.'

Bullshit. No way. Impossible. 'I didn't send him over,' she said.

Mona was knocking on the kitchen door. 'The taxi is here, Miss O'Connell.'

'OK, I'm coming,' she said, putting her hand over the mouthpiece. 'Ask them to hold on.'

'Sure.'

'Jules,' she shouted into the phone when she heard the front door opening, 'stay at home with that nurse, you hear! I'm coming over on Air Afrique, tomorrow night.'

She rung off and stood quite still for a second. The front door slammed. She went back into the front room.

'The taxi is happy hanging on,' said Mona, her scarf slightly askew.

'Thanks.' Eileen shrugged. 'An old friend in bad way. He's losing his marbles.'

'I'm sorry.'

'So am I.' She sounded heartless but it couldn't be helped. 'Can you tell them I'll be right out?'

'Sure.'

She waited for her young friend to shut the front door behind her before turning to her desk and unlocking the drawer. There was no way she was going to start poking around in Cameroon without her gun. By the time Mona was back she'd tucked it into her waistband and had slipped the box of shells into her bag.

'I'll send you a postcard,' she said. 'Mount Cameroon.'

'Thanks. Take care of yourself.'

'Course.' She gripped Mona's arm and looked her in the eye. 'Don't say anything about the document to anyone, will you. We'll talk about it when I get back.'

Eileen held her young friend's gaze for a second longer and a sense of what was at stake passed between them. A shiver of excitement rushed through her: it was like old times.

15

Buea, West Cameroon

Goddammit – arrested for murder. How had he been such a fool? Three explanations came to him: he was supposed to be there to take the rap; or the killer didn't want Castile talking to him; or it was one of those coincidences he didn't believe in. He started to list the people who knew where he'd been going but he hadn't got far before the car lurched and he was thrown against the grid. The gendarmes were talking in an incomprehensible language but for a second he thought he heard the names Ebolowa and Nkumbé.

A whirling carousel of leads filled his head: people with pasts, like ex-Minister Nkumbé, ex-Inspector Takere, and ex-diplomat/agent Eileen O'Connell, as well as Annie Fayol's ex-boyfriend, Victor Castile. Annie had been up against some big players and now he was as well – but they'd got in first. The gendarmes had known about the gun, but he still couldn't believe that Takere had set him up. Takere had been on Castile's trail, no question about it, and Ouweneel had backed Harry too – he liked the big guy, and Mrs Bankole had spoken up for him as well.

He shook his head: nothing was clear except suddenly it was a good thing that Candace was still coming out. She could kick up a stink with the Embassy. Who would've guessed it? Harry Kaplan rescued by a client, and a woman at that. At least he could warn her about Nkumbé. The guy sure had clout.

He looked out of the window: the road had been cut into the mountain with hairpin bends, which they took so fast that the wheels squealed. They nearly collided with some earth-moving equipment and the big cop snapped at the driver. Eventually the road levelled out and opened up onto the bridge with a chain of lights flickering low over the water. On the far side the city sparkled like a Christmas tree. Across the river, they took a few turns off the main drag until the streetlights petered out and the surface became riddled with potholes. A couple of drunks tumbled out of a bar and nearly fell under their wheels. A limping dog sloped away down a dark alley.

They pulled into the gateway of a stone building with wide steps and double front doors. A dim light burned in one of the windows. The gendarmes hauled him out onto the cobbled quayside and he shook himself free but the big cop lifted him off his feet and dragged him down a flight of steps slippery with water.

The light from the lamp was just bright enough to show up a door with an old iron ring for a handle. The driver banged on it with the butt of his pistol. The bruiser's grip on Harry's arm was tight enough to stop the blood and the big man laughed in his ear and told him in bad French he was going to find out what it was like to be a slave. The man's breath was hot on his face and stank of bad fish.

'It's nice and cool in there,' the driver said with a nasty laugh and banged on the door again.

This time the door creaked open, but before Harry could move the big man had kicked his legs from under him. He hit the stone floor and the bastard kicked him in the gut. He tried to get up but a heavy hand in his back sent him flying. His head ached and he wasn't thinking clearly, but he could make out a man with a shaven head who was saying something he couldn't understand.

'He says you're lucky,' the driver said with the same nasty laugh. 'You've got a choice of rooms.'

Harry understood the words but not what they meant and felt like he might throw up his dinner. The shaven head led the way and the big gendarme cuffed his ear just for the fun of it.

'Fuck you,' he shouted and slammed his elbow into the big man's gut, but it was rock hard and the guy just grunted and hit him with a rabbit punch and he crashed sideways into the wall. The driver joined in and kicked him past a door with a peephole crusty with age. The air was clammy and he could hear the rhythmic slap of water. The jailer lit a small lamp and a weak orange flame revealed a low dungeon crammed with bunks.

The big man kicked him forwards and shut the door. The lamplight flickered and nearly went out. Harry got up, his head still spinning. He looked round: he was alone. The ceiling was domed and some of the beds had rough hessian mattresses. He tested one, half expecting it to be crawling with rats. It was coarse and damp and stank of stale flour but nothing jumped out of it. He rolled onto it just as the lamp spluttered and went out.

As a kid he used to brag about not being scared of the dark. He'd had measles badly and had to stay in bed with heavy blankets shutting out the light. He'd come to think of darkness as his friend, scrambling under the covers whenever anyone came in and making up stories about a world where people could see in the dark, but this was different. He didn't have measles and his mother wasn't on the other side of the door.

Near Paris, France

Three thousand miles to the north Marc Benet was landing at a military airfield outside Paris. It was a bare setting with no fanfare, just a low Nissan shack and a 10-foot barbed wire fence. Inside the shack a driver from the Piscine was stamping his feet and complaining about the cold. A tanned SDECE agent paced the floor, barely able to contain his frustration. The driver had been instructed to wait for a second arrival before taking him back to HQ 'to save gas'.

'Damned Arabs,' the agent muttered, fresh from his first posting in Tel Aviv. 'Who the hell is this guy anyhow?'

Just as he spoke the sound of a small plane rattled the window and they watched it touch down and taxi to a halt. The door opened and a set of steps unfolded. In the light of the cabin they could see a short, thickset man descend and make his way across the asphalt. He covered the ground rapidly with a rolling gait that had a rhythmic jerk to it.

'They call him Gitan,' said the driver, turning away with a snort.

'Why didn't you say?'

'You didn't ask. They say he could've had the most celebrated limp in France.'

It was the agent's turn to snort. 'It was actually de Gaulle who said it,' he said. 'Anyhow it's time to go. Nobody keeps him hanging about.'

Among other things, Marc Benet had a reputation for impatience. He was no great talker either and with the tersest of pleasantries over the three men climbed into the DS 21 and took the road for Paris, north along the new ring road, past the Bois de Vincennes and onto the headquarters of French intelligence. The driver flashed a card at the sentry box and the barrier lifted in front of a new building of eight storeys and the gawky look of a stack of egg-cartons.

Marc took the elevator to the top floor.

'M. Benet,' the receptionist said, half getting up. 'Colonel Foccart will see you straight away. Would you like anything to drink; tea or coffee, mineral water?'

He shook his head. He didn't want anything to prolong the meeting or give it a veneer of civility. Foccart's office looked out over the Piscine, the 1920s Olympic pool where the young Tarzan Johnny Weissmuller had won his gold medals. The colonel was sitting behind a massive desk in a chair with an upholstered headrest. He raised a plump hand but didn't get up – a stout man with a double chin and a big balding head like a dome. He looked more like a provincial bank manager than a long-standing and leading player in French intelligence and internal surveillance.

'Sit down,' he said.

Marc hesitated. Even sitting down with this man cut against the grain. Foccart looked up as if Marc was trying his patience. His small eyes blinked and he massaged his fleshy chin. Marc sat down.

'I've come for the passports,' he said.

'And to report back. You work for me, remember.'

'Everything is ready.'

'So I gather.' Foccart studied some papers on the desk in front of him. 'But not without some local difficulty. Seems messy, the way you trapped Pleven into exceeding his brief.'

'The deal was I'd do it my way and you'd send the passports with Pleven. You didn't and that's why I'm here.'

'My sincerest apologies, but the delay is unavoidable on account of my frontline. I told you Geneva is still upset about Moumié—'

'And I told you they're your problem. I've done my part.' He half got up as if ready to take the passports and leave but Foccart made no move.

'And we're very grateful to you,' he said silkily, 'just as we were in 1940.'

'I came for the passports not your gratitude.' Marc clenched his teeth. 'If I don't leave with them I'll pull the plug. One call—'

The smirk faded. 'That would be unwise, an act of treason.'

'Nothing compared to losing your precious uranium.'

Foccart raised his hand in a pose of extreme condescension and Marc was suddenly alert to having made the most terrible miscalculation.

'Well, well, Benet – you've clearly been away for too long.' Foccart leaned forwards, his voice husky with triumph. 'Did you really imagine that I would take you – or Pleven, come to that – into my confidence, or give you an indispensible role?' He tut-tutted and smiled. 'No, no, I would never trust a man like you. You were and remain a pawn in the proceedings, but as a gesture in the spirit of 1940 I'm prepared to make you a present of this.'

He took a Swiss passport from his drawer and tossed it onto the desk, made out in the name of M. Marc Benet with an address in Geneva.

Marc's heart beat faster, his throat dry. 'Where's the other?'

Foccart waved a pudgy hand. 'That's what I was coming to. My local difficulty. Your charming daughter is lamentably the subject of legal proceedings.'

Foccart slipped a thick form across the desk and the name on the first page struck deep into Marc's heart: Madeleine Benet.

'What is this?' He struggled to keep the tremble out of his voice. 'What have you done?'

'Me? Nothing.' Foccart's mock innocence was jaunty with triumph and he flipped through the booklet and pointed to a signature. 'It's your father-in-law you have to worry about. We just helped him with some evidence.'

As he spoke he spilled a packet of photographs across the desk. Marc froze as they spun out in front of him, vivid shots from all angles of his wife in various states of drunkenness and ignominy and a few of Madeleine on his father-in-law's lap.

'Not a pretty sight, eh?' said Foccart. 'Except of course for your enchanting daughter. She's very pretty. Irresistible by the look of it.'

Marc couldn't tear his eyes away and nothing came into his head but a cold hand gripped his stomach. He felt sick. 'You bastard—' He stood up and grabbed at Foccart's throat.

For a fat man the colonel moved quickly, tipping his well-oiled chair backwards out of reach.

'Sit down, you fool!' he snapped. 'You should've known I'd keep a joker up my sleeve.' He spread his hands over the photos. 'The entire community is up in arms, unanimous that this is dereliction beyond repair. The priest, the doctor, the mayor, the schoolteacher – everybody in agreement that a mother this derelict cannot any longer be trusted with an innocent child—'

'You think I don't know—'

'But it turns out that the father is no better,' Foccart continued amiably. 'Maybe not a helpless drunk, but an absentee for weeks at a time and ill-suited to the neighbourhood. A gypsy, dare I say it, a Breton bastard, a mercenary and fortune-hunter – reportedly more at ease in Africa than in France. People in the village even doubt his patriotism and faith. The postmistress says he's scarcely literate and writes to his daughter in childlike language on postcards showing half-naked Africans and primitive mosques. Poor woman lost her only son in Algiers—'

'I know who she is—'

'Of course you do.' Foccart's tone was of a concerned senior citizen. 'So you'll also know that everybody in the village worries about our little Madeleine and supports the view that she would be better off with her grandfather – who, by chance, has just prepared this application to become her legal guardian and ward of court.'

Marc smashed his fists into the desk, scattering the photographs. 'You bastard, I'll kill you—'

'And you'll never see Madeleine again. Like it or not, I'm the only hope you've got. I can stop the process, just like that,' he snapped his fingers. 'But only as long as I have your full co-operation.'

'With what?'

'That's better. Much more sensible. Because, between you and me, I think Madeleine's grandfather has got too soft a spot for your daughter, if you get my meaning. I've got some other photos here that are more graphic but I didn't think you'd want to see them.'

'What photos? Let me see them.' Marc grabbed at them but Foccart was too quick. Red fury was roaring in Marc's ears, blinding his eyes. 'You knew about him.'

'No, but I found out. Information is my forte – you should know that.' Foccart was animated, his small eyes sharp with malice. 'So Benet, if you want to keep your daughter away from that perverted monster you'd better do what I say.'

Marc struggled to control his rage. He couldn't afford to take risks. 'What?' he said.

'*Who*, is more to the point. I'm tidying up loose ends in my office, like Guy Martin.'

'Guy—'

'Yes, and don't tell me you don't know where he is. You were spotted together in Niamey.'

'What d'you want?'

'Tidy him up, as I say. Exactly how is up to you – though I would favour some sort of accident, like in the old days. It would provide a kind of poetic symmetry.' He smiled, his eyes bright with malice. 'Either that or your enchanting little girl will lose her innocence long before she's ready.'

16

Monday, 8 April 1974

Orly Airport, Paris

Thanks to a strong tail wind the flight was early and Candace followed the stream of passengers to collect her luggage, but before she got there she was intercepted.

'Dr Fayol?' A smart, well-built young man was looking at her kindly. He smiled with a bright line of perfect white teeth. 'I work for Mlle Hélène. Her chauffeur.'

He held out his hand and Candace hesitated before taking it. She noticed that he was holding black leather driving gloves in his other hand. 'Hello,' she said. 'Where is she?'

'Waiting for you in the VIP lounge.' He gestured towards a door with flashing blue neon piping. 'She asked me to look after your bags.'

Candace was a bit flustered, since Hélène hadn't said anything about a chauffeur, but she found herself giving into his quiet confidence. It seemed fair enough that somebody else would finally take a bit of the weight. She'd hardly slept on the flight and halfway over she'd looked down on the Atlantic and wondered if she knew what she was playing at. The theory had been fine: she was just going to draw a line, simple as that; but the trouble was that this was the same promise she'd made at her mother's funeral and when she'd sold the house, and yet here she was flying backwards into the past all over again.

If only Karen had been able to come with her. She'd nearly offered to pay and then bitten her tongue, because paying for Karen was the one thing that prickled – and of course she knew that Hélène would be far too busy with her next collection. So she was putting a whole lot of eggs into her basket with Harry, especially when he was none too pleased about her coming out.

She nodded her thanks at the young man and turned to go but he laid a hand on her arm.

'I need your luggage tags.'

'Of course. Silly of me.'

She detached them from her ticket with an apologetic shake of her head. 'They're red, Samsonite. Medium-sized.'

She wasn't good at packing and hadn't really known what to take. She could have asked the Foreign Service but somehow she didn't want people to know she was going; as if the whole project was still nebulous, caught in some limbo between her imagination and reality.

'Candace, *bienvenue!*' Hélène was standing in the doorway to the VIP lounge holding out both hands, immaculate as ever. 'It's wonderful to see you.'

She drew Candace inside and let the door swing shut behind them. There was only one other passenger sitting at the bar behind a newspaper. The room was filled with the aromas she associated with mornings in France: Gauloises, fresh coffee and roasted almonds.

'Let me look at you.' Hélène squeezed her hands gently and pulled her close.

'Please don't tell me I look tired,' she said with a wry smile, 'like you did at Mom's funeral.'

'Somebody had to. You'd worn yourself to a shred. You should've taken time off then.'

'I didn't know about Nkumbé then—'

'For God's sake, Candace, you don't need to know about Annie's boyfriend to take time off.' Her cousin tightened her grip. 'You're old enough to know that.'

She nodded, impatient with herself. 'I know, Hélène. I don't understand why I can't crack it.'

Except that taking holidays on her own was a sad affair, like Christmas, and she'd gotten tired of tagging along behind her old college friends with their dependable husbands and well-behaved kids. She'd turned down an invitation from her old room-mate Nancy for Thanksgiving the same night she'd met Bill Holden and secretly blamed her for going into self-destruct mode.

'You need a total break.' Hélène was still holding her hands. 'Somebody to look after you for a change.'

'Too right.' She'd meant it to sound full of bravado, like it didn't really matter to her either way, but instead her voice caught in her throat and her lip quivered. Her eyes pricked and filled with tears and before she knew it she'd fallen tearfully into Hélène's embrace.

'Hell, sorry—' She pulled back and tried a brave smile. 'I didn't fly all that way for this—'

'Oh yes you did. Nothing beats a good weep; ask Hollywood. Here.' Hélène produced a freshly laundered handkerchief and Candace blew her nose and wiped her eyes.

'Yeah, maybe you're right.' She glanced over at the bar.

'And never mind about him either,' hissed Hélène. 'This is our bubble.'

'Thanks. I'm going to turn a corner, really.'

'Just as long as you know which corner you're turning.' Hélène led her over to a luxurious sofa and they sat down. 'Tell me about it.'

Candace took the battered old bible she'd found in Annie's box out of her bag, the New Testament in some Cameroonian language with a stamp from the American Presbyterian mission at Ebolowa on the first page and below it a carefully written name, Esther Nkumbé. She'd put Didier Nkumbé's photo inside the front cover.

Hélène looked at the photo and nodded. 'He looks right, nice looking and bags of get up and go.' She glanced at the back. 'But he's younger than I imagined, and what's with the bible? Don't tell me Annie got converted.'

'No way,' said Candace. 'It was his sister's and I think they were both educated by the mission.' She took the press cutting out and gave it to Hélène. 'This was tucked inside.'

It was dated June 6 1954 with the headline 'Mission Backs Ebolowa Cocoa Co-op' and a photograph of a group of people standing around some newly planted shrubs; men and women of different ages, a few dressed up in style but most in work clothes and holding gardening tools. Three were white with an older woman with grey-ing hair and the news item referred to 'the mission's personnel, Esther Nkumbé (secretary) and Lillian Fleming (President) expressing their thanks to M. Guy Martin at the Bureau for Rural Development (BPDR) for technical support.'

'Doesn't sound like Annie's big story,' said Hélène. 'A cocoa cooperative.'

'I think it's just where Nkumbé came from.'

Hélène shuddered. 'It's kind of weird seeing him after all these years. Is Harry Kaplan on his trail?'

Candace shook her head. 'Not yet. He wasn't happy about my coming out and said he was concentrating on Victor Castile. He wants me to go after the Ice Maiden instead because he thinks she's up to something.'

'After all this time?'

'That's what I thought, but he says it's his case.'

'That's ridiculous.'

'I know but he's right, we have signed a contract – and anyway I don't really want to track Nkumbé down on my own or for Harry to be difficult about it, like I'm cramping his style.'

Just at that moment a smartly dressed waiter materialised from behind the bar with a trolley loaded with two steaming cups of café au lait, a bowl of fruit and a tray of pastries. Next to it was a sizzling omelette and a basket of sliced baguette. The lower shelf was covered with magazines and newspapers.

'What would you like for breakfast?' he asked.

Hélène glanced at Candace, who smiled and wrinkled her nose. Everything smelled delicious and emotions always made her hungry. 'Everything.'

'Bravo,' said Hélène. 'That's the spirit. A portion of everything – your new motto!' Hélène turned to the waiter who was already sliding the omelette onto a platter and cutting it into two. 'And two glasses of champagne!'

Candace clapped her hands. Why not? It was time to live a bit.

The waiter disappeared and came back with a bottle of Brut and an ice bucket. He popped the cork and poured. Candace watched the bubbles gather and rush to the surface and she raised her glass.

'Here's to a bit of everything,' she said and laughed because it was so ridiculous.

'Everything.'

They clinked their glasses and Candace drank deeply. The bubbles fizzed in her mouth and the sharp taste made her feel fresh. She turned to her omelette hungrily. The outside was bronze, the texture almost crisp, but the middle was moist and flavoured with chives. Her head spun with pleasure and she looked up to see Hélène taking a copy of *Le Monde* from the trolley. A colossal headline leaped off the page alongside a mug shot of a bald man with heavy jowls and small piggy eyes:

'CANARD WIRETAP: PRIME MINISTER BLAMES CIA.'

Hélène laughed. 'Incredible! He's really put his foot in it.'

'Who?'

'Messmer. He had it in mind to be the next president but this isn't a good start.' She gestured at the picture of the balding man. 'It's a long story, but this is Jacques Foccart, ex-Minister for Africa and also a master of the dark arts of political intrigue. They were both devoted Gaullists and Messmer was a key player in the Algerian crisis. He helped keep the army on side against the general's putsch.'

Candace ate another piece of omelette; she'd read about Messmer's plan to sort out the French energy crisis by going nuclear. She refilled her glass and gestured with the bottle but Hélène shook her head.

'I've got to put in a day's work, unlike some.'

'You've just been scolding me for not taking it easy,' she said with a wave of her glass.

'True. And I'll scold you some more if in two weeks you haven't broken every rule in your Protestant handbook.'

'I'm not a Protestant!'

'Then don't behave like one. Indulge.'

They laughed together and Candace felt her spirits lift. 'So what's this long story?'

'It's typically Machiavellian, but basically under de Gaulle the secret service was run by Pompidou from the prime minister's office. Then Ben Barka was abducted in '65, you remember—'

Of course she did: a high-profile leader of the Third World snatched off the street in Paris in broad daylight and never seen again.

Well, most people reckon Foccart was behind it; but de Gaulle blamed Pompidou and transferred the secret service to his faithful old ally at the Ministry for the Army. It's been a bone of contention ever since, with Pompidou and the new director on one side and Foccart and Messmer on the other.'

'Wow—'

'That's not the half of it. You remember the Markovic Affair with Alain Delon's bodyguard turning up dead on a rubbish tip outside Paris?'

'Vaguely. Something to do with drug dens and high-class whores?'

'Exactly. Markovic had access to celebrity parties thanks to Delon and was setting up hidden cameras to blackmail whoever he caught, like Pompidou's wife. The photos of her were never found but the gossip went into overdrive just as Pompidou started running for president and I hear—' Hélène tapped the side of her nose and dropped her voice to a conspiratorial whisper. 'It wasn't Madame Pompidou at all but a prostitute who looked like her, and set up by the old guard in the secret service who objected to the new broom getting rid of good old traditional practices like abduction and drug smuggling.'

'Jeez—'

'Exactly. You couldn't make it up! The hoods she was supposedly photographed with had crazy names out of the movies, like Z and Bimbo!'

'Somebody should write a book about it.'

'Somebody already did, called *Lamia*, but it's banned here as a breach of national security. I got a copy in Montreal.'

Candace shook her head in wonder and mopped up the last of her omelette with a slice of baguette. It all made Watergate look a bit tame.

'Trust the French to pull out all the stops,' she said and picked up the newspaper. She studied Foccart's inscrutable face. 'And these guys are still around?'

Hélène nodded. 'Very much so. Messmer could've made the Élysée but for this mess, and Foccart might have lost his job as Minister for Africa but he's still a power behind the throne not least because he's got a file on everyone, like your Mr Hoover. They're both creeps.'

17

Monday, 8 April 1974

Douala, Cameroon

He tossed and turned his bruised body but all it did was increase pressure on his bladder. He was bursting. He got up gingerly and worked his way from bunk to bunk to the wall at the end. Something scuttled across his feet as he unzipped and urinated all over the stone floor. He zipped back up and counted the bunks back to his pallet bed. He finally fell into a light sleep, only to be promptly invaded by the door being flung open and a piercing flashlight shone into his eyes.

'Get up,' the shaven head said. 'Time to go.'

The two gendarmes were standing in the corridor smoking, the big one leaning against the wall with his thumbs hooked into his belt.

'What time is it?' Harry asked. They'd taken his watch.

'Like the man said, time to go,' said the driver and they bundled him along the corridor and back up the stone steps. The big man seemed subdued and mercifully less inclined to beat him up. The sky was tinted pink with the first light and he could hear the buzz of traffic in the distance. Across the road a woman was blowing on a flickering brazier. He was pushed into the back of the Peugeot and they took off. The city was waking up. Workers scrambled into buses and pushed bikes loaded with baskets and the aroma of charcoal and roasted corn filled the air.

The traffic was light and they got to the Sécurité in no time at all. The front office was brightly lit and they were greeted by the night-shift sergeant stretching and yawning, ready to go home. He jerked his thumb at the corridor behind him and released the bolt on his gate and the driver guided Harry through. The big man brought up the rear and Harry was taken into a side office to be fingerprinted. He didn't bother to raise the question of civil liberties. He needed to talk to somebody nearer the top.

He wiped the ink on his pants and watched the print man gather up his kit and head for the door. Just as he got there it opened and in marched a tall slim man with a pencil moustache and wearing a perfectly laundered uniform. He was as light-skinned as Harry Belafonte and was carrying a thick envelope and a couple of cellophane evidence bags. One had Harry's blood-stained clothing in it; the other had Castile's gun. He put them on the desk and sat down and gestured at Harry to do the same.

'I'm Inspector Atangano of the Douala Gendarme,' he said. 'I gather you understand French?'

Harry nodded. 'But what I don't understand is what I'm doing here. I reported the crime and made a statement to Inspector Takere—'

The pencil moustache cut him short: 'Ex-Inspector Takere.'

'He planted the gun in my car. He let the killer escape and sabotaged your investigation as revenge against the French administration—'

'There is no French administration. Cameroon has been independent since 1960.'

'I know but Takere was fighting old battles.'

'Takere was – is – working for the Lagos oil mafia.'

Harry couldn't believe it: getting people right was part of his job. 'He told me he was going to work for Shell.'

'That's what he told everyone, but we've been watching him for months. Him and Baba Kingibe—'

'Who?'

The pencil moustache gave him a forced smile. 'The man who gave you the gun in Lagos.'

Harry felt the ground sliding from under him. He was back in the world of Uncle Joe Stalin where black was white and the truth turned inside out and people went to the firing squad thankful the ordeal of interrogation was over. Memories of the Hungarian AVH slipped cold steel under his ribs and ran it against his heart.

'I didn't meet anyone in Lagos,' he said. 'And Takere found the gun in Castile's truck.'

Atangano drummed his fingers on the desk with exaggerated impatience. 'Let's not waste time playacting, Mr Kaplan. You're a bit player, a hired gun—' He broke off to give him a pitying look. 'But we're prepared to consider your situation if you co-operate.'

'I am already. I'm telling the truth.'

'Takere and Kingibe are small fry, runners,' Atangano said with icy deliberation. 'What we need is the identity of the man behind them, the shark you did business with.'

'My business is with Dr Candace Fayol,' Harry said, battling to keep his outrage under control. 'I'm a licensed private investigator looking for the story of her sister, Annie Fayol, who worked out here as a photo journalist on *Life* magazine. I'd never even heard of the Lagos oil mafia until yesterday. There's a copy of our contract in my bag.'

'Ah, *monsieur*,' Atangano said with a reptilian smile, 'we already knew about your cover story. Very clever.' He rapped his fingers on the desk and leaned forward with an air of fraternal confidentiality. In his hand was Harry's Illinois gun licence. 'There is one thing you can clear up for me. It's not an important point, you understand, but I'm curious. Colleagues tell me I'm fastidious – an obsession for detail. I just wondered if you specified that the gun had to be the same model as your own, or if it was one of those random instances we call a coincidence?'

The snake was about to strike and anxiety gripped the pit of Harry's stomach. He could see what was going on: Takere was a pawn – they both were – and somebody with a lot of clout was pulling the strings.

'A total coincidence,' he said, 'like everything else. I'd like to speak to the US Embassy. It's my right—'

But before he could get any further the inspector had jumped to his feet and banged the desk with both hands.

'Your rights,' he screamed. 'How typically American to talk about rights!' He leaned close enough for Harry to catch the scent of his cologne. 'But what about Cameroon's rights, M. Kaplan, eh?

Answer me this if you're so keen on rights. Who gave white men the right to carve up Africa? God?'

He straightened up and spun round and walked away. Harry tried to get up but a heavy hand on his shoulder stopped him.

'That's got nothing to do with me and I've got a right to see somebody from the Embassy. I've been falsely arrested. My client will make representations at the highest level.'

It felt as if Candace was all he had.

The inspector checked his stride for a second but then came back and stood over him, still fuming. 'I've already talked to your people in Yaoundé,' he snapped. 'They assured me you would co-operate.'

'I told you I am cooperating – I reported the crime, for God's sake. I could've walked away.'

The man folded his arms. 'This is not some gangster movie you know. Our future is at stake. Oil prices are going through the roof. Your own government understands as much. They're supporting our drive against the racketeers—'

'Sure, I understand,' he said breaking in, 'you've got my support. I did my best by reporting the Hertz car. Whoever was driving it will know the names—'

The inspector slammed his fists onto the desk and leaned across into his face. 'I told you I need names not support, names of the people who run this business and if you want to get back to Chicago you'd better start remembering them.'

And with that, Inspector Atangano of the Douala Gendarme turned on his heel and stalked out of the room.

They'd taken his clothes and left him some baggy prison shorts, a tunic shirt and rough sandals that were made out of car tyres and a size too small. He tried to stay calm but it wasn't easy. He was in a big hole and a long way from home, even if they'd moved him from the dungeons to Douala jail. The scale of the thing bothered him: the coincidence of Castile's death and the way the pencil moustache taunted him about random instances as if they'd been playing him from the moment he touched down.

No matter which way he looked at it the so-called coincidence kept popping up. How did they know he was going out to Castile's place? Was it Stokes, or did Eileen O'Connell have something to do with it? The CIA were capable of anything, but nothing added up and Harry wondered if he was getting paranoid.

He couldn't do anything in jail either. Just being there was bad enough. The perimeter was rough and ready with chain-mesh fences and straggling barbed wire and searchlights as dilapidated as the ones on the border posts in Hungary. There were two long dormitories made of corrugated iron with no windows and a row of filthy latrines with buckets and a couple of spigots and sinks to wash in. He kept an eye on his fellow prisoners. He was an event – a white man from Chicago – and everybody, jailbirds and guards alike, was agog to see what a real-life Mafia hitman looked like.

He heard them calling him Al Capone and Chicago Man, which he didn't bother to correct: maybe a hard reputation would play to his advantage. Most of the inmates kept a wary distance, sneaking glances, and one or two tried to sidle up and touch the hem of his tunic like he was some kind of macho superman, but a couple of others, bigger guys with nastier looks, eyeballed him close-up as if to say they weren't impressed and spat in the dust at his feet. He knew it wouldn't be long before one of them decided to up their prison kudos by taking a crack at him.

The other thing was he was hungry. He hadn't eaten since last night at the Mountain Hotel and the prison didn't do five-star meals. It didn't do meals at all, just dried up maize porridge that pigs would baulk at. On the far side was a compound next to the exercise yard where wives and mothers were herded like livestock and allowed to pass dishes of beans and rice through the barbed wire. A troop of guards spoiled the picnic atmosphere by striding around with baseball bats to make sure nothing else got through.

The noise was as shrill as a parrot house and the smell of food so distracting that Harry almost missed the bulky figure being checked in at the gate. Then his heart leaped and he crossed over to the wire trying to look cool, calm and collected because Chicago hitmen didn't rush anything.

'Jesus, Hans.' He seized the Dutchman's hand. 'Am I glad to see you.'

'Likewise. It was tough finding out where they'd put you. I came prepared.' Ouweneel took a baguette wrapped in foil out of his bag. 'The *spécialité* that the gendarmes so rudely interrupted.'

'Oh my God.' Crunchy bread and moist white meat laced with fresh mayo and green leaves. Harry sunk his teeth into it and wondered if anything had ever tasted better. Mayo squirted onto his chin and he scooped it up. 'Oh Jesus, Hans—' He took another bite. 'It's even better than the other night.'

'Last night you mean.'

'Jesus, yeah. Last night. Feels like a long time ago.'

One of the guards came over with an empty Fanta crate and the Dutchman slipped him some money before sitting down, his big gut resting on his knees. He winked at Harry. 'This is Joseph, good friend of mine. He's going to make sure you don't starve. We've had this arrangement before: a chef I knew who went wild with a chopper. Problems at home.' The guard grinned and whacked his nightstick into his hand before moving off. The Dutchman took a folded newspaper out of his bag. 'You've hit the headlines.'

The words jumped off the page: 'OIL MAFIA MURDER: CHICAGO HITMAN ARRESTED.'

Harry swore. 'Takere set me up. He planted the gun in my car.'

'Never.' Ouweneel shook his head. 'I've known him for years. He'd never do a thing like that.' He took an envelope out of his jacket pocket. 'He sent this up to the hotel for you.'

Harry tore open the envelope. Inside was a handwritten note stapled to a shiny new Shell business card bearing the name of Gideon J. Takere, Head of Security.

Dear Mr Kaplan,
     My card as promised. And apologies, I left something of our friend's in your car by mistake. The car was too

small – it was sticking into my stomach! Feel free to keep it as a memento! Yours, GJT

PS You will always be welcome in Port Harcourt.

Harry exhaled. 'So I wasn't wrong about him.'

'I told you he wouldn't do anything like that.'

'Somebody did.' Harry pinched the flesh at the top of his nose. 'The gendarmes knew what they were looking for and had a photographer ready. They even had a story of where I got it.'

'I know.' Ouweneel passed him the paper. 'It's all in here.'

'That's what I mean. They saw me coming.' Harry chewed some more of the baguette. He studied the photographs in the newspaper: Castile's body, the oil trucks, a close-up of the gun, and him blinking into the flash. 'Whoever it was has got the gendarme helping out big time,' he said, looking up, 'somebody with a lot of clout—'

'Like Nkumbé.' Ouweneel rocked back on the crate. 'You think he's got his finger in the pie?'

'Could be, but can't figure why he's gone to such extremes.' He frowned. 'That's the bit that doesn't add up. It didn't look like a Mafia killing to me.'

Ouweneel shrugged. 'Maybe it's a case of different place, different Mafia.' He took a bottle of wine out of his bag and pulled the cork. 'Drink? Left over from last night?'

'Oh my God, yes.' Harry took a long swig. Waves of relaxation flowed through him and he closed his eyes and it seemed a long time before he opened them again. The Dutchman was smiling grimly. Harry grabbed his beefy arm and said, 'Jesus, Hans, you got to help me get out of here.'

Hans grinned happily. 'Sure, Harry, I know it's tough on you but I've got to say it's a pleasure. I told you it was time I did something else with my life.'

18

Paris, France

When you have only fear and beatings in your life you have to turn them to your advantage. Marc Benet had got that much from childhood. In order to survive the hell his mother called home he had learned to keep his mind clear no matter what, and how to watch and wait. Everything he knew about the world he had taught himself, except the skills of the blacksmith, but even those he'd felt in the marrow of his bones as if they'd been left there by his father.

In school he'd learned nothing except how to fight dirty and hide hurt and now he used his injured hip to deflect pain and panic. For him the bone and socket were a pestle and mortar where he would grind his feelings into dust, like his hatred for Foccart and the terror he felt for the safety of his precious daughter. Years ago, he'd used the same method to dull the agony over Monique's death when he'd torn up over 10,000 feet of Mount Cameroon, lengthening his stride to raise the pain to screaming pitch.

But that night outside the Piscine in Paris he had no mountain to climb and had headed instead for Sacré-Cœur, stamping his left foot forwards on the wet sidewalks to heighten the wrenching discomfort. He couldn't believe he'd been such a fool. He knew he'd made a pact with the devil, agreeing to Foccart's demands in return for a Swiss passport, but he should've realised that nothing Foccart did would be that simple. The bastard had run rings round him, even needling him into losing control. Watch and wait: his childhood self looked on in bleak dismay.

For a while he had fumed in the shadows of the Piscine with the single useless passport in his hand, but he slowly regained control by concentrating on Dayak's wife and family. They had been struck a sickening blow and now their lives were lost in darkness. He had failed them; it was as straightforward as that. He knew about Barbouzes like Dupin and should've done something. Dayak's blood was on his hands and nothing would ever wash them clean.

He tried to think it through; cause and effect. How many other lives had he stopped? Berbers and Tuaregs in the desert, nameless men with families and futures obliterated. Flesh and blood reduced to grief and desolation, the wrong men dead while a monster like Foccart survived to send others to an early grave.

Rain drifted across the city from the west with a swirling wind and Marc's hip protested all the more. He was glad of the overcoat he'd left in the shabby basement room near the Gare du Nord. It was rented from some cousin of Yasmin's and he'd slipped in silently, left his case and then followed his nose upwards to Pigalle and Sacré-Cœur. The view across to the Eiffel Tower was dramatic at night but he preferred the desert. Even so, it gave him the space to think and Dayak wasn't the only old friend preying on his mind. He had to track Guy down – and 'tidy him up'.

He'd told Pleven that he trusted Guy, like he was in a select elite, but now he wondered. He wiped the rain off his face and closed his eyes: friendship and trust were not supposed to be subjected to such an extreme test. He tapped his forehead hard and wracked his memory – what did he really know about Guy and what did he need to know to be able to report back to Foccart 'job done'?

Marc remembered the first time they met. Chance again: they'd coincided in front of a rundown wooden shack in the port area of Douala, both of them thinking of putting a bit of a windfall into a new business. They'd looked round together and saw the possibilities of joining forces and having enough money to avoid going cap in hand to a bank.

The impulse worked out and the shack became La Frégate, the best club on the coast outside of Dakar and eventually good enough to appear in a fashion magazine in Paris as an exotic destination with great music and wild food. Sure, reading between the lines they also said it was an upmarket whorehouse, but when had Paris bothered about things like that? It made him and Guy a tidy income.

Marc winced as he tried to come to terms with Foccart's trap, the ultimate betrayal. Guy was a friend, trusted, as he'd told Pleven, not to crack under pressure and to pass himself off as an American. It was always an American he'd imitate, a New Yorker or 'a good old boy' from the Deep South, and Marc remembered how he couldn't bear to impersonate the British. His passionate refusal seemed out of character but Marc had never bothered to figure out where it came from. Maybe he should have. He just took it for granted as the impulse that drove Guy's inspired campaign in the UN plebiscite in Cameroon and then into deep trouble in the Biafran War. It wasn't as if he was a fervent French patriot. On the contrary: he was a *pied-noir*, an outsider like Marc. It had been an immediate bond between them as they'd clattered around the shell of La Frégate, something shared no matter how different they were. Guy was younger, educated, a prize-winning graduate of the Collège d'Outre-Mer with a powerful patron, while he was just a fucking gypsy with the most celebrated limp in France.

By the 1960s Marc had left Douala for a fresh start and they had drifted apart. He didn't want to dwell on why but, as usual, Foccart's intelligence was accurate: Guy had turned up in Niger not so long ago, a freelance looking for work. He was older and talking about going home and wanting Foccart off his back once and for all. He wanted to go for his Tia Pilar – she'd never taken to the desert and had always dreamed of returning to the Asturias before she died.

He told Marc that after de Gaulle had sold them out in Algeria his aunt had ended up in a pokey little terrace house in the 19th *arrondissement*. It was closed off at one end with steps leading up to the park, which was OK in the summer but downright dangerous the rest of the year no matter how old you were.

By lunchtime Marc's hip was very sore but he had found Passage Gauthier – a narrow cobbled street with stone steps at the north end leading onto Avenue Simon-Bolivar and an entrance to the Parc des Buttes-Chaumont. He walked up and down examining the houses. There were no front gardens and the doors gave straight onto the street. Most of the windows were shuttered and in need of fresh paint. Just as Guy had said, Passage Gauthier was certainly cramped, a far cry from the high skies and Mediterranean balm of Oran.

He had a coffee in the Café de Belleville and weighed up the mood of the waiter. A middle-aged man, overweight, with slicked-down thinning hair and a sallow complexion. Marc overpaid and waved away the change.

'I'm looking for an old pal from the Legion,' he said, his wallet still very visible on the table. 'His aunt lives across the way in Passage Gauthier but I don't know the number.'

The waiter avoided his eye and glanced nervously in the direction of the bar. 'Sorry but I don't live round here.'

'You must have regulars who do.'

He shrugged.

'She should stand out a bit,' Marc added. 'She's a *pied-noir*, must've been here at least ten years – I bet the owner knows her.'

The waiter picked up the zinc tray and said, 'I'll ask her.'

A few minutes later a woman emerged from behind the bar. Marc stood up and offered her his hand. 'I'm Marc Benet. The lady's nephew is my friend. Their family was Spanish and he called her Tia Pilar.'

The woman looked him over and then shook his hand. He was glad he'd had the chance to shave and smarten up. 'You can't be too careful nowadays,' she said.

'No of course not.' He glanced at his watch. 'Maybe you'd prefer to accompany me? If you can spare the time that is?'

'No I'm afraid I can't, but—' She half-turned and waved the waiter over. 'Georges can show you. It'll only take a minute.'

Marc thanked her and followed the waiter into the street.

'Madame must like the look of you,' he said gruffly.

'A lot of people don't.'

'You look OK to me.'

Marc grunted: if only.

They stopped at the third house on the left, number 5. There was no bell and Georges waited while Marc knocked on the door. After a minute, it opened a crack.

'Madame Martin,' said Marc respectfully, 'I'm a friend of Guy's, his old partner—'

There was no answer.

'He might've mentioned me, Marc Benet, or maybe my wife, Monique, from Cameroon. We owned a club together with another friend called Violetta. He calls you Tia Pilar.'

The door opened. A small woman dressed in black stood in front of him. She smiled shyly.

'Yes, Guillermo used to talk about you and Monique—' She looked down and made a quick sign of the cross. 'And your terrible misfortune. I'm so sorry.' Her French was drawn out with heavily accented Spanish vowels.

'Thank you,' said Marc. They shook hands and Georges backed away, saying, 'I'd better get back.'

Tia Pilar looked from one to the other.

'Georges works at the café,' said Marc, waving him off. 'Thanks.'

He followed her inside. The house bore all the hallmarks of rented property with cheap furniture and worn carpets. Several packing cases were stacked up in the corner and there were bare marks on the walls where pictures had hung. Above the mantelpiece two framed photographs were still in place.

Tia Pilar wiped her hands on her black apron. 'I'm sorry, *monsieur*, you must think me very rude not offering you anything, but I'm afraid I've just had lunch.' She spread her hands wide and surveyed the chaos around her. 'I wasn't really expecting visitors.'

Marc shook his head. 'No problem, really, thank you. I just had mine too.' In truth the coffee had been the only thing to pass his lips since his encounter with Foccart. His interest in food had dwindled to nothing.

'Sit down, please—' she said.

Marc glanced at the stairway. 'Perhaps I could use your toilet?'

'Of course. Top of the stairs on your right.'

He reached the top and closed the toilet door loudly before quietly checking the bedrooms. There were open suitcases and cardboard boxes but no sign of Guy except a postcard on Tia Pilar's bedside table of a modest café with green and white striped awning, the Café de la Gare at Vernon. On the back Guy had written a phone number and two names in capitals, ISABELLA and PABLO with the words 'hablan Castellano'. Marc made a note of the number and address before returning to flush the toilet and wash his hands.

Downstairs he crossed the room to the fireplace and gestured at a studio shot of two boys, one clearly Guy, sitting together with a woman bearing a striking resemblance to the woman before him. She was younger and more vivacious but still in black. Marc vaguely remembered the Catholic rules for women in mourning: was it the death of a husband that counted the most?

'That's you and – Guillermo, right?' he queried with a raised eyebrow.

She nodded. 'And his brother Santiago,' she said. Then, as an afterthought, 'We call him Gui, the same as the French. It was easier for him.'

'Sure. I didn't know he had a brother. He never said.'

'He wouldn't. Santiago was killed by the British.' She sat down abruptly and gathered her hands tightly together in her lap. 'It was terrible.'

'I'm sorry.' He wasn't surprised. It made sense. 'Guy never said a word.'

'No. It was such a shock. I think he blamed himself.'

'Why?'

She shrugged a thin shoulder. 'Because he survived and it was his idea to go.'

'Where to?'

'The French fleet in the harbour. The date is carved into my soul, 3 July 1940, the day the British attacked Mers-el-Kébir. Santi was killed outright by shrapnel in his back.' Her eyes welled up and she made a furtive sign of the cross. 'If only I'd stopped them. It was a miracle Gui wasn't injured.' She sniffed and dabbed at her eyes with a handkerchief.

Marc nodded. It made sense. The British had destroyed the French fleet before Vichy had the chance of handing it over to the Nazis. Guy wasn't the only French national who bore them such a grudge.

'Terrible,' he said. They'd never shared their childhood memories. 'How old was he?'

'1940,' she said, momentarily fazed and staring across at the photograph. Her blue eyes, the same as Guy's, were blank. 'Gui was eleven and Santiago sixteen, only two years after their mother died.' She shook her head and wrung her hands as if it'd been yesterday. 'My sister Graciela was taken from us. Cancer.'

She wiped away the tears. 'I'm sorry, *monsieur*, but my sister had already lost her husband—' She blew her nose. 'Our family has suffered so much and I think Gui blamed himself for that as well.'

'How?'

She sighed heavily. 'It was 1934, a Republican rising and General Franco sent in the cavalry. Gui's father was trampled underfoot and afterwards he was convinced his father had been trying to save him, but the poor child was only five and we'll never know what really happened.'

Marc's heart sank. How could he inflict further pain on this family? He knew Catholics didn't believe in curses like gypsies but it looked as if somebody had borne them the most horrific malice.

'Poor Guy,' he said and looked around at the packing cases.

'You're moving?'

She brightened. 'Yes, we're going home. As soon as he gets back from Africa.'

'Guy's in Africa?'

'Yes, Cameroon. He said he had a few things to sort out.' Her eyes shone. 'Nobody could've been more of a son to me.'

'When?' Marc's heart speeded up: was this an opportunity or a disaster? 'I mean when is he back?'

'Sunday.' She clapped her hands like a little girl and picked up a brochure. 'And we're going to celebrate with a visit to Monet's garden! It's supposed to be enchanting.'

Marc glanced at the brochure.

'He's been promising me for months!' she said, 'every time he's been out to his bolthole. That's what he calls it!' She looked girlishly coy. 'Where he hides from me. Some cottage in the forest, like Hansel and Gretel.'

Marc nodded: trust Guy to have a bolthole.

19

Tuesday, 9 April 1974

Orly Airport, Paris

Eileen O'Connell had just used the restroom. Gone was the ex-diplomat and New York sophisticate in upmarket hairpiece and heels; and in her place was civil-rights worker Maeve O'Driscoll in sneakers and trousers and a jaunty beret in Republican green with a Michael Collins pin. She strolled out with her backpack slung over one shoulder and hovered at the bookstall.

The papers were ablaze with the scandal of Canard and Messmer. She smiled incredulously: Nixon's gambit had obviously caught on – if your guys get caught bugging an opponent's office, just blame the CIA! She expected better from the French, but she'd hardly had time to pick up a copy of *Le Monde* when an American voice behind her shook her to the core. She froze, rooted to the spot, and the scales of time fell away.

'She said she took sides as well as pictures.'

Eileen went rigid and looked around her, trying to home in on the voice. So sharp and vivid was the memory that it could've been yesterday, the same tone and exactly the same line. It all came back to her, outside Le Frégate, arguing with Annie Fayol about nationalism she'd been lunching with Alistair, she even remembered the crisp white wine they'd shared but most of all she remembered Annie Fayol's line about taking sides and her insufferable arrogance.

Back in the present a last call for some flight to Cairo boomed out burying the conversation and she moved closer, her heart beating fast. She took up a position behind a revolving rack of maps, unfolded one and peered over it: Jesus, it was Annie's sister, no question, the spitting image, older and slicker maybe with a better outfit and hairdo, but identical.

It was no crazy coincidence either: now that her private detective was in jail Dr Fayol was clearly on a mission to get him out. She kept the map half-open and moved carefully towards the till, straining to hear what the women were saying. The other woman was shorter, almost petite, and beautifully turned out. They were saying goodbye. They embraced before stepping back.

'You take care of yourself, Candace, you hear. Let Harry take the risks – that's what you're paying him for.'

'I promise.'

The petite woman touched Candace's face with an elegantly gloved hand. 'And bring him back this way if you get on.'

Candace grabbed the hand and smiled. Her face lit up and Eileen O'Connell realised she'd never seen the sunny side of the older sister. Maybe she hadn't had one.

There was a last fierce embrace before they spun off in different directions. Eileen O'Connell watched them time their turn back to wave in perfect harmony. It could have been a scene from a movie, but she didn't have the time to appreciate it. Her mind was fixed on what they'd said and how they'd said it. It was obvious that Dr Fayol had no idea Harry Kaplan had been charged with the murder of Victor Castile. She just thought she was going out to find her sister's boyfriend.

Douala, Cameroon

The Air Afrique flight started its descent into Douala and airhostesses glided along the aisles. The cabin lights went out. In the first-class section Dr Candace Fayol reached up for her reading light. She was wearing a beige linen suit over a silk blouse with plain gold ear studs and a gold necklace. Her red lipstick was as bright as a cola can, her finger and toenails painted a colour to match; and her hair had been cut stylishly short, *à la mode*.

She felt deliciously chic. Hélène had hustled her into feeling frivolous, a side of herself she barely knew and trusted less. Never in Chicago would she surrender to the will and expertise of the beauticians, but in a VIP lounge in Paris it felt different, like a fourth dimension. The champagne had helped, of course, and with Hélène bubbling with encouragement it all seemed like an exciting adventure.

'It's high time you pampered yourself a bit,' Helen had chided her. 'It's not as if you're short of money any longer.'

Truth to tell, as a medic she'd never been hard up; but all those years of looking after Mom had made her feel dowdy and so had that louse Bill Holden with his cheapskate afternoon motels and nylon sheets. Life was passing her by and selling the house just had to be a line in the sand.

'Men love a traveller,' Hélène had said, batting one heavily made-up eyelid. 'Ships in the night. No strings. You don't have to feel responsible any longer. You've done your bit.'

Anxiety started creeping back and nerves fluttered in the pit of Candace's stomach. The pilot announced that Mount Cameroon was visible out of the window on her side and she caught sight of a jagged grey ridge in the pale moonlight. She stared down at it and grimaced: it didn't look at all like the place to start the romance of a lifetime – and of course it hadn't been. Truth to tell, Annie's encounter with Didier Nkumbé at more than 10,000 feet had been a tragic catastrophe.

She took a deep breath and switched off the reading light. They were losing altitude and her ears blocked and popped. She thought about Harry and figured they'd get over the phone call pretty quickly. It was good of him to meet her at the airport and of course she was looking forward to seeing him again. She watched the sprinkling of lights below get bigger and thought she could make out a silver sinuous line leading out to sea. The river: somewhere there had to be the bridge and the thought made her nauseous. Why on earth had she come?

The plane jolted as the wheels bounced on the runway and the engines roared. The cabin lights came on and the airhostesses stood up in their full uniforms, every stitch and hem perfectly in place. Her heart beat faster and her stomach tightened up with trepidation: 18

years on, she thought, Cameroon at last, but she couldn't summon a silent cheer or even a secret clenched fist.

The arrivals hall didn't help. It wasn't like anything she'd ever seen. The floor was dusty concrete and the ceiling low, with Customs a deafening babble of chaos and half-opened luggage. Everybody was black, something she was used to in the clinic, but here it felt as if they were all looking at her. Her heart jumped and she scanned the waiting throng for Harry's broad shoulders and thick black hair, but he was nowhere to be seen. Two men in green uniforms and caps started to pester her for her luggage, each promising 'best price', and she tried to keep calm and ward them off but she was losing the battle. This was the last bloody straw. Where the hell was Harry? She'd told him when she was arriving and he'd promised to meet her.

She was just about to cave in to the smaller, older guy when a large florid white man materialised in front of her with 'DR FAYOL' written in big letters on a card and she almost fell on him with relief. He had wispy blond hair and blue eyes and was wearing a crumpled jacket.

'I'm Hans Ouweneel,' he said, waving the notice. 'Didn't really need this, did I? You were pretty easy to spot. Welcome to Cameroon.'

He banished one of the men with something unintelligible and Candace happily let the other take her bag. It was heavy with all her new gear and the night was thick and clammy.

'My God,' she said, relief flooding through her, 'am I glad to see you – but where's Harry?'

He turned towards her with a laconic grin and said, 'Long story. Crazy. Let's get out of this madhouse first. It's tough if you're not used to it. There's so much sneaking stuff through and backhanders. We're over here.'

He paused for her to catch up and they went through the doors into the African night. He stopped next to a battered Citroen and opened the trunk.

'Right,' he said as he paid the porter with a bit of a flourish, 'you're not going to believe this, but Harry is in jail on a murder charge.'

The words took Candace's breath away. 'What? That's impossible—'

'I know but it's happened. He went out to some place near the Nigerian border to talk to a man called Victor Castile—'

'I know who he is,' she said. 'Harry told me he was going to see him.'

'Yeah well, he was dead when Harry got there and like a good citizen he reported it to the police but they went and arrested him instead. Classic.' He took a newspaper off the passenger seat and gave it to her. 'It's all in here. They've cast him as a hitman from Chicago brought over by the Lagos oil mafia to take out some local hood trying to muscle in on their patch.'

'That's absolutely absurd.' She eyeballed the headline with mounting fury. 'He's working for me.'

'He tried to tell them but they're fixated by the idea of Chicago, crime capital of the world.' The Dutchman opened the door for her. 'Sorry the car is such a mess.'

She got in and stowed her bag under her feet. The interior smelled faintly of fish. Her nostrils must have twitched because the big man wound down the window. 'Sorry. I use it to go to the African market – dried prawns, *camarones*. I run the Mountain Hotel, by the way, which was where Harry was staying.'

'So tell me—' Despite the smell she took a deep breath. 'Jesus Christ. How?'

She looked around for the safety belt.

'They don't have them here,' Hans said, glancing at her. 'Well, the gendarmes turned up and found the murder weapon in his car; and like I said—' He rolled his eyes. 'He's from Chicago – the world's capital of organised crime – so he had to be guilty, plus of course there is a mafia-style oil racket going on.'

'That's outrageous.'

'Don't worry, we're on the case.' He started the car. 'The US *chargé* knows. Guy called Logan; I fixed a meeting with him in your hotel eleven thirty tomorrow morning. I already told him there's no evidence against Harry.'

'Thanks, Mr—' she had a crack at his name but he swept the effort aside.

'Call me Hans. Everybody else does. Nobody out here can do the Dutch except some old Boers from South Africa.' He offered her a big hand and she took it.

'OK, Hans. And I'm Candace. I save the doctor stuff for the clinic.'

'Harry told me.' He chuckled. 'He's a good guy, isn't he?'

She nearly said she didn't really know him, but decided to keep it simple. 'Yeah. He came highly recommended.'

Hans braked and swerved to avoid a huge pothole in the road. He glanced apologetically at her and smiled. 'I'm sorry you've had to put up with all this. Can't be easy.' He shrugged his big shoulders. 'Harry told me what – who – you're looking for. Your sister stayed in my hotel just before she met this guy Didier Nkumbé on the mountain – we've kept the old registers.'

Candace tried to swallow but her mouth was as dry as dust. 'Did you meet her?'

'Before my time.' He shook his head. 'It's a terrible thing, the rip-tide I mean, comes out of nowhere. Never seen anything like it.'

'You've been in it?'

He laughed and slapped his stomach. 'No, no, I'm no swimmer. One afternoon I was doing a bit of proselytising—'

She shot him a look. 'You're not a missionary, are you?'

'No, no, far from it I'm afraid. I meant I was drumming up business for the hotel. It's the only beach around and the French go down there from Douala to cool off. One time I was there selling our buffet lunch all calm and collected when – pow! – the ocean suddenly turns into this boiling torrent! It's terrifying.'

They speeded up along a road of even asphalt and Candace put her fingertips on her temples. Her head throbbed from the journey and the booze. And the news: what the hell was she going to do? She sighed, a mix of exasperation and empathy. 'How on earth did Harry get muddled up with the oil mafia?' She banged a fist into her thigh. 'I told him he didn't have to go chasing off after Castile.'

'If you don't mind my saying so, he doesn't look like the type to be told much—'

'He's not.' She cursed silently: he'd screwed up. 'And look where it's got him.'

'I don't know, Candace—' The big Dutchman sounded uncomfortable using her name. 'Out here it's a case of wheels within wheels.'

'It's the same everywhere.'

'But not this old imperial spat between the French and English, takes a Dutchman to see it—'

'I already heard about it. It was one of the reasons my sister came here. She was a photojournalist looking for a great story.' She put her hand on her forehead. 'Look I'm sorry, I'm wasted after the journey. I don't mean to sound ungrateful. God knows what I'd have done if you hadn't been there!'

'No problem, my pleasure,' he said, sounding relieved at her change of tone. 'Only too glad to help. I'm at your service until we get Harry out. I don't want to come over like I'm happy about all this, but the hotel's been dragging me down recently and this has got me thinking.' He grinned. 'I mean, I bet there aren't too many private eyes operating out of Douala.'

'I can imagine.' She nodded grimly: it was an ill wind that blew nobody any good.

20

Tuesday, 9 April 1974

Douala, Cameroon

First-class passengers got through quickly but it wasn't a big airport and Eileen had no trouble keeping Candace Fayol in sight. She hung back and watched her pick up her luggage and frantically scan the hall for Harry Kaplan. Of course, he was nowhere to be seen and she could almost feel the poor woman's relief when a big florid guy turned up waving a card with 'Dr Fayol' written on it and towed her out into the African night.

It took a second for a name to come to his face, or at least an identity. It was the Dutchman who'd taken over the Mountain Hotel just before she'd been relocated to Dakar. She'd never got to know him but she didn't think he was the kind of guy to take advantage of a young woman whose arrival plans had gone to hell.

Meanwhile she had her own arrival plans to deal with. A Customs official was rooting through her stuff like his life depended on it. Eileen had looked deliberately shifty under interrogation and in answer to the question on goods liable to import tax, like a hi-fi, she'd said no, but wrapped in a pair of knickers at the bottom of her valise was a shortwave radio. It didn't take long for the man to find it.

'What's this then?'

'It's not a hi-fi,' she said, stridently defiant.

'Same classification,' said the officer, oozing satisfaction. 'Your passport please.'

He took the details and searched the back of the radio.

'It's just for my personal use,' she said.

'You should've declared it.' The officer completed the form with a flourish and tore off the top copy.

'Normally it would cost you thirty francs tax,' he said, clearly overjoyed to be lording it over the sort of white woman who thought she was above the law. 'But you tried to smuggle it in so I'm confiscating it until your departure. You can pay the fine and reclaim it on the way out or it stays in our storage.'

He thrust the form into her hands and waved her away to make space for the next passenger. She muttered a protest and threw her belongings back into the case and zipped it up. As she walked away the feeling of cold steel pressing into the small of her back was oddly comforting. It had all gone to plan: she'd never been strip searched at Douala whatever passport she'd been on but there was no point taking risks and she'd bought a couple of small radios a while back with occasions like this explicitly in mind. So far so good: she detoured into the restroom and moved the Beretta from her waistband to her purse. Outside in the exit hall she let a mob of taxi drivers gather round her.

'Anybody got today's paper?' she asked in Pidgin.

A young guy with an Afro stuck his hand up. 'It's in my car.'

'You win then,' she said and let him take her case.

'Here it is, *madame*,' he said, giving it to her before opening the trunk. 'You booked into La République?'

She shook her head. 'I want a cheap room in the docks, but not La Frégate.' That would be tempting more than fate.

He slammed the trunk. 'You sure? It's not a nice area. Only last week an officer off one of the boats got mugged.'

'Probably drunk. Anyway it's the mosquitoes I'm worried about.' She got into the front seat and glanced at the paper's headlines. 'In any case the dangerous stuff seems to be happening somewhere else,' she said, reading further. 'Where's this Hi Life place?'

'You know Kumba?'

'I did, once upon a time.'

'Well it's on the old Calabar road. Back door for oil mafia.' He gestured at the paper. 'Idiot was trying to muscle into their business.' He ran his finger across his throat. 'You don't want to mess with those boys.'

The taxi coughed into action and they drew away. He glanced across at her. 'You really want a room in the docks?'

She nodded. 'I'm writing a book.'

'About the Douala docks?'

'In a way. There was a famous demonstration against the French down there.'

'Right.' The driver looked convinced. 'I know just the place. How come you speak such good Pidgin?'

'I'm good at languages.'

It was true: she was. She'd been a good mimic, too, with an Irish taste for blarney, and had been pretty enough to take some of the star roles at college, like Portia in *The Merchant of Venice*, and in those days of male chauvinism she'd liked the idea of getting away with being a man. She still remembered the lines – 'the quality of mercy' – and how Shylock had been cruelly undone by revenge. It made her think about what she was doing and wonder where the world was headed: who the hell prayed for mercy any longer? The modern state's power was without limit.

She made as if to read the paper in the light of a passing street lamp. 'So what's the word on the street? You taxi drivers are supposed to know.' The same the world over.

'They're mostly going with the Lagos mafia.'

'But you aren't?'

He shrugged. 'I just heard the guy was a colon with a lot of enemies. They cut him up real bad. You know—' He nodded downwards. 'And then stuffed it in his mouth, choked him to death.'

'Your business surviving this gas crisis OK?' she asked, changing the subject.

'No, it's hell. Prices are going through the roof.'

'I could help you out.'

He looked at her, his eyes wide. 'How?'

'I need a car for a few days and I'll make it worth your while. Double your daily takings plus 20 US dollars, upfront.'

'Dollars.' He thought about it. 'You want it tonight?'

'Yeah. Tonight.'

He nodded: she was serious. 'OK, 25 dollars and you can have it until midday Saturday.' He glanced at her. 'It's a standard shift.'

'I know.' She counted out the money. 'Just show me where I'm staying and I'll take you back to town. Somewhere in the centre.'

She needed to find a phone.

Candace locked the door. The Dutchman had been kind enough but she still had a lot to take in. Anybody would have, for God's sake: Harry was in jail on a murder charge and she was being minded by an overweight hotelier who fancied he was Philip Marlowe – the whole thing was totally insane. Plus there was Harry's notebook, burning a hole in her bag; confidential, for his eyes only.

'Harry left it hidden under the paper in the restaurant,' Hans had said, relishing the intrigue. 'On purpose. The gendarmes searched his room. I thought you'd be interested.'

She'd looked at him blankly: of course she was interested.

Now she sat on the hotel bed and put her head in her hands. Harry, Hans, Nkumbé, Esther, Ebolowa, Eileen O'Connell, Annie – names, places, emotions ricocheted round and round until she was dizzy. She was tired, jetlagged and alone; she wished Harry was there, or Karen, anybody. Her stomach cramped up and her throat was dry, and the tension built like a tidal wave. She was on the point of caving in and she told herself to get a grip.

She looked around for a minibar but there wasn't one. Just a bed and a shower and French doors onto a balcony – French doors: Cameroon and the French connection, she thought, and pressed hard on her temples. She closed her eyes, trying to clear her head, and told herself sternly that she'd come to find Didier Nkumbé – to wrap things up, to draw a line under it and that was all. He was her priority and, like Hans said, there was no need to worry about Harry, the Embassy would sort it out.

But no amount of internal hectoring could get Harry out of her mind: he was in Cameroon thanks to her and now he was in jail. She tried to picture it, barbed wire and dirt compounds, sheds of sheet metal and horrendous toilets. She rehearsed the arguments: he was obviously innocent, mistaken identity, wrong place at the wrong time, and the whole stupid Chicago Al Capone thing with the gendarmes jumping to crazy conclusions like 2 plus 2 making 20. It was madness, but hopefully it would all be sorted after she'd talked to the guy from the Embassy, Charles Logan – or was it Chuck? – about her and Hans signing affidavits on Harry's innocence.

Her mind settled a moment on the Dutchman. Surely he was a good guy? He had to be; he was helping out – he'd met her at the airport, for God's sake! But he was also pretending to be a private dick, living out a fantasy and gung-ho to help her trace Nkumbé. He'd obviously wanted to hang onto the notebook, but no way was she going to let him and anyway she needed it to contact O'Connell's journalist friend. The Ice Maiden was up to no good, Harry had said so on the phone, and the journalist was one of her connections, so she had to be on her guard.

She took the notebook out of her bag and flipped through it for the man's details, but there was no neat list. Instead the pages were crammed with dense spidery writing as if paper was in short supply. Maybe it had been where Harry grew up, but either way the words were so tiny and crushed together they were barely legible. Plus there were a bunch of abbreviations and it took her a while to figure out that the first pages actually dealt with a different case altogether – a capital M for 'matrimonial' and a Mrs Elaine Kramer suing for divorce. In the state of Illinois you needed graphic evidence of sexual infidelity or domestic violence and Candace saw that Harry had found it.

She flipped further into the notebook until she came to a page with a little more white space and a diagram. Annie, 'AF', was attached to a symbolic skull and crossbones at the centre of a spider's web of connections, with lines and arrows drawing other people into the tangle. Some of these were easily understood like 'VC', Victor Castile, and his links to 'OIL' ('Total' 'Shell' and 'BP'). Total was also connected to 'DN' – which had to be Didier Nkumbé – and a broken line connected him to Annie with a question mark as if Harry still harboured doubts about them being lovers. It bugged her that he hadn't taken her discovery seriously.

She grimaced angrily: why the hell should she care what he

thought anyway? Like Karen said, she was paying the bill. She put her irritation on hold and went back to the notebook. It didn't take long to work out that the initials 'FM' with another skull and cross-bones was Dr Félix Moumié, but 'FS' was tougher until she remembered Uttley's contact Frank Stokes.

She traced his connection back to 'EOC' the Ice Maiden and drew a quick breath: there was another symbol for a dead woman with a question mark. Candace straightened up and clenched her fists – *two* dead women.

The idea bounced around her tired brain; Annie and someone else both connected to O'Connell. She rubbed her forehead and returned to the crazy jumble of lines and abbreviations and was on the point of shutting the notebook when another detail seized her attention, two small bubbles containing the miniscule initials 'CIA' and 'IRA'. Her heart jumped and she thrust the notebook into the light of the feeble bedside lamp: the letters were cramped and tiny, but definitely CIA and IRA with a line back to Eileen O'Connell.

Candace stared across the room, her jaw set: it was *incredible*. The Ice Maiden was connected to the CIA and IRA and Harry had just called her a woman of many parts.

Why the hell hadn't he told her?

It struck her that maybe O'Connell was still an agent – or a double agent, but it made no sense. Sure, the Irish Question was alive and kicking, but how could it be connected with Annie *in Cameroon?*

Candace flopped back onto the bed and closed her eyes. She wasn't paranoid by any stretch and had never swallowed the conspiracy theories about Marilyn Monroe and JFK and the grassy knoll, but this was different. This was her dead sister and the US *chargée* who'd identified the body operating as some kind of double agent. A woman of many parts: it beggared belief! Candace opened her eyes and sat up; her mind sharpened and things began to fall into place. The more she thought about it the simpler it seemed. Just like Watergate and the Pentagon Papers, there was something rotten at the heart of the state. Annie had been murdered and the US *chargé* had covered it up. They'd all been in shock, vulnerable, and O'Connell had taken advantage. Candace sighed: Mom had been out of it but Dad should've been smarter.

She returned to Harry's notes on O'Connell: 'CIA, sacked '73 (NORAID/IRA)'. Then in the same spidery writing, now clear in the lamplight, the shock information: 'US homicide date '54, not Annie Fayol.'

Candace gasped. The murdered American wasn't Annie – maybe she'd just drowned, after all. With a trembling finger Candace traced the line a second time between the skull and crossbones dated '54 and 'EOC'. She took in a deep breath: the woman had been murdered two years before Annie arrived and O'Connell had reported it to the CIA. Candace sat up and snapped the notebook shut. Candace was pissed with Harry for keeping her in the dark, but she was so relieved that Annie hadn't been raped and murdered at Mile 12 that she forgave him. She snapped the notebook shut. A breeze blew up and rustled the flimsy linen drapes and she suddenly felt exposed. She got up and locked the French windows and dragged at the drapes, but one of the runners jammed and refused to come together. Through the gap she could see the last few flickering lights of the city shutting down. Somewhere out there was the river and the bridge and, further north, Mount Cameroon and the beach at Mile 12. She shuddered and clenched her fists, her newly manicured nails digging into her palms. Despite her relief, she felt daunted and alone, but she gritted her teeth and squared her shoulders. It was time to be counted – like some comic-book hero she'd always fantasised about.

21

Wednesday, 10 April 1974

Douala, Cameroon

Despite taking medication, Candace had slept badly with dreams and jetlag and had woken with enough of an ache behind her eyes to make her grouchy, but at least she'd managed to unscramble the details for the old journalist. She marched out into the lobby to call him. Sure, O'Connell and the CIA might have buried the truth but a local journalist like him should've picked up the scent of something that big. She dialled and waited with one hand pressing down on the butterflies exploding in her stomach.

Eventually a woman answered, with an English accent: 'M. Raymond's resident nurse,' she said, with a hint of putting the record straight before anybody could get the wrong idea. Candace explained who she was and asked if it would be possible to drop by and see *monsieur.*

'*Monsieur* is recovering from a serious heart attack and isn't up yet. Can I take a message?'

'What time does he eat in the evening?' Candace asked.

'He has something light,' the nurse replied. 'Cold meat, salad, at seven. It would be fine if you came tomorrow, say seven forty-five.'

Candace thanked her. 'Tell him I have some of my sister's photographs that I'd like him to see.'

After she put the phone down she headed back into the restaurant in a better frame of mind. An appointment with Jules Raymond felt like progress and now she needed a cup of coffee, maybe even breakfast. She poured herself some fresh orange juice from the self-service table and took a seat near the window. She sipped the juice and ran her finger down the spine of Harry's notebook.

He'd obviously done a lot of thinking on the case, even if some of it was up a blind alley. She glanced at the hotel clock, a fifties model reminding her of the one at home, and nodded with satisfaction: she was getting the hang of his hieroglyphics and had plenty of time to go through the notebook again before the *chargée* turned up.

She drained her glass and looked around to order but the waiter seemed to have disappeared. She was aware of a commotion out front with the sounds of a scuffle and was on the point of getting up when the Dutchman blew in looking like a kid who'd been given the day off school.

'Jesus, Candace,' he said, coming over and sitting down, 'it's worse than the airport out there. May I?'

She nodded.

'Sorry to barge in on your breakfast like this, but you need these.' He passed her a set of car keys. 'Harry's car; it's outside, I'll show you, and – well, I'm kicking myself because I should've thought of it last night – but the fact is you're going to need protection.'

She raised her eyebrows. It was far too early for melodrama but it was obvious that last night's knight in shining armour was still in the saddle and enjoying himself. He was bursting to tell her something but she put him off by twisting round impatiently.

'What d'you have to do round here to get a darned cup of coffee?'

The Dutchman shouted something unintelligible and snapped his fingers. A waiter materialised and Hans ordered in what she now knew was Pidgin.

'What d'you mean,' she asked, '"protection"?'

'Well,' Hans said, enjoying the role of the guy who gets things done, 'the thing is they're all agog.'

'What about?'

'You, Candace.' He smiled broadly. 'You're big news, but I fobbed them off with an interview.'

She was stunned. 'You did what?'

'The press is out there and the radio,' he said, irrepressible. 'It's a hell of a story.'

She sat bolt upright and glared at him. 'Hans, exactly what story are you talking about?'

He flushed and looked downcast, a punctured balloon. 'Well you know – Castile and Harry and the oil mafia.' A pink tide rode up his neck and cheeks and he undid another button on his shirt. 'You know—'

She shook her head. 'No I don't know.'

'Well – this whole thing about Chicago being the crime capital of the world. You know the press, they love a cliché.'

She went very quiet and spread yesterday's paper out in front of him. Outwardly calm, she was seething inside. Notoriety was the last thing she'd come to Cameroon for.

'All that stuff is old news, Hans,' she said, 'Castile dead and Harry the hitman for the oil mafia was in yesterday's paper, so what on earth do I have to do with it?'

He flapped his hands so much that a spoon started to rattle against a glass. She put a hand over her eyes.

'For God's sake, Hans, please sit still.'

'I'm sorry, Candace, but the papers already knew Harry was working for you.'

'As well as for the Nigerian oil mafia?'

'Well, what I mean is that you're both big stories out there today.'

'I only just got here.' She leaned forwards, her hands spread flat on the table. 'You sure you didn't mention me to any of your staff last night?'

She watched him frown, going through every conversation he'd had, before shaking his head. 'No, I just said I was going to the airport.'

The image of their meeting came back to her – the only two white people in the building. 'You were holding up my name on a card in Arrivals.'

'Not for long—'

'Long enough,' she said. 'Hundreds of people could've seen it. Damn, damn. What about Harry? He told you about me.'

'Only so there was somebody to meet you. I don't think he told anyone else.'

She wondered but just drew back from the table and lit a cigarette while her gallant companion rushed through his pockets for a lighter.

'You're too fast for me,' he said, finally holding up a lighter with a loopy grin on his face.

She blew smoke in the air. 'Obviously.' She was still pissed with him and he was mopping his brow with a handkerchief.

'Sorry—'

She waved away his apology. 'Forget it; you saved me last night. But I'd actually appreciate knowing what kind of news I am making. Exactly what did you say to the media in your five minutes of fame?' She broke off – it wasn't fair to treat him like Bill Holden. 'I'm sorry, Hans, but you can see why I'm annoyed.'

He flapped some more. 'Sure, sure, Candace, absolutely – but as soon as I saw the scrum I knew they were after you and I just – well – shot from the hip I guess, as usual, my big mouth.'

'By saying?'

'Nothing much, just why you'd come over.' He clammed up, caught in the act. 'What else could I say? It's not my fault your sister is still a hot topic.'

'Jesus, Hans—'

'Well, whatever you call it. She's… *newsworthy*.' He shrugged and met her gaze. 'I might've handled it badly, but you and Annie are a big story and I'm the best shield you've got until Harry gets out.' He gave her the grin and shrugged again. 'Plus I've already got a lead on Nkumbé for you.'

'Really—?'

'I guessed he went to the *lycée* in Ebolowa, which is run by the American Presbyterian mission, so I called them and fixed us a meeting at ten tomorrow with their oldest surviving member of the staff at Ebolowa—'

'A woman called Miss Fleming,' she said, breaking in and watching his jaw drop. 'She's high on my list of people to see.'

The would-be private eye looked dismayed. 'You knew about her?'

She nodded and decided not to show him the cutting. 'I found a reference to her in Annie's things and I think he had a sister called Esther who taught at the mission school in Ebolowa.'

'That's interesting,' he said, recovering his composure. 'I'm impressed. We could drive down there if you like. I've asked around and it's obviously Nkumbé's home patch.'

'Is it—?'

'Yeah, he was a minister and more or less runs Total.' He rubbed his finger and thumb together. 'He's loaded. But you'll need some help down there with Pidgin. Not everyone speaks French.'

'Sure, all in good time, Hans, after I've seen Miss Fleming.' Dismay clouded his broad features and she felt a twinge of guilt. 'I'll need you for the riskier stuff – I mean, who could be less of a threat that a retired missionary? I'll let you know how it goes.'

'OK but what about today? I took the day off so I could give you a hand.'

'Well, I'm going to be pretty busy with Logan this morning and an old journalist contact of my sister's tonight—'

'Who's that?'

'Jules Raymond.'

He snorted. 'Well I got to say I'm happy to leave him to you, snotty so and so—'

'How so?'

'He'd stay once in a while on one of his so-called stories and was so condescending about our cuisine – over this side the restaurants have two menus, one with local produce and one ten times more expensive with imported French ingredients. Good luck.'

'Thanks.'

'Actually, I hear he's been poorly.'

She trumped him again. 'He has been, but he's got a resident nurse, a young English—'

'Fitz!' He jumped and his big thighs smacked into the table. 'I know her too – it's a small place. She used to work in the hospital in Buea and was a regular in the hotel. Sad to lose her, actually.'

He sat back looking relieved and redeemed. The waiter arrived with the coffee and it looked as if they were back to being a team again, but her mind was elsewhere. She stubbed out her cigarette half-smoked and grimaced: Harry was in jail for murder and she couldn't shake the feeling that she was being watched.

Douala jail, Cameroon

They were on the evening perimeter walk when it happened.

He had just had an audience with the US *chargé* Chuck Logan, a fresh-faced young guy who could have been a Mormon in his polished brogue shoes and starched short-sleeved shirt. He'd assured Harry that he was on the case and that affidavits from Takere, who was apparently mortified by Harry's plight, and Hans Ouweneel were being lined up with a lawyer in town. Logan hadn't yet managed to contact the woman from the Hi Life but was still trying. 'She's probably out dancing,' Harry had said and Logan had given him a blank look but promised it would only take a few days.

'You get a sense of the place and how it works,' Logan said as they shook hands but Harry had come away feeling preoccupied and let his mind wander and his guard drop. Either way, he wasn't ready and the big guy who had eyeballed him in the morning hit him from behind. He was thrown to the ground and the guy kicked him in the gut. Harry grabbed his foot and twisted it and the guy stumbled over him into the barbed-wire fence.

Harry knew about blind fury – it had rescued him a couple of times in Vietnam – and it flooded through him again now. Blind to fear, blind to the consequences of violence. He thrashed out with his feet and caught the guy in the groin and rolled clear. The big bastard was roaring with pain but his sidekick hit Harry in the ear with a piece of wood. The pain popped inside his head and he lashed out.

His elbow made contact and bone crunched under the impact before the man fell away. The big guy had recovered and Harry threw a straight right into his throat. It stopped him for a moment but next thing Harry knew the guy was all over him. He fell back and cracked the back of his head on the ground. A huge hand hit him a glancing blow and a foot thumped into his side and almost winded him but he got his fingers into the big bastard's eyes and pushed. He felt the neck snap back and tried to kick himself free but the huge guy was crushing him. A hand was pressing down on his face. He couldn't breathe. He was losing it. Darkness was closing in.

And then there was light. Blinding his eyes. Somebody was hauling the big guy off. His lip was split, there was blood in his mouth and one eye was smarting. There was a knife at his throat and somebody twisted his arm up behind him and frog-marched him across the compound to a small shack. Dim light leaked from the door along with the surreal lyrics of 'You Make Me Feel Brand New'. Inside, the air was thick with stale beer, sweat and marijuana. A bunch of men were playing poker but only one was winning, a very black guy in a stained sleeveless vest with grey stubble and an Australian bush-hat.

'Hey *bwana!*' the hat sneered and Harry waited, flexing his twisted arm. 'You know what *bwana* means, Chicago Man?'

Harry shook his head: he didn't but he was going to find out.

'It's Swahili for "big boss", like Al Capone. You know where they speak Swahili?'

Harry waited to be told.

'On the other side of Africa.'

A couple of the poker players hummed like a chorus line.

'That's where I learned English.'

The chorus line hummed louder.

'I was over there in the King's African Rifles with Idi Amin and look at us now. He's president of Uganda and I'm doing time.'

The poker players hooted and whistled and the hat pushed his chair back from the table with narrowed eyes and looked Harry over with malign calculation.

'What's your first name, Chicago Man?'

'Harry.'

'OK, Harry. You seen *King Rat?*'

'Yeah.' He had watched it on TV: George Segal playing a canny POW in a Japanese camp.

'So you know who you're talking to?'

He nodded; there was one in every jail. 'I just don't understand why.'

The hat leaned forwards with a mean look and banged the bottle. Bubbles spewed out and a puddle spread across the table.

'Because you killed our old friend Victor Castile.'

Harry blinked. He wasn't thinking fast enough. His eyes watered and his head felt as if it was split wide open. His ribs ached and it hurt to breath. He was dog-tired and couldn't decide what to do: keep up the front of a Chicago hitman or come clean. The chorus line had gone quiet, but all he could do was wait for the axe to fall.

The bush-hat was shaking his head. 'They brought you all the way from Chicago! I can't believe it.'

Harry was dumped in a chair. He touched his swollen lip and ran his tongue along the inside of his mouth. It tasted of blood.

'You look a mess.' The hat was peering at him through the smoke.

'A couple of guys wanted to show me how tough they were.'

'Wear this.' He threw Harry a blue denim cap with a big letter B stitched into it. 'Stands for Bamenda, my home town. It's what they call me in here. They won't bother you again.'

King Rat: Harry nodded and put the cap on. It was a bit big but he wasn't about to complain, least of all about the man's softening demeanour. The chorus line was humming along with the music.

'Thanks.'

'My pleasure, Harry. I heard you choked Victor on his balls. I like that.'

'They were actually paper balls. And it wasn't me.'

But Bamenda wasn't listening. 'I'd have made the bastard eat them. How much they pay you, Harry?' He flattened a newspaper on the table and stabbed at it with a thick finger. 'It doesn't say here.'

'I told you I didn't do it.'

'It says you did.'

'You always believe what they say in the papers?'

'I believe the football scores.'

'Exactly. It would be stupid to fake them, but that' – Harry gestured at the headline – 'that's all bullshit. Castile was dead when I got there, killed by a guy in a Hertz hire car who doesn't even get a mention. How d'you account for that?'

Bamenda leaned closer, his eyes widening. 'Then he's the one who deserves a medal! A DSO like Idi, and a bar.' The chorus line hummed louder and the hat turned to a man with a bathtub full of bottles at his feet. 'Give Chicago Man a beer from the bar!'

Harry grabbed the bottle and took a swig. He put it down and wiped his mouth on the back of his hand. 'So what's this about Castile being a friend of yours?'

'We go a long way back, Harry, nearly 20 years. Such a good friend that I tried to kill him.' Bamenda raised his bottle and the chorus line followed his lead. 'Anyway, here's to you or whoever you say killed the bastard. Good health and long life.'

Harry wasn't sure about drinking to a guy who'd helped to get him framed, but the cold beer cleared his mouth of the taste of blood.

'Castile doesn't seem too popular up where he lives,' he said. 'The way I heard it, people are going to be fighting to dance on his grave.'

'I'd be the first.' Bamenda turned away to spit. 'Bastard – I hope he died in pain.'

'He did.'

'I told you that you did it, otherwise you wouldn't know how much pain he was in.' He held out a big hand. 'I wanted to congratulate the man that did in person.'

'I could tell from the mess he was in. Anyhow I'm a private investigator not a hired gun,' said Harry but shook the hand anyway. 'How come you tried to kill him?'

'He killed my brother, slit his throat in cold blood and then watched his family go up in flames, wife and babe-in-arms and three little kids.' He banged the table and spat. 'My brother was the night watchman at the UPC headquarters in Bamenda and Castile was sent to burn the place down. They thought the party leaders were meeting inside but it was only my brother's family; bastard Castile just went ahead anyhow.' The chorus line had simmered down to a reverential hush. 'It took me two years to track him down, but then I messed it up and ended up in here.' He slammed his fist down on the table again and all the bottles jumped. 'The French, they look after their own.'

'I heard he had friends in high places.'

'Fucking bastards.' Bamenda stared off through the smoke. He turned back to Harry and assessed him again. 'If you're a private eye, like you say, what did you want Castile for?'

'You heard of Annie Fayol?'

'Of course.'

'Well, I'm working for her sister. She thinks Annie had a date the night she drowned—'

'She did. It was Castile.'

'What?' He was stunned.

'Yes, she was with him that night.'

'How d'you know?'

He tapped his nose and winked. 'My cousin saw her with him in her car.'

'Why didn't he come forward?' Harry asked but the question died as soon as he'd got it out.

'White man's business,' Bamenda said and gave him a look horribly close to pity. 'He wasn't going to get involved.'

The door flew open and a couple of inmates came in carrying a big black box between them.

'You hungry?' Bamenda was smiling like a benign uncle. 'Groundnut stew, the best on the coast!'

Ouweneel's baguette was a distant memory and Harry always enjoyed a midnight binge, especially if he'd had a beer or two. The atmosphere in the shack was convivial and the aroma from the stew settled the question. The man from the makeshift bar brought him another beer and a knife and fork and the guys with the box passed him an enamel bowl with two waxy white slices of cassava and a wedge of bright-green spinach surrounded by chunks of meat deep in a rich brown gravy. Somebody raised the volume on the hi-fi and the chorus line degenerated into a babble of enthusiasm for the simple pleasures of food and drink.

'Here's to you,' called Bamenda, his bottle raised high like a salute. 'Good luck and good health.'

'To you too,' Harry shouted back and emptied a good third of his bottle. His head was light and his sore lip and ribs forgotten. The cassava was firm and the meat dissolved in his mouth with the smooth flavour of peanuts and a sharp kick of chilli.

'We had you spotted before you got here you know,' said Bamenda. 'Those jungle drums.' He hooted with laughter and pulled a fat cigar from his pocket. He bit off the end and spat it out before lighting it from one of the candles on the table. 'You married, Harry?'

He shook his head.

'You're old enough.'

'Yeah.' It was what Meche was always telling him.

'So what's the problem?'

'It's a long story—'

'Without a punchline,' Bamenda laughed and the chorus line hooted on cue. A love story without a punchline was no kind of story at all.

'The job doesn't help.'

'It's not half as bad as being in jail.' Bamenda clamped his teeth on his cigar and made a thrusting movement with his fist. 'Where there's a will there's a way.'

'Only if you're King Rat—'

'That's what I'm saying. Get to be King Rat. Cut corners and pull strings.'

'There's another King Rat I'm interested in,' said Harry. 'The one that landed me in here. You weren't the only one to have me spotted. I don't know who it was or why but I'm going to find out—'

'It was Takere. Planted the gun in your car.'

'That's not what it says in there.' Harry pointed at the stained newspaper.

'We got other ways of getting the news,' said Bamenda, leaning back to blow a smoke ring. 'I already told you about the jungle drums.'

'Yeah, well, the drums got it wrong this time. Takere left the gun in my car alright, but he didn't set me up for the gendarmes. He can't stand them.'

Bamenda nodded. 'It's the same for everyone over here. They wish they hadn't voted to unify with the East.'

'That's what Takere said,' Harry said. 'They'd been suckered by the campaign promising an end to Igbo domination, and ended up with inflation and French domination instead. He's had enough.'

'It's always been about French domination in this bit of Africa, and if it's not French it's British.' Bamenda paused and tapped the ash off his cigar before looking Harry in the eye. 'You working for Annie Fayol's sister; that's your story, right?'

'It's the truth.'

'So, what's she paying you to do?'

'I told you, she wants to know who her sister was with the night she drowned.'

'And now you know, it was Castile! But I'll tell you something else for free about who calls the shots round here. I told you Castile did dirty tricks for the French, like killing my brother?'

'Yeah.'

'Well, at the time the high commissioner for France was Pierre Messmer – the same Pierre Messmer who's prime minister of France today.'

Bamenda rocked backwards and pushed his bush-hat off his broad forehead to give Harry a long steady look. For the first time since Harry had been dragged off his crib to see him, the King Rat of Douala jail looked deadly serious. He shook his head and something like sympathy glinted in his jaundiced and bloodshot eyes.

'You've picked a fight with some big people, Harry,' he said balefully. 'You'd better watch your back.' He gestured at the cap on Harry's head. 'I can watch out for you in here but not against that lot.'

Harry's situation was suddenly horribly obvious. He'd stepped right out of his league and taken Candace with him.

22

Harry had spent all night figuring it out and the pieces were coming together, the same old story of people in power getting up to no good with Eileen O'Connell up to her neck in it. Who else knew he'd been going to talk to Castile? She was a sharp operator, trawling in dirty water like she said, so she must've known that Castile used to do illegal strong-arm stuff for Messmer.

Like Bamenda said, Messmer was still calling the shots and somebody stirring up the past was the last thing he wanted. That was the core of the case: Annie had been up against some big hitters and they were still around. If it wasn't the Lagos oil mafia that had killed Castile, it looked as if Messmer had decided that he was expendable. They'd either fallen out or Messmer had found someone else to do his dirty work for him.

Harry's head was spinning with questions but it felt as if he was getting somewhere, even from inside prison. His ear was sore and his lip swollen but Bamenda's cap was working. In the exercise yard the young blood had glowered and spat at his feet but had clearly been warned off trying anything else. The guards hustled them on with their baseball bats and the prisoners were halfway round the perimeter fence when there was a shout from the guardhouse.

'Hey, Chicago Man! There's a lady to see you! *Une jolie jeune femme!*'

The cry was picked up across the jail and it rippled over the yard like a flock of birds from one side to the other. He strode across the compound with a swarm of excitement in his train as if everyone was headed for a night on the town. Once he was through the gate the crowd pressed up against the wire, eager for a glimpse of the fair sex or even better a sniff of it.

The chorus simmered down into a murmur of appreciation as

there, at the end of the cinder track, appeared a sight for prison eyes, good enough for the silver screen in cream slacks and a silk blouse with bright-red lipstick and big Continental dark glasses like Leslie Caron. He blinked: here was a new Candace with a fabulous haircut. She stood her ground, head high and shoulders square, a chic leather bag hanging off one, and a hush fell over the jail, every breath held ready for a passionate embrace made in Hollywood.

'Candace,' he said, shaking her hand against a storm of catcalls and whistles. 'That's some haircut.'

'Thanks,' she said poised a moment as if for the crowd. 'And that's quite a reception.'

'The word gets around fast out here.'

'You don't say.' Her face darkened. 'What happened to your lip?'

He shrugged. 'I got into a fight.'

She raised her dark glasses and seemed to roll her eyes as if to say he was accident-prone, but then she said, 'Too bad I didn't bring my medical bag.'

'It's nothing,' he said and steered her round the corner of the shack to a couple of upturned crates. He could feel the crowd break up behind them and drift away on a wave of disappointment. He swept the dirt off the top of one of the crates.

'Thanks,' she said, looking askance at the crate, 'but I'd prefer to stand if that's OK with you.'

'Of course. It's good to see you. And I'm sorry about the last time we spoke on the phone, but it turns out I wasn't so wrong. It was Castile at the beach with Annie; she'd been having a scene with him.'

'According to O'Connell!' she said scornfully. 'Why didn't you tell me she was in the CIA?' She tapped her bag. 'I've got your notebook. Maybe I shouldn't have read it but under the circumstances—'

'No problem.' He shrugged. 'There was a lot I wasn't certain of.'

'But suddenly you're certain about Castile.'

'He and Annie were seen together on the way to Mile 12 the night she died. He was in her car.'

'I don't believe it.' She shook her head angrily. 'More gossip.'

'No,' he said, 'I wish it was.'

'Oh Jesus,' she said. He could see her imagination taking over, like at O'Hare, the worst possible scenario. 'Who saw them?'

'A guy hunting bush meat. He had no reason to lie.'

'But he never came forward?'

'He was black and it was white man's business.'

'Come on, Harry, Nkumbé is black!'

He hesitated, not sure where to start.

'Look,' he said, 'I'm sorry I didn't tell you everything. A lot of it was speculation but, as I told you at O'Hare, Annie's big story was ruffling some fancy feathers—' He broke off. 'Big shots, and apparently the man who really calls the shots round here is Pierre Messmer, the current prime minister of France.'

Her reaction wasn't what he expected. 'I know who Messmer is,' she said, with a gesture of disbelief. 'Come on, Harry, be realistic – how would a guy in jail know anything about him?'

'I know it sounds crazy,' he said, rushing on. He could sense the guards coming back up the track. 'But Messmer was high commissioner when Annie was out here and he was all over the cuttings I found on Castile – the same guy that used to do dirty tricks for the government, like killing women and children. They killed his brother at the UPC HQ—'

'What?' She cut in, shaking her head. 'Sorry but you've lost me, Harry. It's all too far-fetched.'

'I know,' he said. The boots of the guards were pounding up the track. 'But it's beginning to fit. It's insane and dangerous. They're probably the ones who killed Victor Castile even if I can't figure out why.'

She waved him away and said, 'Well everybody else thinks it was the Lagos oil mafia, which makes perfect sense given what's going on in the world right now. Anyhow,' she added, taking an envelope out of her bag, 'the good news is they're letting you out tomorrow—'

'What?' He recoiled, his mind reeling. 'Logan told me it would take longer.'

'Yeah I know,' she said, 'but he did a deal about you tampering with the crime scene and they've cancelled your visa.' She gestured with the envelope. 'You're booked on the first flight to Paris in the morning.'

'I don't believe it.' He was outraged. 'He had no right!'

She looked disappointed. 'I thought you'd be pleased.'

'I'm not,' he said, leaning forwards. 'Can't you see? It's them again; Messmer and his gang getting rid of me before I can start asking questions.'

'I'll be able to do that,' she said and he jumped up.

'No, no, Candace! That's what I mean: you've got to leave with me—'

But she shook her head as if he was going way over the top. 'I've only just got here, for God's sake,' she said firmly. 'I haven't even been to Mile 12 or the cemetery yet.'

'Go today then and we can leave together in the morning.' His voice was urgent. 'I'm serious.'

The guards were back. One grabbed his arms while the other gestured at her like an escort. '*Madame—*'

'Seriously,' he called over his shoulder. 'It's not safe.'

He twisted round at the gate to see if she'd heard but she was gone. She had no idea what she was getting into.

Paris, France

Beware of Greeks bearing gifts. The words kept coming back to Marc and he remembered the baron telling him the story of the Trojan horse and how he should never trust his enemies, no matter what they turned up with. He'd liked the story but hadn't needed the lesson about trust. Although he'd taught himself the most important lessons in life, he owed the baron more than just La Frégate and the house in the Rhone Valley. He actually owed him his life, even though the baron insisted it was his good fortune that fate had brought them together when his horse, a sleek black stallion called Gunnar, had gone lame while hunting in the Breton countryside.

Years later, wherever they were in the Legion, he and the baron would toast the nameless fox for bringing the hunt close to his village, and never a day would pass without Marc wondering how long he would've survived in his grandfather's house if the baron hadn't rescued him. Gunnar and the fox had become characters in a bedtime story he told Madeleine and she loved it. He'd employed an artist to decorate her bedroom in Casablanca with them and he couldn't wait to see how she liked it.

Madeleine.

His mind came back and he gripped his head with his hands: was this another moment of destiny like Gunnar going lame? Could a gift be trusted if the Greek was dead? The question beat a tattoo on Marc's brain.

All around him workers in boiler-suits and railway uniforms were eating lunch, drinking wine, smoking cigarettes, oblivious in their noisy routines with nothing out of place, a regular weekday in workaday Paris: predictable, safe, sound, and the world upright on its axis. He scanned the faces, eyes alight and mouths open, talking, eating, drinking, cursing, their worst problems trifling by comparison, such as an undiagnosed pain or a tortuous infidelity. Nothing like the dilemma he faced with both Madeleine and Guy's lives hanging on a thread.

'M. Marc!'

Through the fog of cigarette smoke he could see the waiter waving his arms and pointing at the phone kiosk in the foyer. 'Your international call!'

He weaved his way through the tables. Inside the kiosk it was quiet. His heart beat faster and he picked up the phone.

'Yasmin?'

'Yes, M. Marc, how are you?'

He pressed a hand to his forehead and rubbed his temple with his thumb. Truthfully, he was exhausted, and had never been less sure of his next move. He was locked in a game of bluff and didn't know how much Foccart knew now that the bastard's network of part-timers had been rolled up. And with Pompidou's new broom at the Piscine, Foccart had a few problems in his own backyard as well as losing his min-isterial post as M. Afrique.

'I'm tired Yasmin,' he said, never so open with her, 'and stuck in France, but your cousin is looking after me very well.'

'I'm so glad. Everything here is fine. I saw the new snake charmer this morning!' She laughed and the sound gave him a welcome surge of joy. 'You know I don't like snakes but this boy is so sweet. He will be a big success.'

'Bravo! A good omen for your new business.'

'Don't speak of it,' she cried, 'I'm still hoping you'll change your mind.'

He wanted to tell her how his mind was but asked after Marcel instead.

'He called yesterday and left one of his funny messages. He said he hadn't found the Greek in the jungle, but your old friend had even-tually suggested he check the suburbs instead. He got the impres-sion people still expected him to be climbing palm trees.' She laughed. 'Quite a riddle!'

'Yes, same old Marcel.' He rested his head on his hand. He was tired. Paris didn't suit him, but he drew some comfort from the thought that in death Petridis had given him a chance of turning the tables on Foccart if Marcel could get to it first.

'I'll call again,' he said to Yasmin. 'Take care of yourself.'

Douala, Cameroon

Fitz knew how pitch-black African nights could be and was careful to take a torch. She felt a twinge of guilt about leaving *monsieur* without any electricity but he'd lived in Cameroon all his life and knew what to expect. The power cuts had been especially bad since the oil crisis and then the generator clapped out and nobody had come to fix it.

As a gesture she lit a couple of hurricane lamps and set the table with candles even though it wasn't her job. She thought of saying it would look romantic for the American guest but didn't know him well enough to make cracks like that. She was feeling good: it was her night off and she was all dolled up for a good time downtown with Rachel and Laura with streetlights and bars and throngs of people, more like home.

She was sick of the suburbs and had decided to give in her notice. *Monsieur* was a difficult patient at the best of times and was getting worse, but the last straw was when she found out that the bastard who'd groped her in Buea was his cousin. They were chalk and cheese, which just went to show you couldn't tell with families, and he was obviously a nasty piece of work but she'd never dreamed he'd end up murdered.

She picked up her bag and gave a little bounce as she slammed the door – she had plenty to talk about: Castile and *monsieur*'s guest, sister of the famous Annie Fayol, as well as Harry Kaplan, the Chicago detective they'd arrested for Castile's murder. Rachel and Laura were going to be goggle-eyed. They'd both lived in Douala longer than she had and normally had the best gossip, but tonight she was going to trump them with stuff even juicier than Rachel's story of *monsieur*'s wife walking into the ocean.

By the time Fitz was sat in a bar and holding her friends in thrall, Jules Raymond's American guest was getting lost looking for his old colonial house. Hardly any of the streets were signed and Harry's Citroen had poor headlights. There was nobody around to ask the way and Candace was beginning to wish she'd agreed to Hans tagging along as 'shotgun' – as if he was John Wayne! The power and reach of Hollywood amazed her and she understood why the French had been desperate to keep them out. 'They knew their whole culture was at stake,' Hélène had said but at the time it seemed a bit farfetched.

But Eileen O'Connell would have had no problem with the idea. She'd seen the struggle first hand – French resistance to American culture in Paris and then France's mission to 'civilise' Africa with Republican ideals, perfect command of the French language and a reverential enthusiasm for the cuisine. It was no wonder that Breton cauliflowers and beef from Burgundy were jetted into the far corners of the Empire as if people were shopping direct from Les Halles.

Eileen also had no problem finding the old journalist's house. It was in the middle of the best of bourgeois Douala, raised up to give a view of the ocean and a refreshing respite from suffocating coastal humidity. It made perfect sense that everyone headed across the Wouri bridge to cool off at Mile 12. She remembered going from La Frégate on the spur of the moment and the delicious sensation of plunging naked into the sea. Oh, to be young again! Instead, she was going down the murkiest of memory lanes, making up for the past.

By the time Candace had found Jules Raymond's house she was running late. She left the car with one wheel cocked up on the side-walk and looked around. The houses reminded her of California – single storey, made of timber, with shingle roofs and surrounding decks spacious enough for rocking chairs and dining tables. Each house was set at some distance from their neighbours' with what Candace guessed were gardens front and back. The air was filled with the throb of diesel engines generating power and most of the win-dows were full of light. A murmur of voices reached her from the far end but otherwise the street was deserted. Number 12, the journalist's house, was cloaked in shadow with dim candles flickering in the win-dows and for the second time that night Candace wished she'd taken up Hans' offer to ride shotgun.

The hotel staff had reacted with surprise at her decision not to take a taxi and one of them had pressed a flashlight on her. He'd said they were expecting a power cut and there was no moon and he was right, but the flashlight was a poor substitute and she had to navigate her way through the gate and down the path by peering into the dim pool of light at her feet with the occasional look up at the candle she adjudged to be nearest the front door. She only just saw the lowest step in time and nearly tripped. She cursed and deliberately tapped the flashlight on the wooden balustrade to announce her arrival, but nobody came to the door.

Her heart beat faster: she was expected and running late and the place was pitch-black. Surely a bourgeois like Raymond had staff – or servants, as they called them? She swallowed and tried to turn her nerves into annoyance but her bravado drained away as she reached the door and it swung open in front of her. The hallway seemed cavernous and a guttering candle on the sideboard went out.

'Hello—' Her mouth was dry and the word seemed to hang in the air. 'M. Raymond – it's Dr Fayol.'

No answer; not a word. She was a city girl used to streetlights and people and she'd never, even on summer camps, been in such darkness. Something was wrong and she'd started to turn when her professional duty got the better of her. The man was convalescing. His nurse had told her. She told herself to calm down and took a deep breath. He was probably just dozing in his chair but you could never tell with convalescence.

'M. Raymond,' she called again and forced herself forwards. The hall door creaked open and the beam of her flashlight swept over a dining table laid for dinner with unlit candles.

'Oh God.' She caught her foot and cried out, a ruck in the rug. She shone the flashlight into the shadows, her heart hammering against her ribcage. Somewhere a dog was whining and Harry's words came back to her: 'It's not safe'. What the hell was she doing? She turned to leave but stumbled and her hand brushed against warm flesh – a body. She stifled a scream and scrambled back on her feet. She started to when suddenly the lights came back on.

Back to normal – a room ready for a dinner party, but her heart was racing and all she wanted was to get out of there. She stood rooted to the spot, she couldn't move and a terrible thought gripped her: he needed her help. She exhaled and forced her eyes back to the body on the floor. It lay face down with the head turned to one side. She hesitated and then crouched down on one knee to check for a pulse. Nothing. She strained for the faintest movement, willing it to register, but after a bit she sighed and gave up. The man was dead. Jules Raymond had suffered a fatal coronary.

23

Douala, Cameroon

Candace pulled up opposite the jail. The air was thick with warm mist and water was dripping on the thin tin roof with annoying regularity. Somewhere she'd read about prisoners being tortured by a dripping faucet. She looked at the paper: Harry's prison mugshot appeared under the headline, 'MISTAKEN IDENTITY', and below there was a photograph of a white car.

She groaned and fumbled in her purse for a cigarette. She hadn't slept a wink after the chaos of last night, although it could've been a whole lot worse. Raymond's nurse Fitz had come home mercifully early and had taken over. She said it was her job and she'd been ready for it. But even though they were both medics they were still in shock and only felt better once they'd covered the body with a sheet and could wait for the ambulance in the other room with some of *monsieur's* best cognac.

She looked across at the prison gates. The eerie silence was suddenly broken by the whine of a motorcycle and Candace caught sight of a dim light approaching. It came to a halt and the rider cut the engine and kicked out the stand before sauntering across towards her. He had a camera and flashbulb round his neck. She swung the door open and got out and the man jumped backwards.

'Apologies, *madame*, I'm from the press—' he said and held out a battered card.

She felt like pushing him over. 'Did you follow me?' she asked.

'No, no, *madame*. They sent me to get a picture of Chicago Man.' He looked at his watch. 'He's supposed to be coming out any time.'

'It's supposed to be confidential.'

'Confidential.' His tone sounded sad and he shrugged. 'It's today's story—'

The man looked at his watch again and shook his head. 'Maybe he won't be coming.'

'He is,' she snapped without thinking. 'He's leaving the country on the eight thirty flight—'

'It's grounded,' the man said. 'Air traffic control are on strike. That's today's other story.'

'What d'you mean?'

'Orly is paralysed, so we are too: twenty-four hours.' He looked across at the gate. 'No flight, so maybe no Chicago Man today.'

'Jesus—' She slammed the car door. Logan hadn't said anything about a strike. She'd called him late last night about M. Raymond and he'd said not to worry, he'd make sure Fitz was OK. There wasn't a British presence in Douala and he was used to helping out instead.

She made a move to get back into the car.

'Wait, *madame*,' the photographer said, holding his hand to his ear. 'I hear other things too, about the guy they call Bamenda fixing things for Chicago Man. Looking out for him. Come.'

He took a step towards the gate. Something seemed to be happening. Keys rattled, a bolt was pulled, the gate clanged and a voice called out 'Regards to Al Capone'. The photographer jumped forwards and Candace's instinct was to trip him up but she was too slow. A bulb popped and Harry was caught in the bright light. He punched out at the guy but wasn't close enough. The guy got astride his bike and kicked it into action before roaring off.

'Am I glad to be out of there,' Harry said, smiling. She remembered his dimples. 'Thanks for meeting me. It's more than I could do for you.'

'My pleasure,' she said. 'And the good news is you've got twenty-four hours' reprieve. Air traffic control are on strike.'

'I just heard,' he said. 'Got a cryptic message from Bamenda telling me I had time to go dance on Castile's grave.'

'Will you?'

'Maybe. I've never been so famous,' he said.

'Infamous you mean,' she said and he laughed.

'OK, infamous.' He gave her a steady look. 'But seriously, it's great that we've got more time.'

She wilted. She didn't want to talk about it but she knew she had to. 'Jules Raymond died last night,' she said. 'Just before I got there. His nurse was expecting it – he was still smoking and eating all the wrong stuff.'

'Candace,' he said very quietly, 'you're a medic so you will know, but was there anything to suggest he didn't die from natural causes?'

She shook her head. 'No, but I know what you're getting at – he was the second person you were lined up to talk to who's dead—'

'Exactly. Which also makes sense of me being thrown in jail while they got to Raymond.'

'OK, it might look like that,' she said, 'but who the hell are "they"?'

'I told you—'

'Yeah and I've been thinking about what you said,' she said, breaking in. 'I can't believe it. I mean, the prime minister of France, for God's sake. He's got to be above stuff like this.'

'What about Nixon and Watergate?'

'That's different. No one was killed.'

'It's the same compulsion,' he said. 'Conspiracy and cover-up.'

'But it's insane, like pulp fiction.'

'So was Watergate and Ben Barka, not to mention the French Connection drugs case.'

'I know,' she said leaning back against the car, 'I saw the movie, but I still can't believe it. Messmer just doesn't look the type.'

'Do they ever?'

'Nixon did. Anyhow, all the more reason to find Nkumbé.'

'Have you got the photograph with you?'

'Sure.'

She gave him the studio portrait and watched him turn it over. He was frowning. He looked at her, his expression set for something serious.

'You can't be sure this is for Annie,' he said. 'There's no name.'

'It's obviously for her,' she said hotly. 'It was in her things and he says they climbed the mountain together.'

'It still doesn't mean it was for her.'

'Sometimes you have to go with your hunch. You said so yourself.' She got the keys and his notebook out of her bag and gave them to him. 'I'd sooner you drove.'

'OK.' He shrugged; he was looking troubled and unconvinced. 'Where to?'

'The beach,' she said, getting into the car. 'I don't want to go on my own and we've got an appointment at the mission at ten thirty.'

'OK. Mile 12.' He started the car and looked at her hard. 'But I meant what I said yesterday: it's not safe for you to stay on. First Castile and then Raymond – you've got to see what I mean.'

She gestured with the paper and tried to laugh it off. 'The press will look after me,' she said. 'And Hans.'

They drove back into the city in silence. She stared out as another new day started, people waiting for buses and buying breakfast with the air laced with charcoal and coffee. She glanced at him. The side of his head was bruised and there was dried blood below his ear and she had to stifle an urge to wipe it away. In the port district the coffee and charcoal gave way to seaweed and dried fish.

The Wouri Bridge emerged from the mist, leaping low and flat across the river with dark jungle on the far side. The air seemed chilly with foreboding but halfway across she summoned up the courage and asked him to stop. She got out and leaned over the railing. The water was as grey as pewter and a tangle of debris had caught up around the pillar.

Where they'd found her.

Images invaded her mind and she tried to shut them out and gazed upstream instead. Two pirogues were so low in the river that the fishermen seemed to be walking on water. The thin mesh of their nets shimmered like fine mist in the morning light. Three men were dragging a boat along the shore and they stopped as a grey car pulled off the track, but nobody got out. She put a hand on his arm. 'It's going to be tough enough for me at the beach, OK?'

His face softened. 'Sure, sorry,' he said again, but his expression clouded. 'Whoever these guys are, they're serious – and my money is on the same big hitters Annie was up against. Digging up the past has stirred them out.'

She nodded dumbly. She didn't know which way to turn. She looked up river again and shivered. 'Can we go please?' she asked. 'This place gives me the creeps.'

'Sure.'

On the other side of the river the jungle gave way to ranks of palm oil and a road of smooth asphalt. They passed a bunch of men on bikes and a ramshackle factory of corrugated iron surrounded by a tattered chain-link fence. A metal stovepipe spouted black smoke; and heaped at the gates was a pile of palm nuts like huge red porcupines. A mile or so further on the road turned into a pitted track and the oil palms gave way to the monstrous tangle of jungle. Vines whipped against the hood and in the distance she could hear the ocean crashing on the shore. Her mouth went dry and she tried to calm herself.

'This is it,' Harry muttered as the car pushed through the creepers into a small clearing. Beyond them stretched the beach, a bleak expanse of coarse red sand strewn with spirals of seaweed, uprooted trees, and a rusty oil drum bearing the Shell logo. The jungle crouched at the edge like a huge malevolent force poised to leap.

'Welcome to Cameroon's answer to St Tropez,' he said and cut the engine.

It wasn't funny and she barely nodded. Her stomach was in knots, but she pulled herself together and got out. 'I want to go and check the water.'

'Be careful,' said Harry. 'Remember it's dangerous.'

'I won't be long and it's OK at the moment.'

'Hans said it comes from nowhere.'

'I'm just going to dip my toes in,' she said. 'For Annie's sake.'

The ocean was an unwelcoming grey in the early light, an undulating sheet as far as the eye could see, and she pulled her jacket tight and set off with her head down. At the shore she kicked off her shoes and watched the waves while trying to conjure up some connection with Annie – anything – but all she was aware of was a solitary screeching gull and the flow of the water around her feet. She felt down and lonely and looked back for Harry, but there was no sign of him. She'd felt wretched enough on the bridge to want to put her head on his shoulder, just for once to have someone take the load, but she barely knew him.

Gazing out across the water she lost herself in the past and with her eyes tightly closed she tried to summon up Annie's spirit. But still nothing. Then suddenly came a surge of water from nowhere with a torrent rising rapidly up her calves. She gasped and pulled her skirt up just as the water reached her knees. She turned back to the beach but it was gone. In its place there was a boiling cataract of white water. With mounting panic she tried to stride out for the shore but the rocks and shingle were giving way under her feet and the water surged high up round her thighs. Her legs were being pulled from beneath her and she struggled to get a grip but the current was over-whelming. She felt herself fall, sucked down, and screamed for Harry.

He was leaning against the car and the scream ripped right through him. He tore his jacket off and sprinted across the beach. He caught sight of her but by the time he reached the shore there was nothing more to be seen but a raging river of angry water. He stood frozen with indecision, Hans' words in his ears – 'let it take you' – and then his own reminding him that he was no great swimmer. His body strained forwards but his feet were rooted to the spot, head and heart pulling him in opposite directions.

He was still rooted to the spot when she broke the surface again, her hand thrown up in a desperate grasping movement, and his name screamed out but abruptly cut short. The sound spurred him to action and he kicked off his shoes and trousers and strode into the surging water. Within seconds his own feet were torn from under him and he too was being swept out to sea. He used the strength in his arms to hold his body up and his legs like a rudder. He rode the current to where he'd seen her and swivelled round to face the shore. The full force of the water crashed into him and it was all he could do to keep his head above water.

There was no sign of her and he couldn't hang on. His arms and legs ached and his heart felt close to bursting. All he could see were the whipped crests of the tide and the vast ocean beyond. The car looked toy-like in the distance and he felt his willpower dip. He told himself he'd been in worse fixes, but none of them had been in water and suddenly he was dragged under. Bubbles burst around him. He looked up at the light and thrashed out but something heavy was hanging onto his ankle. His lungs were searing with pain and his ears thudded.

He kicked again and freed his leg from the weight. Roaring noise filled his ears and as he twisted round to make one last thrust for the surface his hand smacked into something – or someone. Candace materialised in front of him, her body at first eerily loose but then jerking into life and grabbing at him with both hands. His heart pounded and his lungs were close to bursting but he took hold of her and kicked out with all his strength.

Together they moved towards the light and soon he could make out her face and mouth and he wanted to shout. Her arms and legs moved with his and the light came closer but it seemed an age before they burst through the surface. His lungs filled his head cleared, his ears stopped thudding, and he held her up. The expression in her eyes was dark and deep, intense as if she wasn't ready to be beaten. Her mouth sucked in air and he felt her breast fill against him.

'Let it take you,' he gasped, the words a hoarse croak whipped away on the water. 'Don't fight it.' And he pushed her out to sea. The water powered them from behind with terrifying force, but his panic was fading and his arms and legs were strong with new life. He struck out with a smooth breaststroke and turned towards her. 'It's OK,' he mouthed and thought he saw her nod.

They swam together, letting the rip take them until it weakened and finally faded away. Then he called her and they made a wide turn back towards the shore. The swell carried them and gathered up into waves and rushed them ever nearer to safety and his heart filled with relief. In the final stretch his feet touched the rough shingle and he dropped down to crawl out. His head was spinning and above him the sky was still a leaden grey but it felt as if the sun was beaming down.

His heart was still beating fast but his body was so still and heavy it felt as if he was sinking deep into the sand. A wave slapped up against him and pulled the shingle from under his head. He opened his eyes and Candace's profile took shape. She was lying on her side with one arm thrown out. Her face was pale and still. Her skirt was caught up around her thighs. She sighed and drew her legs up like a foetus. He could feel her seek him out with her eyes.

'You saved my life, Harry,' she said, her voice weak and husky like a whisper.

The sound of his name touched him and he remembered how close he'd been to giving up.

'You saved yourself,' he said. 'You grabbed my leg.'

'Instinct. I saw you diving in.'

'That's strange,' he said, 'I've never dived before. Nothing so decisive.'

'That's what I saw.'

Maybe it was, but he'd stumbled in, half hearted. But it would do. He'd saved her life even if he hadn't known much about it. They lay together in a silence wrought by a shared brush with death, a kind of intimacy that was new to him, and it occurred to him it was why the French called making love *la petite mort*.

24

Douala, Cameroon

It was a new feeling for Candace too. She looked in the mirror for any external sign but all she could see was a deathly pallor. She pinched some colour into her cheeks and decided that her new lipstick would look too garish. The large cognac Harry had sent up with room service hadn't calmed her racing heart and she was still trembling. She felt drained and elated all at once, a weird high. She'd nearly drowned and although she knew it was hippie mumbo-jumbo, she just couldn't shake the feeling that Annie had been watching over her.

No matter how down-to-earth she was supposed to be – a medic, a child of the Enlightenment, for crying out loud – it felt as if Annie was nudging her from the grave: first with the card, then Nkumbé's picture and now with what happened at the beach with Harry. She looked closer into her eyes and a thrill ran through her; she'd been totally drained, exhausted in mind and body, and yet there'd been a moment as they lay on the beach when they'd been about to kiss. Trouble was she couldn't remember who'd pulled back.

She shivered and headed down to the bar. Harry was in the banquette at the end. His hair was brushed and he looked smart in a freshly pressed blue shirt, which somehow didn't quite suit him.

'I ordered us some breakfast,' he said, half getting up. 'OJ, scrambled eggs, croissants and coffee – alright?'

'I know I should, but I'm not sure I'm up to it.'

'It'll do you good. You've – we've – had a bad shock.'

'The cognac helped, thanks.'

'I needed it myself.'

'You earned it.' She looked him in the eye, wanting him to soften. 'I meant what I said out there you know.'

'I shouldn't have let you go into the sea on your own.'

'But I needed to be on my own—' She shook her head: she couldn't explain it so retreated to the banal. 'I know this isn't how you normally run your cases—'

'I don't normally get to play in the big league.' He slipped a flimsy, discoloured cutting across the table. 'Take a look at this. It confirms my suspicions about who we're up against. It was written by Jules Raymond.'

It felt ominous: her heart pounded and her hand trembled. She skimmed the first lines: an obituary for Dr Nikos Petridis, a Greek medic born and bred in Alexandria, Egypt, and trained in Athens before collaborating with the Nazis. She glanced up. 'Where did you get this?'

'I found it on the floor of the car when you were on the beach. It must've fallen down there when I was checking the cuttings at Castile's place.'

She nodded and went back to it.

'*Dr Petridis,*' she read, '*eluded justice after the war and escaped to Africa with nothing more than the shirt on his back (as he liked to say). However, such inauspicious beginnings didn't hold him back and during the guerrilla war he became senior pathologist in the Douala Gendarme with responsibility for some of the most controversial (some would say falsified) autopsies of those troubled times, including Ruben Nyobé, Elizabeth Palmer and Annie Fayol.*'

'Oh my God,' she said, 'he faked Annie's autopsy.' The thought turned her stomach. This was the man who'd manhandled Annie's dead body. She shuddered and froze the image out of her mind to continue reading.

'*Dr Petridis was a lifelong non-believer but in the last weeks of his life he returned to the Orthodox faith of his birth to repent of what he had done (with the collusion of others) in his official position as senior pathologist. It will come as some compensation to those that cared for him to know that he was at least able to make a death bed confession and receive the last rites.*'

'So there was a cover-up,' she said.

'Yeah, that's the way I see it. Jules Raymond put it out in the open and Castile picked it up and now they're both dead, before I could get to them.' He leaned across the table to point at the obituary.

'This was stapled to the obituary.'

There were only a few lines, typed and with no address or date.

Dear Victor,

It's a very interesting proposition but I'll need time to make the big-shot contacts you suggest to see if it'll fly. We've all been through a lot of changes (not just the Greek) since the "good old days" and it's a lot to digest without any warning.

Yours, G.

'It's blackmail,' he said, 'Messmer wanting to keep a lid on the past.'

She read it again. Of course: 'proposition' smacked of blackmail, almost a cliché; the Greek was obviously Petridis; and the 'good old days' were back when he was covering up with false autopsies. Smoke and mirrors. She sighed and looked up at Harry.

'But who the hell is G?' she asked.

'Right, whoever he is.' Harry was massaging his temple, his eyes closed. 'Messmer's trusted intermediary. Somebody from the old days on first-name terms, probably from the same operation.'

'OK, Harry, fair enough,' said Candace getting up, 'maybe Messmer is at the bottom of it all, but let's find out what the mission has to say about Didier Nkumbé first.'

They drove to the mission in thoughtful silence and he glanced at Candace as they arrived. She was pale but holding up. The beach had been bad enough but now she had to bear the load of knowing for sure that her sister had been murdered. He wondered what that felt like. It was bad enough for him knowing what had happened to Judit, a raw place that hurt every time he went near it.

As soon as they got inside the mission building he could tell that they'd been waiting for their visit, the kind of event that only came round once in a blue moon.

'Dr Fayol – welcome.' A tall, thin, white woman with steel-rimmed eyeglasses and a coil of grey hair stepped forward with an outstretched hand. 'I'm Alison Fleming, the mission archivist. I'm sorry your visit is laden with such sadness.'

Candace shook hands. 'This is Mr Kaplan,' she said, half-turning. 'You may have seen him badly misrepresented in the papers.'

'Please come through to my office,' Miss Fleming said with a quick birdlike nod in his direction. 'It's more suitable.'

The office was small and boxed in with books and files as high as the ceiling. Facing into the room was a wooden table with a chair and a small set of steps leaning against the open window. The archivist indicated the single chair in front of them.

'Please, Dr Fayol,' she said, 'take a seat. Mr Kaplan, excuse me—' She steered past him and took a folding chair from the corner. 'We were only expecting one of you.'

'Thank you.'

The old missionary sat down and put a hand on her chest as if to calm a beating heart.

'The Good Lord moves in mysterious ways,' she said and tapped a box file in front of her. 'I've been praying for guidance for months but for the first time in my life He's left me on my own. Are you familiar with the bible story of Jacob and the fleece?'

Candace glanced at her and shook her head.

'Oh well, it's just a question of faith, but you haven't come all this way for a divinity class. I gather you're trying to trace one of our students from Ebolowa.'

'Yes,' Candace said, 'a good friend of my sister's.'

Miss Fleming took a thick ledger off the shelf. 'She was here in '56, if I remember right.'

'Did you know her?' Candace asked, leaning forwards.

'I met her once. A chance encounter in Ebolowa, just to shake hands. Now,' she said and opened the ledger, 'what was his name?'

'Didier Nkumbé,' Candace said, passing the studio portrait across the table.

Miss Fleming flinched. She straightened her spectacles in a move born of habit and wrapped her hands together in a white-knuckle grip.

'Dear God,' she muttered, 'I wasn't ready for this.'

'For what?' Harry asked.

'I'm very sorry, Dr Fayol,' she said turning to Candace, 'but Didier was never a friend of your sister's.'

'But they climbed Mount Cameroon together,' said Candace, cutting in.

'They couldn't have done,' the old missionary said. 'Didier died the year before she got here, in 1954.'

Candace recoiled, lost for words, but Harry filled the space. 'How did he die?' he asked.

The old missionary took a moment to reply. 'He hanged himself,' she said, 'out of shame. He'd been charged with the rape and murder of a young colleague of mine called Beth Palmer—'

'You mean Elizabeth Palmer?' he asked.

'Yes.' She nodded. 'We called her Beth. Everybody did. It was the most difficult test of my life and at the time the circumstances seemed cut and dried. Didier was a bit of a tearaway and his sister Esther—'

'Esther?' Candace took a battered bible out and flipped open the cover. 'Annie had her bible.'

Miss Fleming nodded and sighed, 'I should've known better.'

'About what?' he asked.

'About the world, Mr Kaplan, about the earthly powers that drive us—'

'You mean sex?'

'Lust for carnal pleasure and power.' Her voice was so husky she was barely audible. 'I'm sorry, but this is the cause of great anguish for me. Esther persuaded me to include Didier on an outing to Mount Cameroon that Beth had organised for her bible-reading group. He was mixing with the wrong crowd and she thought he'd benefit from it.'

She hung her head before looking up.

'But it just gave him the wrong idea about Beth and the night she was killed he'd been bragging about what they'd got up to on the mountain. The case against him was very convincing: he had no alibi for the time of the assault and he had scratches on his neck and face and Beth had black skin under her fingernails. He was charged with her murder and held in jail, but tragically took his own life for what he'd done. His sister Esther always protested his innocence and now I wonder if she was right.'

'What changed your mind?' he asked.

'Bizarrely, something that came to light a couple of years ago in the US.' She took a sheaf of press cuttings out of the file. 'You'll probably remember it. The so-called French Connection case, when a shipment of heroin was found in an imported VW camper. The owner, a man called Delouette, turned out to be an agent in the French secret service and under oath he spilled the beans.'

'I remember,' said Candace, 'it was all over the news. They tried to extradite a couple of big wheels from France.'

'That's right, but I didn't pay much attention until a friend told me Delouette had worked in Cameroon for an organisation I knew well, the BDPA: Bureau for the Development of Agricultural Production.' She took an old black-and-white photograph out of the box. 'They helped us on this project in Ebolowa. A cocoa cooperative.'

Harry took the photo from her: a young white man was shaking hands with a large African in full traditional robes next to a freshly planted shrub and a spade stuck in the ground. A crowd of gleeful children were gathered round with a few men in suits, a couple of black women in long skirts and turbans, and a pretty young white woman with a blonde ponytail. She was wearing an open-neck blouse and a full skirt. One leg was bent slightly at the knee in a pose that was somehow coquettish.

'BDPA was named in the trial as a cover for the French secret service,' said Miss Fleming. 'It turned out that all their people had been agents, including this man here, Guy Martin.'

She pointed at the handsome white man.

'Gee—' Candace murmured and nudged Harry under the table. He nodded and nudged her back.

'They closed the organisation down and called everyone back to Paris. There's no doubt that Guy Martin was, as they say, working undercover.'

'What was he doing undercover?' Harry asked sharply.

The old missionary shrugged. 'I haven't wanted to think, but it's made me wonder whether Didier was actually responsible for murdering Beth.'

'Do you think he was?' asked Candace, brandishing the studio portrait.

'Originally, yes I did, like everyone else except Esther.' The old missionary looked away. 'The gendarmes said there was no forced entry and that Beth let Didier in. They said it made sense because they'd just been up the mountain together, and then there was compelling forensic evidence. It's only since the French Connection trial that I've started to have doubts.' She gestured at the photo. 'Beth had fallen for M. Martin's Gallic charms and I blame myself because I chose to close my ears to the gossip.'

'What gossip?' Harry asked.

'Guy Martin's reputation as a ladies' man. I cautioned her about him, but she was headstrong and a rift had already developed between us. It's the cross I have to bear.'

He looked at the photo. It was obvious who Beth's pose was aimed at. 'What sort of rift?'

The old missionary waved his question away. 'Oh, just the way she chose to bear witness, that's all.'

'How exactly? It's important.'

'I don't see why. It was a private matter.'

'Maybe it was, but Beth Palmer was raped and murdered and the gendarmes framed an innocent man with a suicide-in-cell trick, and now you tell us she'd been associating with an agent in the French secret service. It stinks to high heaven, and the situation between you and Beth is relevant.'

Miss Fleming pursed her lips in displeasure. 'I don't see why,' she said, 'but if you must know, Beth had insisted in the teeth of my advice to make her own idiosyncratic interpretation of Jesus' fourth beatitude.'

'What? I don't even know the first.'

'Blessed are they who hunger and thirst after righteousness—'

'How did that cause a rift?'

She swallowed.

'She used it to justify the UPC's actions against the government. She said they had natural right on their side.'

'You mean she was treading on their toes?'

'Look, Mr Kaplan,' she said with a sniff, 'you have to understand that the French weren't used to having us in their colonies. This was a UN mandate and they couldn't pick and choose who they let in.'

'Somewhere else you'd have been kicked out for misbehaving like Beth?'

'Yes.' She sighed. 'I didn't want Beth to get too far out of line and antagonise them.'

'But she didn't listen to you?'

She shook her head. 'Unfortunately not.'

'What was she doing with the UPC?' asked Candace.

Miss Fleming grimaced. 'You've got to remember it was the fifties,' she said, 'the height of the Cold War – and, well, paranoia I suppose you'd call it – anyhow, it doesn't sound like much now but Beth was working with the UPC translating the Bible into tribal languages—'

'My God,' Candace started forwards in disbelief. 'Is that all?'

'I know how it looks now, but then it didn't seem so innocent. The UPC was supported, and subsequently armed by the Soviet Union, a Trojan horse for atheist communism. I'm not condoning them but I knew what the government was doing and I tried to counsel Beth but as I said, she was stubborn and headstrong—'

Harry bust in: 'I get what you're saying,' he said. 'Beth Palmer was an enemy of the state, enough to get her killed by them, as you say. But who were they? Who gave the order to rape and strangle her and then pin it on Didier Nkumbé?' He leaned across the table and said accusingly, 'Where I grew up it was always the anonymous "they"; but that's not how things actually work, is it, Miss Fleming? There has to be a somebody to decide and act – in this case, to rape and strangle Beth and to string Nkumbé up so it looked like suicide and whoever they were sat around planning it like a day at the office.'

He stared at her and she flinched.

'Didn't it ever cross your mind to try to find out who they were?'

She blinked at him behind her steel-rim glasses and coloured slightly.

'I'm not on trial here, Mr Kaplan—'

'We all are. We all collude.'

'Harsh,' she said, looking at him closely, 'but I suppose you're right. I trusted the word of the government; *their* word, if you must. It was easier, I grant you that. You should talk to Esther. She stood out against them on her own when everything was stacked against her.'

'Must be a brave woman,' Harry said, pushing back his chair. 'Where can we find her?'

'She's got a stall in the market. She'll be there now.' The old lady looked forlorn. 'She won't welcome my best wishes, and I understand why not, but please pass them on.' She passed him the box file. 'Take this. It might help.'

He nodded his thanks and turned back at the door. 'By the way did you know a Greek medic called Petridis?'

'Not personally,' she said. 'The mission has its own medical staff.'

'Did you know he just died?'

She frowned, her forehead creased with deep lines. 'Vaguely. As I said, I didn't know him personally.'

'But you knew of him?'

'I knew he used to work for the colonial government.'

'Did you know he did the autopsies on Beth and Didier?'

She shook her head and avoided his eye. 'As I said, at the time—'

'Yes, you said. You thought the case against Nkumbé was cut and dried. A young tearaway: guilty as charged.'

25

Friday, 12 April 1974

Douala, Cameroon

Harry came out of the mission in front of her with the box file under his arm and dumped it on the back seat. He slammed the door.

Candace got in alongside him. 'You were a bit hard on her,' she said.

He snorted. 'I could've been a lot harder. You don't have to be too smart to know that people need a lot of help to hang themselves in jail. I had too many friends who jumped out of windows in police custody in Budapest with the same sort of help. It's always easier to accept the official verdict – you don't have to do anything.'

'Like us you mean, me and Dad?'

'No, I'm talking about bystanders like Miss Fleming. She could've asked the gendarmes a few tough questions with her status. So could O'Connell.'

He turned onto the main drag. She leaned over the seat for the box file and took out the photo of Guy Martin. She stared at it in silence, one hand balled tight into a fist, the knuckles white.

'So G stands for Guy Martin,' she said. 'Messmer's trusted intermediary.'

'And longstanding fixer.' Harry grunted. 'They must've known one another here years ago.'

Candace studied Martin's handsome face. Fine-boned, thick black hair swept off his high forehead, nearly six foot and comfortable with himself – arrogant.

'He looks so convincing,' she said. 'The cool guy next door.'

'Selection and training,' Harry said.

She looked harder into Guy Martin's face and realised shamefully that she'd got used to reading character and capacity from the mug shots of condemned criminals. Annie's voice came back to her berating her: 'Remember, Candy,' she'd say, 'it's not a person you're look-ing at, it's a position.' Annie's line was always that she took sides, not pictures.

'I know all about the hidden power of photography,' Candace said, 'and how it's nonsense to say the camera never lies, but it's still real hard to be on your guard the whole time. This SOB just doesn't look as if he could murder in cold blood.'

'Right,' said Harry. 'Appearances deceive, but in any case he may not have.'

'But Beth let him in—'

'She certainly let someone in,' he said.

Someone... Candace flinched: that word again. She looked at the photo again and said, 'Beth was in love with him – or had fallen for his Gallic charm or whatever Miss Fleming said; it must've been him. Who else, for God's sake?'

Harry nodded as if he agreed with her.

'It's terrible.' She shuddered. 'How old do you think he is here?'

'Mid-thirties probably, but he's got that kind of face—' He broke off and shrugged.

'With sex appeal? Is that what you were going to say?'

'That's for you to say.'

She put the photo away and shut the box. 'Quite enough for an innocent like Beth, that's for sure,' she said. A bad feeling crept over her: maybe the Frenchman had enough for a smart woman like Annie as well. She was still thinking about it when Harry suddenly pulled off the road in front of a bar with a telephone sign painted on the win-dow.

'What's up?' she asked.

He cut the engine and put a hand on her arm. He had that soft look in his eye that turned her stomach over, like at O'Hare when she couldn't tell if it was just him or what he was going to tell her. Her mouth was suddenly dry.

'What?' she asked again, a tiny tremor in her throat.

'Er—' He glanced out of the window. 'I need to use that phone to call Hans.'

He was holding something back. The tremble got worse and she swallowed hard. 'Come on, Harry,' she said, 'you're freaking me out. What, for God's sake?'

'Could be nothing,' he said. 'I can't remember exactly, but you know I checked the hotel register?' He broke off and waited for her to nod. 'Well, I found Annie's name but not Nkumbé's—'

He shook his head and she started to feel a rising panic.

'No,' she said, a hoarse husky voice. 'No.' But the surge of certainty was too strong. 'You think Martin was there, don't you? Oh God.' She felt sick. 'No.'

'We have to check, that's all,' he was saying gently. 'There were a lot of names.'

'Damn him.' She wrenched open the door and stamped out. 'I'll do it.' She couldn't bear any more waiting.

'Let me—' Harry said, getting out. They stood for a second on the muddy sidewalk.

'I need to,' she murmured. 'In case it was him.'

Harry nodded. 'Let's do it together.'

She went into the bar and looked around. It was all guys; all suddenly silent, watching her. She bit her lip and felt Harry's hand in the small of her back. A couple of the guys were gaping at him and the words Chicago Man rolled across the room like thunder. She pitched forwards and fumbled for her purse. The barman was lost for words. 'I need to use the phone,' she said and gestured at the booth. 'Local call. Buea.'

'Sure, *madame*.' The barman wiped his hands and ducked under the counter to unlock the booth. It was small inside, hardly enough space for them both.

'I'll wait here,' said Harry, giving her his notebook open on the right page. 'Hans' number is right there.' He shut her in, a sudden capsule of silence, and all she could hear was her beating heart above the metallic dialling and the long tones ringing out the other end. The old Bakelite instrument trembled in her hand and she turned to look at Harry through the window. She mouthed the words 'It's ringing' and he put his thumb up.

Suddenly Hans was on the line and she jumped.

'Hans, it's Candace,' she said, praying for him not to be his normal jaunty self.

'Candace, hello.' He stopped, sensing her tension. 'What is it?'

'Your register for '56,' she said, trying for a calm, even voice and gripping the flesh of her stomach wall until it hurt. 'I need to know who was staying at the hotel the same time as Annie.'

'I've got the register right here.' He sounded breathless. 'We never put it away.' She could hear it being moved and paper rustling and she squeezed harder, digging in her nails.

'Got them.' Hans sounded like a surgeon ready to make an incision. 'How – I mean, d'you want me to just read out the names?'

'No. Not all of them,' she said, gathering her strength to get the name Guy Martin out – just three easy syllables, that's all. She glanced through the window: Harry was leaning against it, close by, waiting too. Somewhere in the bar the jukebox was playing and the men were talking again. The world was abuzz, but she was floating away, far away, gripped by fear.

'Thanks, Hans,' she said, forcing herself. 'Just checking for somebody called Guy Martin.' There, all done. She breathed out. It wasn't so difficult, but her stomach was still clenched tight and her mouth bone-dry.

'OK, Guy Martin,' Hans repeated and the name echoed back to her. 'Let me see.'

And then nothing more; close to total silence except for the sound of her beating heart and Hans muttering as he went down the page. Nothing, glorious wonderful nothing, she said to herself and was on the point of shrieking with relief when Hans' voice exploded in her ear. 'Yeah, Candace, here he is: M. Guy Martin. Address in Douala. In room number 8, next but one to Annie's.'

Candace stifled a howl. There was a feral beast trying to escape. She just stopped herself from banging her forehead on the window. Harry was looking at her, soft eyes questioning. Hans was talking again, checking that she'd heard.

'Thank you, Hans,' she heard herself saying, crisp and in control. 'That's all we needed to know.'

She put the phone on the cradle and cut the line. It wasn't an illusion. Time had stopped. She'd been finally skewered by the Truth: Annie's *someone* was a Frenchman called Guy Martin – rural-development worker, Gallic charmer, secret agent and murderer. The mystery of who Annie had fallen for, 'sky high', had been solved in one cruel moment and the words kept on coming at her like when the needle got stuck on a record.

Outside Candace couldn't find anything to say. She stayed quiet and balled up her fists again. The bastard Martin had enjoyed 18 more years on this planet than Annie, 20 more than Beth Palmer – but for him, she thought, they'd both be alive and thriving, women in their prime leaving their mark on the world. It sickened her. Two whole decades and their stories had never been told.

Her head swam and she looked around: she was outside on the sidewalk with Harry holding her arm and saying he was very sorry. She was still reeling. That bastard. She folded her arms and gripped tight but the pain was deep down inside and out of reach. She couldn't believe it, but her big sister Annie had fallen for a two-faced murderer. A lady-killer.

'How?' She looked at Harry. 'Why?' she demanded of him. 'For God's sake, why?'

'I don't know yet,' he said, 'but Annie said she was up against some big hitters and Guy Martin was one of them.'

She ran her hands through her hair and wanted to scream. 'On top of Castile,' she said, 'and the prime minister of France! They don't really come much bigger, do they?'

'No, they don't.'

Her head felt ready to explode.

'What I don't get is why she went to the beach with Castile,' she said. The Frenchman Martin, with all that Gallic charm, shit, well, she could understand the appeal no problem, but the Charles Atlas type – it didn't make sense.

'Maybe she didn't go with him,' Harry said. 'He was only seen in her car; and now we know Petridis faked the autopsy it's quite possible drowning wasn't the cause of death at all.'

Candace went quiet, taking it in. Over the years she'd got used to the idea of Annie drowning. That image was bad enough but at least it was fixed.

'OK, Harry, that's it for now,' she murmured. 'I've got to put my imagination on hold.'

They got into the car and she took a deep breath.

'Where to now?' she asked, very quiet.

'Airport,' said Harry. 'Hertz – to see if they can tell us who hired the car.'

He turned onto the freeway for the airport. Heading towards them were three military trucks full of soldiers, mostly white.

'Jeez,' she said as they swept past, 'no wonder Logan says Cameroon is in Paris' pocket.'

Another truck bore down on them and a couple of the men waved. They drove the rest of the journey in silence. Harry pulled into the parking lot and Candace got out and looked around. It was almost deserted. Incredible: there was a strike at Orly in Paris and everything in Douala had closed down except the neat rows of French MiG fighters parked on the apron as if it was a military airfield. Paris was still calling the shots. Candace walked towards Arrivals. The asphalt was fresh and tacky under her feet. Harry bought a paper from the kid on the steps and folded it into four and stuck it into his inside pocket and patted the bulge.

'Do I look like I'm carrying a gun?' he asked.

She smiled bleakly. 'You playing to your fans in the gallery? There was an awed hush when we walked into that bar.'

'That was for you.'

'Ha ha,' she said, and put a hand on his arm. 'Nice try. I appreciate it after the day I've had.' She looked him over. 'Yeah, you could just about be from Chicago.'

In the Arrivals hall some kiosks were doing business and a few passengers were standing in line. The Hertz unit was open but unattended.

'I'll do this,' she said, as if she needed something to keep occupied.

'Sure.'

She walked over to Hertz and leaned on the counter. 'Any chance of someone serving here?' she asked the women in Avis next door.

'Avis have cars, *madame*, and the best deals. Better than Hertz.'

'Thank you but I'm not looking for a car. I've just got a query for Hertz.' She glanced back at Harry.

'There's Antoine.' The Avis woman was pointing down the line of locked kiosks. 'He's coming.'

'Thank you.'

A short man was hurrying towards her in a smart Hertz shirt. He slipped under the counter and popped up on the other side.

'We're looking for a friend,' she said, smiling at him like an airhead, 'but I've lost my purse—'

'Stolen more like,' said Harry, picking up the ploy.

'That's not right, darling,' she said with an irritated look over her shoulder. 'You know we're guests here. It's not polite.' And then she put the smile back on for the Hertz man.

'I'm sorry to hear that, *madame*,' said the Hertz man, but his smile had faded and he was staring at the infamous Chicago Man. 'I can't really help.'

'You underestimate yourself,' Candace said, with the kind of simpering smile she'd learned in high-school drama classes and had hardly ever used since. 'Hertz is an international company and we use them all time – Paris, Hollywood, New York, New Orleans, Chicago—' She leaned closer to the man with every new city. 'We're always so impressed by your efficiency. Aren't we, honey?' She half-turned away from the counter and winked at Harry.

'Wouldn't use anyone else,' Harry said.

'Thank you,' said the man, his attention caught between this attractive woman and the dramatic celebrity from Chicago. 'But I don't see how I can help.'

'Your records,' she said, leaning over to put her hand on the stack of counterfoils. She almost stroked them. 'I know you need a local address as well as a passport ID and that's what's gone missing in my purse.'

The Hertz man now focused his admiration on her and she narrowed her eyes jokingly and said, 'And you know what Chicago is famous for, don't you?'

The man gawped.

'The Blues,' she said. 'And that's how we'll feel if we can't track our friend down, won't we, honey.' She didn't wait for a response before adding, 'He told us he was going to hire your best car, a white Renault 12 so we just couldn't miss it.'

The man said, 'Ooh, well, *madame*, that's all we have – white Renault 12s – at least in cars. Hertz stocks only the best.'

Candace cursed silently. 'I bet,' she said and made to reach for the stack of counterfoils. 'Our friend is French. That should narrow the field.'

'That information is strictly confidential,' the man muttered, fidgeting with a company ballpoint just as Harry materialised at Candace's elbow with a five-franc bill. With the other hand he conspicuously nudged the ominous weight in his armpit.

'The Hertz new-style management system is all about rewards and penalties, isn't it?' asked Harry, pushing the bill nearer to the edge of the counter and hunching his shoulder. 'Just like it is in Chicago.'

The bill tipped off the edge and fluttered down onto the counterfoils. The man rescued it and swallowed hard.

'French, you said?' His eyes were jittering from one side to the other.

'How many white Renaults does Hertz run out here?' Candace asked, as if it was the most fascinating question.

'Seven,' the man said.

'A very small fleet then,' she said in a withering tone with a glance at her expensive watch. 'We should be out of here in no time.'

'We're building it up,' said the man defensively. 'Next year we will have twenty.'

'Next year,' she said brightly, 'we might all be dead.'

The man didn't like the sound of her prediction and leafed through the counterfoils with practised speed.

'You could count money with that skill,' she said, 'couldn't he, honey? A bank or a casino.'

Harry grunted. 'Can't be too many Frenchmen,' he said.

'France has a big military presence in Cameroon,' the man said, 'and a lot of technical-aid workers. Most of our renters are French.'

He had separated three counterfoils from the stack. 'Only three French today,' he said peevishly. 'Normally we'd have more. Some Americans occasionally.'

'Sure, sure, I bet you do,' said Candace, relieved that they wouldn't have too many addresses to follow up. 'But we're only interested in our friend.' She reached for them but the man pulled them back.

He raised himself to his full height and listed the names. Candace held her breath.

'Two men and a woman,' he said, raising an eyebrow. 'We don't have so many women clients. Mme Jocelyn Boulstein, and Marcel Blanc and Guy Martin.'

Martin's name rang out and took Candace's breath away. She gripped the counter. Harry leaned forward, brushing her arm. 'That's who we're looking for,' he said, folding another bill in front of the Hertz man. 'Our good friend Guy – where's he staying?'

'La Pleine Lune in the docks.' The man wrinkled his nose. 'I'd have recommended somewhere else. He's returning the car on Saturday.'

Harry put the photo of the Ebolowa cooperative on the counter and pointed. 'That's him, right?'

The man looked surprised and then peered closely at the photo as if he was short-sighted. 'It's quite an old picture,' he said, looking up, 'and now he has a beard and was wearing dark glasses—' He peered again and shrugged. 'I'd make a bad witness.'

'Not so bad,' Harry said and drew Candace back into the main concourse.

'Jesus—' she said. Her heart was jumping and she scanned the white men in the lounge. Most of them were in French military uniform. 'I can't believe it.' She was seething. 'He's here and isn't even using an alias. The nerve of it.'

'Maybe he doesn't have to,' said Harry. 'He's been calling the shots for so long. But still—' He broke off. 'I wonder if the beard is just a style thing or if he's trying for a disguise. Whichever, it's just as well we know.'

26

Douala, Cameroon

They went through the exit doors and the newspaper boy waved as if something had jerked his arm out of the socket and his face broke open into a wild grin.

'At least somebody's happy to see us,' Candace said.

'Right, but now you can see why it's not safe to stay on – because you stand out like a sore thumb,' he said as they got into the car. 'We both do.'

The truth ebbed up and caught her unawares. She had got what she came for and he was right here. They were breathing the same air and walking the same streets.

'What's the place he's staying at called again?'

'La Pleine Lune,' said Harry. 'In the docks. One of the places O'Connell calls rough.'

She put her head in her hands. It was crazy – how could it matter? – but she wanted to know how long.

'Does it take one or two nights?' she asked. 'I mean, to climb the mountain?'

'One in the hotel, according to Hans,' Harry said, 'and one on the mountain. There's a hut at ten thousand feet.'

Tears stung her eyes. 'She said she was "sky high".'

He just nodded.

'Jesus.' Bile rose up inside her and she fought it back. 'And to think he's still—'

The word stuck in her throat: here.

'That's why I'm not leaving without you,' he said.

She ran her hands through her hair. Pictures jerked through her mind like frames of a film that had got stuck. The way old projectors used to.

'You OK?' he asked.

'Just about.' She jutted her chin out. 'It's going to take more than Guy Martin to chase me out of here before I'm ready.' But the words were full of bravado and she knew she couldn't stay on without him. It was insane, unbelievable, but Harry was right – it was dangerous. 'OK, Harry,' she said, 'I'll go with you tomorrow; but only as long as you help me bring him to justice, even if that wasn't in the contract.'

'No problem,' he said. 'We know he's here and what he looks like – and why he came back.' He pulled the door shut and adjusted the mirror. 'And we know who he's working for.'

He drove with Candace deep in thought. She had a lot to take in. The road got rougher as they got closer to the market and finally turned into a pitted lane. Straight-backed women walked by with huge baskets on their heads crammed with shopping. A couple of crowded buses were parked on the sidewalk with guys unloading live chickens and bags of potatoes from the roof rack. The air was hot and dusty.

As soon as they got out people stared. There was a lot to stare at: Europeans shopping in the African market were about as common as white guys in Douala jail – and in this case the spectacle comprised a beautiful woman and a famous mafia hood from the front page.

The market was made up of rows of stalls. A few had corrugated-iron roofs but most were open or covered with canvas canopies. The first they came to were butchers. Slabs of meat were sitting in the sun and entrails hung from hooks. An entire liver, glistening bright purple, was laid out and a flank of pig fat was cooking in a cauldron of oil. A kid with a fly-whisk was fighting a losing battle with the flies and he turned his attention to a couple of ragged dogs scrapping over a bone.

They turned up the next alley past a fish stall and a run of vegetables and fruit. Mangoes were piled high and whole branches of green bananas were leaning against the front of a stall. At another there were small boxes of herbs and roots with the promise of good health and infinite virility. A tailor was working feverishly on a shirt at a treadle sewing machine and beyond him a man was cutting leather for a pair of shoes. Everywhere they looked there were things for sale and jostling shoppers, a few of them fighting off the mid-morning sun with umbrellas.

'You OK?' Harry asked her, breaking the silence.

'Just about but that's what we need, an umbrella,' she said. 'This heat is unbearable—'

The sun beat down on them, a palpable weight. He took her arm for a second. 'You sure you're alright?'

'Yeah,' she said and puffed out her cheeks. 'It's just the sun. Remember the Chicago cold I just left behind.'

'Try this,' he said, picking up a raffia sunhat from the clothing stall opposite.

She tried it on. 'Yes, *madame*, very beautiful,' said the woman trader, holding up a pink plastic mirror.

'How much?' she asked.

'To you, *madame*, twenty francs.'

It was far too much but it promised blissful relief and she bought it. Harry was just about to suggest a cool drink in the shade when she pointed at a sign: 'Esther Nkumbé BA: School Books and Stationery'. The front of the stall was piled with textbooks and behind it was a woman with glasses and hair plaited in criss-cross patterns serving a mob of school children all reaching forwards and shouting at once.

He waited until the children had dwindled to a handful before introducing himself. He judged her to be about fifty and in full possession of a shrewd mind behind her horn-rimmed glasses.

'I've seen you in the papers, M. Kaplan,' she said.

'Somebody else falsely accused by the Douala gendarme,' he said, 'like your brother. This is Dr Candace Fayol, Annie's sister.'

But Esther Nkumbé had already noticed: she was shaking her head from side to side and laughing.

'I'm sorry, Dr Fayol,' she said, finally holding out her hand, 'but I thought I'd seen a ghost. You're the spitting image of Annie and she had a hat just like that.'

The two women shook hands and Esther took both of Candace's

in hers and smiled into her face. To all the world it looked like the happy reunion of long-lost friends.

'I'm so pleased to meet you,' said Candace. 'You're the first person I've met who actually knew Annie.'

'She was a wonderful person,' said Esther, letting go of one of Candace's hands. 'Come—'

She drew Candace down the aisle to a small café shaded by striped awning and furnished with a few tables and rough wooden chairs.

'Sit down. We must have a tea or Fanta.'

Candace nodded. 'Tea will be just fine.'

'Mr Kaplan?'

'The same thank you.'

They sat round a table and Esther beamed again. 'You even sound like Annie!'

A young man brought them a tray with three glasses of tea, a jug of milk and a bowl of sugar cubes. Esther passed them round.

'I keep having to pinch myself,' she said and her smile faded, 'because this is exactly where I saw Annie for the last time. We were talking about poor Didier and how she was going to clear his name in *Life* magazine. She called it an outrageous conspiracy and had taken lots of photos.'

'What of?' Harry asked.

'Me and the family.' Esther smiled bashfully. 'Our house, Beth's quarters at the mission in Ebolowa, even her old bedroom—' She broke off and gesticulated. 'She was amazing and told the gendarmes she was doing a story on everyday life in the police. She certainly knew how to be persuasive! She had them round her little finger and even got them to let her take photos of the cell Didier had been in. She said it proved he couldn't have hanged himself, which is what I always said.'

Harry shot an urgent look at Candace with the message that a bunch of Annie's photos had gone missing. The question was where from.

'So you thought it was a conspiracy from the beginning?' Harry asked.

Esther polished her spectacles and nodded vigorously. 'Maybe my brother was guilty of having a big mouth but he would never have hurt Beth and he most certainly wouldn't have committed suicide.' She let out a heavy sigh and spread her hands out wide. 'But who was going to listen to me? Anybody who raised their voice got crushed.'

Candace showed her the old cutting of BDPA and the cocoa cooperative.

'You knew that Guy Martin had been working undercover, didn't you?' she asked.

'It was all over the news. Everyone in BDPA had been undercover. They closed it down.' She shivered. 'I can't believe it now, but I used to enjoy Martin's company. He was so clever at playing the charming rural-development officer, so civilised.'

'Have you seen him since?' Harry asked, catching Candace's eye.

Esther shook her head and toyed with her glass of tea. 'No, thank God.' A big woman passed by and called out a greeting and she waved back. It occurred to Harry that without justice for her brother Esther Nkumbé was caught up between the past and the present.

'What about Victor Castile?' he asked.

She made a face of disgust. 'Pig,' she muttered. 'He was a racist, as bad as your Ku Klux Klan. A lot of people are very grateful—' She smiled at Harry and added, 'Even if you didn't do it.'

'He didn't,' said Candace.

'I know,' she said, 'but people like the idea of Castile being eliminated by an avenging angel from Chicago.'

'Ha, ha,' he said. 'That's the first time I've been called an angel.'

'But maybe not the last,' said Esther with a twinkle. She got up with a glance at her watch. 'I'm sorry but I have to go. I'm already late.'

'Can we give you a ride?' asked Harry.

'No, no, thank you.' She waved her arm down the line of market stalls. 'I'm only going down there.'

They all shook hands and said goodbye but just as she was turning away Harry stopped her. 'Did you know Dr Petridis?'

'I knew who he was.' Esther's lip curled. 'And I hope he fries in hell. Annie had arranged to get him on film as well but they got to her first. Maybe he was the one to smell a rat.' She turned to Candace and said, 'I'm sure you know already but Annie never went skinny-dipping at Mile 12. I don't know how she died, but I'm sure she didn't drown in the riptide and Petridis faked the autopsy.'

And with that Esther Nkumbé enveloped Candace in a hug before pulling away with a sob. Harry and Candace watched the figure disappear into the melee of people and without a word walked back to the car.

Vernon, near Paris

Marc watched the Normandy countryside flash past. The rhythm of the train lulled his mind and he half-dozed. Two items had been waiting for him in Poste restante at Saint-Lazare. A telegram from Marcel saying 'No Greeks in the suburbs either; maybe Chicago has it? M', and a postcard from Madeleine that brought tears to his eyes. 'Papa I am writing this because I miss you so much. XXXX'. His co-conspirator Marie Therese had added, 'I'll mail this in town.'

He nodded grimly: the village postmistress was intercepting his mail, as Foccart had taken pleasure in informing him. It occurred to Marc that Foccart might be losing his grip – maybe the effect of the oil crisis at home coinciding with the ominous situation in Niger – but Marc wasn't counting on it.

He looked again at Madeleine's postcard, pushing thoughts of his father-in-law out of his mind, and filled up with pride – only five and her writing was as good as his! Better! School had been a hell of persecution for him and he'd truanted most of the time, but one lesson had stuck in his mind: the Good Samaritan, because everyone had passed by on the other side until the baron and Monique. He put the card in his pocket and made sure his gun wasn't showing.

It was after two o'clock and drizzling when the train got in but the Café de la Gare was still doing desultory business. Marc glanced through the window – a short dark man with a thin moustache was drawing a beer: Pablo he guessed. His wife was nowhere to be seen. He pushed through the doors and loosened his coat. Pablo was wiping down the zinc counter. The air was fuggy with damp warmth and the fire was smoking as if the chimney needed cleaning. Three tables were occupied: a young couple looking at the clock as if they were already late, a single man reading the paper and a noisy trio playing dominoes. Marc took the table nearest the door and made a note of the open and closed sign. He pushed himself away from the table and crossed his legs to ease the pressure on his hip before catching Pablo's attention. '*Oui monsieur*,' Pablo said, tapping his pad with a chewed ballpoint.

'A bottle of water and a black coffee please—' Pablo nodded and moved away with another angry look at the door. The couple got up to leave and he watched Pablo make the coffee and take a bottle from the fridge while casting hostile glances at the clock in exaggerated impatience. Then the door opened and a young woman entered with an anxious look on her face. Isabella. She shook her wet umbrella and avoided her husband's eye.

'*Por fin – puta*,' he hissed at her.

She shrugged and hurried behind the bar to put an apron on. Pablo flipped the top of the bottle and poured it into the glass.

'Working overtime?' Marc asked him.

Pablo grunted: 'She's late—'

'Your day off?'

'Yes,' he said, and strode away, the tray swinging at his side.

Marc stirred sugar into his coffee and watched the fierce body language behind the bar. The trio of men rattled their dominoes and the single man stubbed his cigarette and slid a handful of coins onto the table. He put his coat on, picked up his bag and umbrella and gave the fire a disgruntled look as if it was time someone attended to it.

'*Bonjour*,' Marc said.

'*Bonjour*,' said Isabella.

Marc sipped his coffee and watched her come round the bar with a broom. She leaned it very deliberately against the wall and straightened up. Her buxom shape was accentuated by the way she had tied her apron strings. One of the domino trio waved at her.

'Alright, alright, Isa,' he called drunkenly. 'We're going! Then you'll be able to clear up, on your lonesome—'

'When the cat's away—' another said and blew her a kiss.

She blushed and swept furiously along the wall banging the skirting board. The men joked and laughed some more and finally piled the dominoes into a stack and pushed them into a box. They got up together and bowed drunkenly before jostling their way across the café with a chorus of hooting 'Isa-bella'. She followed with the brush like a peasant driving geese and as soon as they were outside slammed the door with a bang and a heave of her pretty bosom.

'Drunken idiots,' she muttered.

He grunted and watched her clear away the glasses and dominoes. Suddenly her husband emerged from the back, his hair parted and combed and wearing the eager look of a man about to go out on the town. He opened the till and it rung with an old-fashioned bell.

'Not all of it!' she said with a reproachful look, but he ignored her and left with a roll of bills in his hand. Marc heard a car start up and watched until she had cleared away the last of the glasses. He put his cup down with a deliberate clatter and caught her eye.

'*Combien?*'

She came over with a weary smile and he smiled back but as soon as she was within reach he leaned back in one lithe movement, took the gun from his pocket and lifted her skirt with the barrel.

'Get off,' she said with a casual slap. She hadn't seen his gun and it was as if customers were always trying it on, but then she gasped as the cold metal touched her thigh. She froze and dropped the broom.

'Do exactly what I say and you won't get hurt,' he said slowly letting her skirt fall back.

She stared at him, her big brown eyes wide with fear.

'Lock the door and turn the sign,' he said, 'same as usual.'

She swallowed, her hand grasping at her blouse.

'Right now,' he said sharply, getting up and pressing the gun into her side.

She did as he said and he came up beside her and walked her to the bar pressing the gun into her back. She was trembling with fear.

'Don't hurt me, *monsieur* – please—'

'I won't touch you,' he said. 'As long as you do as I say.'

'There's nothing in the till,' she cried, her voice breaking. 'Pablo took it all.'

'I don't want your money,' he said, easing her into the back room with a worn sofa along one side and a sideboard stacked with dirty glasses. He took hold of her waist and turned her round. Her cheeks glistened with tears.

'Please, *monsieur*,' she whispered, 'please—'

'All you have to do is tell me where Guillermo's bolthole is—'

'Gui—'

'Yes, Guy.'

He lifted her skirt again with his gun and her knees suddenly buckled and she crumpled and fell.

'*Merde.*' He hadn't meant to make her faint.

He rolled her over and put his hands under her arms and pulled her over to the sofa. Her head lolled to one side and he put a cushion under it and slapped her a few times. Her mouth hung open and her eyelids fluttered and then she opened her eyes, half-conscious – and then she saw him and her eyes popped and she drew a deep breath. He clamped his hand over her mouth.

'I told you,' he hissed in her ear, 'just do what I say.'

He eased the pressure on her mouth and let her breathe. She nodded and he helped her to her feet. She wobbled and he sat her down on the sofa.

'D'you want a glass of water?'

She nodded and he took a clean tumbler from the side.

'There's some Evian in the fridge,' she said weakly.

He poured some into the glass. She gulped at it and splashed a little on her blouse. She was still very pale.

'Something stronger?'

She made a face and shook her head.

'I told you, nothing will happen to you. Just answer my questions.'

She nodded and swallowed.

'Where's Pablo gone?'

'Playing cards with friends, he says—'

'You don't believe him?'

She shook her head angrily and bit her lip. 'I think he's with—' She broke off and spat out in Spanish, '*Su puta* in Paris, for the weekend.'

He crouched down, lifting her chin with his gun. 'Quite sure?' he asked, looking into her eyes and squeezing her thigh hard enough to hurt.

'Yes—'

'On your mother's life?'

'Yes,' she said, emphatically. 'Yes.'

'OK,' he said. 'I know Guy has a place here – his aunt told me – and you and Pablo look after things when he's away, don't you?'

'I do.'

'OK – so you're going to tell me where it is and then forget you ever saw me. You don't tell anybody, not Guy or Pablo or even the priest in confession. If you do, I will find out and come back and hurt you—' He looked deep into her eyes and touched her between her legs with his gun. 'So bad you'll never have a baby, *compris?*'

She flinched and nodded.

'OK. Show me on the map.'

She looked panic stricken. 'I can't – I'll have to show you. It's not far, but it's hard to explain, the back roads, tracks really, they're not on the map—'

He glanced at his watch.

'Is Guy out there now?'

'No – he's coming tomorrow from Spain. He's going back there with his aunt.'

He nodded and softened his voice. 'He told me. I'm a friend.'

He knew he wasn't acting like one and she looked at him, her eyes still wide with fear.

'But he's not on the phone out there?'

'Now he is. Before there wasn't even a toilet.' For a second she looked the way she should have, a young woman with everything ahead of her. 'I used to tease him about it.'

He stood up and picked up the phone.

'Call him, just in case.'

She dialled and he pulled her close to him, the muzzle of his gun against her throat. 'No tricks.' She turned away but he was close enough to see a bead of sweat glistening on her upper lip. He listened as the phone rang unanswered for a long time and she looked at him and shook her head.

'He's not there. I told you.'

He held her a second too long and felt the panic seize her. She trembled in his grip.

'It's going to be alright,' he said, as if he could be trusted. 'I gave you my word.'

She gave him a look that seemed to draw on generations of women's experience and he let her go.

27

Douala, Cameroon

There was a lot of traffic on the road back into town. Candace sat back in the seat and tried to keep her mind blank. It was sort of working when Harry touched her arm.

'Don't turn around,' he said, 'but we've picked up a tail. Grey saloon, tinted windshield.'

Her heart jumped and she had to make an effort not to look round. 'Is it him?'

'Yes. He's good. See that turning,' he said, nodding across the traffic.

There was a track about 100 yards away. 'Yes.'

'Hold on tight.'

No safety belt. Her heart was racing. The engine roared and they jolted forwards. She grabbed the seat with both hands as they pulled up close behind a bus before he whipped the wheel around, swinging the car across the traffic. A saloon flashed its lights and a big truck blared its horn but they got across and hit the sandy surface of the track. The car skidded and she braced herself. The bonnet leaped up as they vaulted a bank and she thought they were going to turn over but then the car crashed down and she lurched forwards and banged her head. She felt the wheels swivel and grip and come to rest next to a ditch.

'Jesus Christ,' she said, puffing out her cheeks, relieved and thrilled. 'Was that strictly necessary?'

'Sorry, but yes. Anyhow you look as if you enjoyed it!'

'It feels good getting one over on him, even if I have broken a nail.' She looked ruefully at her left hand.

'It could've been a lot worse.'

'I don't normally have nails like this.'

He laughed and made a three-point turn and headed back. She searched the traffic coming out of the city for the grey saloon.

'What happened to the white Hertz?'

He shrugged. 'Maybe it was a bit obvious; and I noticed a grey saloon when we were on the bridge.'

'I remember,' she said, fighting off paranoia. It came back to her: three men dragging a boat across the sand and a car lurking on the shore. 'Anyway,' she said, trying to lighten up, 'I thought you were just showing me you're worth the money?'

'Bit of both.'

'I don't need convincing,' she said. 'Seriously. Not after this morning.'

He just nodded.

'Do you think he'll double back?'

He shook his head.

'So we've shaken him off?' She felt like pumping the air with her fist.

'Only for now. He's a pro.'

She looked at him. 'What you said at the mission about it all being like a day at the office for guys like Martin – is that what you mean by a pro?'

'Yeah.' He glanced across and she caught his eye.

'A professional killer,' she said to herself, turning the words over in her mind and feeling the chill creep up her spine as she thought back to how Hans had gone down the list: Annie had signed in first and Martin afterwards and it occurred to her that all that 'sky high' business hadn't been a random thing at all – he'd tailed her there and turned on his famous Gallic charm!

It'd been a cold-blooded, clinical act. She remembered the one time she'd had to deal with violent death at the clinic, someone she'd treated: homicide in the heat of the moment and a kitchen knife to hand – it'd all been over in a trice and about as far from a regular day in the office as you could get.

'A regular day at the office,' she said out loud, as if it was the least-regular thing imaginable.

'Yep,' he said, 'that's how they do it. A careful calculation, pros and cons.'

She shuddered and forced herself. 'But how – in Annie's case, actually?'

'I don't know yet.' He paused at a red light and looked at her. 'You OK to get to Jules Raymond's house?'

'I found it in the dark.'

'Good.' He glanced across at her again, a meaningful look, as the light changed. 'If we're right about the Greek, and I think we are, there's a dossier out there that Messmer and Martin are desperate to get their hands on.'

She nodded: it did make sense – the stakes were that high. She directed him off the highway and up into the airy suburbs. A couple of times they nearly went wrong but pretty soon she was gesturing a final right.

'This is it – here – number twelve.'

The street was lined with trees and the houses were spread out, colonial residences for top officials with big porches and large gardens. Before he had even pulled up at the kerb the front door flew open and a young woman rushed out followed by an excited, small white dog.

'Thank God you've come, Dr Fayol!' she cried, 'I've been ringing you all morning. I'm sorry to drag you out here again but I didn't know who else to call.'

She was holding a hefty tumbler of what looked like strong gin and tonic with ice and lemon. With her nasal Liverpool accent Harry couldn't be certain, but it sounded to him as if it wasn't her first drink. Her make-up was smudged, her curly hair dishevelled and her freckled face streaked as if she'd been crying. Candace put a hand on her arm.

'It's OK, Fitz, we're here now. This is Harry Kaplan.'

'We talked on the phone,' he said and steered her back into the house and sat her down on the sofa. The dog jumped up beside her and she gathered it into her lap.

'Now, what's the problem?'

'We were burgled last night! As if things weren't bad enough already, and *madame* is coming later.' She gave the dog a loving squeeze and lowered her voice, saying, 'and we don't like *madame* do we?' She straightened up. 'Come on, I'll show you.'

She crossed the broad parquet floor to the open French windows with the dog leaping after her. Harry caught Candace's eye and she nodded as if she understood what he was thinking. Beyond the porch a neatly clipped lawn swept down to an outhouse and they followed the English nurse inside. The space was tight, poorly lit and reeked of cigar smoke. It had been ransacked. Papers were everywhere and a whole shelf of box files were strewn across the floor. In the middle of the desk there was an old Remington typewriter that took Harry back to his grandfather's study.

'He always smoked in here,' said Fitz, pushing open the window and gesturing at the splintered latch. The wood was dry and rotten, dusty with woodworm. 'This is where they broke in. Easy. Must've been the middle of the night.'

'Didn't you hear them?' Harry asked. 'Or the dog?'

'You've got to be kidding!' She sort of laughed. 'After everything that happened last night I went out like a light, and so did Ollie.'

Harry nodded: 'Any idea what they took?'

'That's just it,' she said and swigged at her drink. 'I haven't a clue. There was nothing valuable down here; it was just where he worked – and smoked, where I couldn't catch him! He wasn't very careful either. Lots of times I'd find it unlocked.'

'Really—' Harry said. 'I thought everyone worried about security nowadays. Crime stats are as high as inflation.'

'I know,' Fitz said. 'It's the same in Liverpool; and *monsieur* worried too, but only after his second heart attack. It made him very paranoid.'

'When was that exactly?' Harry asked.

'I'm not going to forget in a hurry,' she said. 'It was New Year's Eve.' She grimaced and finished her drink. 'I was all set to go out and instead I spent the first two weeks of nursing him back to health. We didn't think he was going to make it.'

'We?'

'Me and the rest of the unit.' She smiled. 'We actually had a good laugh together. We had to. The other bed was a terminal case, some Greek called Petridis. He died and there was quite a palaver over his last rites. He wanted some Orthodox priest to read them.'

Harry's mind sharpened. The case was breaking open.

'Did M. Raymond know Petridis?' he asked.

'Yes.' She nodded. 'From way back I think. They chatted when they were conscious. They were both smokers and went on about how wonderful Cuban cigars were.'

'Did Petridis get any visitors?'

'Nobody.' She shook her head. 'It was pretty sad. It was M. Jules who sat with him at the end. He was recuperating by then, but I was still surprised—'

'Why?'

She shrugged and looked sheepish. 'You're not supposed to speak ill of the dead but M. Jules wasn't a kind man. He wouldn't put himself out for anybody.'

'What happened to the priest?' Harry asked.

'They couldn't get one.'

'D'you remember the exact date he died?'

She frowned and cracked her knuckles. 'I could look it up in my records,' she said, 'but it must've been about the 20th of January. He died a couple of days before *monsieur* went home and I remember *madame* arrived a couple of days later, on the 25th. Her visits really stick in the mind I can tell you.'

'You don't get on?'

Fitz hooted. 'You could say so! Old biddy thought I was a gold-digger. Such a bloody insult, I could've socked her one. She actually warned him to keep me out of his bedroom! I heard her. My French isn't great but I understand a lot more than she thinks.'

Harry and Candace exchanged fleeting smiles: there was no stopping the young woman.

'Like when I picked them up from the airport before Christmas,' Fitz said, waving her arms around. 'She'd come over for a holiday and he was up in Niger doing a story about Gaddafi. I remember because I had to get the flights – one of the little errands that came with the job – anyway, he was in a real state when he arrived and I told him to calm down, professionally, because it was bad for his blood pressure; right, Dr Fayol—?' She glanced across at Candace before carrying on. 'But he wouldn't listen and all the way back the two of them were going hammer and tongs in the back of the car like I was a taxi driver or something about these two guys who used to own this night club in the docks called La Frégate—'

Harry interrupted. 'You mean the Romany with the famous limp?'

'Yes, yes, that's right, the gypsy,' she rushed on excitedly. 'But it was the other one who had an affair with his wife, or Olivia Godiva as we used to call her.' She looked at Harry sheepishly and added, 'I know I shouldn't call her that but everyone in Buea does.'

Inspector Takere's comment came back to Harry: Lady Godiva, the suicide who'd walked into the riptide at Mile 12. 'Why Godiva?' he asked.

'Oh right,' Fitz said, realising he didn't know the story. 'They were both naked. The original Lady Godiva rode a horse through town naked to win a bet and Olivia Godiva walked into the riptide at Mile 12. Anyway they were going on about the man she'd an affair with, calling him an effing *pied-noir*, which is some kind of racist insult—'

'No, it's not,' said Candace. 'It's what they call French Algerians.'

'Oh.' Fitz stopped mid-flow but not for long. 'I didn't know,' she said, 'but anyway it was him they were ranting on about for wrecking *monsieur*'s marriage.' She broke off abruptly and jumped up. 'Oh my God, look at the time. I've got to pack. She's arriving at six and I want to be ready to go.' She leaned over and rumpled the dog's ears and said in a quieter voice, 'She doesn't like you either, does she, Ollie?' She added, 'She's a cat person.'

Candace smiled wanly at Harry and they watched Fitz and her dog disappear up the lawn. 'Phew,' she said, blowing out her cheeks, 'that's some head of steam.'

He nodded and faltered for a second: it wasn't a good idea, her coming with him to the docks – for a kick-off they might find Guy Martin down there – but he didn't want to bug her by being patronising. 'Fancy a trip to La Pleine Lune and La Frégate? You remember those shots of the Scots in a bar—'

'Yeah,' she said, 'O'Connell's favourite dive.' She grimaced and shook her head. 'But I'm kind of bushed, Harry. It's been quite a day—'

'Sure has,' he said. 'Why don't you take it easy at the hotel?'

'Yeah, I'll get changed for—' she said, breaking off and laughing, 'our last night in Cameroon. I'll book a table at the hotel, on me, to say thank you.'

But before he could answer there was a strangled mixture of shock and excitement. They burst out of the office to see Fitz outside with a large envelope.

'Look what I've found!' she shouted.

Harry and Candace exchanged glances and turned to cross the lawn but they were immediately stopped in their tracks. A grey Peugeot saloon was approaching and slowed up as it passed the gate before accelerating away in a cloud of dust.

'Damn. Bad timing,' Harry said, tilting his head towards Fitz and the big envelope.

'It's all about her affair.' Fitz lowered her voice, as if someone might overhear. 'Monsieur had hidden it in Ollie's basket, look—'

They joined her in the house. She had taken a file out of the envelope and was shaking the contents onto a desk, a bound booklet and a stack of black-and-white photographs. 'This is the man Olivia had the affair with,' she said, holding one of them up. 'He's called Guy Martin.'

She spread the rest out: shots of Martin kissing a beautiful young woman in a white bikini on a beach, the two of them walking hand in hand through a sunlit street market and eating tête-à-tête at a fashionable terrace restaurant. Harry opened the booklet: St Tropez. It was a PI's report. St Tropez, 25-30 July 1962.

He flipped through it. 'Well, well,' he said, looking up at Candace. 'We got lucky. There's a Paris address for him here.' He glanced at Fitz and said, 'And yeah, you're right: he's a *pied-noir*, born in Spain and moved to Oran when he was a child. In 1936.'

Candace was pale and her face pinched. She was holding one of the more risqué photos. 'I don't care where he's from,' she hissed, 'he's a son of a bitch.'

Fitz was gawping, looking from Candace to Harry and back again. 'You know who he is?' she asked. 'I mean, from somewhere else?'

Candace looked away and Harry nodded. 'Yes, from somewhere else.' He picked up the envelope: it was heavy in his hand and he turned it upside down. A thick spiral-bound notebook fell out.

'Oh my God,' muttered Candace. Their eyes met.

He ran through the pages, each one covered with a dense Arabic script, until he found the Roman letters 'BP' written in the margin.

'Yeah, Beth Palmer' he murmured, 'this is the Greek's dossier. He sent a copy of this page to O'Connell and I thought BP stood for British Petroleum.'

It should've been a moment to celebrate but instead the blood-stained image of Victor Castile came back to him along with Bamenda's warning that they'd picked the wrong guys for a fight.

28

Friday, 12 April 1974

Douala, Cameroon

Harry shuffled the St Tropez photographs into a stack and returned them to the file. He put the file and the Greek dossier back in the envelope and looked up. Candace was still as pale as a ghost and by contrast Fitz looked as flushed as a dairymaid. He glanced at his watch.

'Time to get moving,' he said with a deliberate look at Fitz. 'Remember, you've got to pack before *madame* arrives.' To Candace, with a softened look in his eyes he said, 'And you look all in—'

'I'm fine,' she said. 'But we can't leave Fitz here on her own.'

'It's OK, really,' Fitz said. 'Rachel said she'd collect me by four. She's coming with her boyfriend and his van.' She laughed and added, 'You really don't have to worry about me. He's quite a tough guy. Actually from the underworld in Yaoundé, though you'd never know it. Rachel says he wouldn't hurt a fly.'

Candace was standing upright with her arms folded like someone at the prow of a ship looking out for land and Harry was moved by her stamina. She'd taken quite a beating and had come away looking gaunt but beautiful.

'You sure that's OK?' he asked Fitz.

'Sure it is,' she said, squatting down to rub the dog's chest as it rolled over on the rug. 'You're quite the hero, aren't you, Ollie. Imagine if there'd been no bed to hide the file in. We wouldn't know who Olivia's lover was.'

Harry grunted. 'Well,' he said, taking one of his business cards out of his billfold, 'we can hardly say it's been nice meeting you, Fitz, but if you ever make it to the Windy City, look me up.'

'That's a deal,' she said with a cheerful smile.

'Me too,' said Candace reaching across for the card. 'Let me put my phone number on the back of that; then you've got us both.' She dug deep into her purse for a pen and Harry took the chance to ask Fitz a last question, the way Columbo always did, as if he'd covered everything and was leaving.

'There was just one other thing,' Harry said, 'about those errands you did for M. Raymond—'

Fitz groaned. 'Errands, my God, there were hundreds of them.'

'Like you were his secretary?'

'Exactly! I actually heard him tell someone on the phone to ring back and not to worry when because his secretary would always take a message. Bloody cheek.'

'Right,' said Harry. 'So I was wondering if you remember taking any calls or mailing anything to someone called Eileen O'Connell with an address in New York?'

Fitz slumped down on the sofa with another groan. 'Yeah, yeah, definitely, a few times,' she said. 'And he sent her a book for her birthday. I hadn't been here long and he asked me to go out to get a card, so it must've been the end of November—'

She blushed. 'I'm sorry, Harry, I haven't been completely honest with you, but when I started I didn't know anyone and me and M. Jules were sort of thrown together.' She shrugged and said, 'Rachel said it was bound to happen; and anyway one night it almost did happen – which is why his sister went on about all that gold-digging rubbish – anyway, like I said, it didn't go anywhere but that night we did drink too much and he kind of poured his heart out—'

'In French?'

She shook her head and momentarily her blonde curls caught the afternoon sun in an unlikely halo.

'No, no,' she said. 'He could get by in English. Anyway, as I said, he got a bit maudlin – weighing his life up, the things he'd done and hadn't done, like writing the book he was always going on about.' She leaned forwards and wrapped her arms round her knees. 'It's standard fare for us nurses with blokes suddenly facing up to things, isn't it, Dr Fayol?'

Candace nodded knowingly.

'I had one feller actually propose!' Fitz added. 'Anyway, that one time we got close Jules blurted out he wanted to get back at the bastard who'd killed his wife – I was gobsmacked and wondered if I'd heard right but he clammed up and never mentioned either of them again, or that night either. I think we were both a bit ashamed of the whole episode.'

Fitz stopped and glanced at the envelope in Harry's hand before saying, 'But now I understand and I feel bad about all that Olivia Godiva stuff. He'd actually hired a private detective to find out the truth and had it rammed in his face—'

Fitz's dog suddenly started barking and she broke off and got up. 'It's dinner time,' she said. 'He always reminds me.'

'Right,' said Harry. 'Clever.'

He and Candace watched the young English nurse shake a heap of biscuits into a metal bowl before standing back proudly. 'He's smarter than he looks,' she said fondly.

'Well, he's certainly done us a good turn,' said Harry.

'Come on, Ollie,' she said. 'Time to pack.'

As Harry pulled away from the gate Candace waved out of the window and drew a deep breath before starting on the private investigator's report.

The photographs were numbered and they weren't only of the lovers having a ball at St Tropez. Guy Martin had been caught on a zoom with a bunch of other people, including Pierre Messmer, listed as President de Gaulle's minister for the army. Entry 15 was for 'Café de la Gare, Vernon' and Candace picked it out – striped awning over a few tables and chairs on the corner of an ordinary French street. No sharp shadows, Candace thought, like somewhere in the north. Photos 16 to 20 were of Martin at La Frégate with two more beautiful women, called Violetta and a very pregnant Monique.

There were also a couple of pages on his background: born in 1929 in Pamplona, Spain, as Guillermo Martinez Caceres; moved to Oran, Algeria, in 1934, changing his name to Guy Martin with a powerful patron, also a *pied-noir*, General Juin, the only Vichy collaborator ever accepted into the ranks of the Free French. The report noted that Guy Martin was a very gifted linguist, could pass perfectly as an American and nurtured a fierce hostility for the British after his brother had been killed in the unilateral demolition of the French fleet at anchor in 1940.

In the late fifties Martin apparently used this anti-British hostility to good effect in running a pro-French slant to the UN's Cameroon plebiscite and got the entire coastal belt to vote in favour of unifying with the old French mandate.

'Wow, this guy was thorough,' Candace said, looking up. 'Almost as good as you.'

Harry smiled and concentrated on overtaking a truck belching diesel fumes. She shuffled through the St Tropez photographs and sighed again.

'The poor woman was obviously smitten,' she said. The bastard looked so charming, so charismatic – no wonder they'd fallen for him; not to mention the glamour of a week on the Côte d'Azur or a seemingly random encounter sky high on Mount Cameroon. What a two-faced operator, thought Candace. With those assets it was hardly surprising he'd ended up Messmer's right-hand man.

'D'you realise, Harry,' she said, 'Annie's *complication* took us up the blind alleys of infidelity and race before we found out that Martin was a spook—'

But she broke off and gaped as the words echoed through her head.

'Wait a minute,' she said and turned towards him. 'That's not right! *We* know he was a spook but Annie didn't. It only came out years later.' She put her head in her hands and pressed tight. 'Annie must've been talking about something else.'

Damn.

Candace shook her head and tried to clear it – there was so much to take in. Only two days ago she'd scoffed at the ludicrous notion that Prime Minister Messmer was involved, but now she took it for granted along with the secret dossier that stood between him and his presidential ambitions – and that he'd trusted Guy Martin to get hold of it for him. *They* were Annie's big hitters.

She shoved the report and photos back into the envelope and flipped through the Arabic dossier making sense of the initials in the margins standing for Beth, Annie, Didier Nkumbé and Ruben Nyobé.

'Jesus,' she said, trying to contain her fury. 'There're more than fifty here! How many d'you think O'Connell knew about?'

'Certainly just Beth. That's what was in her desk—'

'Eileen O'Connell lied to Dad, Harry, a darned barefaced lie,' she cried, 'and then pushed us into this mess – it's obvious she's been in touch with Raymond and has been mixed up in this business from the very start.'

'Right, but maybe not on their side—'

'Goddammit, Harry,' she flared. 'You're giving her the benefit of the doubt again!'

He put his hand up. 'I'm just trying to make sense of what's happened and why.'

She looked at him and her anger subsided. The hotel was in sight.

'Right now,' he said, pulling up in the car lot, 'I'm working on getting us out of here in one piece.' He cut the engine and pulled the handbrake. 'Not to mention getting back in time for dinner. We both deserve a break.'

'I'll second that,' she said, 'but I just keep seeing Annie with Martin and it totally throws me.'

'I bet it does,' he said. 'Those photos can't help.'

'Exactly.' She shuddered; that's what had done it. Martin and Raymond's wife looked like a couple of film stars. Just reminded her of the power of the image again.

'Let me have it,' he said, relieving her of the offending envelope. She was happy to get shot of it but raised her eyebrows as he shoved it under the seat. 'Is it safe there?'

'As safe as anywhere else,' he said. 'Remember they've got the gendarmes on their side.'

She nodded: he was right; there wasn't anywhere safe until they got out of the country. Suddenly that felt like an immense burden, but she brushed the feeling aside and said brightly, 'Well, having it evens the score doesn't it?'

'As long as we can get it into the right hands.'

'So it's one for Annie,' she said. 'Or something anyway. She hated losing.'

'So do you.'

She turned to look at him. Her eyes shone and for a second he thought she was blinking away tears. 'Yeah, you're right, Harry, I do.'

She got out and slammed the door.

'The trouble is they know we've got it,' he said.

'And it's not as if we can unload it onto the cops.'

'No way.'

'What're we going to do then?'

He didn't know. 'Get on that flight tomorrow.'

A shout went up from the street. 'Hey, Chicago Man, you've got your beautiful woman!'

Harry curled his lip and glared at the man, who whooped and took off on a bike.

She burst out laughing. 'You're really enjoying playing the tough guy, aren't you?'

'It makes a change from being the scrawny kid at the beach.'

'You never were—'

'Only because I never got to the beach.'

'What about the Black Sea?'

'Party faithful only.' Like his brother.

'Oh, you poor deprived thing! I'll take you to the lake when we get back to Chicago.'

'Thank you, ma'am, but maybe I don't have the right beach-wear—'

'We'll get you something in the Champs-Élysées.'

They went into the hotel and hovered in the lobby.

'So what time tonight?' Harry asked.

'Eight in the bar? A drink before dinner?'

'No problem, partner.' He gave her a light buddy-type punch on the shoulder. 'We got a ways to go yet.'

She returned a dazzling smile. 'I'm not tagging along any longer?'

'Couldn't manage without you.'

The words were out before he realised what he'd just said. The elevator arrived and the doors opened. She waved and the doors shut. She was gone and his head was suddenly full of memories of Judit. The last time came back to him: the dank cellar and low ceiling, the splintered box of ammunition in the corner and the hush broken only by the rumble of Soviet tank tracks on the street above them. Judit, typical Judit, was quoting Marx to him in German about men making their own history, '*Die Menschen machen ihre eigene Geschichte*', not under conditions of their own choosing but within the limits of the past.

She had led him across the concrete floor and crouched down to take a pistol out of the box, a brand-new CZ52. She'd pressed it into his hand, the metal cold and slippery with oil.

'We're going to make history,' she'd said, their hands clasped together around the gun. He'd gone to embrace her but she'd put a finger on his lips and pushed him away. 'Today. Now. And then we'll make love.'

Three days later she was dead and he was scuttling across the Austrian border with the gun unused and still in his pocket; and now, years later, there was another attractive woman talking to him about doing the right thing. He went down the corridor and unlocked the door to his room and dropped his bag onto the bed and went out onto the balcony for a smoke. He wondered for the nth time if they'd just dumped her in an unmarked grave and why the hell he'd never tried to find out.

After a shower and a change of clothes he went down and drove around town until he found a hardware store and bought a six-inch hunting knife with a belt. The light was beginning to go as he set off for the docks. He turned a corner and caught sight of the bar with the stripper-and-snake act.

The sign was broken so it was hard to know if it was called Exotique or Érotique but either way the place was closed up tight and he drove on into the kind of seedy back streets that spend the best part of daylight recovering from the night before. The only life moving was a dog rooting through the garbage and a guy in a dishevelled suit looking as if he'd forgotten his way home.

Harry took another turn and spotted another club. Next to it was an empty lot with a couple of cars parked and one of them was a white Renault 12. He slowed down: the Hertz logo was just visible in the fading light and he drove in and stopped alongside. The doors were splattered with red mud but he couldn't see inside. His heart beat faster as he walked round to the dilapidated clapboard façade at the front. Above the first-floor balcony the name La Pleine Lune blinked weakly across the image of a dim crescent moon, and he remembered it from one of the cards in Castile's wallet.

He climbed the broken steps onto the porch, holding the knife in his pocket. In the light of the sign he could make out a couple of stained leather chairs and a low table covered with empty bottles and an overflowing ashtray. To one side there was a threadbare hammock loaded with a huddled shape. One leg was hanging off the side and moving in time with a nasty gargle of a snore that sounded as if a blowfly was caught in the man's throat.

Harry started across to the door but was beaten to it by a man from inside. All he could see were the whites of his eyes.

'*Se fermée*,' the man said, stepping forwards into the light.

He was carrying a broom and had nothing on his feet despite the broken glass strewn across the decking. Harry stepped back and the man stopped and leaned on the handle with the air of someone who'd been a bystander at too many banquets.

'*Bonsoir*,' Harry said, looking around like someone in real estate. 'I was just passing. A friend recommended this place.'

'The place or the pussy?' the janitor asked and without waiting for an answer jabbed the sleeper in the balls with his broom handle. The gargling snapped off midstream and turned into a groan, but the man's eyes stayed shut.

'Bastard's too tight to pay for a room. Fucks them up against the back wall instead and then sleeps it off out here!'

Harry nodded and made another move for the door.

'I told you, we're shut,' the man said and barred his way with the broomstick and then gestured with it at the neon sign. '*C'est une boîte de nuit.*'

'Yeah,' he said, not really wanting to pick a fight about the difference between dusk and day. 'But how come this guy got served?'

'He paid special rate,' said the man rubbing his thumb and forefinger together. 'We got a couple of girls in the back if you want a quick deal—'

'I didn't come for a girl. I'm looking for a man.'

The man squinted at him. 'Don't I know you from some place?'

'Maybe—'

'I remember now—' The janitor stood back and looked him over. 'How much did Lagos pay you to kill M. Vic?'

Harry made a face as if to say it was confidential and the janitor cleared his throat and spat over the rail as if he had his own views and was sticking to them. He brandished the broom like a weapon.

'I heard you cut his dick off—'

'So?'

'So what're you doing snooping around his old haunts?'

'I'm looking for someone else, a friend of his.' Harry put the photo of Guy Martin on the beach at St Tropez and a five-franc bill on the table.

'Nice tits—'

'The man. Used to be a player around here. Still might be.'

The janitor gave him a scornful look. 'Not here. This is Victor's patch.'

'So you know him?'

'Course I do! Bastard used to fuck at Violetta's. He used to fuck her—' He waved into the darkness. 'But you're barking up the wrong tree.'

'How come?'

'It'll cost you double.'

'That depends on what you've got.' Harry took out another bill and waited.

'Guy Martin was no friend of Vic's—'

'The way I heard it, they worked together when the French were in charge.'

'Maybe they did, but they fell out.'

'Over what?' Harry held the note out.

'Money. What else? Martin double-crossed him in Biafra big time.' He made a grab at the money.

'I know what they got up to in Biafra.' Harry made to put the money back in his billfold.

'Sure you do but I've got something you don't know.'

'I'm waiting.'

'He's been staying right here, that's what!'

'You've got to do better than that. I even know he's driving a Hertz hire car, the white Renault 12 that's parked in your lot across the road.'

'Maybe, smart guy, but what you don't know is that he's disappeared again, this time for good.' He drew a finger across his throat. 'Some other guys got to him first.'

'Who?'

The man made to grab the money again. 'Old man who paid me to keep an eye on him.'

'Who?'

He shrugged. 'One of them I seen before down here, a Belgian. Way back. Anyway they got him!' He snapped his fingers nastily. 'All his stuff is inside, his passport, fancy Japanese camera, clothes, the lot, but his bed hadn't been slept in. Hertz are coming for the car in the morning.'

'What about the gendarmes?'

'What about them?'

'Didn't you call them?'

The man looked blank. 'Where's the body?'

'Right.' No body, no worries. Harry let him take the money and started back down the steps.

'Anyway, Vic had the last laugh!' the man crowed after him.

'That bastard Martin wouldn't have been seen dead here in the old days, but it's where he had his final fuck.'

The cackle pursued Harry down the street and left him with the thought that even Messmer's trusted intermediaries could run out of time and end up like Castile – the price for knowing too much.

29

Friday, 12 April 1974

Douala, Cameroon

Harry took a turning towards La Frégate and the stench of rotten mangroves filled his nostrils. The past came flooding back with memories of some poor health freak from their neighbourhood in Budapest who'd made the same smell by rotting her kitchen waste into compost in her back yard. She claimed it would save the planet, an eternal cycle, but the apparatchiks had her marked down as a dissident and she was so mercilessly persecuted that she hanged herself.

Harry had been just a kid, and he knew he wasn't to blame, but he'd tagged along with the mob and could never forget the look of wounded betrayal in her eyes. Now he wondered what point she'd been making and if Olivia Raymond's choice of when and where she'd killed herself had been more than just a tragic coincidence. As Sal would say, he didn't believe in coincidences; but as she'd also say, there was always an exception to the rule – and maybe that's what it had been, just a tragic coincidence. But he wasn't convinced.

One more turning took him within view of La Frégate, less derelict and with better lighting than La Pleine Lune. A few people were whooping it up on the steps as if a party were going on. He cruised to a halt in the shadows and a few snatches of the hullabaloo reached him: 'Incredible!' and 'Mme Violetta is upstairs!' He had her picture in his bag, numbered and indexed, a woman who'd banned Victor Castile from her club. No shrinking violet then.

The group disappeared and Harry considered his options. He belted the knife round his waist. The door of the club swung open and two men emerged still hooting with laughter before disappearing into the darkness of the parking lot. A gate clanged shut and he could just make out the flare of a match and the glow of a cigarette. He doubled back and worked his way down an alley between two deserted warehouses until he reached the swamp. His foot sank into soft slime and he pulled it out with a muttered curse. In the dusk, he could make out a rough balcony at the back of the club.

He cursed again as his foot slipped further into the mire. What the hell was he doing down here at all? He jumped as something scuttled between his legs and slipped into the water. He told himself to calm down and scanned the dark surface of the swamp: was Guy Martin out there, floating face down with his throat cut, surplus to Paris's requirements? It seemed possible, but since when had Harry taken the word of a guy like the janitor at La Pleine Lune?

He moved forwards and suddenly slipped in further, the thick mud sucking at his shoe. He imagined leeches wriggling up his leg and shuddered. Give him a bad guy with a gun any day. He grabbed a hold and pulled free just as an external light lit up the club's back balcony. He ducked down and worked his way to the corner post. Above him parallel lines of light shone through the decking and excited voices reached him over the metallic whirring of the air-conditioner.

He forced the knife between the post and the joist and rammed it right in to make a step. He tested it with his weight before reaching up for a grip. With a deep breath, he pulled himself up and scrambled over the edge of the decking. He stood up and cursed the noise of his squelching shoe but the balcony door had stayed closed and the drapes hung straight and still. He moved forwards quietly and pressed his ear to the window.

He wasn't sure why he'd come or what he was expecting, but La Frégate was Guy Martin's African home base – and, according to Raymond's PI report, his business. Surely the man would have stopped by to say hello; but, according to the voices inside, the party atmosphere was down to a woman.

'What ever happened to Alistair?' one of the women was asking in an accent reminiscent of a Brazilian friend in Chicago. 'I always thought it was a match made in heaven.'

'Ha,' the other woman scoffed, 'his marriage mattered more to him.'

Harry strained his ears: the second accent was patrician Parisian and the French sophisticated, but who was Alistair? One of the Scottish oil crew?

'And you?' The Brazilian accent again.

'I like my own company. Always did.'

'Wait.' The smart accent stopped and Harry heard the pop of a champagne cork. 'Brut Superior. It was always your drink. We used to keep a bottle chilled ready for you.'

'My God, Vi, what a memory!'

Harry made the connection and smiled with satisfaction. Vi was the club's owner, Violetta, and, long ago, Guy Martin's mistress.

'Remember your customers and they'll remember you,' she said with a rich gurgle. 'I learned that in bed! *Salut!*'

He could just hear the clink of glasses followed by a pause of silent pleasure.

'Perfect.' The Parisian patrician.

'Now, *chérie*,' said Violetta, 'tell me why you've come back after all this time, incognito? That outfit does you no favours by the way.'

'It's my Irish Republican aid worker and anyhow I'm not a VIP anymore.'

Irish. Harry made a tight fist: right. Of course, the smart accent was Eileen O'Connell.

Why wasn't he surprised? She'd half shown him her hand all the way through, like she had an agenda and actually wanted him along. He tried to get a glimpse of her but all he could see was the ice bucket and bottle of champagne.

'You never behaved like a VIP,' said Violetta, 'hanging out in a dive like this! Nobody else from the Foreign Service came down even in broad daylight.'

'Probably not,' said O'Connell. 'No doubt another pretext for kicking me out.'

'They kicked you out?'

'Yeah, they did. You remember Connor?'

'Connor! Of course! How could I not?' The club owner threw her head back and let out a peal of laughter. 'What's the rascal up to now?'

'The same old glorious struggle for a united Ireland.'

Harry tried a different angle but all he could see were framed photographs, and then suddenly O'Connell came into his view. Her Republican disguise really worked: she looked like a mature student, downbeat with a flat hairstyle and glasses, but the Long Island glamour came out in the way she leaned forwards to light a cigarette from Violetta's Bic lighter. The tobacco caught fire and smoke curled into the air. It was O'Connell all right.

Eileen O'Connell smiled: chilled champagne and a French cigarette made for a pretty good preparation for the tricky business ahead. She looked round the office: the same old desk with inlaid green leather; a slow-moving fan in the ceiling even though the club now had air-conditioning; subdued lighting; and the same gallery of framed photographs on the wall. She was swept back into the past, a time of extremes when she'd been in her prime and fighting to stay true to the Atlantic Charter.

Violetta was pressing her about Connor and her abrupt departure from the Foreign Service.

'All I did was make a donation to NORAID after Bloody Sunday, for God's sake,' she said, 'but they jumped at the chance – "inappropriate association", they called it – and threw me out.'

'Shame on them.'

'Yeah.' She winked. 'But don't worry, I'm getting my own back.'

'Of course you are.' Violetta raised her glass. 'Bravo.'

'They were mighty wary, though.' She put a finger to her lips. 'I had to sign a gagging clause. No spilling the beans.'

Eileen sat back and ran her finger down the stem of her glass. It was good to be back, and she'd always liked the vibe at La Frégate, but this wasn't a trip down memory lane. This was a chance to set things right and put the record straight, even though it'd threatened to go off the rails once Jules' cousin had elbowed in and put the squeeze on Messmer. She'd warned Jules but he'd gone ahead with Castile and they'd both paid the price. The only question now was where the Greek's dossier had ended up.

She looked across the table at Violetta, a woman who'd taken herself from working in a whorehouse to owning it, and wondered if she'd offer a helping hand now that her plan was falling apart. It was time to go for broke.

'Thing is, Vi,' she said, watching the champagne bubbles fizz and rush to the surface, 'I'm sixty and free from rules and obligations and I just want to put the record straight. When I worked for the Service there were always things I couldn't talk about and coming down here was a relief from all those stiff collars and whalebone stays.'

'That's what we're here for.' Violetta nodded and sipped her champagne.

'Yeah,' Eileen said, 'I used to think of La Frégate as a bubble I could escape to. Anyway, one of the things I couldn't talk about was the Beth Palmer case and how I got leaned on to toe the French line. You remember, the pretty American missionary at Ebolowa who was raped and murdered by that young tearaway Didier Nkumbé?'

'Of course I remember.' Violetta looked away.

'Yes, of course you do.' Eileen paused and then continued, 'You know, Vi, in all the years I worked out here we only had two US citizens die from unnatural causes. Beth Palmer and Annie, and both their autopsies were done by Dr Petridis.'

She'd very carefully dropped the name and now she watched for Violetta's reaction. Inside her bag was Mona's translation of Petridis' autopsy detailing the extensive bruising to all of Beth Palmer's orifices and no sign of black skin under her fingernails.

'That Greek pig!' Violetta reared up. 'I couldn't bear to have him anywhere near me after what he did to Monique.'

'Well, he's dead,' Eileen said bluntly. 'That's why I'm here.'

'Good riddance.' Violetta spat the words out. 'I hope he burns in hell.'

She raised her eyes to the framed photograph of herself and Monique leaning against a palm-oil tree. Hidden high up among the leaves was the kid they called the Monkey. Her eyes were glistening with tears when she turned back.

'I still miss her terribly,' she said, 'but it was even worse for Gitan.

He went back to the desert and sold me his share of the business cheap so I could afford it. He said Monique would've wanted me to have it.'

'You ever see him?' she asked.

'Unfortunately not. The memories are too much for him; but he has another baby now, called Madeleine. Very pretty, same deep dark eyes like his, and her middle name is Monique.'

'I barely knew him,' Eileen said.

Violetta nodded. 'He wasn't easy to know, always the outsider – like Guy; something they shared.'

'Guy didn't seem an outsider to me; if anything, the opposite – a man making and taking his chances.'

'Maybe not to you, but he was deeply divided inside. *Pieds-noirs* always feel excluded, on the outside—'

'Of course; I'd forgotten.' She remembered Guy's rhetoric, an intense conflict between pro- and anti-French feelings, as if he was an eternal adolescent caught between rebellion and deference. He'd always identified with Camus.

'Presumably he was called home after the revelations of the French Connection trial?' she ventured.

'You know he was.' Violetta's eyes flashed and her tone changed. 'And before you ask, no, I didn't know he worked undercover. I wasn't interested and we didn't do pillow talk – isn't that what you people call it?'

Eileen held up a hand in truce. She couldn't afford to piss Violetta off even if she didn't believe her.

'Anyway we've parted ways,' Violetta added in a more conciliatory tone. 'I bought him out and he didn't like my offer, said I was taking advantage.'

Eileen nodded and glanced at the gallery of photos on the wall, which still included Guy Martin. It seemed a strange way of falling out.

Violetta nodded as if she knew what was in Eileen's mind. 'Whatever's come between us,' she said, 'they're still precious memories, and I haven't fallen out with Gitan.'

'I can see.' There were more shots of him and Monique with Marcel than Guy.

'He was even more extreme than Guy,' said Violetta, sipping her glass. 'No affection for France at all. Hatred. The complete anti-hero in 1940.'

'I remember all that,' Eileen said. Summer 1940: momentous times. How could she forget? France had fallen to Hitler and she'd gone to London to monitor and liaise with de Gaulle's fledging Free French. 'That was another thing I couldn't talk about.'

Her heart was beating fast: nothing got past Violetta and the moment would have to be timed to perfection.

'What about the Monkey then?' Eileen asked, gesturing at the photo. 'He must've been totally lost when Gitan left.'

'Gitan took him with him to Niger,' Violetta replied. She shook her head sadly. 'Poor Marcel. When he heard about Monique he climbed the tallest tree he could find and wouldn't come down until Gitan came.'

'The kid always seemed very insecure—'

'Of course he did! Monique had no one in her life until Gitan. They were outcasts in Fernando Po, bullied from pillar to post.'

Eileen held her breath and gripped the stem of her glass. She had to ask; it was now or never. 'Vi,' she said steadily, 'can you tell me if you've seen Marcel recently?'

Violetta kept a poker face, giving nothing away. 'I told you,' she said without a flicker, 'he's in Niger with Gitan.'

'Then how come I saw him last night?' Eileen said, keeping her eyes on Violetta's. 'He was coming out of Jules Raymond's house at a hell of a rate. He nearly knocked me over.'

'Must've been somebody else.'

'No, Vi,' she said, leaning across to grip Violetta's arm, 'I swear on Monique's grave, it was him.'

Violetta retrieved her arm. 'It couldn't have been.'

'I saw him, Vi,' Eileen said, raising her voice. 'It was definitely Marcel.' She took a deep breath and pitched in further. 'Look, I'll come clean about why I'm here and how come Marcel is too. Jules

Raymond got me into it. He shared a private ward in hospital with Petridis and discovered the bastard had kept a secret record of the autopsies he'd faked, including Beth Palmer's and Annie's. Jules thought he could make something of it with a bestselling exposé but that thug of a cousin of his, Castile, spotted the chance for quick money by blackmailing Pierre Messmer – if you remember him?'

'Not really, no,' said Violetta, unmoved and unsurprised. 'High commissioners never graced us with their company. They sent their henchmen or women.'

'Sure,' Eileen said, stung by the jibe and clearly getting nowhere. It felt as though her chances were fading fast. 'I need that dossier, Vi,' she said urgently. 'Can't you just tell me if Marcel has got it?'

'I told you, he's in Niger with Gitan,' Violetta answered, cool and aloof. 'I'm sorry I can't help.'

'I just want to know where it is, for God's sake,' Eileen pleaded. 'I don't give a damn if Marcel killed Jules – he was going to die anyway – but this is my big chance. They screwed me last time and I'm not letting it happen again.'

But Violetta remained impassive and tight-lipped. She had other prior loyalties and a business to run.

30

O'Connell's plea echoed round Harry's head as he twisted away from the window and slithered off the roof. Marcel, the Monkey, had killed Jules and was hell bent on getting the Greek's dossier. Castile had been blackmailing Messmer and had paid the price: Harry had been right about that, but wrong about the signature 'G' being Guy Martin. It stood for Gitan! Gitan was Messmer's trusted intermediary, not Guy Martin, and the package of cuttings had been mailed in N – I – G – E – R not Nigeria.

Damn – he'd thought the case was connected to oil and OPEC by the energy crisis and it'd made OK sense at the time, but now he could see that it was actually about uranium and Messmer's dash for nuclear power. That was the story Jules Raymond had been following in Niger when he saw Gitan and Guy Martin together.

And it'd been the Monkey driving the Hertz and the 303! The realisation chilled Harry to the bone. It was obvious the Monkey would do anything to get Gitan the dossier – he'd already killed Castile and Raymond for it and was still looking. Harry sloshed through the swamp as fast as he could, swearing all the way. Marcel knew they had the dossier and Candace was on her own in the hotel. What the hell had he been thinking of!

The sound of the band on the hotel terrace below reminded Candace how long it had been since she'd been out to a club. Caring for her mom and long hours at the clinic had seen to that. She got into the new underwear Hélène had given her and looked in the full-length mirror. Vanity wasn't one of her vices and she didn't spend too long admiring herself but she had to smile at the effect. Then she sat on the edge of the bath and shaved her legs and wrapped herself in her dressing gown. The music lured her onto the balcony, where she lit a cigarette, popping her head out first to make sure there was no one to observe her. The smoke filled her lungs and the hit ran up her spine and she closed her eyes and rocked for a moment, steadying herself on the railing.

She was tapping her foot in time with the music. It was catchy and it crossed her mind that she and Harry might check it out as a kind of send-off after they'd eaten. She watched the couples on the dance floor and wondered whether Harry liked to dance. A breeze picked up and caressed her neck and shoulders and she stretched out her arms and shivered. Out to her left she followed a figure patrolling the fence and while she watched a car slid up the track on the other side and cut its headlights. The figure pointed a flashlight into the darkness and picked out a clump of banana trees and then swept across the track before going out.

She narrowed her eyes as the figure receded and merged into the darkness and she stubbed out her cigarette on the railing. Sparks flew into the creeper, which seemed to shake in the breeze. She was poised by the French windows as the mosquito netting billowed around her when she was startled by a sound like a bird fluttering in the foliage. She listened, her heart beating faster and her mouth dry: there it was again, the same rustling but too big for a bird, but before she could move inside the room the curtains whooshed again and her heart leaped so hard that it hurt.

A man stepped onto the balcony wearing a balaclava like a hijacker, arms looping down by his sides and a body poised like an athlete. She jumped into action and bolted inside for the bathroom, slamming the door just as he crashed against it. The wooden panel seemed to bend and the lock nearly gave and he slammed against it again. Somewhere a phone was ringing.

She cried out. Her hands trembled as she searched her toilet bag for scissors – anything – and the contents clattered out into the basin.

Harry was driving so fast that the car bounced over one huge pothole and nearly crashed into another. He hammered on the wheel in frustration at a red light and then made a perilously risky left turn in front of a huge truck. Now he could see the hotel. He cursed again as some idiot stopped in front of him to let out a passenger. He banged on the horn and looked sideways up the track alongside the hotel garden. Two weak lamps in the chain-link fence cast a dim light over the banana thicket and a saloon that looked ominously like the grey 303 with tinted windows.

He pulled off the road and cut the engine, wondering whether to take the dossier or leave it under the seat. He took it out and stood for a second scanning the back wall of the hotel. There was only one light on the third floor and he could see the fine mesh of the mosquito netting waving in the open door, but there was no sign of Candace. He was just about to turn away when the shape of a man rolled out of the creeper and landed deftly on the balcony. It had to be the Monkey. Harry spun round and sprinted down the sidewalk into the hotel lobby. The clerk on the desk jumped.

'There's a man in Dr Fayol's room,' Harry said, breathing heavily. 'Give me the key!'

The clerk stared at him for a long moment before taking it off a hook and handing it over.

'Come with me,' Harry shouted just as the elevator doors closed in front of him.

The man nodded and took a baseball bat from behind the desk.

Harry took the stairs three at a time, his lungs bursting and pain stinging his thighs. On one corner he nearly knocked over a tall woman carrying a doe-eyed baby; the woman cursed him in a language he couldn't understand but with a sign that he could. On the third floor he thought he heard screaming but it was the mix of the vocalist and a saxophone in the band on the ground floor. Her door was locked. He rammed in the key and turned it, holding the dossier like a weapon.

'Candace,' he shouted, wrenching the door open and blowing through it. He could feel the desk clerk at his shoulder bearing the bat. A shadow flitted across the balcony and out of sight. He sped round the double bed and through the French window onto the balcony. The sax was still going but now he could hear Candace.

'It's OK, he's gone,' he called from the balcony. Below in the darkness he could make out a figure floating smoothly down the creeper. He took the knife by the blade and leaned over the railing straining his eyes to get a good sight but the man was already barely a blur – and moving like a monkey. Harry hurled the knife into the wooden floor at his feet and it stuck.

'Bastard.'

His hand was bleeding. He put the dossier down on the bed.

'Candace.' He tapped on the bathroom door. 'It's OK. It's me, Harry.'

He stood awkwardly, listening to her breathing deeply. He stepped back on the balcony in time to hear a car door slam and the 303 disappear down the track.

'*Monsieur*,' a voice called from the corridor. The reception clerk was standing in the doorway with the baseball bat. There was another man behind him, his eyes popping out of his head.

'He got away,' Harry said, waving towards the perimeter fence. 'He was parked up the track, a grey 303 saloon.'

The clerk returned to the corridor. 'We'll go and look, sir,' he said shutting the door. 'I hope *madame* is not too shocked.'

'Thank you,' said Harry, reaching out with a restraining gesture, 'but we don't need to call the gendarmes – though you could get someone to trim that creeper.'

'Yes, sir.' The desk clerk nodded with relief and shut the door. Nobody wanted the gendarmes around. Harry could hear water running into the basin. 'Candace,' he called, 'you OK in there?'

The toilet flushed in reply. The water stopped running and she pulled the lock.

'Wait.'

Her voice was a dry whisper. In the dim light her eyes looked dark and hollow and her face as white as the towel she was holding. Her mouth opened to speak but nothing came out. He stood back from the doorway.

'You need a doctor?'

It sounded ridiculous and she sort of laughed. 'Hardly,' she said, 'I'll be alright in a minute.'

He went into the bedroom and waited. She came out and sat

down heavily on the bed. Her shoulders shook, but she made no sound.

'He had a mask—'

He put a hand on her shoulder. She seemed out of reach.

'Tissue, please—'

He went into the bathroom. He pulled paper from the dispenser – it was coarse.

'Sorry, it's pretty rough.'

'It'll do.' She blew her nose and crumpled the paper into a ball. 'Idiot! I asked for it, wandering around on the balcony like that. He must've been watching.'

He rested a hand on her back and felt the muscles tremble. She straightened up and he stepped back.

'I should never have left you alone.'

'It was my fault. I was so dumb,' she said. 'But it never crossed my mind somebody could climb that creeper.'

'That's why he's called the Monkey,' Harry said and followed her onto the balcony. They leaned over the railing. A couple of the strongest vines were broken and hanging down. He looked at her, wan but defiant, the whites of her eyes smudged with bloodshot. A breeze was blowing off the ocean with the scent of seaweed and cargo boats.

'Let me get you a cognac,' he said.

'No really – I'm OK.'

'Something else then?'

She shook her head. 'No, I just want to get him.'

'Well we've got his aunt's address in Paris,' he said, deciding to leave the revelations about O'Connell and Guy Martin for the morning. They'd have time and energy to make sense of it all on the flight. 'Did you get to the cemetery OK?' he asked instead.

'Yeah.' She nodded. 'I put flowers on the grave but it was weird: I felt closer to Annie in the riptide.'

'Too bad there wasn't an easier way of persuading you to leave,' he said with a sardonic smile.

'My fault for being so stubborn,' she said. 'Headstrong and impulsive. Runs in the family, remember?'

He nodded: so did the good looks.

31

Paris, France

On special occasions, like the launch for a new line or an anniversary of an old favourite, Candace's cousin Hélène employed a new young chef called Henri to do the cooking *à la nouvelle*. It was the kind of extravagantly modern gesture expected from a woman producing lingerie for the top end of the market and she did nothing to discourage rumours about a liaison in the kitchen. The risqué gossip was good for her business and she liked the public associating her light, silky creations with a revolutionary new cuisine noted for its freshness and visual flare.

'He was the sous chef on a publicity trip I made on Concorde,' she was saying. 'Dining faster than the speed of sound is incredible, the modern equivalent of a romance on the Orient Express.'

Candace had never broken the sound barrier and although the new French cuisine was the talk of the New York gourmands she didn't think there was a *nouvelle* restaurant in Chicago, even on her side of town. In any case her taste inclined towards the Mexican food at El Nuevo León with its bold flavours of chilli and charcoal. Funnily enough Mexican was Harry's preference too, and he'd told her how it reminded him of the kitchen maid in Budapest pounding dried peppers to a dark-red powder. It was the only time he'd mentioned his childhood to her and a sad look had come into his eyes.

'Harry won't mind if we start without him,' Candace said. 'He wouldn't want it to spoil.'

Henri's culinary creations had been timed to come to the table in Hélène's Parisian town house at nine o'clock, which had looked like a viable schedule before they'd run into the chaos at Douala airport. The strike had marooned planes and passengers all over the place and Harry's ticket, courtesy of Messmer's henchman, whoever he was, had been routed through Dakar. No amount of Candace's charm or extra money would persuade the airline staff to give him a seat on her flight and they'd had to say *au revoir* at the gate with the promise that someone would meet him at Orly.

'I asked my driver to wait for the Dakar flight with a placard,' said Hélène.

Candace smiled. It was Harry's turn to have someone waving a placard with his name on it. 'Come,' said Hélène, taking Candace's hand and drawing her through into the palatial lounge. 'At least we can celebrate your safe return with a glass of champagne.'

By rights Candace should've been dog-tired.

She hadn't really slept at all last night even though Harry had changed rooms with her and made sure the balcony door was locked. She'd been too full of adrenalin to relax and on the flight back she'd been mulling over Harry's garbled summary of what he'd overheard at the back of La Frégate. The biggest surprises were Guy Martin's death or staged disappearance; the 'G' signature standing for Gitan not Guy; and Eileen O'Connell being out there, intent on 'getting her own back' – whatever that was supposed to mean.

Candace threw herself into Hélène's deep sofa and suddenly felt exhausted: the plot seemed impenetrably thick. All they could be really certain of was that Guy Martin had been Annie's SOMEONE and that Petridis' record of falsified autopsies had been used by Castile to blackmail Prime Minister Messmer.

Hélène flicked a switch and the room was filled with the soothing sound of a tinkling piano like an ad for menthol cigarettes. The centre light was broken into a mass of splinters by a chandelier and Hélène dimmed it to a soft glow. A bottle of champagne was waiting in an ice bucket and Hélène poured them both a glass.

'Well, Candace, *chérie*,' said Hélène, smiling at her and holding up her glass, 'there's so much to drink to. But like I say, no question, we must start with a toast to your safe return. My God—' She shuddered. 'To have nearly lost another dear cousin to the same riptide off the coast of Cameroon – it doesn't bear thinking about!'

Candace smiled back, her eyes pricking with tears, and clinked her glass. In the hectic chaos of their meeting at Orly she hadn't had the time or space to give Hélène a tidy methodical account of what'd happened so without thinking she'd started with the trip to the cemetery. And that'd done it: the whole horror of the riptide poured out, the beach and the jungle and that Shell oil drum, and the way the placid ocean suddenly turned into a raging torrent ripping shingle and rocks from under her feet.

In the soft enclosed luxury of Hélène's BMW she'd relived the whole horror – the surge of the water, the bubbles bursting from her mouth and hurtling towards the light, and then Harry rescuing her. All the emotion of the experience tore through her again and she'd only just kept a grip on her tears.

She sipped her champagne and gazed around: she couldn't believe it, but it was only four days since she'd last been in Paris and ten days since she'd found out about Didier Nkumbé – ten days! It felt like a lifetime! Her world had been turned upside down by an apparently harmless decision to employ a private investigator to find out who Annie had fallen for in Cameroon.

Together she and Harry had found out – mission accomplished – but it didn't feel the way she'd imagined. She'd been hoping that Annie's *someone* would have a good reason for not getting in touch and that he would turn out to be a nice guy worthy of Annie's affections, but now she knew better.

Now she knew the truth: he was a French secret agent called Guy Martin, already complicit in the murder of Beth Palmer, and he'd conspired with the thug Castile to get rid of Annie as if she'd been a bag of garbage. They had done the bidding of senior officers in the French state, Pierre Messmer or Jacques Foccart, with additional collusion from the pathologist Petridis and the US *chargée* Eileen O'Connell. It had been a fully blown conspiracy to kill and cover-up involving at least five people!

Ten days ago she would've scoffed at any such claim, but in those ten days she had changed and now she knew the truth could indeed be stranger than fiction. She knew what had happened in '56 and that the same powerful people had conspired to kill again to stop the truth from coming out.

'Candy—' A voice was coming at her from the far side of the room. 'Candy, you OK? You looked totally spaced out.'

She shook her head clear: back to reality. It was Hélène; they were in Paris. Candace drained her glass and the sharp, cleansing sensation of champagne zipped through her.

'Yeah,' she said, 'yeah, I'm OK – just blown away by what's happened; a whirlwind—' She shrugged and looked up at her cousin. 'There's still too many loose ends; but like a big operation – heart surgery or something – you want it over and done with, closure.'

Hélène filled her glass and put the bottle back in the ice bucket.

'You bet you do, sweetie,' Hélène said with another toast ready. 'Here's to closure.'

Before Candace had a chance to respond Laurent was at the door with Harry – and the Petridis dossier in his bag. He smiled at her and tears filled her eyes. She wanted to throw herself into his arms, but instead she burst out laughing and said, 'My God, Harry Kaplan, am I glad to see you,' as if they were old buddies and hadn't seen one another for months. 'It's been a long time.'

And he laughed, showing his dimples, and said, 'Yeah, Candace – you're right, it's been too long,' as if he understood.

'And you're just in time to eat,' said Hélène, reaching out a hand. 'I'm Hélène.'

Midway through the meal the conversation shifted from the food to the Petridis dossier and what to do with it. Candace was keen to get hold of her cousin's contact at Canard but Hélène didn't think it was a good time because of the break-in and attempted bugging at their new offices.

'It'll be a few days before they're back to normal,' she said.

'I suppose we could always mail it,' said Candace.

'Bad idea,' Hélène said. 'Their stuff is intercepted.'

'But we need somebody like them on our side.'

'You seriously think they're that driven to find it?' Hélène asked.

Harry nodded. 'They've already killed Castile and Raymond to get it.'

'Yeah, Candy gave me the gist.' Hélène got up. 'Let's take our coffee into the lounge.'

She offered him a cigar.

'Genuine Cuban.'

He shook his head and picked up the newspaper from the glass coffee table. The headlines were all about the anti-French rioting in Niger but the Canard break-in was still running on the inside page. He ran his eye down the article.

Hélène crossed her elegant legs and let one high-heeled shoe slip from her foot. Harry looked from one cousin to the other. They could have been sisters: the same slate-blue eyes and thick dark hair, the same full lips and intensity. The only difference was 10 years – and some very expensive make-up.

'Petridis' dossier is clearly dynamite,' said Hélène. 'Messmer's pitch for the presidency might survive this Canard fiasco but the dossier will sink it altogether. I'll get the office to translate it ASAP. We must have someone fluent in Greek—'

'It's Arabic,' said Harry.

'That'll be easier.'

Harry hesitated. 'OK, thanks, but we need somebody we can totally trust,' he said. 'We've got to remember it'll put them in danger.'

'I see what you mean.' She nodded. 'Candy told me that's what might have got Guy Martin killed.'

'It's possible,' said Harry, sipping his coffee, 'but the more I think about it the less I buy it. It was all too neat. He's up to something.'

'Why would he want to disappear?' Hélène asked.

'Maybe he needs a new ID. He was seen in Niger with Gitan.'

'What's Niger got to do with it?' she asked.

'I don't know,' said Harry, 'but right now it's big news. Messmer is staking France's future on nuclear power with Niger's uranium and Colonel Gaddafi is stirring the mix with calls to nationalise the mines.' He gestured at the newspapers on a side table. 'Things are boiling over and Messmer is worried sick they'll go ahead and leave his nuclear plan high and dry.'

'So you think he's planning to do something about it.' Hélène grimaced. 'Like a coup – and that Guy Martin might be running it?'

'Who knows.' Harry shrugged again and said, 'All we know is that

Martin was working undercover for the French secret service until the French Connection trial a couple of years ago.'

'But the other guy, Gitan, wasn't – right?' Hélène asked. 'You said he was running a tourist company in Niger – or that's his cover. It could be—'

'Yeah,' Harry nodded. 'It could easily be. All I know is that he didn't work for them in Cameroon, but all of a sudden he's popped up in Niger and is sorting out Messmer's blackmail problem.'

'So he's back on the team and pulling the strings in Cameroon,' said Candace. 'And the question is why he got you thrown out. My guess is he didn't trust Jules Raymond not to give you the dossier, or at least not to tell you about it.'

Harry nodded. 'No question,' he said. 'I'm sure they killed Castile before I could talk to him and then threw me in jail while they got to Raymond.' He broke off and snapped his fingers. 'If only I'd gone to see him first.'

'D'you think Annie was onto them the first time round?' asked Hélène. 'Her big story?'

He shrugged. 'I'm sure she was convinced of Nkumbé's innocence—'

'But at the same time fell for a guy who was in cahoots with the whole bunch of them?' said Hélène, her voice echoing with disbelief. 'Doesn't sound like the Annie I knew. She used to be the smartest cookie on the block.'

'Right, but he's pretty plausible,' said Harry, spreading the St Tropez photos across the table. 'She wasn't the only smart cookie to be taken in by him.'

Hélène caught her breath, 'Jeez, he's handsome—'

'Isn't he just?' Candace said.

'God, what a smile. No wonder she fell for him.'

'They all did.' Harry said and put the mission's photo down. 'This is Beth Palmer, the young American missionary who fell under his spell.'

'Now we know what he looks like,' said Candace turning to Hélène. 'And where his aunt lives – I forgot to say – in Belleville.'

'Belleville! How could you forget?' Hélène sat up, smiling. 'The cradle of my business empire! Where exactly?'

'Passage Gauthier. Near the Buttes Chaumont.'

Hélène clapped her hands. 'Just round the corner from my first workshop.' Her smile faded. 'Imagine, I might've passed him in the street.'

'You were long gone by the time she arrived, at the end of the Algerian war.'

'I know, and anyway Gauthier is a cul-de-sac—'

The women laughed as if it was a secret joke.

'Gauthier is the name of Hélène's ex,' Candace said. 'He was a Resistance hero and thought his laurels should last him forever.'

Hélène put her hand on Candace's arm. 'Now then, if he hadn't been so idle I'd have never started my own business.' She looked up at the glittering chandelier and raised her glass. 'Here's to silver linings.'

'I wish I could say the same for Bill Holden,' said Candace and immediately looked as if she regretted it.

'You weren't married to him.' Hélène turned a teasing smile onto Harry and said, 'What about you, M. Kaplan, are you married?'

'No.'

'Single, just like Guy Martin. So why did Annie originally say he was complicated?'

'There's one explanation,' Harry said, 'of his Casanova reputation – Annie might've baulked at that, but somehow it doesn't seem quite big enough.'

'On the contrary, for Annie it might've been part of his appeal,' said Hélène. 'She always loved a challenge.'

'Right,' Harry said, 'so maybe she suspected something. She was digging into the Beth Palmer case and it must've been common knowledge that Beth had fallen for him, so maybe she'd turned up something complicated—'

'Wait—' Hélène closed her eyes and frowned. 'Let me get this straight. Annie's out there, running around getting the best stories – she's got the Englishman on a string and is flirting with Castile, and then she meets Guy Martin. She's excited, she writes to Candy about him, he's SOMEONE, finally a guy she's really fallen for – but she's not going to say who he is because it's complicated.'

She looked at Harry and then Candace. 'OK so far?'

They nodded and she carried on, 'But at the same time she's working on a big story with big hitters, the Beth Palmer and Didier Nkumbé case, right?'

'Right – we think so—'

'Fine – so far so good, but there's a problem. You're saying she had her suspicions before she wrote you that postcard and that's what she meant by "complicated"?'

'Yes,' said Candace. 'It makes sense of all the bits.'

'Not to me. This is Annie we're talking about, a smart cookie who's been round the block a few times. She gets the feeling that the guy she's fallen for is complicated in some bad way and still arranges a rendezvous at some Godforsaken beach in the middle of the night! That doesn't sound like Annie to me.' She scuffed angrily at the photos. 'No matter how damned good-looking he was.'

'You're right,' Harry said. 'We don't think she was at the beach at all, which is why we have to get Petridis' dossier translated and find out what actually happened that night. Chances are Castile took her car to Mile 12 to make it look as if she'd gone down there, but she was probably killed in Douala and her body was thrown off the bridge.'

'My God—' Hélène sank back into the sofa and exhaled loudly. 'And that takes two. Somebody to help dump the body and give him a ride back from the beach.' She looked at Candace but didn't say anything. It was all too horribly obvious: Beth had let Guy Martin in and Annie had agreed to meet him somewhere after dark. The thug Castile had done the rest. Or at least that was the very best tilt you could give the story. At the very least Guy Martin had been the bait. Either way, they desperately needed that translation and to track him down.

Candace was wasted. She stretched and got up from the sofa. 'Time for bed,' she said and caught Harry's eye. 'We got to be ready for the big rendezvous in Belleville in the morning.'

32

Paris, France

Harry and Candace were sitting round the breakfast table with Hélène sipping coffee and eating croissants. Hélène got up.

'These are for the apartment,' she said, giving Candace a bunch of keys, 'and the car. It's parked on this side of the square, a blue Volvo. The number is on the back of my card.'

The buzzer went and she jumped. 'Laurent.' She leaned over and shook hands. 'Nice to meet you, Harry. Visit again when this is all over and we'll have fun. You know the song "April in Paris"?'

'Let me help with your bag—' he said, getting up.

'Don't get up; I'll do it,' said Candace pushing him back. She linked arms with her cousin and headed into the hall. 'It's such a shame you have to go.'

'Make sure she takes a break, Harry, you hear,' Hélène called and winked at Candace. 'You too.'

They embraced downstairs on the doorstep. Hélène's driver was standing by the open door of a smart saloon. She took both Candace's hands in hers and looked her in the eye. 'I wish I didn't have to go. There's so much happening here; and Harry's right – these guys have got their backs to the wall. They're not taking hostages. No disrespect but they're out of Harry's league.'

'I know; and I wish you weren't going too.'

'I could cancel—'

'No way. You said it's a huge deal.'

Hélène squeezed her hands and Candace squeezed back. Their eyes shone.

'Stay in touch,' said Hélène. 'Night and day. I want to know exactly what happens when it happens. Jeanne in the office is looking around for someone who might provisionally do the translation. She'll call you, and use my answering service.'

Upstairs Harry was leafing through his notebook.

'She's pretty impressive,' he said.

'Isn't she,' Candace said. 'She gets on with everyone and she's so sociable and smart.'

'Sure.'

He drained his coffee and got up. They were alone and standing close – it felt to her for the first time. Furious with herself, she blushed.

'You ready?'

'Absolutely.' He threw his satchel over his shoulder. 'Time to track him down.'

'Good thing I brought a coat. We're going to notice the difference from Cameroon.'

She was right. In the square below the trees were barely in leaf and the air was sharp with the threat of snow. She turned up the collar and walked quickly across to Hélène's electric-blue saloon.

'I might've guessed,' he said. 'Flash.'

'She had style before she made any money. When she moved here after the war this place was full of poor immigrants—'

'I'm surprised you can remember—'

'I've got a good memory—'

'I'd better remember that,' he said, getting into the passenger seat. It was sunken and in soft grey leather. She flicked the key and the engine caught first time.

'Nowadays immigrants head for Belleville,' she said, pulled out and drove east into the weak winter sunshine. It slanted down from above the steep tiled roofs and picked out the plant pots and washing lines on the wrought-iron balconies. He wished he had a map, the way he always did when he was in a new place.

'Where are we?'

'Rue de la Roquette,' she said. 'There were two prisons just here, one for each sex. They've only just pulled down the women's. They used to do public guillotining out front.' She nodded ahead. 'Those trees up there are in the Cimetière du Père Lachaise – where Piaf is buried, and this was the route the hearse always took.'

He wrinkled his nose. 'The hearse?'

'Don't tell me you're superstitious—'

'Not really.' The grey-white walls of the cemetery entrance came into view. 'It's just that we've had our quota of corpses.'

She took a left turn alongside the cemetery and he glanced at her legs as she shifted gear and only half-listened to the list of famous French buried on the other side of the wall. Quite suddenly there were Africans and Vietnamese on the street.

'See,' she said, 'this is the new Belleville.'

She turned right and pointed out the Parc high above them and the club Java where Piaf used to sing and then made a left and pulled into the side and cut the engine. She took her Michelin guide out of her bag and opened it on a marked page.

'That's Buttes Chaumont,' she said, 'designed by the guy who did the Eiffel Tower, and Guy Martin's street is here.'

He got out and watched her stretch. She looked radiant, despite the circumstances.

'How're we going to play this?' she asked.

'By ear I guess. Who knows, his aunt might've moved.'

'And left a forwarding address – so,' she said, taking his arm, 'what're we waiting for?'

They walked briskly to the junction: Passage Gauthier was on the other side of the road. They crossed and she stifled a giggle. 'We need a disguise, like the Barbouzes.'

'A beard wouldn't suit you—'

'Thank you very much.' She made to hit him with her Michelin guide. 'We'd better be American tourists doing "April in Paris".'

The door of the aunt's house was the middle of the narrow street. There was a 'sold' sign standing in the tiny front garden. A few cars were parked on one side, including a VW van painted with psychedelic colours and a NZ sticker with 'Britain or Bust' on it. Alongside was an old Citroen on blocks with a spreading oil stain underneath.

A taxi turned into the street from the top end and overtook them.

Harry tensed up and watched as it stopped outside the house. She gripped his arm and they drew close as a short dark man emerged from the back seat. He had grizzled silver hair and dark glasses and was dressed in a woollen overcoat.

'A Barbouze,' she whispered.

'Maybe,' he nodded, half-inclined to join her in the game until he saw the way the man limped up the path.

In the same instant, she grabbed him and hissed in his ear, 'It's Gitan.'

'Yeah.'

The man turned towards them and Harry made to duck his head but suddenly the street echoed with the sound of Candace's exaggerated accent.

'Oooh, honey, thank you!' she cried. 'This is just so romantic – Paris in the springtime—'

The words bounced up and down the tight passage, the vowels stretched out in a drawl that was pure Hollywood, but what came next was even more of a shock. She twisted round and slipped her hands inside his jacket. She kissed him, sucking him in deep, her eyes closed and her supple body pressed against him. She tasted of geraniums.

His ears thumped with the sound of his heart. Across the street Guy Martin's aunt had opened the door and was speaking to Gitan. The name Marc floated over and something about a train to Spain but that was all – the rest was Candace, her fingertips like butterflies on his face and her body pressed against his. Out of the corner of his eye he saw Gitan's famous limp turn back down the path and she pulled him even closer.

Eventually he broke away, breathing heavily.

'Jesus. Candace—' he said.

'Mmmm, Harry—' She looked elated.

'Yeah—' The blood was swirling through his ears like waves crashing on a shore, his eyes locked on hers.

'Did you hear what they said?' she asked breathless.

'Not really—' He pulled away.

'Guy Martin is alive alright. He's going to meet Gitan in the café Belleville. That's where he's going now.'

'Jesus—' He shook his head, battling the urge to seize her again.

'I'll follow him.' She skipped up on tiptoes and kissed the end of his nose. 'You bring the car.'

And then she was gone. His eyes followed her Levi's and he shuddered, standing there with a hard-on in his pants and the keys to Hélène's fancy car in his hand.

Gitan was moving fast. He took quick jerked strides, slightly hunched with his hat pulled down, and Candace had to walk briskly to keep him in sight. Her heart was racing but it wasn't the pace – it was the kiss, Guy Martin, the sudden excitement of playing the spook, all crammed into the same crazy second. Her adrenalin was running wild.

At least Gitan was an easy target for her first shot at playing the sleuth. On the main street he stopped at a kiosk for the Sunday papers. People were coming in and out of the Park in the tepid sunshine and she acted like a tourist, wandering around as if she had time on her hands and consulting her Michelin. Out of the corner of her eye she saw him go into a café. She loitered a moment before buying papers from the same kiosk and idling up to the door.

The decor was classic belle époque, all brown wood and frosted glass and wrought-iron railings. It was barely half-full but the air was already hazy with smoke. She hovered in the doorway, taking in the rumble of conversation and clatter of crockery before spotting him at a table obscured by a pot plant on a yellow jardinière.

She took a vacant place a couple of tables away with the plant still between them. Her heart was pounding and she tried to get a grip and told herself nothing could happen: she was in Paris, for God's sake, Dr Candace Fayol, reputable Chicago medic and US citizen, out in the open and in full public view – they couldn't touch her.

But still her heart pounded and she took Hélène's card out of her purse: maybe she should leave a message, tell the office where she was and remember to state the time, the way Harry said if they got separated. She'd waved him away; it seemed ludicrous, too cloak-and-dagger, but now she could see the point and it crossed her mind to get up and walk away and pick up with Harry where they'd just left off. Maybe she should've followed Hélène's advice and taken a break.

Gitan's hat and raincoat were on the chair and she could see his unfolded paper with the headlines on the crisis in Niger – his patch and Messmer's uranium. The waiter brought him a black coffee and a glass of water and left a check on a small tray. She bit into her lip and tried to keep her panic from rising. She realised she needed the toilet.

'*Madame?*'

She jumped. It was the waiter, coming around the plant and leaning slightly towards her. He had a pencil-thin moustache, brown eyes and a clean black apron. She ordered a café au lait and immediately kicked herself for forgetting to screw up her French as if she was the typical American abroad, but mercifully the limp was deeply into his paper and paid her no attention. She busied herself with her own and flipped through the glossy supplement, a profile of bankrupt crime-ridden New York with shots of syringes and addicts and tag lines on soaring heroin use and Nixon's War on Drugs.

She sipped her coffee and wondered what Harry was doing and reminisced about the look he gave her after the kiss, the shock in his eyes as if his head was swimming like hers, and the sound of his voice – 'Jesus. Candace' – all throaty and breathless. She remembered pulling him close and how he'd resisted a split second before folding into her and running his hand up her back. She shivered – but then her waiter came back with her order and a little tray with the check on it.

She thanked him and took hold of the cup. It rattled in her trembling hand so she let it sit and pressed a nail into her thumb and counted breaths the way she told kids to in the clinic. Stay calm, deep breaths, raise your diaphragm, nothing was going to happen: one, two, three...

She had reached five before her hand felt steady enough to pick up her coffee. It was so hot it nearly scalded her tongue and she put it down again with a clatter. Damn. She cursed silently again and again.

She couldn't believe she could get into such a state over nothing, but deep inside her lurked the gruesome sensation that at any minute the man who'd lured Annie to her death – killed her probably and maybe worse before tossing her body off the Wouri bridge – was going to walk through the door.

Panic seized her and she wondered if she was too close and almost got up to change tables before telling herself to keep cool and not attract attention. She opened the paper and hid behind it, but the newsprint and even the pictures were just a jumbled blur. Everything was out of focus, but in her mind she pictured him arriving in precise detail like a clip from a movie: the shadow behind the glass door, a handsome profile and smoking cigarette, and then his entry, Guy Martin – Annie's SOMEONE; Beth Palmer's and Olivia Raymond's nemesis – tanned, handsome, raffish, his dark eyes taking everything in, composed and in control, so mannered and theatrical she wanted to scream. The sheer gall of the man took her breath away and she doubted she'd be able to cope with him in the flesh. She'd freeze or throw up.

She closed her eyes and slowed her breathing and tried to look casual by taking another sip of coffee. A shadow appeared at the door and her heart leaped but it was only another Frenchman taking time off for a late breakfast. She was so relieved that she didn't notice Gitan get up until he'd come round the pot plant and got close enough to nudge her elbow.

Her heart jumped so hard it hurt but he barely broke stride and simply tilted towards her with a murmured '*Pardon, madame*' and disappeared into the phone booth. She watched him go, her heart beating furiously and her mouth as dry as dust. She got up unsteadily. Now she really needed the toilet.

33

Paris, France

The phone rang several times before Guy answered.

'Guy,' Marc said, 'I was beginning to think you hadn't got back. *Bienvenido.*' It was one of the Spanish words he had learned in the Legion.

'*Gracias.* Tia Pilar told me you dropped by.'

'I'm in the Café de Belleville.'

'I thought you were in Niger,' said Guy.

'I was. Did you spot anyone on your tail?'

There was a muttered curse on the other end of the line. 'I thought I'd shaken them off.'

'Who?' said Marc.

'Bounty hunters, Foccart's men. He's still trying to catch me with the money but he's too late. The deal is done.' His voice was suddenly jaunty, that boyish tone and infectious enthusiasm. 'Instead I have half a hectare of Tempranillo and a gorgeous view. You must bring Madeleine—'

Marc broke in. 'I can't, not yet. Look, I need you to pick me up at the back of the café.'

'I can't. Sorry, but I left the car at Vernon.'

'*Merde.*' Marc paused, weighing up the risks and options. 'You'll have to use mine, a white Renault 4 parked on the corner of Rue Carnot.'

'What about the keys?'

'There aren't any. It's stolen—'

'Where are we going in it?' asked Guy.

'Your cottage. Don't worry, the car hasn't been reported yet. The owners are away for the weekend.'

'How d'you know?'

'A kid came round to feed the cat. Anyhow, you know the back of the café where they deliver?'

'Shit, Gitan, of course—' Guy exhaled loudly. 'I've been going there for years.'

'Right, so you know the waiter with the pencil moustache called Georges?'

'Yes. Why?'

'He needs to do us a favour.'

'He'll do it, but I don't like the idea of driving around in a stolen car when Foccart has put a price on my head.'

'I'll handle it.' Marc took a breath. 'I need you to do this for me. For me and Madeleine.'

'OK. When?'

Marc looked at his watch. They didn't have long. 'In fifteen minutes. Out the back at eleven fifteen. OK?'

'As long as the car starts.'

'It will. Reverse up as close as you can and bring a blanket.'

'You planning a picnic or something?'

'Or something.' Marc rang off; they'd have time to catch up later.

Candace watched Gitan go from the phone to the toilet. For a minute, she was worried he was going to slip out the back; she'd seen a couple of the staff go that way. But he came back and sat down. She hid behind her newspaper and tried unsuccessfully to concentrate.

She turned away and focussed on Paris instead: a Sunday morning in April with ordinary people passing ordinary time, a young man leaning over locking a bike, a nun heading for Mass, a woman with a shopping bag and a bundle of daffodils, and a couple leaning against a tree.

A world of bliss and normality, but it was in the real world – and for a second she was tempted to jump up and join them. It was where she belonged. She glanced again at the time and was on the point of paying the check when the waiter came over.

'*Madame*—' He seemed a bit uncomfortable. 'Doctor Fayol?'

She was shocked. 'Yes.'

'From Chicago?'

'Yes. What is it?' she asked, her heart beating fast.

'It's M. Harry Kaplan—' The waiter dropped the 'H' in classic Gallic manner. It was endearing and she managed a half-smile. 'He's outside, at the back.'

She shot up in fright, 'I understand, thank you,' she said, paying the check and clutching the papers to her bosom. She looked for Gitan, but he was gone. The waiter led the way and she followed with an anxious look over her shoulder.

'M. Kaplan told me,' he went on confidentially, showing her through the door, 'that the man outside is an old lover you don't want to see—'

'That's right. I'm finished with him.'

And she meant it. She waved her thanks and set off down the narrow corridor to the back exit. Boxes were stacked high on both sides with logos and brands of flour and coffee and sugar. A large cardboard drum full of chocolate was open. The heady aromas of a French café invaded her senses and she drew in a deep breath. The musty smell of hessian bags mingled in, dust too, stale tobacco, and then something familiar and shockingly out of place, antiseptic, medicinal – chloroform.

She opened her mouth to scream but a cloth covered it and something hit her hard on the back of the neck. Her knees buckled and everything went dark.

Guy was waiting outside the back of the café, the car already in place with the trunk open. His eyes widened in horror as he saw who Marc was dragging out.

'What the hell you doing with her?'

Marc rolled her into the trunk and pulled a cloth and rope from his jacket pocket. 'Gag and tie her up.'

But Guy was rooted to the spot. 'I said what the hell are you doing, Gitan, with Candace Fayol?'

'Do it. I'll be right back.'

He turned on his heel and went back through the stores into the phone booth and dialled Foccart from memory. Georges was watching and he gave him a curt nod as if to say it was all going to plan. Foccart's hotline, 'any time day or night', was ringing in his ear. Bastard. Soon enough he might get the shoe on the other foot.

'Foccart.'

'What now Gitan?'

'Madeleine's passport,' said Benet. 'Today is the day.'

'And all going to plan I'm glad to say—'

He cut in. 'Forget the plan, Foccart. Think about this instead: you remember that Greek pig Petridis?'

Silence: it sounded as if M. Afrique had been stopped dumb in his tracks. Marc imagined him gasping, taken by surprise, his fat mouth hanging open, his brain struggling to pick up the pieces, for a split second losing control.

'Who?' Foccart asked, wrenching it back.

'Petridis. The creep who faked the autopsies for you – hundreds of them, remember? Like Nyobé, Nkumbé, Beth Palmer and Annie Fayol. Castile killed her and Petridis kept a record, like an insurance policy. Canard can't wait to get their hands on it. It'll be the biggest national-security scandal since Ben Barka.'

'I told you I wanted Guy Martin.'

'I've got him too, but you don't really care about him. You care about matters of state security and headlines in Canard and everyone else covering them, not just in Paris but all over the world. You care about you and Messmer finally copping it, just when you thought you had Niger under control.'

An audible intake of breath: Foccart was on the back foot, scrambling for a grip.

'You're going to have to do business with me,' Marc said, 'The passport—'

The sound of something slapped down on the desk interrupted him.

'I've got it right here,' said Foccart. 'I've been waiting for your call.'

'I've called—'

'You could be lying—'

'Why would I? You haven't given a thought to Petridis for years. You dumped him like Dupin and Castile and they're all coming back to bite you in the arse—'

'Prove it.'

Was that a quaver of uncertainty in the fat bastard's throat? Was he was still scrambling, trying to figure out how he'd let such a detail slip when there'd been so much hanging on it? Heads would roll in the Piscine.

Gitan allowed himself a smile. 'I don't have to prove it. You can't risk taking a gamble on a Swiss passport against matters of state security – come on, Foccart, you know you're going to save your ass and do the deal. Messmer will be indebted to you for saving his. You might even get your job back.'

'You're right.' M. Afrique sounded calm. 'Where do we do it?'

'Café de la Gare in Vernon. Four o'clock this afternoon. Be there to take a call. And leave your muscle in the Piscine.'

Marc put the phone down nice and gently but his insides screamed hatred and revenge – and subsiding confidence. When had anyone like him told Foccart what to do?

Candace came round. Her head ached horribly. She opened her eyes. Her vision seemed blurred but she couldn't tell for sure because it was dark. She was rolled up in a heavy blanket and dust filled her throat and nostrils. She was gagged and the back of her neck hurt. She moved her head and pain stabbed at the back of her eyes. Under her was a cold metal floor throbbing in slow-moving traffic. She tried to move her arms but her wrists were tied and her heart sank as she made sense of it all.

Somebody had hit her from behind. Her mouth was still acrid with chloroform. She closed her eyes and moved her head carefully. She was a medic, and she knew about blows to the head, concussion and brain damage. But it didn't feel that bad and suddenly memories of Belleville came back to her: Tia Pilar's house, following Gitan, the café, smells of coffee and pastries – and Harry's kiss.

Waves of jumbled images washed over her: the taste of him, him saving her at Mile 12, crushing herself against his chest – and the waiter giving her a message from him. She was too afraid to think. Dread overtook her and all she could do was register the bare facts: she was under a blanket in the back of a car, going somewhere; a prisoner.

What were they going to do to her? Men usually abducted women for one reason. Her heart vaulted with fear and a scream formed but couldn't escape. The gag in her mouth stopped it and her chest was so tight she could scarcely breathe. She had never felt so lost and like a complete sham she started to pray. Please God. Please.

She couldn't beat the question off. It kept coming back to her: what were they going to do to her? She prayed again. She prayed that Harry knew what'd happened and had called the police. But then, with a twist so brutal that it hurt, she remembered that the men running things in Cameroon were the gendarmes. Higher up even, and it came back to her who they were, a nightmare but true: the French prime minister, Jacques Foccart and Guy Martin – the man Annie had fallen for, a secret agent working undercover.

And the celebrated limp – the man pulling the strings in Douala who she'd followed to the Belleville café. It came to her like a hammer blow: she was his prisoner, Gitan's. After that it took every grain of her courage just to hang on. She told herself that she hadn't survived the riptide at Mile 12 to die in the back of a car. The Fayols didn't give in without a fight. Annie hadn't made it easy for them, so nor should she. She had to focus and tune in to every clue where she was going and what they were going to do.

But there was nowhere to go inside her head. Nothing in her life had prepared her for this. This wasn't normal mortality. She'd seen victims of violence in the clinic, too many times – she'd treated them, for God's sake: gunshot wounds, stabbings, horrendous abuse – and some had been to the brink and come back, but those guys were different. Their lives had been chaotic and hers had been ordered, even after Annie's death and her parents' divorce. A wave of panic surged through her and her mind began to unravel. She was on the very edge of breaking down and she grasped at the straw above: his voice. She could hear his voice.

Concentrate on that accent.

She hammered the words onto her mind like nails into a wall. It was the voice from outside the old lady's house. Harry hadn't been able to understand it. Marc Benet. The man's name came back to her, dark enough for an Arab, short silver-flecked hair and a strong aquiline nose. He could have been handsome – and for sure he looked powerful, fearsome. Candace reached back to the fragments and pieced them together: Cameroon, Niger, Bamenda, Pierre Messmer – what chance had she, a broken reed in the teeth of their storm?

Annie was dead. Like Harry said, nothing was going to bring her back. Candace shut her eyes tight and wished she could hug herself to sleep and wake up to find it'd all been a nightmare. Why, oh why had she been such a fool to imagine she could play with fire? She forced herself with every fibre to still her mind and just listen, syllable by syllable, word by word, sentence by sentence to that accent and what Gitan was saying.

'I told you, Guy—'

Her heart stopped and her mind froze. Guy – Benet was talking to Guy Martin. Annie's SOMEONE was sitting within feet of her head. She clenched her fists and her arms and shoulders cried out in pain. Every nerve and muscle in her body screamed with agony and she told herself to try to relax – some kind of Buddhist mantra that she'd never mastered – but how could she with Guy Martin so close?

Benet's accent came again – 'He thinks he's got me by the balls—' – followed by a slamming noise of a fist beating against the dash and a curse cut short by the sound of a police siren close behind. Her heart leaped. Harry had done it, mission impossible! She was safe!

'Merde—'

Benet's accent clashed with an educated voice; she imagined this was the Left Bank tone of Guy Martin. 'You said it hadn't been reported.'

'They must've come home early.'

The sirens: Candace could hear two, piercingly beautiful, miraculously loud and getting louder and the car was slowing down. It lurched and bumped and she heard the sound of crushed gravel. Guy Martin was swearing – he didn't need any hassles with the gendarmes. The car bumped again and there was a short squeal of brakes and it came to a halt. The engine died, the throb stilled and the screaming sirens fell away.

'Leave it to me.' Benet: she heard him get out.

'What about Candy?'

'Watch her.'

The sound of her pet name in Guy Martin's mouth crashed through everything else. Candy – how dare he? Only her father and Annie had called her that, along with her best girlfriend and the boy who'd taken her to her first prom. Bill Holden Jnr had tried and she'd nearly spat at him, but now her eyes filled with tears. She was shaking with anger and relief.

She couldn't wait for the back to fly open and the blanket to be swept aside. Harry would be with them. She wriggled and waited, but it stayed shut. She strained her ears, but there was no sound of Harry, only the distant murmur of two voices, one of them Benet's. It started low and insistent and rose to a bullying threat. Slowly but surely, and with mounting horror, it dawned on her that something was wrong. She wasn't going to be rescued.

Gitan was still in charge, the man who'd been pulling the strings from the very start. She tried kicking out. She tried screaming. She could hardly move and produced not a murmur and nobody took a blind bit of notice. The sounds of Benet's voice softening to an '*Au revoir*' and the door slamming hit her as hard as an express train and her hopes were dashed to ruins.

She closed her eyes and darkness closed in as the engine kicked into life and the floor shuddered. She listened to the noise of gravel spitting under rubber and the crashing of a gear. Speed took over – a smooth lift like the moment of take-off in a plane.

'Shit—' Guy Martin said, exhaling loudly. 'What did you say?'

'I told them it was a matter of national security and to call Foccart on his hotline. I gave them the number.'

Candace curled up in dread with the words ringing in her ears. Foccart and national security: Annie's big hitters, a lethal combination with a long reach and no questions asked. She lay there helpless and alone, her will to fight and hold on wasting away. She told herself again and again that she was not ready to die and that these men had no cause to kill her. She believed in reason, didn't she? Deliver us from evil.

The hushed words from the Lord's Prayer came back to her and she was caught between God – a concept she'd ridiculed in every working moment of her life – and a mounting dread that evil did exist – and was right here, a raw uncivilised id, turning her life inside out. How and why could she ever have doubted it after what these men had done to Annie and Beth Palmer? How could she have put her faith in such a puny weapon as reason? They'd trash it without a second thought.

The car was slowing; the occasional stop, like a red light, and a longer one when they both got out and then somehow there was a quieter feel to the world outside her bubble of hell – a different tone to the tyres on the road and an uneven surface. It felt as if they were getting somewhere and the car stopped and the engine died.

'Isabella told me where to find this place,' said Gitan as they both got out. 'I didn't give her any choice so don't blame her.'

'I won't.'

The trunk opened and Candace was lifted out. She struggled against them and Gitan cursed. He was holding her legs and his grip tightened. Keys jangled and a door creaked open. They were breathing harder like they were going upstairs and her hip banged against a hard edge. She winced and Gitan cursed again. Guy Martin said something in a language she didn't understand, maybe Arabic, and Gitan just snorted contempt. 'You think Foccart has a soft side,' he said.

'Of course not.'

She bumped against something again and Guy said, 'In here,' and it sounded as if a door was being kicked open. She prayed they'd at least untie her gag.

'On the bed.'

She was lowered and half-dropped.

'Jesus, Foccart, of all people,' said Guy Martin, and something else in Arabic – an expletive. 'What the devil were you thinking of?'

'He came to me because he'd had to dump all his old part timers.' He cursed. 'He baited the trap with the passport and I thought I could handle it—'

'You could've. You didn't have to dance to his tune.'

'Fuck you, Guy. He changed the terms – your head on a plate or no passport for Madeleine.'

'Why didn't you just take Madeleine and cross at one of those unguarded border posts that ETA use?'

Gitan cursed, a cry of frustration. 'He'd thought ahead, the way he always did. He had the house covered. They showed themselves to me, like a warning not to run, and then that fucking colon popped up with a wildcard. Wanted me to tell Messmer about it, so I sent the Monkey—'

'But Castile didn't have it, the Americans did—'

'Yeah, but now we've got the girl, they'll have to give it to me—'

They were moving away from her. The door creaked and shut. The last thing she heard was Gitan telling Guy to get out while he could and that one sister from the Fayol family should be enough for any man.

34

Paris

Eileen watched Harry pull up opposite the café and disappear inside. To all outward appearances she was a fashionably dressed mature woman with one serene eye on the colourful stream of people passing and the other on the headline story of Niger's threat to Plan Messmer, but inside she was churning.

She'd had her stint on the analyst's couch in the past and knew all about her neuroses and shortcomings – and she couldn't believe she'd let illusions of grandeur sabotage her normal measured assessment of reality. She'd been fool enough to entertain the idea she'd been in control. It would've been laughable if she hadn't put people's lives at risk.

She put her hand in her jacket pocket and gripped the butt of her gun. It didn't do much to reassure her: Gitan, reluctant hero and rogue agent, was flying solo and she wished she understood his desperation. It didn't add up, but like a quail with a broken wing he'd limped his way to the Café Belleville and taken Candace Fayol with him.

He was the guy in control except he didn't have Petridis' dossier. She'd tell Harry that a straight exchange, Candace for the dossier, was the best deal they could muster. She got up and tucked the paper under her arm: there would be time enough for her to play her wild-card. Maybe, just maybe, she wasn't fooling herself and could still get even.

The café door flew open and Harry hurtled out carrying a map and crossed the street without a glance at the traffic. He nearly collided with a Vespa and a young woman riding pillion screamed at him. As he got in on the driver's side Eileen opened the door and slipped into the passenger seat. She pointed the gun at his chest and he recoiled in shock.

'Jesus, O'Connell—' His eyes darted from hers to the gun, his body poised to lunge.

'Don't even think about it,' she said, jerking the gun up into his face. 'We both need to be at our best.'

'What's the "we" bullshit—?'

'We're on the same side.'

He swore. 'I already heard you say that at La Frégate.'

'Really?' She was impressed. 'Where were you?'

'Outside on the back porch.'

'So you overheard us talking.' Like how she wanted to get even with the bastards who'd compromised her over Beth Palmer and Didier Nkumbé. She'd sent two reports to Langley on how dumb it was to support the French, years before they'd been suckered into Vietnam, but the idiots had just filed them both under 'dissent'.

Harry grunted. 'I already knew about Martin and Beth Palmer and him operating undercover. And about Castile dumping Annie's car at the beach.'

She smiled. She'd always figured Harry Kaplan was a cut above the average. 'Nice work.'

'Yeah, and I tracked him to some dive near La Frégate where he'd done a disappearing act. Left everything behind, including the Hertz car and his passport.' He cast her a sidelong glance. 'I haven't worked out why, except there were some guys on his tail.'

She looked at him: it was true, they were on the same side, always had been really, so there was no point keeping him in the dark. 'He got his hand in the till in Biafra,' she said, 'some dissent over strategy. Anyway, I think I know where we're going now – Vernon.'

He blinked. 'How the hell did you know?'

She shrugged amiably and smiled at him: he was an attractive man. 'The up side of Raymond's obsession with Guy Martin. He showed me.'

'You're lying. The PI report on his wife's affair only gave Tia Pilar's address.'

'Very good, Mr Kaplan,' she said, 'but Raymond wouldn't let it alone. He got his investigator to track Martin to his hideout in the forest—'

'I don't give a damn about that now!' He brandished the map. 'They've got Candace, for God's sake.'

'I know. You let them lure her.'

'I don't need you to tell me,' he said.

'Right, they have her but I assume you have Petridis' dossier.' She glanced at the bag on the back seat and raised an eyebrow. 'I'm surprised you let it out of your sight. Lucky I was here to keep an eye on it.'

He shook his head. 'Bullshit.'

'We all make mistakes.' She patted his thigh with the gun and put it away. 'Now, what are we supposed to do next?'

He threw her a bitter sidelong glance. 'We—'

She nodded, 'I told you, you need me more than you know.'

'OK.' He nodded emphatically, accepting the situation. 'We go to Café de la Gare at Vernon. They'll call me there with further instructions.' He started the car.

'That's better.'

He took a deep breath. 'They said no harm will come to her – bastards!' He slammed the dash with his fist. 'That's what bastards like that always say.'

The way she figured it, Gitan and Guy Martin weren't quite 'they', but she let it go.

She directed him north and they picked up the new ring road going west, Sunday lunchtime and traffic was light. In 10 minutes, they were up to the Nanterre turning and onto the main road for Normandy. At Bonnières they took a right turn at some lights, which ran steeply down to the Seine and within another 10 minutes they were on the outskirts of town with the bridge and the wooded bluffs in clear sight.

The signs took them through the centre to the railway station and the Café de la Gare was nestled into a corner site with tattered green-and-white striped awning. Plastic tables and chairs were stacked up to one side of the terrace, still waiting for spring, and a dim light burned in the window. The notice hanging in the door said it was closed.

'I don't like it,' she said.

Harry nodded. 'We're supposed to take their call here. Maybe they told them not to open.'

She looked around. 'Maybe, although doing something different only attracts attention.'

He hammered on the door and eventually a young woman appeared. She looked very anxious but opened up.

'Hello,' she said.

Eileen O'Connell moved forward and smiled. 'Can we come in for a minute please?'

The young woman hesitated and then stood back.

They moved into the café area. A tray of dirty crockery had been left on the zinc bar and the fireplace was heaped with ash. The place smelt of wood-smoke, floor polish and the memory of fresh pastries. Over the mantelpiece was an ancient shotgun and a pair of 12-point antlers dated 1966. To one side of the fireplace was a glass trophy case exhibiting a medium-sized wild boar.

'You heard from M. Martinez this morning?' Harry asked. 'Did he tell you not to open?'

'Yes.' She swallowed and closed her eyes. 'He stopped by on the way to the cottage to tell me you were coming.'

'Was he on his own?' asked Eileen O'Connell.

She shook her head. 'Another man was driving.'

'What car?'

She shrugged. 'White. Boxy.' She looked over his shoulder nervously, her eyes darting around the station car park and up in the sky.

Harry grabbed her arm tight. 'What's wrong?'

'Nothing.'

'Something else is bothering you.'

She swallowed again and her eyes shone with tears. 'We're illegals—' she said as if that said it all.

He understood. 'You don't want anything to do with the gendarmes, is that it?'

'*Si, si*,' she spluttered.

He nodded and pointed at the stuffed boar. 'Who shot that?'

'My husband.'

'Where's his gun?' He gripped her arm tight, his thumb pressing into her flesh. 'Show me.'

She led the way to a locked cupboard in a utility room off the kitchen. 'He's got the key,' she said.

Harry grabbed a big kitchen knife and slammed it into the wood and levered at it. Splinters flew and he worked it in again. The cheap pine split easily and he ripped at it and wrenched at the door but it wouldn't shift. Out of the corner of his eye he caught sight of an old-fashioned set of scales.

'Where are the weights?' he asked, pointing with the knife. 'The heaviest.'

She dropped to her knees and reached under the cupboard, pulling out a 5kg weight. He took it and hammered at the lock and clasp, smashing it repeatedly until the door hung free. Inside were a double-barrelled 12-bore shotgun and a hunting rifle with a pair of binoculars hanging from a brass hook.

Neatly arranged in the well were boxes of cartridges and shells. He put the binoculars over his shoulder and took the shotgun down and tested the trigger mechanism before loading and stuffing his coat pockets with cartridges.

Outside he glanced at O'Connell. Her face was pale and her features pinched with worry.

'Whose side are they on?' he asked.

She shrugged. 'Depends who's coming. Either way it would be good to get the upper hand before they arrive.' She gave him a long sober look. 'I've seen too many innocent people caught in the crossfire.'

'Me too.'

He followed her directions deep into the forest.

'This track here,' she said and he drove past slowly enough to catch sight of the cottage at the end of the track with a white Renault 4 parked out front. About 100 yards up the road there was an opening in the forest where a tree had been felled. Harry eased the Volvo over the soft verge and across the carpet of sawdust and tucked it in as far from the road as possible. He cut the engine and they listened. A tractor passed on the road and in the distance a chainsaw was working.

They got out quietly and he gave her the keys.

'It'll take you at least ten minutes to work your way round to the back,' she said. 'More if they've let it get overgrown since I was here. Let's say in fifteen minutes I'll drive up the front and bang on the door, enough to distract them, and you come through the back.'

He nodded. 'If it's open.'

'It should be.'

'Right, but they're going to figure something's wrong—'

'For sure. That's what I'm worried about. It's not going to be the 5th Cavalry.' She looked at her watch and waved him on his way. 'So fifteen minutes from now. Good luck.'

The trees were just coming into leaf, giving the canopy above him a wispy light green, and he was glad he'd found the husband's camouflaged hunting jacket. The pockets were bigger than his coat and the colours blended in. Underfoot there was spring garlic with white flowers. The sky was grey and there was a hint of rain in the air. He reckoned he was about 300 yards from the cottage. A dry twig snapped under his foot and a jay dashed through the trees in a flash of colour. It was very quiet.

He moved through the trees, staying as far as possible out of sight. After a few minutes, he stopped and used the binoculars but he was still deep in the forest. He edged forwards, running from tree to tree and checking out the way ahead. His head was clear but his heart was racing. He listened for sounds: there was still nothing but he thought he detected the scent of wood-smoke. He had to be near. Suddenly he heard the unmistakable thwack of an axe splitting logs.

Stooping low he set off at a trot to his right, sweeping round towards the back of the cottage and the outbuildings. A pigeon started up a love call above his head and then clattered away through the branches. He stopped and waited with a beating heart but the rhythm of the axe ran on uninterrupted and he let out his breath in relief. Leaving the sound of the axe behind he moved away from the cottage and came across a stream rushing headlong for the Seine.

It was swollen with rain and tumbled brown and white over the rocks, too deep and turbulent for him to cross without getting wet. On the other side rose an outcrop of moss-covered rock interspersed with fern. He slithered across, stumbling from one visible stone to another and more than once slipping into the water. Once he was on the other side he scrambled up the rock face and collapsed panting on the flat surface.

The rock was cold against his cheek, his feet tingled with the cold water and his breath came in deep gasps, but it had been worth it. Through the trees he could make out a chimney and tiled roof, and by positioning himself further to the right a part of the cottage came into view. He took the binoculars out and adjusted them. He was looking at Martin's new bathroom extension, a lace curtain modestly covering the window. To one side he could see the back door, slightly ajar, and the hood of a red saloon, but the axe man was out of sight.

He raised the binoculars to the flat roof and the spare room. There was a water butt gathering rainwater and Harry calculated that it would be easy enough to use it as a platform to get onto the roof. He focussed on the windows but the drapes hadn't been pulled back. Suddenly a figure flitted across the yard at the back and shut the door. Harry rolled away and dropped down the edge of the rocks and ran through the woods until he could see the cottage only 20 yards away. He glanced at his watch: less than five minutes to go.

His chest was heaving and sweat ran into his eye. Working round to his right, he used the woodshed as cover and broke out of the forest without being in view of the windows. He pressed himself up against the wall and got his breath back before inching round the side. Nobody was in sight.

He strained his ears but all he could hear was another pigeon cooing and the rustle of wind in the trees. He gripped the gun and scanned the windows. The back door was open; he didn't need to force the bedroom window – he had a shotgun and surprise on his side. He could walk straight in. He heard the Volvo coming up the track and a shout from inside. Sixty seconds to zero.

The drapes were closed but in the dim light Candace could make out where she was. They'd carried her out of the car and upstairs still wrapped in the blanket and laid her on a double bed. Her head ached but her mouth was not so dry. One of them had loosened the gag before lifting her out and she'd pretended to be only semi-conscious.

She stretched her legs gingerly. Her ankles and wrists were tied but she could move her hands and arms in front of her. She moved her head. Her neck was stiff and she could feel where they'd hit her. She looked around slowly. Dim light came in from around the drapes.

There was a chest of drawers on the other side of the room with a mirror on it and a few ornaments. Outside she could hear someone chopping wood and a little way off the sound of a car passing. A pigeon cooed and in the distance a chainsaw whined. She was in the country – most likely near Guy Martin's mailbox address at the station café in Vernon.

She closed her eyes and tried to hold down her panic. She told herself that Harry would be looking for her. He knew who'd kidnapped her and would figure out where they'd taken her, and anyhow they'd make contact. The whole point was to get the Petridis notebook and she was the trade. They had no reason to harm her because they were secret agents not violent rapists, although the thought didn't do much to quell her fears.

On the edge of her consciousness a voice kept whispering that Annie had been naked when she'd been found and that Beth Palmer had been raped before being strangled. She bit her lip hard and took a deep breath and counted to 10 before taking another. She told herself to put her imagination on hold and that she couldn't afford to turn into a jelly.

She stretched her legs again and reached out with her arms. Her wrists were tied with cord but by flexing her fingers she loosened the bonds. She drew her legs to the side of the bed and let them slide over.

The movement sent a piercing pain through her head but it helped her sit up. Her head swam and waves of nausea rose through her.

She gasped at another breath and strained her ears. She could still hear the steady everyday rhythm of someone chopping wood. She stood up slowly, steadying herself on the bedside table as her knees briefly buckled. She closed her eyes. What the hell was she doing? She had no answer but she bent her knees and fell gently forwards onto her elbows and arms. She held her breath and listened but all she could hear was the same rhythmic sound of splintering wood.

She reached out by wriggling her wrists and elbows and then drew her legs forwards and arched her back like a caterpillar. In this way, she made her way laboriously towards the window. She was doing something, fighting back, and her spirits lifted. She made the same move again and calculated she needed two more before getting to the window. She wanted to see who was chopping wood and to let in a little more light.

Her heart was beating hard and she was out of breath by the time she reached the window. The walls of the cottage were more than two feet thick and there was a deep sill. Below her she could see Gitan. She watched him swing the axe and split the log. He took another from the pile and set it up before another lithe and accurate swing cut it neatly in half.

Time stood still: the man who'd pulled the strings in Cameroon was splitting firewood and stacking it in a basket – an utterly normal act. As she watched a thought struck her. Secret agents kept guns in their bedrooms. She pulled the drapes open a fraction to let in more light and rolled to one side before getting back onto her knees. She looked around.

On the far side of the room there was a low set of drawers. She looked back at where she'd come from: there was a drawer in the bedside table as well. She rolled over a couple more times and then worked her way caterpillar-like back to the bed. Outside the sound of the axe had stopped and she could hear logs being thrown into a basket.

She pulled the drawer open but it jammed against something at the back. She prayed for a gun – she could hardly bear to look – and her heart leaped. It was something shadowy and black almost out of sight and in her rush to get at it she scraped her knuckles. She stifled a curse and tried again, this time flattening her hands together and twisting her arms sideways, straining to reach and fighting off thoughts that it wouldn't be loaded. What would be the point of keeping it there otherwise?

She stretched her fingers out further, her face resting on the top of the chest of drawers. Her nail caught at something and she hooked it. At first it felt as if it was stuck fast but it suddenly gave and swivelled loose and she gave a stifled cry. But it didn't feel right. It wasn't metal. She slumped over as it came free in her hand. It was an old photograph album and as she opened it her heart froze. The pictures were of Annie smiling happily; in one of them she worked at her typewriter, smoking a cigarette and naked from the waist up.

Candace barely had time to flip through the pages before a car pulled up outside and someone started hammering on the front door. An American voice was calling for them to open up, a woman. In the distance, she could hear the insistent throb of a helicopter approaching. The voice quietened down and the front door slammed shut. Somebody was coming up the stairs, two at a time.

35

Vernon, near Paris

The bedroom door opened and she turned with the album still clutched in her hands: Guy Martin. He crossed the room and she flinched and fell back but all he did was open the drapes. Light filled the room and he dropped onto one knee beside her. He was holding a knife but his movements were calm and gentle.

'I was going to show you that,' he said, undoing her gag and cutting through the cords. He helped her to her feet and she flexed her arms while he stooped to gather the photos and album, as if he was rescuing them.

'I was in love with her,' he said and words and images rushed through her head with just one thought making it out the other side.

'You were in on it—' She was trembling.

'I tried to warn her, but it went wrong.' He sagged. 'They were only supposed to take her film and scare her off, but it was the chance that Castile had been waiting for, so—' He faltered and gestured at the room and then the door. 'We've got your man Kaplan and the US *chargée* downstairs. I'm sorry but we needed the Greek's dossier. If we'd got hold of it in Cameroon none of this would've happened.'

Her head swam. She and Harry had figured Annie had never been at the beach and guessed Castile had been involved, but nothing much else. She lunged at the album, furious indignation replacing fear. 'You bastard. She was no more than a trophy to you—'

He managed to look forlorn and misunderstood. He put the album back in the drawer and closed it. 'I told you the truth: I was in love with her.'

She clenched her fists and wanted to batter him. Monster – she struggled for the words. 'You stood by and let it happen; helped them.'

He shook his head. 'I didn't. I warned her to put the film into the British mail.'

The words reverberated in Candace's mind: Annie had mailed it and she'd got it developed nearly 20 years later. With the card: SOMEONE – sky high...

She looked at him: her big sister's *someone*. Really? She felt her certainty wilt. 'She said it was complicated—'

'It was,' he said, still a man unjustly misunderstood. '*I was*. We were trying to figure a way out.'

'Of what?'

'Our predicament.' He shrugged. 'We weren't ready for the way it took us, neither of us. Like a storm.' He closed his eyes and shook his head, muttering under his breath so quiet she hardly heard. 'I never got over her.'

She lost it. 'You never got over her!' she screamed. Bastard—' She threw herself at him, clawing at his eyes, but his hands moved faster and caught her wrists. Their faces were close, her body against his, his breath on her cheek. 'What about Olivia Raymond then?' she spat at him. 'Did you get over *her*?'

He recoiled and his hands dropped to his sides, momentarily unsure.

'Well? *Did* you, or was it just another trophy, another death—'

'I didn't know—'

'That she'd kill herself?'

He sighed. 'No, I had no idea, although I knew she was angry. I told her to go back to her husband.' He half turned back to the bedside table. 'But then she found the album. She shouldn't have gone looking but she was dead set on finding something about Annie. She said she'd suspected all along, as if I was only ever half there.'

His words took Candace back to Mile 12, deep down in the dark, bubbles of air and light above her reaching for the surface. Olivia Raymond had walked into the riptide with only one thing in mind, to commemorate Annie's death with her own. Candace tore the drawer open and seized the album, brandishing it in Guy Martin's face.

'She killed herself because of this, didn't she?' she said. It was suddenly obvious. 'You broke her heart – her will to live. You must've known.'

'Unfortunately.' He nodded. 'She said I was still in love with Annie, the album proved it and that she was just a stop gap.'

'She was right. You took her to St Tropez. I've seen those photos.' She looked him over: a weak man, vain, self-regarding, yes; but a murderer? It didn't seem so likely anymore. 'Did you tell her that it was *complicated* too?'

'No, no, never,' he said, shaking his head. 'It wasn't. I'm not proud of it, but it was just an affair, part of what went on, bored women with too much time on their hands and the steamy weather. Annie was different. It was complicated for her. She was in love with her work. You must've known.'

Candace did. 'Yes.'

'And it was complicated for me too.' He pulled open the lower drawer and took out a couple of *Life* magazines, the top one from 1944 with a photo of a man on the front. 'General Juin, Hero of the Battle of Monte Cassino,' he said.

He flipped it open and her eye travelled across a number of shots of troops in wild terrain, the Benedictine monastery perched on the rugged peak and the same soldier on a tough and inelegant horse. The other magazine was from 1956, with the main story from the Battle of Algiers and the number of French troops approaching half a million.

'General Juin was my patron,' Martin said, tilting his handsome head at the portrait. 'He supported my aunt and paid for my education. He exhorted me to get to the top like he had, trusted me to, both of us *pieds-noirs*, colons caught up between France and the Maghreb, rejected in the one and resented in the other.'

He stared at her defiantly. 'He always opposed Algerian independence and was put under house arrest at the time of the army's putsch. That's what I told Annie: I couldn't quit the French secret service just like that. There was too much riding on it. I needed time.' He put the magazines back in the drawer. 'I told her it was complicated for me as well, but she was on the side of the angels.'

He shut the drawer with a curt finality that suggested he still harboured a grudge either against Annie or France, or maybe just circumstance. The sound of the helicopter grew louder and changed pitch as if it was landing. Guy Martin gestured at it and said, 'That'll be Foccart. We'd better get moving.'

Downstairs they found Gitan holding a shotgun, with Harry sprawled on the sofa looking dazed and a sharply dressed woman in her mid-fifties sitting in an easy chair. Candace caught Harry's eye and was on the point of crossing over to him when the woman got up and stepped forward with an outstretched hand.

'Dr Fayol,' she said, smiling a trifle grimly. 'We should've met under better circumstances. I'm Eileen O'Connell, US *chargée* in Douala at the time of your sister's untimely death.'

After a second's hesitation Candace took her hand. The malice she'd felt for the Ice Maiden had dissipated, although she still wanted to know why the woman had kept her secrets hidden for so many years. That she couldn't easily forgive.

'I'm Marc Benet,' said Gitan, reaching out his right hand with the shotgun in his left. Petridis' dossier was on the table beside him. 'We haven't really met either.'

She thought he was taunting her but the expression on his hard, sculpted features was calm and serious.

'I'm sorry we had to bring you out here against your will.'

'Really.' It was surreal. She accepted his hand and returned the firm grip. He looked her in the eye and she was momentarily stilled. 'And now you're pointing a gun at me.'

He put a hand on the dossier. 'I'm just guarding this.' He swept the gun over them and came to rest pointing at the door. The throb of the helicopter had changed tone again as if it was just ticking over. 'You all should get out while you can.' He glanced at Guy Martin and gestured at the map on the wall of 'Euskadi', the Basque national homeland as claimed by the terrorist organisation ETA.

'Especially you, Guy. Foccart is gunning for you as well as me,' he said.

'But I'd rather like to take advantage of this opportunity to meet the ex-Minister for Africa and Madagascar,' said Eileen O'Connell with a smile. 'To my knowledge our paths have never crossed, which is surprising given how close he was to the late General de Gaulle.'

The words were barely out of her mouth before they were drowned out by the raucous bellowing of police sirens. Blinking blue lights flashed round the walls of the cottage as the cars swept up the drive and screeched to a halt.

'It seems it's too late,' she said, holding Gitan's sombre gaze. 'But, in any case, M. Benet, I think you might be glad of my support.' She dropped her eyes to the dossier and took a folded sheet of paper from her bag. 'After all, what's to stop the ex-minister from walking out of here with that irreplaceable evidence of his government's criminal past in Cameroon? You don't have a back-up copy and by the sound of it' – she glanced sadly at the shot gun – 'you're definitely out-numbered.'

Marc Benet was beating off memories of the past just when he needed to focus on the present. Figures and images spun round him, and stupid questions jumped up, like whether the US *chargée* had been with de Gaulle in 1940. She had changed since the last time they'd met but she was still eye-catching. He remembered Monique being there, big with the baby and wanting to go home early. So had he. He'd never liked those parties Guy threw at the bar, whatever kind of 'honey trap' was planned.

He shook the memories out of his head and gripped the stock of the shotgun. Any minute Foccart would be joining them, their deal hanging on the thread of Petridis' dossier. He cursed: he shouldn't have asked the Monkey to deal with it and gone himself; but the guns had needed him – my God, so they had too, every last ounce of his attention and still he hadn't been able to save Dayak. The thought fled through his mind just as the door burst open and three uniformed gendarmes with sub-machines fanned out across the room.

He shot out a hand and caught the slender biceps of the American medic. She cursed him but with one sharp twist he'd flipped her across him like a shield and forced the barrel of the gun into the soft flesh under her jaw. He felt her quiver and dug his chin into her neck and whispered, 'Just do as I say and you won't get hurt.' Even Foccart would have trouble explaining away the death of an innocent American, especially the sister of a photojournalist drowned in suspicious circumstances in one of his many back patches. They didn't call him M. Afrique for nothing.

And here he was, with his balding dome, double chin and trademark smirk, looking like a bank manager wearing his crumpled winter suit well into spring. Beads of sweat sparkled on his brow. Behind him was the young toff Pleven brandishing the Marakov, now every inch the seasoned agent.

'Get them out of here,' Marc said, his gaze settling on each gendarme in turn. They stared back, waiting for the boss. 'Or I'll blow her pretty American brains all over the ceiling.'

Foccart nodded at the gendarmes, the smirk still in place, guns down, and gave his young assistant a look. The Marakov disappeared and the gendarmes relaxed. Kaplan came across and Marc released the woman and rested the gun on the table.

'My, what excessive drama, Gitan,' Foccart exclaimed, glancing casually round the assembled company. 'Quite a gathering too.'

'Witnesses,' he said. 'Americans. Out of your reach.'

'Yes indeed,' Foccart said, taking a small transistor radio from his pocket and putting it on the table. 'International witnesses to a momentous event for France.'

He flicked a switch and a clear triumphant voice filled the room. The communication had been issued earlier that morning from Niamey, capital of Niger. It announced that an armed rebellion against the incumbent president had been successful. The TV and radio stations were in rebel hands and the presidential palace had been sacked. The welfare and whereabouts of the ousted president and his family were not known for certain but the Nigerien people had been reassured that the old regime had been crushed and superseded.

Colonel Seyni Kountché had taken over the reins of power and was setting up an interim government. He had made a short address to the nation and international press corps to the effect that recent political agitation over the uranium mines at Arlit would be a thing of the past and that Paris was guaranteed full and indefinite future co-operation over the resource.

French personnel would remain in post and production levels would be boosted in accordance with Plan Messmer and making France self-sufficient in energy by the year 2000.

Colonel Kountché had concluded his message with a tribute to the tradition of long-standing co-operation with Paris and a clipped rebuttal of any possibility of Niger entering into a political alliance with neighbouring Libya and Colonel Gaddafi. Libyan personnel temporarily based in the country were being rounded up and transported back across the border. The world was waiting for a reaction from Tripoli.

'Marvellous news – and virtually bloodless,' said Foccart, switching off the radio and beaming round the room. 'You are privileged witnesses to this momentous event. It's only just happened.' He gave the radio an affectionate tap and put it away.

'With a little help from the Paras?' asked Eileen. 'Or was it just a coincidence they were crawling all over Douala airport the last few days?'

Foccart lifted himself on his toes as if he'd only just noticed her and raised his eyebrows. 'Aaah, *madame*, I don't think we've had the pleasure—'

'No we haven't,' she said. 'Although we might've attended the same events.' She stepped forwards with an out-stretched hand. 'Eileen O'Connell. I was US *chargée* in Douala at the time of the war of national liberation but I don't believe our paths ever crossed. I'm sure I'd remember.'

His hand was soft and moist. His small eyes flicked from hers to the seething figure behind her. 'No, no, no help at all from the Paras—' He paused, clearly unable to let an opportunity for self-aggrandisement pass him by. 'Although it must be said that the fraternal exercises in Douala between the Paras and the Cameroonian army were a fortuitous coincidence. The Niamey regime was clearly expecting some kind of intervention from the air—'

'The normal French pattern—'

'You might say so, but in this instance our thanks are not due to the Paras but to the man standing behind you.'

'Marc Benet—?'

'Exactly, or – as we used to call him – Gitan: famously the hero of General de Gaulle's first victory over Vichy in Douala, 26th of August 1940, when he singlehandedly assaulted the collaborating barracks and took a bullet in the hip.' He smiled with sickening condescension. 'A wound, as the general subsequently said at his bedside in the military hospital, that would become the most celebrated limp in France—'

'Fuck you, Foccart,' Gitan cursed.

'And now we owe him yet another debt,' Foccart sailed on. 'His first heroic action secured titanium for our struggle to liberate France; and this one frees France from the grip of OPEC.' He tut-tutted. 'I can't think why we didn't bring a bottle of champagne – except our hero is also famous for not celebrating France, right Gitan?'

'You know I didn't do it for France.'

Foccart tossed a roll of fresh bills onto the table in front of him. 'But you still demand your thirty pieces of silver. To feather your nest in Casablanca—'

'You bastard—'

Foccart turned his head. 'Ah, Guy. Or I should say, *Guillermo*. I wasn't forgetting you.' With grandiose elaboration, he swept a prolonged look around the room, settling finally on the map of Euskadi. 'But surely, Guillermo, your new identity should be Basque now that you've decided to throw your lot in with ETA—'

'I haven't,' Guy said, his face haggard with hatred. 'I'm just bringing my *tia* home.'

Foccart snorted. 'Some home!' He looked around again. 'I know enough for our friends in Madrid to give you and your precious *tia* a very rough time indeed. A terrorist cell. I already told them what you said to Violetta about sharing the Biafran spoils with ETA and your aunt.' He took a Polaroid photo from his pocket and flung it in the direction of Guy Martin. 'Take a good look, my friend. She held out for a touchingly long time. A tribute of her affection for you before she succumbed to her interrogators. It's a common enough pattern.'

A strangled cry came from Guy as he jumped forward. The nearest gendarme kicked out a heavy boot and his knee cracked and he fell. Before he could regain his feet the snub end of a sub-machine gun was rammed into his neck. The photo lay within sight, the image burned on his retina like a brand, Violetta sprawled on her chaise longue with her skirt above her waist. He roared with futile fury. How much more pain could he cause?

Foccart returned his attention to the trio of Americans. 'I'm sorry you've had to witness all this,' he said, emollient. 'Especially on a day of such good news. In time to come you will look back and celebrate the moment France became the world leader in nuclear power.'

'Just as I look back at my days in Douala,' said Eileen, 'and regret that my hands were tied and my mouth gagged.' She took out Mona's translation of Petridis' autopsy on Beth Palmer and waved it in his direction. Her heart was beating fast and her mouth dry. She clenched her fist, angry that a tremble had crept into her voice. 'Your squalid Greek coroner did your bidding with false autopsies on so many victims of the war of liberation—'

'It was a Soviet-sponsored insurrection –'

'History will not absolve you—'

'It already has,' he sneered. 'Cameroon is one of France's most loyal allies.'

'Imagine how they will react to reports in Canard of how that loyalty was secured.'

The ex-minister smiled. 'There is no such report.' He looked across at Marc Benet and took a passport from his pocket. 'Gitan is here to give me Petridis' papers, in exchange for a Swiss passport—'

Eileen O'Connell was drowning and the translated document felt like a lifeline. 'Annie Fayol was close to exposing how you'd raped and murdered Beth Palmer and framed Didier Nkumbé—'

'Mlle Palmer was out of her depth; ask Guy Martin,' said Foccart.

'I tried—' Guy began.

'She liked you Martin,' Foccart said, 'she let you in.'

Guy groaned. 'I left.'

'You followed orders.'

'You bastard,' spat O'Connell. 'I'm going to hand this—'

'A fiction—'

'Not so. It reveals the truth about Beth Palmer—'

'Pure fiction,' said Foccart, 'and sadly Castile is no longer here to deny it.'

'I'll still publish it,' said O'Connell.

But before she could move the nearest gendarme had pounced. For a large man moving with grace and agility, his fist crashing into the side of her head. Her ear exploded and she keeled over. By the time she'd been helped back on her feet by Harry and Candace, the translation was in Foccart's hands. She watched as he set fire to it and let the flames turn the paper into a pile of charred ashes.

'Gone,' he said, and held up his hand. 'And please don't tell me you have the original safe in New York.'

She started. Blood drained from her face.

Foccart consulted a business card. 'Hogarth and Palacios?' He looked up '*Plumbers*, I think you call them, broke in last night – a strange case, the police say, because nothing seems to have gone. They didn't even have to force the filing cabinet. Old fashioned, apparently—'

Eileen had never been so bettered in her life and Colonel Jacques Foccart, ex-Minister for Africa and Madagascar, had another sworn enemy.

'You bastard.'

'With thanks to your ex-colleagues at Langley,' he said with oily insincerity. 'They were especially keen to help after your dalliance with the IRA.' She baulked: what a fool she'd been. They *had* bugged her phone.

Foccart brushed his plump hands together as if cleaning something off. 'Business done, I think,' he said, 'except for the non-existent Petridis papers.' He moved forwards to the table with the passport in his hand. A gendarme followed and covered him with the sub-machine gun. 'All's well,' he said amicably. 'The Swiss eventually backed down and our man is living out his retirement on the Côte d'Azur. Give me the dossier.'

Gitan felt his spirits crash. His arch enemy had defeated them all, thanks to superior intelligence and a righteous certainty. Always acting in the national interest for the greater good of France. He could resort to any means and come away unscathed.

Bastard.

Focus on the future. Madeleine.

Together at last: school, college, Casablanca. Marc's heart lifted. At last.

His head swam and he felt the gendarme take the Greek's document from his grip.

No evidence; no crime, no conspiracy, no retribution. No justice.

Foccart gave him the passport. Madeleine's lovely face looked back at him and his heart surged. But – there were two photographs. The other was of Agnes. His wife.

Foccart was watching carefully, a hint of a terrible smile. Pure malice. Gitan went rigid, his body consumed by hatred.

'She's a minor,' said Foccart. 'Can't travel without a parent.'

Gitan was blinded by fury. He grabbed his stick and wrapped his hand round the knob. At least – but out of the corner of his eye he caught sight of Pleven pulling out the Marakov.

'He's got a knife!'

Something exploded. Burning-hot metal ripped at his throat. He was knocked backwards. Blood pumped out of him. The American medic, Candace Fayol, was on one knee at his side, her face a blur of concern, one minute resembling Monique, the next Madeleine. Her hands were pressing his throat but the pumping went on and the darkness was closing in. He floated. He couldn't hold on; he was sinking.

'He's gone,' said Candace, heart heavy in shock and reaching up for Harry.

'Justifiable homicide,' said Foccart brushing his hands again. The ex-Minister for Africa and Madagascar was already leaving.

Postscript

In the wake of the revelations of heroin smuggling, high-class call-girls and counterfeited money at the 1971 French Connection trial in New Jersey, the French secret services had been under pressure to clean up their act, but in 1985 they once again shocked the world by sinking Greenpeace's antinuclear boat *Rainbow Warrior* in Auckland harbour and killing the Dutch photographer Fernando Pereira.

After Jacques Foccart's dismissal as Minister for Africa he was reprieved and reinstated by both presidents, Giscard d'Estaing and Jacques Chirac and ended his working life as consultant to the president of Gabon, a country enormously rich in oil revenue but with some of the world's most extreme levels of inequality. The agent Foccart sent to assassinate Dr Félix Moumié in Geneva was revealed as Resistance hero William Bechtell, or Big Bill. Swiss attempts to extradite him dragged on unsuccessfully but he was then arrested back in Switzerland and bizarrely allowed to return to the Côte d'Azur to die in luxury.

The case of the raped US Presbyterian missionary and faked prison-cell suicide has never been reopened.

Pierre Messmer did not run for president in 1974 but remained a faithful Gaullist for the rest of his political life, including as the elected deputy for Moselle. Despite his outstanding war record in opposition to German Occupation and the puppet Vichy regime, he took the stand in 1997 to support Maurice Papon on a charge of crimes against humanity for collaborating in the Nazi policy of Jewish persecution and the Final Solution. In another instance of contested versions of the past, Messmer called for Papon's pardon and argued that 'the time had come for Frenchmen to stop hating themselves and to begin to grant pardon to themselves'.

The 1974 government, under Giscard d'Estaing, adopted Messmer's plan for nuclear power. The target he had set for 170 plants and national energy self-sufficiency by 2000 turned out somewhat too ambitious (they achieved 75%) but the French state-owned company EDF has emerged as the leading nuclear-power producer in the world. Their emergence has required a secure supply of uranium from Niger, the fourth-largest producer of uranium in the world and the only one enjoying a 'special relationship' with France.

The 1974 Niger *coup d'état* removed the threat of nationalisation and restored the privileged position commanded by France during the colonial period. The coup was fronted by Colonel Seybi Kountché, a pupil at a special school in Senegal for children of the military run by a close confidant of Colonel Jacques Foccart.

As a result of President Kountché's pro-French politics, Niger has remained, in the words of the former president of France Nicolas Sarkozy, 'a highly important strategic partner'. Sarkozy was visiting the uranium mine at Arlit in the Nigerian Sahara in March 2009 to celebrate fifty years of 'close co-operation' between France and Niger and to sign an agreement for the opening of a new mine nearby at Imouraren. The new agreement guarantees an investment of €1.2bn and an annual production of 5,000 tons, with only one third of the revenue going to the people of Niger – one of the poorest countries in the world.

The Agadez region is also at the centre of the ancient homeland of the Tuareg people, who for centuries have used their knowledge of the desert to sustain trans-Saharan trading routes between West Africa and the Mediterranean. Enforced French colonisation was never accepted by the Tuareg and the social and environmental damage inflicted by the mining operation has been the subject of extreme tension between the French owners of the mines (AREVA) and Tuareg nationalists.

When the 'one-eyed' Tuareg terrorist Mokhtar Belmokhtar attacked the gas facility in neighbouring Algeria in January 2013 (an incident that saw 39 hostages lose their lives) extra French troops were immediately drafted in to guard the mines in Niger. As the IAEA (International Atomic Energy Agency) had stated in a critical Report in the 1980s, the French government and the mining company AREVA have treated the area as if it was a part of France.

And finally, as to the fictional characters in Ebolowa, I can only report that late in 1980 Eileen O'Connell received an invitation to the opening of an exhibit at a fashionable new gallery in the Village. She turned it over in her hands: the photography on show had been gathered under the theme of 'Taking Sides: Women Behind the Lens' and included a selection from the work of Annie Fayol (1930–56).

Eileen noted the prestigious list of exhibitors, and the signature in a hand she vaguely recognised. 'Eileen,' it said, 'With best wishes, Harry Kaplan'. The omission of Candace's name struck Eileen as curious – and disappointing. She'd known her reputation with the Fayol family as 'the Ice Maiden' would be hard to shift but she'd hoped that Candace had finally put it behind her. The only way of finding out was to attend – and in any case she'd wanted to see Harry again – so she put a note of the location in her diary and the date: 15 March 1981.

Only then did she recognise the significance of the date.

Dramatis Personae

In order of appearance

Harry Kaplan Chicago-based private investigator

Sal Harry's receptionist

Dr Candace Fayol Chicago medic and Harry's new client

Annie Fayol photojournalist on *Life* magazine, (dcd.)

Bradley Hastings US Foreign Service IT specialist

Eileen O'Connell US *chargée d'affaires* in French Africa

Bill Holden Jnr Candace's occasional married lover

Karen Candace's Afro-American co-worker and friend

Hélène Candace's rags-to-riches cousin in Paris

Ronald Uttley English textile manufacturer

Marc Benet, a.k.a. Gitan (Gypsy) tourist agent in Niger

Madeleine Marc Benet's young daughter in France

Jacques Foccart Gaullist politician and eminence grise

Yasmin Marc Benet's office administrator

Frank Stokes retired English colonial in West Cameroon

Victor Castile French colon (settler) in French Cameroon

Luc Pleven young agent in French secret service

Louis Dupin redundant part-timer in French secret service

Mrs Bankole owner of Hi Life bar in Cameroon

Inspector Takere policeman in West Cameroon constabulary

Dr Petridis Greek pathologist in Douala Gendarmerie

Hans Ouweneel manager of Buea Mountain Hotel in Cameroon

Jules Raymond colon and local journalist in Cameroon

Jenny Fitzgerald resident nurse caring for Jules Raymond

Mona Iranian PhD student at NYU Stony Brook

Esther Nkumbé friend of Annie Fayol

Miss Fleming senior US Presbyterian missionary in Cameroon

Guy Martin French aid worker (Note: the pronunciations of 'Guy' in French and 'Gui' in Spanish (abbreviated from Guillermo) are identical, sounding the same as 'ghee').

Inspector Atangano inspector in Douala Gendarmerie

Bamenda prisoner on attempted-murder charge in Douala jail

Olivia Raymond wife of Jules Raymond (dcd.)

Chuck Logan US *chargé d'affaires* in Douala

Tia Pilar *pied–noir* aunt of Guy Martin in Paris

Monique wife of Marc Benet (dcd.)

Marcel, aka the Monkey first child of Monique

Elizabeth Palmer young US Presbyterian missionary

Pierre Messmer Gaullist prime minister of France in 1974

Isabella Spanish tenant Café de la Gare in Vernon

Acknowledgements

A great many people have helped me with the writing and publication of *Ebolowa*. More than a hundred generous supporters pledged money in the crowd-funding process and their names are listed here with heartfelt thanks.

I'd also like to mention people who pointed out scenes or characters that didn't work. It's difficult to offer such comment and I'm indebted to you all for giving it alongside sensitive solidarity: Andrew Grieg at the very beginning; fellow members of the South Manchester Writers Group; the UEA-Guardian Master Class group taught by Gillian Slovo especially Sandy Hogarth Scott; Tony Cook and the crew of valiant readers at ABCtales.com; Francis Byng, Lew Sargentich, Val Bradley, Gérard Balloteaud, Paul Kelemen, David James, Nonie Miller, Max Farrar, Nick Davidson and Jenny Keating.

I'd also like to thank the people at Unbound who have guided the book through the final phases of editing and presentation with great skill and patience: Xander Cansell, Sadie Mayne, Molly Powell and Mark Ecob (for the cover design).

Finally, I'd like to say that this is a work of historical fiction binding together the past and present. I have been lucky enough to experience the same continuous thread of time thanks to Su, Sam, Joe, Kate, Benny, Lucca and Louis.

Patrons

Hildegard Atherton
Celia Atherton
Nicky Atherton
Tony Dowmunt
Chris Evans
Paul Gerhardt
Jonathan Gosling
Verity Groom
Karl Hallam
Gary Herman
Leslie Holmes
Dai Hughes
Ruth Johnson
Patrick Kincaid
Peter Kirkham
John Latsis
Beth Miller
Mary Miller
Paul Miller
Rachel Morgan
Kevin Mount
Ben Newman
Jack O'Donnell
Toby Partlett
Jane Radford
Waldo Roeg
Geoff Shepherd
Nicola Turner
Tom Williams